Vigilante Nights

Vigilante Nights

Erin Richards

F+W Media, Inc.

Published by Merit Press
an imprint of F+W Media, Inc.
10151 Carver Road, Suite 200
Blue Ash, OH 45242. U.S.A.
www.meritpressbooks.com

ISBN 10: 1-4405-6235-0
ISBN 13: 978-1-4405-6235-8
eISBN 10: 1-4405-6236-9
eISBN 13: 978-1-4405-6236-5

Printed in the United States of America.

10 9 8 7 6 5 4 3 2 1

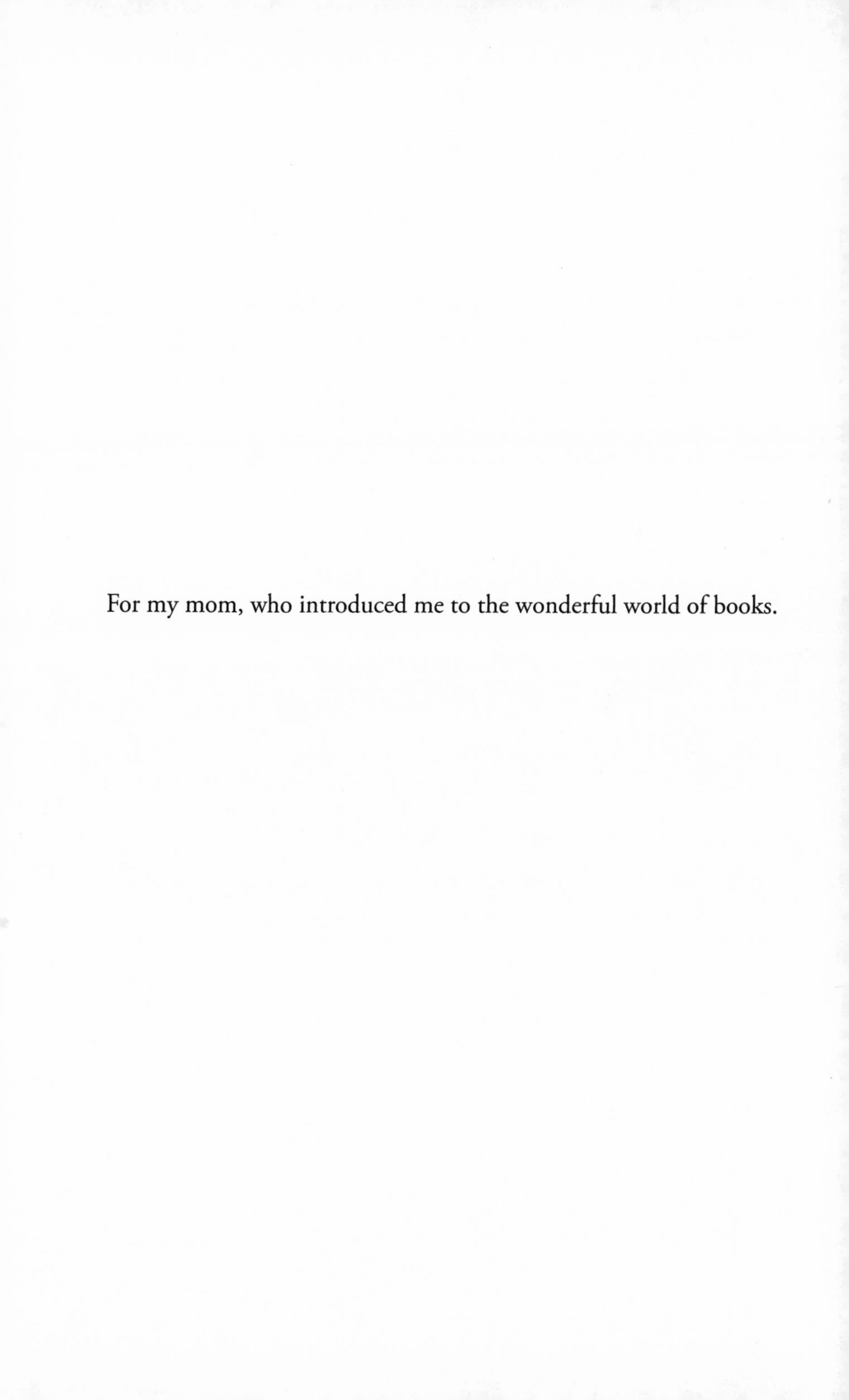

For my mom, who introduced me to the wonderful world of books.

Chapter 1

Silver's babbling continued at racecar speed. Seriously, I didn't want to hear about the new target of my sister's *lust*. The fallout of her last crush with one of *my* friends still jacked me up. Memories surged and my gut pinched. *Ex-friend now.*

A blissful moment of silence descended. I peeked at my twin in the passenger seat. Brow puckered, she sucked on the straw to her daily iced mocha. My gaze slid past the speedometer clocking me at ten over in a fifty-five zone.

"Something feels weird tonight, Lucas." Her tone turned somber. "Maybe you ought to slow down."

"Meaning?" I felt her apprehension, a feeling I'd grown used to over the last week since she'd kicked Raymond—our collective ex—to the curb.

She shrugged. "Just a weird vibe I've had since we left the mall."

"Raymond still bothering you?"

Silver looked out the passenger window. She didn't have to hide the tears I *felt* from her in our weirdo twin bond. Hoping to lighten the mood, I gunned the car on a clear stretch of the frontage road. Despite her heebie-jeebies, I knew she loved the speed as much as I did.

Night had sneaked up on us as we left Monterey behind. We zoomed past the dimly lit *Welcome to Sea Haven, California* sign. Population 28,342, give or take ten million in an influx of farm workers from the inland counties, yearly tourists, and summer resort peeps.

The thumping drone of the Red Renegade's new headers oozed '68 perfection. Or as sweet as the Camaro SS should've sounded back in 1968. "Camaro sounds badass, you think?"

"I guess." Silver sighed, knocking her cup on her thigh. "Do you think I did the right thing?"

"Dumping Raymond?" Incredulous, I glanced at her. "Hell, yes."

"He's still your friend. He keeps calling me."

"We're football teammates. Nothing more. I'll make sure he stays away from you." I tweaked her hair. "You know he's gunning for my spot."

"You're the best quarterback the school's ever had. Coach would never," Silver said thoughtfully, jingling her silver bangle bracelets.

Good enough to get three scholarships to killer schools. "I am perfect, aren't I?" I teased, wanting to slide her mind off douche bag Raymond. He'd never know how much I hated him for the way he treated my twin. If I didn't continue to keep the peace, he'd get all vindictive on her, like he did with other girls who quit taking his crap. I'd bite my tongue into pieces before I let on how much I knew about him . . . pressuring her . . . before she was ready. A slow burn spiraled up my chest. Screw him.

Dropping my speed, I felt for the glassy shift of the four-speed transmission. I'd spent junior year restoring the Camaro, using all the money from my weekend gopher job for my mom at the resort. I finished the last engine mods in time for summer break in two weeks. I was raring to open up the Red Renegade on the public track.

"I'm still ticked about my cell," Silver said, her long blonde hair streaming out the open window, her mind already switching gears as usual. "Karma's like a boomerang." She swished her drink. "It always comes back 'round."

I snorted. "In your case, it always bites you in the butt, and I gotta wipe up the mess."

"Not always, Lucas." I deflected her playful backhanded slap. "You owed me a trip to the mall. Besides, I didn't *lose* my cell. Someone stole it out of my purse." She danced her fingers on her silver bangles into a tinkling vibration. "I needed a new phone anyway. Screen was shot." A giggle slipped out. "Karma's a bitch."

As we neared the speed trap on County Coast Road, I eased up on the gas. The small-block engine thumped and growled, the exhaust burbling defiantly. Few cars zipped past, driving south toward Monterey. Cops wouldn't clock me going more than seven over north of the Sea Haven sign. This stretch of the frontage road had already earned me a speed warning. Lucky for me, I weaseled my way out of a ticket by promising to install a Borla exhaust on the sheriff's Corvette. Killer small town bribery.

Silver traded my quick grin with her evil squint. Her evil squint was one of her poker "tells." That particular tell meant the hard drive was spinning in her head. Which led me to believe she knew who nicked her cell. Man, I felt sorry for the poor sucker.

She slurped down the dregs of her mocha and tossed the empty cup in the pristine backseat, missing the trash bag by a mile. "Oops."

"Silver! My car's not a trash bin." I knocked my fist on the gearshift, glowered for half a tick. We approached the STOP sign at the Ocean Avenue intersection. I downshifted and rolled to a full stop. The streetlight across the intersection bathed the red car in amber fire and ghosted the stickweeds along the side of the road. Light glinted off a small spot in the ditch to our right.

"Jeez, go find your happy place, will ya? I'll get it when we . . ." Silver cranked up her window so fast I thought she'd just discovered that sea air killed genius brain cells. She mashed her elbow on the door lock. "Someone's hunched over in the ditch."

The seat harness squeaked as she squeezed closer to the center console. "Oh. My. God. A body's lying down there, too."

Did someone get hit by a car? I rammed the gearshift in park and reached to unbuckle my racing harness.

She swung her head in my direction, her hand gripping mine before I unlatched the buckle. "Don't go out there! Let's just go."

The streetlight on this side of the intersection was toast, making it hard to fully scope out the situation. "Someone could be hurt." I pushed her hand away, unhooked the seatbelt.

"Call the sheriff." She jabbed her new smartphone into my side. "Stay inside. I told you something felt weird about tonight."

Her unease twitched along my nerves. My twin's intuition was usually right on, where I acted without a second thought. We balanced each other in freakish ways I'd probably regret the rest of my life. After locking my door, I stretched across her lap to peer out the passenger window. The trench caught a scant glimmer from my headlights, enough light to make out two shadowy shapes.

Shrouded in dark clothing head to foot, a small man or woman crouched over a prone body in the shallow, weedy ditch. Cat eyes gleamed. Not moving. Just staring toward the car.

Staring at Silver.

"Hey," I yelled. "You need help?"

Silver grabbed my hand so hard I flinched. "Lucas! I'm scared."

"We can't leave if someone's hurt." I flexed my fingers to loosen her vise grip, gave her a reassuring squeeze. "Just stay in the car, 'kay? Keep the doors locked."

The slightly illuminated eyes in the ditch flicked from right to left. A low keening, like a death dirge from some creepy ancient ritual, emerged from behind us.

Silver's voice wobbled. "I'm calling the sheriff."

The second she tapped in 911, the keening grew to two voices, then more, rising in an undulating wave.

Ah, hell. Gang initiation? Gang activity and crime had tripled in Sea Haven over the last few years since the seaside resort town had boatloads of dough and good job opportunities. Way out of my league. "Screw this." I jerked back in my seat, slammed my foot on the clutch, thrusting the stick into second.

Before I could punch the gas pedal, a dozen dudes flowed out of the ditch, a black tide encircling us, blocking our getaway. I wanted to plow into them, but the idea of hurting someone stopped me cold. I'd wait for them to make the first move. Maybe they just meant to scare us. They blended into the night, the weak streetlight dying on their dark clothing. Voices became a chant of jumbled words. They surrounded the car, bouncing on their feet, watching us from a yard away, arms folded across their chests. Doing nothing but chanting that ridiculous sound. Until Silver brushed her hair over her face to cover her actions and put the phone to her ear.

They leaped at the car. Masked faces pressed to the windows, grinning, tongues lolling, making smacking kissing sounds. They licked and kissed the window on Silver's side, some rubbing their crotches, eyes latched onto Silver's breasts in her low-cut, skintight tank top. *The shirt Dad will kill her for wearing without a jacket over it.*

Nearly incomprehensible, Silver sobbed to the 911 dispatcher. I tapped the gas, advanced three feet, slamming the brake before I hit the three goons blocking us. The trio stood rooted to the pavement, arms crossed, not moving, expressions blank as cardboard. Silver's fright pooled in my head, her silent pleas hitting every guilt receptor.

I searched the interior for a weapon of any sort. "Damn it," I muttered. Car was cleaner than a padded cell, except for the mocha junkie's empty cup. My tools were in the trunk. "Might be a gang initiation," I whispered. "Stay calm."

They all wore black—from their beanies to their shoes. No gang colors, no designation, except for the color of their skin—Hispanic dark from what I could make out around the eye and mouth holes of their masks. Which meant nothing near a valley of farmlands where the Mexican population topped any other ethnic group. The tall dude front and dead center unbuttoned his pants, the zipper followed. He waggled his tongue at Silver. A lump grew in my throat, threatening to cut off my air supply. I pressed on the gas, inched forward. The three didn't budge, and I had only inches to spare. The Camaro's engine shook into a rocky idle.

"Is the sheriff coming?" I forced a calmness I didn't feel into my voice to keep Silver from totally freaking out.

"I think so." Heaving in ragged breaths, her left hand gripped my arm so hard her nails felt like they'd pierced my hoodie sleeve.

The ten or so other guys surrounding the car began to beat on it with the flats of their hands. All geared to trip us out rather than cause damage. Every thudding, vibrating slap amplified my anger. Anger because they played their dumbass games in our exclusive oceanfront community. Anger because they dared touch my ride. Worst of all, I was furious that they scared the piss out of my twin.

The streetlight sparkled on the earring dangling from the left ear of the tall leader in the center. A stylized cross. *Oxymoronic Christian?* I white-knuckled the steering wheel and tapped the accelerator again. That time the car chugged forward against the prick on the left. He struck out his arms, palms flat on the hood as if to push us backward. An earring on his left ear winked in the light too, but I didn't let it distract me.

Laughing, the tall leader started pissing on the front grill, his gaze never leaving my face. Piss splashed onto the radiator and thin threads of steam spiraled into the air. The gang whooped it up, egging him on. Slaps against the fenders continued, and the sound grew deafening.

Yet it was Silver's crying that unglued me.

Screw it. I plowed into the three losers at the speed of a snail. The burly dude on the left vaulted to the side, rolled into the ditch. The Pisser lost his footing and landed face forward on my hood. His enraged roar broke through the clamor. Asshat on the right followed him, thudding onto his side on the hood. I jammed the shifter into gear and shot forward. Pisser gripped the front edge of the hood and the other dude rolled off the right fender onto the asphalt.

"Go, baby. Go!" Silver slapped the dash, excitement replacing her fear. Her tension melted away with my relief.

I shifted the Camaro into second, ready to haul ass and shake the sucker off the hood. The car sputtered, lurched. It stalled in the middle of the intersection, jerking us into our seats.

I punched the steering wheel, turned the key off and on, gunned the engine. It died the second I tripped first. Interior lights dimmed. *Oh, mother, not the alternator.* To save power, I flipped off the headlights. Again, I turned the key on. Nothing.

Pisser hauled himself onto his knees. Someone shoved a knife into his hand. The gang surrounded us again, their angry din bouncing against Silver's whimpering piercing my skull. A baseball bat shattered the rear window. Every dull thud on the safety glass echoed in my chest. The car rocked side to side, jolting with every hit.

"Lucas, do something." Silver's cloying floral perfume wafted her renewed fright to me, clogging my sinuses.

The carburetor caught and whined until I flooded the engine.

Through all the noise, familiar sounds arose, like a symphony of Metallica to my ears. The realization that we were stuck in the middle of an illegal street-racing path seemed to rip a ragged claw down my chest. Two hotrods were approaching. Lightning fast. The gang must've also heard the distant roar, as they fell silent and the Camaro stopped rocking. Sirens pierced the distance, drowned out by the advancing growl. As if on cue, the gang scattered into the night.

"Out of the car! Run to the ditch," I screamed at Silver, yanking on her harness buckle. The latch clicked open. "Go!"

Too late. We never made it out of the car.

From out of nowhere, twin sets of headlights flashed on seconds before two hotrods hit the intersection. Tires squealed, screeched. The drag racers slammed the passenger side of the Camaro. Barreled into Silver.

Metal scraped metal, tangled, rolled. The strong odor of gas filled the air. Heat whooshed up, a scorching, blinding plume. My head thundered. Metal tore into my side, scalding a crisscross trail through my middle. An anchoring weight crushed my left leg, and my entire body fell numb.

Silver's faint voice cut through the static shutting down my brain, "Oh, God . . . Lucas. It hurts."

Chapter 2

The moment I awoke in the beige, sterile hospital room, I knew I'd been in a coma. Cloudy thoughts collided with echoes of Silver's gibberish in my fried brain. My eyelids twitched and opened. Silence finally reigned, but my head throbbed as if a zombie had eaten half my brain. I hurt everywhere. Even my hair hurt.

Mom and Dad's faces swam above me, eyes brimming with tears, hands touching me as if to ensure I was real. My wonky gaze landed on the doctor, a short Eastern Indian dude, standing on the other side of the bed. He adjusted the beeping machines with the gyrating green and blue lines.

"Hello, Lucas. Can you hear me? I'm Dr. Sharma."

Through my scratchy and dry throat, I tried to say yes. Epic fail. Mom brought a cup with a bendy straw to my lips.

"Small sip," she said. It barely wet the fuzz sprouting in my mouth.

"I can hear," I croaked. "How long have I been out?" I looked around the room for Silver. Didn't see her. Where'd she go?

Mom smoothed her hand over my covers and Dad looked away, both of them avoiding eye contact. But not before a skosh of relief relaxed the tight skin of their tense faces.

"You've been in a coma for a month," Dr. Sharma answered.

Shock impaled me. Pain knifed down my left leg. "A month?" I echoed.

Sharma nodded. He consulted my charts, then gave me the download on my injuries. "After several surgeries, you've spent the month in a medically induced coma, mainly due to brain swelling and extensive internal injuries." He fiddled with a monitor and grinned. "Welcome back, Lucas."

I tried to bend my left leg until I realized a cast encased it from above the knee to my foot. "What else?" I whispered, afraid to hear the answer, scanning the floor for a puke pan.

"Three cracked ribs, punctured lung, ruptured spleen, intestinal damage. Your left leg is broken in two places—"

I sucked in my bruised and sliced gut. "Will I play football again?"

Mom squeezed my arm and I had to look away from Dad's swimming eyes before I lost it. Sharma didn't even have to respond. The bad news bigmouth did anyway.

"I'm sorry, son. You'll never play football again. We did the best we could, but the damage . . ."

The room spun. Sharma's voice faded off as the horror hit me. I could kiss my scholarships goodbye. *Finito.* Life over.

My life *had* consisted of my Camaro, football, and Silver. Thank friggin' God I had Silver. Otherwise, just kill me now.

I needed to speak to my twin. She'd talk me off the ledge. I opened my mouth to ask about her when the full extent of the accident careened into my sluggish memory. I experienced the pain of the two hotrods slamming into my body, the crushing weight of metal, the searing heat of fire, the suffocating stench of gas. The split moment of oblivion when I believed I had bitten it.

I remembered Silver's screams.

The screams that still filled my head.

Panic thumped in my mending ribcage. "Where's Silver? Is she okay?" I tried to sit up, but it felt like I was at the bottom of a dog pile on the football field. Cleansers and medications assaulted my nose. The lingering scent of sick bodies filtered into every pore. I gagged, wanted to spew, but my empty stomach contained only piped-in fluids.

After a moment of awkward silence, Dr. Sharma nodded at my parents. Tears rolled down Mom's cheeks. Dad's summer tan faded to honky white.

"Honey." Mom took my hand in her small moist grip. "She was hurt so bad . . . she . . . couldn't—" Mom choked up and sobs shook her.

Dr. Sharma squeezed a safe spot on my arm. "Lucas, we worked on her all night. Silver was strong and fought to the end, but she was hurt too badly."

"Is she in a coma too?" My mind had a hard time following. My heart clenched as if it predicted the next words to come.

"I'm sorry, son. We lost her." Dad laid his trembling hand on my leg as if to comfort me. "She never regained consciousness . . . the night of the accident," he continued as if giving a statement in court. It was the way he hid his emotions as the cold, lawyerly dad. "She didn't feel any pain."

I narrowed my eyes. "Silver's not dead," I replied, my throat dryer than a heat wave in hell. "I heard her talking. Is she okay? Is she still in the hospital?" I knew she'd suffered the worst hit from the street racers. And I refused to believe that sickening dead body smell of the hospital belonged to my twin.

"No, honey." Mom wiped her nose, but the tears continued to flow.

Were my parents smoking dope? "What? I don't . . ." My mouth hung open. I tried to move my right arm to hide my face, to hide the sissy tears about to rampage, but the tubes cut my efforts short. My insides burned. I must've imagined Silver yakking up a storm. *Like now.*

"Don't be a weenie, Lucas. Car accident. Check. I'm dead. Check. Moving on. Check. But you're still here," her voice softened. "One of us had to live."

The overhead light flickered. No one noticed it. I shook my head to clear her voice, scowled at the tubes stuck in my arm.

Mom and Dad did that eye-play thing parents do. You know, the unspoken message. The one that said they'd tolerate me until I tripped over some stupid imaginary line. I think I scared them, though. Mom grew flustered and fussed with my pillows. They acted weird. Something had changed between them. They avoided touching, as if guarded against each other, something I'd never witnessed. Yet, they stood united on calling in the head doctor.

As we waited for the shrink, I witnessed more of my parents' evasion. Evading each other, evading *my* certainty that Silver lived somewhere. *Their* truth dawned on me. Silver *really* was dead. But I refused to believe she was gone. *Gone* wasn't my reality. True Reality was a lie, a tool of deceit. My twin was still in my head. I didn't know how she managed it, and I had a tricky time thinking about the possibilities over the guilt blazing up my chest. All the pain Silver suffered destroyed me. Fucking Reality.

A lanky sixties reject jetted in and introduced himself, "Dr. Beranger." He patted my shoulder, flipped his pencil-thin ponytail over his shoulder. Mom and Dad anxiously hovered behind him, waiting for word that I suffered delusions or brain damage.

My parents didn't know of my weirdo empathic connection with Silver. Mom and her twin sister never possessed the same bond we did, although they experienced a touchy-feely thing. None of us believed in telepathy, if that's what was happening at that moment. Hella freaky. How did one have telepathy with a dead person? Had I totally lost my marbles?

Beranger reviewed my chart, consulted with Sharma. "Hmmm, head trauma. Your stats look good. What's going on,

Lucas? Anything I can help you with? We can talk now, or later. Whatever you want."

I didn't want to share her, so I lied. "Yeah. I must've had nightmares of the accident while I was in a coma."

"Are you sure?" Dr. Beranger looked at my chart and muttered to himself, "Could be auditory hallucinations. Nothing here indicates a drug reaction."

Hallucinations? How badly did the accident pound my head? I didn't want to freak my parents out any further. "Uh, no big deal. Just a dream." I'd freak out on my own later.

In a low voice geared for my parents' ears only, Dr. Beranger said, "He could be making her up to cope with the trauma. Manifestations of his subconscious. Situational delusions." He raised his voice for my benefit. "It happens. Not all that unusual. It's probably going to be temporary." He smiled and winked at me. "Spend your time healing and let us worry about the other stuff. We'll get you right as rain soon."

The tension sliding out of the room was practically touchable.

Dr. Beranger's stained teeth beamed dull as cement. "We'll talk when you're ready. Things will get better. Okay?"

Will my guilt go away? I wanted to feel hope, rage, anything to halt the horrible remorse threatening to burn me to a crispy critter. Wanted to let it all go. I willed myself not to feel, but the consuming guilt refused to take a hike. A terrible emptiness settled in my chest. In honor of Silver's need to tag everything, I called it "May 12 Mayhem."

"Can I be alone now?" I choked back a sob. Reality had finally hit me hard.

Mom and Dad split for an hour, and the doctors left. The emptiness of the room gave me a semblance of false peace. It was better than the void inside me. Until I heard Silver babbling that she was thankful I had awoken from my coma. I clenched my eyes shut to kill her voice, to kill the inevitable nightmares.

No dice. The horror of my new life continued.

Monotonous days dragged by. The nightmares dug in even as I tried to forget how the accident had destroyed football and the car I spent so much time rebuilding. If nothing else, I still had Silver. Sort of. Her incessant chattering helped me handle the nightmares.

Between crying jags and babbling, Silver grew calm and confident in my head. "We have our twin power," she said. "Don't let them take it away."

What choice did I have? She was in my heart, always would be. And if I suffered from hallucinations, bring it. Memories and Silver's voice kept me sane where nothing else did.

• • •

Two weeks after I'd awoken from my coma, I hobbled on crutches between Mom and Dad to Silver's gravesite on the way home from the hospital. I saw *their* truth. They'd picked a high-rent site beneath a eucalyptus tree on a narrow cliff overlooking the Pacific. Finally, the fresh sea air scrubbed the nasty hospital odors out of my body. Eucalyptus branches fluttered, sifted together like sandpaper, adding their cleansing tang to the air, washing death off me.

Mom brought my twin's favorite silver roses. They were actually purple even though called "silver." Shaking off Dad's hands, I managed to lean like the Tower of Pisa on my own and place a flower on the stone marker rising out of the plush grass. "Sylvia Rose Alexander, beloved daughter, special twin, we love you" the stone read, along with the years of her birth and death, and the words, "too soon." They had a trio of roses engraved at the top of the marker and above it "Silver."

I touched my fingers to the letters of her first name. Sylvia was an old family name on Dad's side of the family. When I learned to talk, I couldn't pronounce Sylvia and everyone thought I was saying silver. The name stuck. "Half of us," I whispered.

"The better half," she replied in my head. "The pretty and smart half," she teased.

Startled, I caught myself on a neighboring headstone. Panic flitted across Mom's face. Dad grabbed my arm as if he feared the ground might split open and suck me into the coffin. I was all they had left, so I suffered their paranoia.

I imagined drama queen Silver loving the spot, clapping her hands, whooping it up.

I knew it for fact at that moment: death couldn't sever our bond. *Explain that.*

My Camaro and football were gone. I refused to let go of Silver. She was my cornerstone, my anchor. Silver lived. Somewhere.

Drained and supremely confused, I hobbled to the wrought-iron fence that protected mourners from flinging themselves into the aqua-blue Pacific. I searched for an opening wide enough to gimp through.

• • •

The crutches never made it past the garage, let alone into the Pacific Ocean. I loathed the wimp sticks. Too many reminders of the reeking hospital of death. The car parts graveyard in the garage earned the sticks and my avoidance. From that day forward, I dodged the zillion reminders of the Red Renegade Camaro, tossing all pictures and reminders of it in the back of my closet.

My strange new life continued. My physical healing pleased the doctors. No one expected me to use the crutches much anyway. The hike up to the second floor of the house winded me, and my leg ached constantly. Someday, normal lung function might return. I had months of physical therapy on my leg to go. Not that I cared. I'd never play football again.

One day, in a lame fit of despair, I dug out my letterman jacket. I sat on the bed fingering the haunting symbol of my former status, remembering Silver's happiness the day I earned the letters. She loved the status I brought to her table.

"Will you miss football?" she asked.

"What do you think?" I said aloud before I whipped my head around to look for her. *Holy. Crap.* The air in front of my desk lamp wavered as if a cloud floated in front of it.

"Silver?"

"Who'd you think? Casper? Bloody Mary?"

"Right. Sure. Okay. Whatever." I paced the room, looked at the lamp. Waited.

"Raymond will take your place as team captain and first-string quarterback now."

"No shit, Sherlock," I said as if it was natural talking to the air. "He'll be first to boot me off the A-list." I slammed the jacket on the floor.

"I know," she whispered. "I'm sorry. I hate him now and I want to burn him."

"He didn't cause the accident," I yelled louder than I intended. Then I understood. Her hatred went back further, to a horrible day in April. Son. Of. A. Bitch.

"Not once did he come to the hospital. Half the team, Raymond's minions, will shun you."

My fists curled and I stared in the mirror. Windshield glass had left a network of tiny scars across my face. *Safety glass, my ass.*

"Bunch of losers. They've all wanted Raymond as top dog from day one. Well they can have the jackass." Raymond's family practically ruled the town. When I made lead quarterback instead of him, I imagined things eventually changing. *Fat frigging chance.*

Anger fueled my movements as I schlepped out to the backyard. I tossed kindling in the fire pit and set it blazing, adding lighter fluid until flames shot up three feet. Slowly, I fed the jacket into the fire. Flames devoured the material inch by inch. I squirted on lighter fluid until the fire blinded me and the charred leather and wool stunk up the backyard. I dropped the lid on the smoldering ashes of my childhood. They represented relics of a life that no longer existed.

It was that conversation with Silver when it dawned on me she wasn't merely a figment of my imagination. I couldn't possibly know about the smack Raymond spread while I was in Comaland. The convo left me epically disturbed. Also freakishly sane.

The rest of summer passed by in a blur of grief and anger. I remained home lounging by the pool in misery, soaking up the rays, eyeing the diving board. Most days I spent holed up in my bedroom. My best friends—my *true* friends—Chris and Kev visited often, just like the old days after football practice and on weekends. I first met Kev boogie boarding the day after my family moved to town. I was a newb at it and Kev had a blast laughing at my million faceplants. He promised to teach me to boogie board, if I promised to teach him football. We both sucked at teaching. Kev stuck to boogie boarding and I stuck to football. Chris, on the other hand, was a stray dog loner. Kev was his only bud. When I came onto the scene, he became my bud. Like Silver, my football status elevated his status. Girls finally noticed him. He eventually taught me how to surf. All three of us had a knack for pranking, which became our biggest bond.

Anyway, we played video games and watched apocalypse movies that summer. They swam. We talked about nothing. They didn't know what to say, how to act. *Welcome to Awkward.* We balanced on a strange ground we'd never trod. Once, I was the life of our clique, the king prankster, the star quarterback, the brother of one of the hottest and smartest chicks in school. Then I became nothing. The night of the accident, my light winked out, leaving me dark and hollow. Though I lived in body, my spirit had died. People say, "what doesn't kill us, makes us stronger." Screw that.

A stranger residing within me operated the strings on my limbs and my emotions. I needed to keep living and not evaporate into that creature that had stolen my body. How? Through lame mental therapy?

The shrink wanted to hand me off to another doctor after the first month because I refused to talk about anything. Except for the nightmares. I told him about the hell I traveled every night, where my mind replayed the crash scene. Beranger forced sleeping pills on me. I hobbled out of his office and tore the prescription to shreds, letting the pieces float toward the sea. I needed the nightmares to keep me sane. To keep me from forgetting. I needed Silver's voice to keep her alive.

Toward the end of summer break, in a rare bonding moment, I sat at the dinner table with my parents in the formal dining room. The first time we'd eaten together since before the accident when we used to enjoy family dinners several nights a week. Until then, either Mom or Dad worked late each night, or I chilled in my room. I may have killed family dinners, too.

Silver's presence was achingly absent. Mom and Dad were like strangers having met for the first time. They creeped me out. Having spent so much time away from them in the hospital, I wondered if the accident had destroyed their marriage.

The dinner scene weirded me out even worse when they centered all their attention on me. Silver always used to gobble their interest when we weren't talking about football or my latest failed school prank.

"Two more weeks until school starts, huh?" Mom took a slug from a gigantic glass of white wine.

"Whatev." I shrugged, shoveled in a forkful of buttery baked potato.

Dad clinked his fork on his plate and gave me a frank stare. "Your mother and I were wondering how your sessions are progressing with Dr. Beranger."

Ambush alert.

"Doesn't he tell you everything?" Screw doctor-patient confidentiality. More like doctor-parent download. Sinking lower in my seat, I continued to shovel food in my mouth, not tasting, just needing something to occupy my hands, something tangible to chew on.

"Only his impressions of how you're coping," Mom replied.

"How am I coping?" I challenged.

"As well as can be expected." Mom twirled the wine in her glass before taking another guzzle.

"Then there's nothing more to say." I slurped down half my milk. "You want me to go. I go. Doesn't mean I have to like it."

"Honey." Mom touched my arm. Like old times, I let her fingers linger. "What about Silver. Are you still . . . hearing her?"

Ambush played.

I yanked my arm away from her touch. A flush worked its way up my chest, stopping short of my neck. "I'm fine. I must've been hallucinating." I shoved my plate away. The saltshaker took a header into my potato and I shoved it in deeper.

Relief smoothed out the lines on Dad's forehead, sent color back into Mom's face.

Of course, I lied. Silver remained. I think.

The flaming, consuming ache of revenge against the unidentified gang also persisted. Before the accident, I cared nothing about revenge unless it was a defensive football play. Yet I wanted to kill those loser gang members. I thought Silver would talk me off the rails. Nope.

Revenge consumed Silver, and she consumed me.

That night after dinner, I hung in my bedroom, skipping past preseason football on TV. Still battered, I floated in a sea of emptiness wondering how I was going to survive senior year.

"God, Lucas, get over yourself. Get a life! It's time for revenge," Silver shouted. I imagined her standing over me, hands on hip, lips in a wide sneer. *Next up: finger stuck in my face.*

I gritted my teeth. "What am I supposed to do, get a gun and mow down every gang and street racer in town? Jeez, Silver, I'm not into first-degree murder."

"You wanted more consumer days at the race track, right? That's a start."

"That won't stop illegal street racing." I had enjoyed street racing occasionally, but I never played the boneheaded games of chicken those racers played, driving with their lights off. "Besides, both drivers are serving their sentence at the boys ranch until they're twenty-one." They'd settled on reduced charges from vehicular manslaughter, reckless driving, and street racing. Dad, the lawyer, also got the court to order their families to pay restitution. What a joke. Money couldn't bring back what my family had lost. We would never experience Silver's smart, quirky life again.

The gang members escaped as if they never existed.

"Come on. Think!" Silver's voice drove me up and down the wall. "Do I have to do all *your* thinking still?"

"Get out of my head. You're dead." I slammed a pillow at the wall. "You're not even a ghost. I can't see you."

"What're you talking about?" Her voice wavered. "Lucas, I'm here. For *you*."

Oddly, I felt her sadness pinch my heart the way I used to when she lived. Maybe it was my own sadness. *Yeah, that's it.*

Tears pricked the corner of my eyes. "Leave me alone." Silvery stars on the black ceiling twinkled from the spinning globe light, hypnotizing me. Stars my sister had insisted painting on my ceiling to match her room.

Silence greeted me, for two lucky minutes. Not that I wanted her gone; I craved a break. From her, from myself, from the hell I lived.

"Lucas?"

I rolled onto my side, studied the butt end picture of our old Labrador retriever, Bullwinkle, in a silver frame. A black frame in Silver's bedroom held the head shot. Her twisted twin humor. Pain shot up my left leg, dissipated into my thigh. "What?"

In that moment, I wanted nothing more than to see Silver kicking it. Bitching me out even. Calling me her name of the day. I used to get off on her twisted verbal creativity, and she knew it.

I focused on my cluttered desk, wishing with all my might. The air shimmered. I blinked rapidly, knowing my parents would eventually fit me for a straitjacket and ship me to crazy-town. I cleared my head. My vision of Silver remained in my imagination. *Duh.* The air above my desk grew blurry. I rubbed my eyes, felt something prickle across my arms. "Silver?"

"You're such a doofus." Silver laughed.

Excitement accelerated my pulse. "Screw me. I'm losing it." I whacked my head. It didn't help. Silver *was* in the room. I reached forward to touch the air. I know it sounds lame, but the hairs on my arm rose.

"No thanks. I'm not into *doing* brothers."

I heaved myself into a sitting position, planted my feet on the *solid* floor, and reached for the bottle of prescription tranqs on my desk. Willing for something to shake me up, I stared at the label. Didn't remember when I last took one. No matter.

"Keep taking those and they'll have to peel your hands off your pecker." Silver's gleeful tone stopped me cold. I tossed the pills into the overflowing trash basket beneath my desk.

"You're . . . a ghost? Are you really here?"

"Been here since May 12."

"Um . . . Silver." Heat rushed up my neck. "Did you . . . did it hurt? You know . . . the accident?"

"No." Her voice quivered, and I imagined her twining her long hair around her index finger, her bottom lip trembling.

"Don't lie."

"Argh . . . okay. For, like, two stinkin' seconds. I mean long enough for me to tell you it hurt. Then I blinked out. Snuff city."

"I'm so sorry." I dipped my head to hide the tears threatening an infusion of girly hormones.

"I know, Lucas," Silver said softly. "I don't blame you. But can we make my death mean something?"

Monster knots that had pained me since Comaland ejected me loosened in my shoulders. "Like what?" I rubbed my cheek, felt the healing scars along my right jaw, traced them to the tiny cuts crisscrossing my upper lip.

"Remember what I told you in the 'Maro about karma?"

The memory was so vivid my gut crimped. Like I'd ever forget her last words. "It always comes back around," I repeated slowly. "Like a boomerang."

"Bingo." I almost saw her fist pump the air and rub her hands together in excitement. "We're gonna help karma along." Her evil, cackling laugh filled me with adrenaline. "It's war, baby. Boomerang wars."

Ideas bubbled in my wrecked brain. Revenge pumped a new crop of endorphins into my veins. Every member of the gang who initiated the chain of events on May 12 may live to regret they ever woke up that morning.

"Welcome to vigilante nights, Sea Haven." My somber grin turned gleeful.

Chapter 3

Dad's sorrow and his desire for me to snap out of it ate at him so badly he bought me a new, metallic red Camaro SS. Actually, insurance money and court-ordered restitution financed the car. Doctor's prescription to replace the car, supposed to help me heal, you know, in the old noggin. At first, I didn't go near the car, wanted nothing to do with American muscle again. Parents shook their heads, buzzed the shrink.

Eavesdropping, I heard Beranger say on speakerphone, "Give him time. He's healing in his own way."

Right. What did he know? Had he ever lost his flipside? Not that anyone knew the odd bond Silver and I had shared as twins.

Strangely, with Silver "plaguing" me in that weird airy sensitivity, my light burned brighter each day. I dare not say I lived again or that Lucas Alexander had returned, but I did my damnedest to fool the masses. I walked. I breathed. Okay, in reality, I limped and wheezed. At least my body had awoken. I think I wanted to live again. I just didn't know how. Although guilt lit my way, something still needed to jumpstart within me. Revenge and vigilantism were the first words to spring to mind.

On the first day of school, I awoke to Silver prattling about a change in the air. "Something pretty's gonna hurl all over the jockstrap stench in your bedroom. Like moonlight and lavender." Sunlight streamed through the windows, stroked half my bed in bright slashes. That tickle drove up my arms. It was warm. Silver.

"You're just as weird as, whatever the heck you are, as you were . . . um . . . alive." I tossed a smelly T-shirt over the picture of her on my dresser. It fell in a heap on a stack of empty soda cans on the floor. My recycling chores had fallen into the crapper this summer, too. Light reflected off an upstairs window on the empty house next door, painting a rainbow across half my body. I scanned the window for a prism. *Nada*.

"That's what you love about me." The Silver presence wavered. She would've simultaneously preened and sneered at me in real life.

I tugged on beach shorts and a faded Linkin Park tee. "Right." Part of me was relieved, the other part supremely disturbed. It was cool with her "here," though. The hollowness remained from her bodily death, but without a bottomless hole I'd feel if she were totally gone. In a crazy way, she lived. *Call me a psycho.* How long would it last? I slipped my feet in my Reef flip-flops, the pair Silver gave me for our birthday in April.

I almost felt and saw her gaze rake me up and down, lips curling, hands on hips. "Seriously? Did they banish the school uniform just when I get killed?"

"Screw the uniform."

"Jeez, Luc. You going all rebel now?" Silver's laugh echoed in my ears as I slunk downstairs. "I love it. Matches your face. Fun times are coming."

I grabbed a cinnamon-raisin bagel and snagged the Camaro keys off the pegs over the kitchen desk. Rendered my parents so speechless they didn't blast me about my threads. They'd receive the note later. If the school had the balls to smack down on me. Who knew how administration would treat the gridiron king of faceless pranks since I didn't have my football star status to buy me out of trouble. I touched the scars on my lip, sketched my fingers over the fading scars across my cheek.

"Later," I said to my mute parents. They followed me out to the driveway. I hopped into the Camaro and returned their stiff waves.

They might want to reserve the shrink's couch for a session or two. After they visited a doctor to fix the broken hinges on their jaws.

Silver's warmth hovered in the passenger seat. "Do the scars bother you?" she asked softly. I knew they bothered her for my sake.

"They don't hurt." I backed out of the driveway, gunned the car down the street, the stock exhaust emitting a low growl. I missed the Red Renegade's loud roar. I inhaled the new car smell, missing the old Armor All scent. The new car kicked ass, though.

"That's not what I meant, dillweed."

"They give me a hardcore, villain look, don't they?" I swished my right arm through the air in the front seat, glomming onto the prickly warmth.

Silver giggled. A sound I missed so much. "You look perfect for your new life."

I parked in the student lot, taking the last spot in the front row to avoid door dings. The football bowl of Sea Haven High School loomed, displaying the glossy green grass, the aluminum benches, the bright yellow goal posts. I gulped the lump clogging my throat. Why did I park facing the field? Sharp sympathy twinges traveled down my left leg. My gaze flicked to the Spanish-style buildings.

"You'll take a hike while I'm in school, right?" I turned toward the passenger seat. Hairs rose on my head, and air whooshed out the window. The sound of Silver singing the school anthem—totally off key—filled my head. Creepy answer enough.

The scent of freshly mowed grass stunk up the parking lot. Trim bushes and trees surrounded the lush lawns and rainbow flowerbeds. Windows were spit-shined, and fresh boring beige paint brightened the walls. School district must've gotten an infusion of cash over the summer.

A small crowd gathered outside my car, a sea of smiling tanned faces. Telepathy not necessary to know my ex-friend—Silver's ex-boyfriend—Raymond Randall was stoked to be top dog of the football team. He sneered and took off without a word. A few dudes glared at my car, jealousy flashing across their faces. Several girls from the vapid princesses and future MBAs smirked, ecstatic that they might be crowned one of the hottest or smartest to replace Silver, not that Silver had been a vapid princess. Some cast expressions of sympathy. For the most part, everyone appeared glad to see me. Even if the other half of the Alexander twins was absent. *Oxymoronic shit.* Once I was sure no one was going to deck me or hug me, I slid off the virgin leather seat into the crowd.

The condolences began. Half listening, gritting my teeth, I suffered.

People repeated the words of sympathy because it was a given. How many really cared? They lived in their own miniscule worlds, drove over the potholes of excitement at eighty miles an hour. They cared only about what they got from the next pit-stop: the offensive drive down the football field, a class prank to lighten their day, a popular date to the dance, a coveted hookup, a ride in a hot car. Then they raced off to their next destination having forgotten the road traveled. My pit-stop was closed. How easily the high and mighty got booted off the A-list. *Simply off your sister, wreck your leg, and annihilate your hot ride.* Nothing had changed and everything was different.

Welcome to Sea Haven, California, the seaside town dripping in bliss and delusion.

After tearing myself away from the well-wishers, I walked alone toward my locker in the open hallways. My so-called friends, most of the varsity football team, avoided me. They had become

Raymond's cling-ons. A few waved at me, but played the game and let Raymond rule the kingdom. Had I been that bad as top dog? As I shook off the thoughts, my gaze landed on a willowy redhead girl I'd never seen before. The type I'd horn-dog after in a heartbeat. Before Accident (BA).

"Who's the newbie?" I nodded my head at the tall redhead as Chris and Kev took up my flank in a flurry of pummeling jabs and laughter.

"Jillian. Hot transfer from the corn state," Kev replied, leering at her. "Too hot to handle." He made a sizzling sound to accompany the song title. The varsity football team quickly surrounded her, leaving the cheerleaders and their looks of jealousy and fury in the dust.

"Way out of your league," I teased Kev, not at all interested in her.

Chris and Kev walked me to first-period P.E. We passed by clique after clique. Everyone stared at me as if I were a pariah, half practically willing me to stay away, the other half luring me toward their easy smiles. I no longer belonged to the jocks, unless I formed the Reject Jocks. Rastas, cowboys, A/V geeks, coffee cliques, future MBAs, and nerds did nothing for me either. I couldn't even muster interest in any of the vapid princesses. Girls just weren't on my radar.

"You're a Nomad, like us, buddy boy," Kev mimicked his stuffy father. "Get used to it. It's better this way. You can hang around all the cliques, get the lay of the land, and jet off to the next one."

"Yeah. You get away with so much more." Chris chuckled.

"A Nomad, huh?" More like a Nomad's nomad. "Cool." Maybe there was something to being a Nomad . . . on the surface. Especially considering my plans.

"Luc, why're you going to P.E.?" Chris scuffed his shoes on the cement tiles.

"Referral to study hall." P.E. was off my class roster for good, thanks to May 12. Study hall and I were well acquainted. I'd spent hours snoozing through detention or pranking on the other inmates. I always took the rap when Kev, Chris, and I did our pranks. When we got caught. No one wanted to suspend the quarterback who led the team to district championships two years in a row. I'd visit study hall until I bounced into another elective class. Home Economics might work for my broken body.

After a jaw-clenching day, the last bell pervaded the halls, killing a few eardrums. My classmates rose from their seats eager to claim the waning days of summer on the beach. I remained seated.

"Hold on," yelled the strict new English teacher in room thirty-two. "I haven't dismissed you yet."

Twenty-seven seniors returned to their assigned seats. A disappointed murmur raced up and down the neat rows of desks.

"Um . . . Mr. Dalton, sir," I said in a mock display of Stupid. Unaccustomed embarrassment ignited in my chest. BA, I would've gotten off on the class clown act. After accident, I played an expected role. The one thing I counted on to keep my crown of barbed wire.

"Yes." Dalton studied his seating chart. "Mr. Alexander."

"It's Lucas, *sir*."

"*Mr. Alexander*, if you don't mind getting to the point." Exasperation clipped his tone.

"Yes, sir. Uh . . . Mr. Dalton, sir . . . um, when the bell rings, doesn't that mean we're dismissed?" Normally, I'd fake stutter. No faking going on now. My prankster genes had taken a powder.

"That's why they installed those things called bells," I managed to blurt out.

Stilted sniggers escalated from one corner of the classroom to the others.

"Oh, jeez, here we go," someone mumbled sarcastically.

Wilted, hollow thorns pricked my scalp. The class-clown act no longer gave me joy. I fidgeted on the wooden seat, my butt growing numb. I wanted to get out. Wished I'd shoved my foot in my mouth.

A muscle in Dalton's neck throbbed, ready to explode. I fought to keep from shielding my face from the blood about to spurt. He slammed an eBay-special clipboard on the desk, the sound bouncing up to the twelve-foot-high ceiling. Soon as the classroom fell silent, he asked one of four beach-blonde cheerleaders in the front row to repeat his earlier rule concerning dismissal, "for all to hear, especially the hearing-impaired Mr. Alexander." He'd already shoved the subject of dismissal—one of his commandments—up our backdoors at the beginning of the period.

I almost took verbal umbrage—Silver's calendar word of the day—at the "hearing-impaired" remark, but I had pushed my luck with my classmates. Not that my bum leg allowed room to disobey the rule and jump out of my seat earlier. Small favors.

Lead cheerleader Suz Williams clearly enunciated the stupid-ass law, "Students must remain seated at all times. Class is dismissed when Mr. Dalton so instructs."

"Now, Mr. Alexander." Dalton's slitty-eyed glare nailed me. "You may learn the rule by writing it longhand one hundred times. Due at the beginning of class tomorrow." He paused for emphasis. "Class dismissed."

Gasps and tittering erupted. The punishment was a first for me. Dalton earned my long, low whistle. After the last person

filed out the door, I sauntered past the smirking teacher, a go
grin plastered on my face. Once outside in the covered breezew
Chris and Kev ambushed me.

"Schooled you." Kev's long dark hair blew across his pale fa
No matter how long he baked under the sun, he couldn't ca
a tan if his old man paid for it. His real name was Kevin, l
we shortened it to Kev, 'cause his hoity-toity parents hated
Anything to rile up the parentals.

"Dalton's got guts."

"Yeah, anyone who gives you extra homework as a rap has g
for miles." Kev punched Chris's arm.

"I'll break him down." I leaned against a bank of turd-bro
lockers. Ever since I'd whirled into town in seventh grade, teach
never knew what'd hit them. I pushed their buttons, always shy
suspension. BA, I was king of harmless pranks. Everyone expec
it. All hail the lofty expectations of the delusional. Regardles
needed the wiseass façade. Needed it to kill the guilt gnawing
my gut 24/7. Needed it to lead my vigilante club.

This year, I'd become the Revenge King—after I got
sidekicks onboard. The unidentified May 12 gang won't kn
what hit them. My new life's purpose.

Chris slanted me a sly look. "So what's on the agenda for sen
year? Got any killer pranks we should start planning?" He to
a step back as if afraid I'd flatten him, afraid I'd go psycho
him. Or melt into a stinking puddle of grief. Living with a sin
mother, Chris had always been more emo. One of the reasons
fit in with us. We balanced him out, gave him balls. In turn,
and Silver helped Kev and me understand girls better.

Soon, I'd crush the seashells everyone moonwalked over. "H
yeah." I plowed my fingers into my spiky hair, tugging the gel

locks into random disorder. "You ready for some hardcore stunts?" *Of the revenge kind?* My gang of two salivated like winter-starved wolves.

We moseyed toward the student parking lot, cracking jokes at the nerds and freshmen, rating the girls from one to ten. The good old days. Well-wishers continued to welcome me back. I smiled until the skin of my face prepared to splinter into a desert road. With the optimism they expected, I thanked everyone. But if one more person spewed out another Hallmark greeting, I'd lead them all on a tour of the cemetery followed by a jaunt to the junkyard to show them my wrecked car. Then I wanted every one of them to stroke the lacerations around my knee and torso, take a glimpse into the emptiness of my soul, and then ask how I was doing.

"Yo, Lucas, you with us?" Chris pointed to a chunky, crater-faced freshman. "There's a ten for you."

I yanked my head out of my sorry butt. "You saw her first. She's all yours." I propelled Chris toward the girl. Reddening, she bolted in the direction of a late model hybrid in the pickup zone.

"Hey, little lovely," Kev yelled. "Lover boy wants to suck your lips." He dragged a grumbling, balking Chris toward the silver Ford.

"Come on, you wankers." Impatience burned through me. The sun beat down from a hazy blue sky. Seagulls wheeled overhead, screeching a greeting, a warning, who knew what. As long as they didn't dive-bomb me. BA, we'd hit up the beach and catch waves on our boards. Those days of fun and innocence died on May 12.

Hell, I sound like one of those lamo literary novels they made us read in English lit last year. *It is what it is, though.* Death had barreled over me at a hundred and twenty miles an hour. Fun and innocence never had a chance. Nor a choice.

"Dildo, you started it." Kev loped over to me. He'd adopted Silver's use of pet names the day he *discovered* her. It was head over heels for him a year ago, for a minute. Not so much for Silver.

"Effing prick. You ripped my new shirt." Chris flattened the tear in the shoulder of his navy polo. Standard school uniform they made us wear to keep the dress code on equal footing.

"Is mommy gonna spank you?" Kev mimicked Chris's mother yelling, even managed to imitate her evil witchy squint.

Chris burped into Kev's face, swatting at Kev's finger pointing. "Funny. You're a chum bucket of laughs. My mom works for a living, unlike yours who lazes in her mansion on the vineyard and orders servants around all day."

"Hey, giving orders is hard work." Kev gave Chris a friendly slug on the arm. "Hefting wineglasses to her lips is exhausting."

I rested my weight on my right leg. "You want a ride or not. Don't have all day."

"Heck, yeah. Been waiting to check out your new ride." Kev picked up his backpack, digging out his earbuds. Chris and Kev exchanged skeptical looks. "What hardcore stunts you dreaming up?" Kev asked.

Vigilante ideas warred for emergence. First, I wanted to run ideas by Silver before I spilled. My right foot skipped a step. Whoa. Did I just think that? Sweat grew under my pits.

"Let's roll." The two stooges followed me into the car. Kev sprawled across the backseat, Chris rode shotgun. The second my wheels squealed out of the parking lot, I met Kev's expectant brown eyes in the rearview mirror. "It's epic. We'll be heroes."

"You gonna bang down Raymond for talking smack about you beating him up last spring?" Kev dry-washed his hands, ready to make a move. "He had a torso full of bruises to show for it."

"What about turning the team against you?" Chris shrugged. "He's telling everyone you threw the last two games because you didn't want him dating Silver."

I white-knuckled the steering wheel, wanting to plant my fist in Raymond's face. For Silver more than anything else. "Screw that lying pissant. He'll get his soon enough. I'm talking the majors."

Their anticipation chomped through the awkwardness in the cab. "My house tonight," I said.

Chris unbuckled his seatbelt as we approached his house in an older neighborhood between my mini-McMansion 'hood and the school. Fresh Pepto Bismol paint coated the small house. Chris must have been working on the grass-green trim since half the windows were still painted in humdrum white. His summer job when his scary, whacko mom didn't have him slaving at her new-age shop while she brewed fake witches potions in the back. Kev would hang out until Chris's mom got home and swept him out with her broom. One of the vineyard hands would swing into town and cart him home. New day, same old shit. Time to end the status quo.

"You're never this mysterious. Must be good." Chris slammed the door shut, rocking the Camaro.

"Hey," I called to their retreating backs. They turned. Their excitement fed my adrenaline. "It's for Silver." I stomped on the clutch and gunned the accelerator, taking a deep breath of new car smell.

New everything.

Chapter 4

A titanic moving van hogged the street between my house and the house next door. They'd spared me just enough room to slip into the far right spot of our three-car driveway.

Musclemen movers hauled a gargantuan water fountain toward the open front doors. In the four years I'd lived in upper-middle suburbia, a revolving door of families lived in the lone rental on the street. The last residents had turned the five-bedroom pad into a white-trash commune. Best count, ten kids and eight adults lived there. The three oldest boys were drug dealers. One of the kids roasted a neighbor's cat in a backyard fire pit. A steady string of petty thefts kept the cops on speed dial. The 'hood heaved a humongous sigh of relief when the landlord evicted them six months ago. They'd left the house a waste, the yard weedy and littered with trash and dog crap. Did I mention the four pit bulls? Slumlord sold it, and contractors had been in and out over the last two months.

"Maybe we'll get lucky with a normal family," I muttered.

I needed normal.

After I headed into the house, I checked downstairs to ensure Mom hadn't come home early, hovering and suffocating. She'd done that a lot since the accident. Before, she worked until seven, an hour before Dad got home from the law firm in Monterey.

"Mom, you here?" I called up the stairs, waited. Radio silence.

I dumped my backpack on the granite island and ransacked the kitchen for non-diet Coke and a bag of corn chips. No need to watch what I ate since coaches no longer dictated my diet. One killer bonus.

The snick and hiss of the soda top filled the too quiet lull. Usually Silver would be home blabbering away, pouting enviously at my can of Coke. Thoughtfully, I studied a blotch of coffee on the tile floor.

"Hello, numbnuts. Whatcha doing?" Silver's voice filled my head.

Welcome home, kid. "Thinking about revenge." I snickered. Her presence was inevitable whenever I skid into a funk. Coping mechanism, Dr. Beranger kept spouting off his textbook crapola. More like sanity checker, keeping the memories active, and keeping Silver happy. Not that I ratted Silver out to the shrink.

"Quit thinking. It so hurts to watch." Her words hung in the air.

Smiling, I stuffed a handful of chips in my mouth, dropping crumbs on the floor. I threw a chip at *her*. It fluttered to the floor. "I'm thinking for the two of us now. Hope it doesn't hurt too much." I loved this rapport with her. Felt like old times.

Silver sniffed. "I need you, you know. Who else will avenge me? Us. God, Lucas, I hate that you've lost football too. You can replace your Camaro, but—" her voice faded off.

"It is what it is." I lumbered up to my room. It felt weird being home after school instead of at football practice. May as well change things up, do something new . . . like homework.

Later that night, takeout Chinese dinner consisted of Dad eating in the den, Mom in the kitchen, and me in my bedroom. Silver remained absent. I didn't know where she went, or if she went anywhere. They didn't exactly teach Creepy 101 in school. Anyway, I'd just finished my writing assignment for Dickhead Dalton when the Nomads barged in.

They sprawled on the beanbags in front of the flat screen, turned on Monday night football. I put the TV on mute. While Chris checked out my unopened iPhone, Kev drooled over my new laptop. I swear all you had to do was off your sister and your parents handed you the world. My lungs stung. I quickly booted the guilt and morbidity to a hole in my brain.

"I've been thinking." I paused to find the right words to frame my idea.

Kev lobbed a clean roll of socks at me. "You mean the accident didn't fry your brains." He clutched his heart in mock horror. "School's already rubbing off on you?"

Chris smacked Kev's arm and shot him a death-ray look.

"Quit wussing out on me." I slammed my fist into a pillow. "I'm not gonna go postal."

"Told you." Kev knocked his shoulder into Chris and they piled onto the floor amid grunts and fake jabs. They used to tackle me, but they knew better now. In time, after I healed, we'd travel to the State of Semi-Normal.

"We square?" I looked at Chris. He nodded, tomato-faced.

Kev grinned triumphantly. Over six feet tall and lanky, so nonintimidating, he appeared the perfect basketball player. Except he hated sports. Too much exercise, too much sweating. He earned his crooked nose from a bully's fist six years ago. He had a wide, goofy grin, which usually evoked grins from anyone who didn't get his incessant wisecracks. My perfect counterweight to go along with any idea, no matter how farfetched. Where Kev followed, lost pit-bull Chris tagged along.

I straddled my desk chair, resting my forearms on the top of the chair back. Gauging them once again, I swallowed the crud that kept forming in my throat. Dynamite might be necessary.

"Did you call us here to stare at us all night?" Chris asked. "If I'd known that, I'da worn Silver's favorite mini." We'd all squeezed into Silver's clothes for Halloween last year. Hairy legs and all, Chris won first place in the costume contest.

Chris was back. 'Bout time.

"Okay, here's the deal." I massaged my throbbing left thigh. "I lied to the sheriff about the accident." Puppet strings seemed to jerk Chris's thick torso straight. Kev's caterpillar eyebrows lifted to his hairline. "The nine-one-one call Silver made, I remember it. After I awoke from coma hell and gave my statement, I only told the cops my car had stalled in the intersection. I told them I didn't remember any nine-one-one call that night." Before I gave my statement to the sheriff, I had a weird conversation in my head with Silver at the hospital. At that time, I didn't know if I had dreamed her or not. She wanted me to zip it about the gang. She feared retribution against our family if I narked. By that point, the seeds of revenge had already been planted in my head.

"Your memory's not toast?" Chris's face darkened. "You lied to us too?"

"Yeah, what of it?" Like I planned to tell them about Silver's bizarre postdeath intrusions. Right. Nor fess up to the fact that it hurt like a mother to remember. *I'm a dude for cripes sake.* I held up my hand to forestall Chris's rant. "Point is . . . we were attacked by a gang, Mexican I think. Some sort of gang initiation. It's their fault the car stalled when we tried to escape."

Storm clouds settled over the room. Before they uttered a word, I told them what happened from the moment Silver and I first stopped at the intersection to when the street racers slammed us. By the time I finished, they paced the room. Anger, sorrow, and anticipation jerked their movements, fisted their hands. They understood my consuming need for vengeance. For the existence I'd lost. For Silver. For the innocent others at the mercy of gangs of all types. A growing problem troubling our seaside resort town. Gangs and crime followed the money. Tourists dropped a boatload of it in Sea Haven. Even half-Mexican Kev was once beat up because he refused to join a Latino gang just because his family owned business employed Mexican family members. I mean, geez, talk about racial profiling. Gangs came in all colors. Even white.

"This year's gonna be different. Screw the kindergarten tricks, the Friday night football games, lame dances." I stood, shook out the kinks in my left leg the way the therapist taught me.

"Whoa, dude." Kev's head shot up. "What's wrong with having fun?"

Fun? I wasn't a quarterback anymore. Dancing no longer existed in my bag of tricks. Alcohol and drugs flipped parties into stupid territory. Those days of fun had died at the intersection of Screw Lucas Road and Dead Silver Street. "Nothing wrong with fun." I relented.

"Quit stalling. Give us the DL." Chris threw up his hands.

"Street gang." I held my head high. "Vigilante style."

"Huh? You want to join a street gang?" Confusion painted Chris's square face, darkening his five-o'clock shadow.

"Form one." The whirl of the attic fan invaded the room, the sole sound riding a long, silent moment. "Let's do our part to ax crime in town. I don't mean causing trouble, just watching out for trouble, reporting it." While we hunt down my sister's killers. An inner infectious excitement grew.

"Shiver me timbers." A wide smile transformed Kev's pasty face. "I'm in."

"Second that!" Chris high-fived me.

"The boomerang wars have begun," Silver said.

"What're you—" I snapped my mouth shut.

Chris screwed his finger in his ear, tilting his head to the side as if Silver had invaded his air space.

Silver laughed loud enough to wake the dead. *Wait . . . she is the dead.* I knew then that only I could hear or feel Silver. Straitjacket, anyone?

"Got fleas?" Kev squinted at Chris. "Something kinky in the water in town?"

Sweat formed on my palms. Leaning back against my desk, I knocked a six-inch-long, narrow object onto the floor. Enough crap teetered on top of my desk that a fly landing on it could cause a serious crapslide.

"Bite me." Chris retrieved the switchblade off the floor, his hand clenched around the shaft. "Where'd you get this?" The two stooges honed in on it. Chris flicked the four-inch blade open. Two twisting and turning lava lamps cast red glimmers on the glistening steel. "Are you serious?"

Bug-eyed, Kev stalked over to Chris, nearly frothing at the mouth. "Aren't these illegal?"

"Several black-market dealers at the flea market." I shrugged. "We need to start somewhere."

"With weapons?" Chris closed the blade, and Kev snagged it out of his hands.

"Just for protection." I didn't know if I lied to Chris or myself.

"They'll never know what hit them." Kev lunged, thrusting the blade in the air. "We can attack under the cover of darkness, in subtle ways, invisible." He stabbed a bed pillow. "Die, you suckers." Another jab. "Enter sandman."

"You and your song references." I gripped Kev's arm before he decimated my pillow.

"Hey, life can be summed up in song titles," Chris mimicked Kev's usual response.

"Invisible like a ghost." I high-fived Chris and ogled Kev over his shoulder. "We'll call ourselves Silver Ghost."

"I'm a ghost. Hey, Chris, did you know I'm a ghost?" Silver's voice spiraled. An evil cackle followed. "I'm gonna get you suckers," she mimicked Kev. Song references. Movie lines. Maybe Kev and Silver should've hooked up.

A ten-pound sack of creepy dropped onto me, sending shivers down my spine.

Chapter 5

Something pliant wrapped around my face, forcing me awake. Denim? Grunting, I thrust the pair of jeans off, recalling that I hadn't cleared off my bed before I crashed last night. Then I heard the faint clink of metal against metal. Sounded like someone messing with my car.

Pale moonbeams pooled on the foot of my bed. Too early for school. I peered out the window. The automatic coach lights at the sides of the garage were dead. I bounded out of bed, sprinted to the closet.

I snagged a baseball bat, flung my door open. I bumped into Mom in the hallway, knocking her against the wall outside Silver's bedroom across the hall. "Sorry."

She closed Silver's door, eyes red-rimmed and cheeks puffy. I knew she'd been holed up in the room crying again.

"What's wrong?" Mom combed her fingers through her mussed, shoulder-length hair, returning me to the present.

Trying to keep the pressure off my bum leg, I bolted past her and limp-sprinted down the circular stairs. My leg was always stiff and sore when I first woke up.

"Lucas, where are you going?" She grabbed at my arm, missed.

"Someone's outside."

"Mitch," Mom whisper-shouted for Dad. Despite the early morning hour, he hid in his office downstairs. He'd distanced himself from Mom since the accident and slept more times in the den than he did upstairs. But I refused to dwell on who hated who more. I was the one who deserved their hatred. Nothing I said or did convinced them to see it my skewed way. Not that I'd tried hard enough in the face of my other troubles. Pale green eyes that mirrored Silver's and the same blonde hair should be enough for them to want to kill themselves. Or me. Hell, I was surprised they hadn't ordered my straitjacket or shipped me to some radical boys' ranch to shake me out of their hair.

I scattered the natty cobwebs from between my ears. The den door opened off the foyer and Dad rushed out, dressed in work slacks and a wrinkled shirt. Maybe he *was* working late. Whatever.

Brushing past him, I twisted the deadbolt, forgetting about the security system until it was too late. But it remained silent as I eased the door open. Dad was definitely working. Setting the alarm was the last thing he did before snoozing. Maybe there was hope for them yet.

"What's going on?" He seized my arm, his long fingers unable to curl around my biceps anymore. Goose bumps sprouted as I dreamed of the implications. Not that I'd ever get physical with my father. Just that I liked the guns. They made up for the gimpy leg.

"Someone's screwing with my car." Dad and Mom parked their cars in the garage.

"Should I call nine-one-one?" Mom already had a phone in her hand.

"Let's not overreact." Dad dug another bat out of the closet. "Might be a cat. Stay behind me. I don't want you getting hurt."

Yeah, *hurt*. Cheering swirls blossomed in my stomach. Felt like old times. Dad and me at batting practice together. Maybe we'd get in some hits.

In stealth mode, we crept down the cool stone walkway, bats held at strike position. We had to round a corner of the U-shaped house to view the driveway. Motioning for me to halt, Dad peeked around one of the upright coffin-shaped bushes flanking both sides of the garage columns. He made a phone gesture with his thumb and pinkie to Mom peeking out the den window.

Someone had knocked out the dusk-to-dawn coach lights, leaving the driveway dark. Faint slivers of light cut through the clouds scuttling across the full moon. Neighboring lights rendered enough illumination for us to make out shadowy human shapes. So much for cats.

The metallic crunch of a tool hitting the concrete drifted over from the far side of my Camaro. The neighbor's motion lights beamed across half the driveway.

"What the—" A Hispanic voice carried to us.

"*Vamos,*" another guy uttered in a low voice.

Dad darted out from around the bush. "Hold it right there!"

Right, Dad, that'll stop 'em. Two shadowy bodies dashed across the lawn. I'd never catch them chasing on my bad leg, so I swung the bat toward the legs of the second runner. Thunk. First base hit.

He toppled, planting his face in a bed of river rocks. Running lights flicked on an older Mustang parked along the side of the corner house next door. The first thief made a beeline straight to the car. I jogged to the downed runner, took a flying leap on his back before he escaped.

"Lucas, let up." Dad ran to me, tossing his bat on the ground where it clanked against mine.

Intermittent sirens pierced the night. The getaway car squealed off down the street. *So much for standing by your teammates.*

The short, wiry boy beneath me bucked and rolled in the gravel, trying to knock me off. Curses hemorrhaged out of his mouth. I understood enough Spanish to recognize the threat to kill me if I didn't release him.

I wrapped my fist around the punk's short ponytail, savagely pulling his face out of the rocks. The world around me went red. The dark skin and the switchblade gripped in his fist sent me spiraling toward hell.

I jammed his face into the grass. "You greaser pig!"

Hands clawed at my shirt, tried to pull me away. I slammed his head down again, then again until someone pinned my arms back and rolled me off him. Sweat stung my eyes, blinding me. My heart beat so hard, I feared it would implode. I didn't know how long I sat paralyzed, my fists clenched on my thighs, Mom's arms wrapped around me until the deputy cuffed the thief.

Through it all, I heard Mom's soothing voice, Dad talking to the sheriff, the buzz of the lurking neighbors. I felt Silver beside me, like her hand petting mine. I rocked on my heels, my chin almost touching my chest.

"Luc? You okay?" I caught Mom's whisper above my thunderous breathing. She tried to massage my neck. I ducked beneath her touch. "Leave me alone." Without seeing, I absorbed the circle of neighbors who'd left their safe havens to witness my freak-out. The lure of excitement in an otherwise mundane life was like telling a crack whore to stay out of the medicine chest. Head held high, I clambered to my feet.

Sheriff Masterson Mirandized the cuffed thief. I recognized the pain of revenge in the dark slits buried in the bloodied, dirty face of the teen punk. I may have signed another death warrant. But it felt stupid good slamming his face on the ground, wishing he were one of the gang members from May 12 Mayhem. Wanting each slam of flesh to take his last breath.

But I refused to stoop to the level of a murderer. My little vigilante gang of three would rock it without reducing ourselves to criminals. Much.

Turning, I spied two of the new next-door neighbors standing along the edge of the driveway near my jacked car. The man scrutinized me as though he totally regretted moving his family onto this street. A boy my age grinned and gave me thumbs up.

Hooray for my one fan.

Chapter 6

I awoke the next morning, head splitting. Took a tick or two to recall why my feet were dirty, why my room was blissfully quiet. I'd shut Silver down before I crashed for the second time that night. For a change, she obeyed without a snarky comment. I had stepped over the line in my own fright department and I think it scared her off.

After the altercation with the wheel thieves, Sheriff Masterson chased off the gossipy neighbors, then took my statement. The thief brandished a blade and Masterson deemed my actions self-defense. At least that's what my *lawyer* said. Dad the civil litigator did enough *pro bono* criminal work to know the score. Or how to bend the truth.

The jerkwads stole three wheels off my Camaro. With the brilliance of idiots, they gave the car the *white glove treatment* by jacking it up on landscape bricks. They tagged the CrimsonX—one of the two big Mexican gangs—logo on the trunk lid. Nice calling card, dumbasses. I had to resist scanning my back in the bathroom mirror for the CrimsonX bull's eye. Until I realized the gang probably wasn't CrimsonX but another gang setting them up for a fall.

"Hey, Lucas." Silver's voice floated to me as I combed my wet hair. My short period of quiet took a nosedive and I latched on to her voice.

I threw my comb on the vanity, bouncing it into the sink with a clatter. I tucked my navy polo into the waistband of my khaki shorts, parodying the poster teen for the Hamptons in the school uniform. Mom got the smackdown e-mail from school administration yesterday about my first-day attire. Guess my new Nomad status didn't rate the slacking.

"Suppose I have another shrink appointment after school." I slammed the cap to my cologne bottle in the sink.

"Nice that you don't have football anymore." Silver's snarky giggle turned glum.

"Wonderful." The bottle slipped, clinking loudly on the granite.

"Ugh. Crap reeks like a whorehouse," she said. Nothing I hadn't heard before.

"You gave it to me." I was kind of used to her ghostly shenanigans. Most of all, I didn't want to be mad at her. Besides, annoyance made my lungs ache.

"Thought Chris and Kev might like smelling it on you."

"You were evil."

"Still am," she purred. "It's super easy when you're dead. Ghosts rule. Ghosts rule dead people."

"Ghosts *are* dead people."

"Lucas?" Mom called. "Who are you talking to?"

My pulse tripped. Silver vanished. "Jeez, can you knock?" I faced Mom. She still wore her bathrobe. Normally she'd be dressed for work in a dress or skirt outfit. For the first time since I had no clue, I noticed she'd cut her hair to shoulder length. She used to wear it long like Silver's hair. People used to think they were sisters.

"I did knock."

"I have a shrink appointment, right?" I brushed past her into my adjoining bedroom.

"Four o'clock. You need someone to talk to since you won't talk to your father or me." She folded her arms over her chest and took the stance. *You know the one I'm talking about.*

An aggravated heat stormed my chest. "I'll talk to him when you and Dad do."

Mom reached for me, dropped her hand as I edged away. "We're only going through a rough patch. Things between your father and I will get better. We need time . . . to adjust."

"That's all I need." My defiance practically ripped the tight skin from around my eyes.

"It's not the same. Your anger—"

"Hello! You're right. It's *not* the same." Irritation elevated my pitch. "I rebuilt the car. I was driving. I stalled in the intersection. Not you. Not Dad." I stomped off and grabbed my backpack.

Mom rushed after me, catching my wake. "The accident wasn't your fault. We don't blame you."

I was sick to death of the MP3 on replay. Despite the words tumbling out, I knew she directed some of her emo toward me.

Our mini stare-down ended. Mom sighed. "Take my car. I'll call insurance and have your Camaro towed to the shop."

Reverse psychology to get me to the shrunken head pit. Whatever. One hour was better than thirty hours in lame anger management classes. Next on the Fix Lucas List, I bet.

My seven forty-five alarm buzzed. "Gotta go." I shoved past her, turned. "Mom?"

She spun around so fast her head almost careened out the door. "Honey?"

"I like your hair cut." That'd get her off my back for a time. I rushed out before she got all crazy sweet on me.

Morning sunlight slashed the sky in gold and amber streaks. The temperature already neared seventy, summer's final grasp. Might be a good day for a swim with the gang after I got my brain cells fried. I avoided my defiled Camaro, burying it under a mountain of denial. Instead, I checked out a Beamer and a small U-Haul parked in the driveway next door. Another perfect family. Perfect on the outside, until you unlocked the front door and the loonies slunk out of the closet.

I remembered the man and kid from last night. *Kid?* Damn, he was my age. I stroked my temple. Summer had robbed ten years of my life. Years I'd never recover. Going by age, I was still a kid. Any other measure and I didn't know what I was any longer.

I backed Mom's silver crossover out of the garage. Just as I was about to hit the street, the front door of the neighbor's house opening caught my attention. I tapped the brakes. A girl my age stepped out, Silver's height—five-five—with extra pounds of curve, more than I usually liked, but on her, the weight was healthy and alluring. Touchable. Totally unlike the tall, skinny girls I used to go out with in their painted on jeans and skimpy second-skin T-shirts. Quarterback cliché. It once defined me. Now nothing defined me.

Something unnamed drew my senses to her, a weird radiance I was powerless to resist. Yep, "radiance" fit. *Corny, huh?* She inclined her head, her freckly skin soaking up the morning sun. I drew in a whistle of surprise. "Hello there."

Thick and short, golden-brown hair framed an angel's face. From this distance, I saw her long dark lashes flutter over bright blue eyes. Her sunny smile caused my throat to clog. I had the strangest desire to touch her, to sift my hands through her hair, to absorb her energy forever. To fill my black hollowness. How crazy was that? Was mystical fairy magic storming the horizon?

"I think I'm gonna like my new neighbors." Instinctively, my right hand covered the scarred side of my face in a phony scratch.

The girl checked me out, her hooded gaze roving over the visible part of me in the Lexus. An unaccustomed sheepish grin cracked my face. She returned my smile with an about face and dashed toward the front door. Jeez, Louise. I was something scary. I sped off toward Chris's house, her image engraved into my mind.

Reason for living number two. Time to remake myself. For real.

"What took so long?" Chris complained. He and Kev climbed inside the Lexus, strewing coffee cups—empty I hoped—and Pop-Tart crumbs all over. Mom was so going to kill me.

"What I saw was hella worth the wait."

"Dude, where's your car?" Kev tossed a crumpled napkin on the floor, laughing at his movie joke. "And what was the grand illusion?" He segued on to the usual classic song reference. Kev was the biggest classic song nut. He could recite the lyrics to all the greats. Kev used to think he'd be a rock star one day. But his guitar-playing days ended when cats and dogs bolted. He admitted listening to music suited him better. With cotton stuffed ears, Chris and I agreed.

"One of my new neighbors." I zoomed toward school, barely hearing the sewing machine engine, missing the sounds of Chevy muscle. Finally, really missing it.

"Bet it's a girl." Chris smirked.

"Why else would he look so dazed and confused?" Kev wobbled his head.

"Man, you should see her," I blurted out with more enthusiasm than I'd felt since May 12. "Hot doesn't even compute." Cute was the word I refrained from voicing. Whenever we used that word, the jokes about dogs surfaced. Blood might fly in that case.

"Does she go to Sea Hag?" Chris studied the kids flocking from the school parking lot to the open hallways.

"I bet he'll know by the end of day." Kev plucked earbuds out of his ears and stuck them in the seatback pocket. Immediate detention if caught using earbuds during school hours. He never trusted himself to keep them in his backpack. A sucker for white noise. And detention.

I parked the mom-car and the first bell rang. All visions of the mystery goddess fled. "By the way, I might have a CrimsonX hit on my head. Ready to bust some ass, vigilante style?"

Chapter 7

The morning went smoothly. No threats from CrimsonX or anyone else for that matter. No sense in dropping my guard, I kept my eyes peeled. Not exactly known for blatancy, CrimsonX's game was subtlety.

Third period delivered a text from Mom. She needed me home at lunch to meet the tow truck. An emergency at work, she'd texted. Someone must've broken a stem on a flower. Seriously. That's how important her event manager's job was to her. Okay by me. I wanted to ensure I hadn't hallucinated the girl next door. Like I sort of did with Silver.

My lucky stars must've aligned in my alternate universe. The mystery goddess was catching rays and reading on her eReader on her front lawn. *Bookworm?* Girls I used to date only read fashion and gossip rags. Her gazed alighted on me, zipped away, head bowed as if she were studying her purple toenails. I climbed out of the Lexus, practicing my most suave moves. My disjointed efforts backfired big time as my knee buckled and I banged my arm on the open door catching my balance. Stars flickered in my vision as I rubbed my elbow.

"School out already?" Her voice carried to me, sultry and hot enough to melt chocolate. The breeze tousled her hair and she made no attempt to smooth it down.

Wow. My tongue got all tied up for the first time ever. I wanted my initial words to be epic. Stupid Epic refused to emerge from the brain sludge. I strolled over to where she sat Indian style on the new lawn in a loose black T-shirt and baggy cargo shorts. "I need to meet the tow to snag my car."

"Bummer about your Camaro." Lacking any grace, she stumbled to her feet, brushing grass off the rear of her white shorts, seeming not to care about grass stains. Most girls I knew would've beelined it for the closet. Strangely, I liked that she didn't care. "I'm Tara Harrison," she added. She sipped green gunk out of a clear plastic cup.

Her name jingled a distant bell. Dad probably mentioned the family to me during my Summer of Delirium—in honor of Silver, my moniker for the worst summer of my life. The parentals used to visit my hospital room and babble about nothing. The pits of despair kept me from remembering much.

My gaze traveled from Tara's bare feet to her blonde-streaked brunette hair. Weird flutters plagued my stomach. A freakishly intense need to move closer to her kept my feet rooted to the new sod in a fierce battle. "Lucas Alexander. I live next door."

"I figured as much."

Feeling the idiot gene sprout, I mentally kicked myself. We traded an easy laugh, and I resisted the urge to scratch my itchy facial scars.

"You have awesome eyes. Like spring grass." A blush colored her neck, flushed down her chest.

"Uh, thanks." Total moron reply. Man, everything had changed after the accident. My defective brain couldn't keep up with the new Lucas Alexander.

"Do you play football?" A breeze kicked up, and Tara brushed a lock of glittery hair off her eyelashes.

Several disconcerted moments slipped by before I realized I wore my football team polo, the first shirt my hands snagged in the closet that morning. Regret radiated through me. I attempted to unclench my locked jaw. Time to bite the bullet. Beranger told me every time I discussed the *tragedy*, it'd get easier to tackle. Those hundred bucks an hour weren't a total waste. That piece of advice was worth a bill.

"Used to," I mumbled, honing in on a beetle crashing into the damp grass.

"Did I say—" Her eyes grew misty. "Oh, I'm sorry. The realtor told us about the . . . about what happened."

I waved off her concern. "Where you guys from?"

Her full bottom lip trembled. Honestly, I was glad she'd heard the story. Saved me from having to download the gruesome details.

"L.A. My dad's the GM for the town expansion project. We're from San Jose originally, but we haven't lived there in a few years." She seemed to babble, unsure what to say. For the first time, it was cool that a girl wasn't hanging all over me trying to impress me or snag all my attention.

I smiled, really feeling the smile to my soul. "Lot of San Jose transplants here."

"Tara!" A male voice boomed from inside the house.

"Out front," she hollered. "You better watch out," she said in a stage-whisper. "My brother digs your car." A crimson tide stained her neck and face.

"Not much to dig at the moment," I grumbled, watching the yellow tow truck speed toward the house.

Tara's brother loped out to the front yard, smiling crookedly. "Wow, did Tara glom onto you? Don't let her suck you into whatever book she's reading." She nudged his arm. "I'm Denny."

"Hey, man." I shook his hand, eyeing him as a prospective candidate for the new gang. "Lucas Alexander." My gut warmed up to Denny, and I instinctively knew we'd be friends. *Must be my newfound psychicness.* He looked like Tara, except he was my height and built like a linebacker.

And he was a dude. It would totally suck if he played football. "Tara tells me you've been eyeballing my car. Anytime you want a ride, say the word." I grimaced. "Once I bail it out of the shop."

"Dude, does that happen often around here?" Denny hauled up his surfer shorts before they slipped off his butt. "My dad about busted a vein last night." He took in Tara's cup of gunk, cringed comically. "She offer you some of her New-Age goop yet? Pass and run."

The tow driver parked. Reluctantly, I replied, "Gotta roll." Tara shined me her butter-melting smile. I grew an inch or two in my southern hemisphere and quickly turned on my heels.

Halfway to the driveway, an idea whomped me. I spun around. "Friends are coming over later for a swim. Join us about seven if you want. I'll give you the scoop on the 'hood."

• • •

"Her name's Tara Harrison." I plopped down next to Kev in English class.

"Huh?"

"New girl next door."

Kev's forehead turned scrunchy as he attempted to corral his brain parts. "I used to know a girl named Tara Harrison. I mean, her brother and I were best buds."

"Denny?"

"Yeah." He bolted upright in his seat, fingers drumming his desktop in his excitement.

Dalton launched a glare our way. He had one minute before he usurped reign. I waved a peace sign, and scarlet disgust stormed his face. Dude had some serious issues. An idea I might explore later. Never knew what kind of crap I could use against a teacher. *I'm just sayin'.*

"They moved to Looney Tune land when I was living in San Jose before my parents bought the vineyard."

"They're here now." I saluted Dalton, hoping he'd switch focus to someone else. His scrutiny weirded me out.

"We were best friends. Went to elementary school together."

"Seriously?"

"Serious as a herpes breakout. Dang, they live next door to you." Kev's foot tapped the floor. I thought he might tap himself into an apoplectic fit any moment. "That's rad. Man, I can't wait to catch up." The tardy bell pealed through the school at illegal decibels.

"I can't wait to see his sister again," I said in an undertone.

"Eww. Tara." He stuck his index finger in his mouth, pretended to gag.

"Yeah? What's wrong with her?" My defenses kicked in.

"Short, chubby, pimply Tara?"

"She smokes any chick here." I opened my English book, pretended to read, then turned the book right side up.

Kev grinned ear-to-ear. "Denny's perfect for our club." His face darkened. "But what about our no dating the sister rule?"

"New life. New rules." I winked. He kicked my right leg. Silver never would've dated Kev anyway.

Dalton pinned a disarming glare on me, checked his seating chart. "Mr. Alexander, your new seat is right here." He rapped his red pencil on a vacant desk in the front row next to ditzy Suz. Buzz spread across the classroom. Suz blistered me with a look of part hunger and part loathing. Once hot for my Johnson, she'd vaulted up the pole to the next star athlete after I rejected her for Silver's best friend, Ciara Mitchell. A chick I believed wouldn't hand *it* out like gum. I wasn't that much of a horn dog. Ciara turned out to be another user. I dumped her once I found out all she wanted from Silver was to get to me. Silver never knew how Ciara used her. I loathed the poser for that. Silver deserved better.

"Sweet. Didn't know I wanted a new seat." I hefted my loaded backpack and limped to my new desk.

Sound erupted. Dalton slammed a book on his desk. The room grew so quiet you could hear a fly fart.

"Mr. Alexander, your homework." He sneered as if he expected me to beg out.

"Have it here somewhere." In a mock display of clumsy, I spilled the contents of my backpack around the legs of my desk. "Oops, my bad." Muted laughter mushroomed.

"I'm such a doofus." I bent to pick up one item at a time. "This may take a while. Do you wanna wait?" Dalton's disdain morphed into anger, evidenced by the explosion of color over his face. I returned to picking through my scattered folders. "Aha! Found it," I cried with phony glee and handed the crumpled papers to Dalton. His hairy eyeball inspected them before he stuck them in a shredder beside his desk. The whirl of the shredder's teeth drowned out the collective gasps among several snickers of the students.

"Are you quite through, Mr. Alexander?"

"Uh . . . yeah. Think so. Go 'head, start your lesson, *sir*."

The period crawled by, and I remained on my best behavior. By the time the bell rang, I was glad to escape to Beranger's office. He loved hearing that I finally had normal things to occupy my energies: a new girl to obsess over, a teacher to complain about, beating up carjackers, and forming a vigilante club. Okay . . . I withheld the last one. Of course, I copped to the incident last night after his subtle prompt. He empathized with my fury toward someone messing with my new car after having my old car totaled, the car I'd restored from a shell. Boy, could I smoke the mirrors or what? According to Beranger, I experienced a textbook reaction last night. I just needed to learn positive ways to expend my anger, to redirect my negativity toward something positive. Like a new hobby or working out. He suggested a punching bag. I told him I was considering a few darker-skinned models. Session over. Halle-effing-luyah.

I didn't feel like going home yet. Too many memories. I needed to escape my life, including Silver, for an hour. Instead, I headed to the overcrowded touristy beach my friends and I usually avoided near the wharf. No memory triggers there.

Weekday afternoons along the coast were less crowded. Still enough places to get lost among the tourists, resorts, and various beaches and alcoves along Sea Haven's stretch of the Pacific coast.

I parked in the main wharf parking lot. Shoving my shoes into the back, I scuffled barefoot into fine sand, scattering a flock of scolding, screeching seagulls. A sea lion barked to my right underneath the pier holding tourist shops and restaurants. I rolled off my polo shirt and hung it from my back pocket. The scars on my torso stood out from my summer tan, angry pink badges of the seventeen-year race I unwittingly ran and lost. I didn't plan to chat with anyone I'd have to explain them to. Townies I knew didn't hang on the main beach drag.

Skirting the sun-worshippers, toddlers building sand castles, and kids hooking up, I scrambled over the rocks until I found a secluded inlet.

The sinking sun rested its final rays upon my scarred body as I lay flat on my back. The half sun floated over the water like a fiery ball at the edge of the horizon. Not meaning to crash, I did until sounds of yelling jolted me awake.

The wharf and Ocean Street lights didn't penetrate this side of the cliff wall. I stumbled up, putting on my shirt in one fell swoop, focusing my sleepy eyes on the growing twilight. Latino boys taunting someone grated on my ears like a whiny car starter. Slowly, I sidled over to the rocky outcropping to hide in the shadows, and waited for the right moment to intervene if necessary. My first vigilante move?

The voices grew heated. Three 'cans circled another boy, their target for one slight or another. I swear all it took was one look at a gang member's girlfriend and you hit their shit list for life.

"It was an accident," the unrecognizable boy blubbered, holding his hands up to block his face. Three gang members forced him into the rocks. He had nowhere to go but up.

"Accident or not, punk, you stole something that belongs to us," the Mexican in the middle said. He sported a CrimsonX jacket from what I could tell by the leather backside.

What would a punk-ass white kid steal from the town's most fearsome Mexican gang? I glanced around and snagged a four-foot-long chunk of driftwood. As I began crawling over the rocks, the CrimsonX member on the right lunged forward and punched the kid in the stomach, holding him up as the boy doubled over for another round from the Mexican on the left. The third guy shoved a hand over the boy's mouth to stifle his cries.

Without a second thought, I jumped off the last boulder into the fray. *Death wish, much?* Silver's voice resonated. I shook her off. Too distracting.

"Rico, what's up?" I spun on the oldest of the three CrimsonX members, holding the driftwood stick like a cane. No sense in taking a defensive stance. Yet. I knew Rico from auto shop last year. We got stuck on the same team in the yearly Rebuilt Engines for Kids competition. The idiot stole parts from other teams and got our team disqualified. He ended up flunking out for using nitro on his final project.

"*Loco* Luca, wha'chu doing here?" Rico rounded on me, his bulldog mug going all snarly.

"Just walking the beach. Saw the haps over here. Need help beating on this punk?" I offered, poking my stick into the boy's side. He looked vaguely familiar, but not someone I'd met. I'd remember the spiky blond hair that looked freakishly like mine and the red '68 Camaro on black T-shirt. I swallowed the memory lump lodged in my throat.

Rico barked out a laugh. "What help can a broken *chico* like you gonna give? I got my *mijos*." He swept his arms out to encompass his silent, scrawny wingmen.

Guess not all CrimsonX members were bulls. One hit from my driftwood and both weenies would go down. Rico was another story. I sized up the kid leaning off kilter between the two scowling boys, one arm wrapped across his gut, his other hand loosely protecting his junk.

"That's cool. I'll split. Have fun with the punching bag." I turned as if to leave, noticed the ranger's jeep approaching down the beach, his lights bouncing up and down. I wasn't stupid. Better to let beach patrol take the rap than me. Hiding my hands in front of my body, I waved the ranger over.

As expected, Rico grabbed me from behind. No way would he just let me walk away. A friendly grab or else I would've spun swinging.

"I'm giving you a free pass, *loco* Luca. You did me a favor beating on that little bitch the other night. He got caught. He never should've gotten caught, eh, *mijos*?"

His circus pals grunted out a few chuckles and good-naturedly punched each other.

The jeep stopped ten feet away and the lone ranger hopped out. "I don't want trouble on my beach." The tall, wiry ranger stroked his leather shoulder holster. He looked at me, a questioning slant to his brow.

I didn't move a muscle or say a word. Rico would dig his own hole.

"No trouble." Rico held up his hands. His two minions sidled away from the relieved boy, who slumped to his knees in the ice plant.

"You okay, kid?" Ranger Rick pulled out his radio. "You look green. Want me to call someone?"

"The kid's okay." I stepped over to help him stand up, murmuring under my breath, "Shut it." If he voiced one word against CrimsonX, he'd have a target on his back forever. A very short forever.

"Then break it up and get off my beach." Ranger Rick sent a meaningful glance at Rico before sauntering off to check out a dead seagull a few feet away.

"Another free pass. Next time you won't be so lucky," Rico hissed at me before he and his goons scattered toward the parking lot.

And so began my vigilante nights.

"Thanks, man," the kid gushed out. "You totally rocked it. I can't believe it's you, Lucas."

I slanted my head, gave the kid the once over. "Do I know you?"

A grin split his face ear-to-ear. "Dude, you're not gonna believe it." We both limped toward the parking lot. "We met on the First Generation Camaro forum last spring. I'm Mikey Dalt from

Arizona." He whistled. "I can't believe my dad moved me to the same town where the Red Renegade lives. You're flippin' famous."

My online persona rocked a tidal wave of nausea in my gut. "You're the new transfer sophomore? Mikey Dalt?" For about six months before May 12, I mentored him on the Camaro forums on how to be cool. He wanted to rebuild a '68 Camaro, but his dad wouldn't let him. We talked about football and pranks, and he followed me to the Pranx 'R Us forums, too. The kid was trying to clone me. Except for the football. His father forced him to play, but he wasn't any good.

"Yeah. My dad's the new English teacher." He scowled.

Screw me now. "Dalton?"

"The one and only. He and my mom split up. We moved here for a fresh start."

I searched my brain for a missing element to this wacky coincidence. Then it hit me. "Your dad was a cop in Arizona. A gang expert of some sort, right?"

"Yeah. School district hired him to crack down on gang activity in the region. He works with local law enforcement."

We neared the Lexus. "Need a ride?"

"Really? Too bad about your Camaro." Mikey scrambled into the passenger seat as if afraid I'd renege on my offer. "It'll be badass when you start mods."

I grew thoughtful. "Maybe," I mumbled. When hell freezes over, thaws, and freezes again. An idea flickered. "Has your dad always been an ass?" I studied him, looking for telltale signs.

My question drew the desired response. Hurt, anger, humiliation flitted across his face, hardened his eyes. Not toward me, though. "He's Class A. Every nasty thing you hear about bulldog cops is true."

I hid a smile. "How do you feel about revenge?"

He clutched his gut. "Against those . . . jerks?" His voice wavered.

"Sort of. Behind the scenes stuff. Little chance of us getting caught."

His face lit up. "Like the pranks you talked up on the Pranx forum?"

"Sure."

"Cool. Count me in."

I nearly had to wipe his drool off the dashboard.

"So what'd you steal from CrimsonX?" I asked instead.

His back pulled taut in his seat. "I didn't steal anything. Those butt-wipes stole the carburetor off our rebuild in auto shop. I just took it back."

The kid was A-okay.

• • •

The house was empty when I arrived after dropping Mikey at home. No big surprise. Not even a ghost. Until I entered my bedroom. That silvery presence danced like dust motes in sunlight over my bed. Silver and I had spent a lot of time up here. It was too easy to slip into the past and the weird afterlife Silver that dogged me.

"Oh, man, I *luv, luv, luv* Denny Harrison. He's smoking hot."

I knew one look at Denny Harrison and Silver would've been all over him. "You're not gonna haunt him, are you?"

"Don't be silly. We're twins. I can only haunt you. I think." I almost saw her incline against my desk, her boobs thrust out in an exaggerated pose. The switchblade moved on a stack of DVDs teetering on the desktop. "Will you kill him for me?"

I gaped, cringed. "God, Silver. When did you become so callous and evil?"

"Oh, I don't know." She paused as if she were tapping a purple fingernail on her chin. "Like, maybe, the night a Charger and a Mustang mowed through my body."

I sank down on the bed, my hands pressed to my stomach.

"Lighten up, Luc. I'm kidding." The knife crashed onto a pile of folded clothes. "I kind of like living in the afterlife."

"You're not living. You're . . . dead."

"You know what I mean."

"Don't you miss your friends?"

"Of course I do, dumbass McGhee." She sniffled. "I miss Mom, Dad. I miss Ciara, the End Zone Gang." Her clique of football groupies.

Blood rushed to my groin as my thoughts slipped to my last date when Ciara gave me a pole dance striptease in the end zone. Silver would die—again—if she found out how horny her best friend was, how she only wanted me for status. Ciara's since latched onto Glenn, the new backup quarterback, exactly as I predicted. The reason why I never banged her, as much as she begged me. I didn't need that reputation following me like a vengeful ghost.

Silver babbled onward, "I can't believe Ciara's best friends with that twit Suz Williams. And she joined the cheerleading team." She faked a gag. I bet she even stuck a finger in her mouth. Had Kev and Silver been doppelgangers? Never noticed it before.

I studied an old grease stain on my formerly white sneaker. "Are you lonely?"

For a long moment, she remained silent. "My loneliness has a purpose. It ties me to you, maintains our bond, don't you think?

Keeps our revenge pact alive. My death gives me a truer purpose than life ever did."

My eyes watered. Screw my wussy genes. "I may not always be enough. Then what?"

"I don't know," Silver's whisper burned through me. "Will I be enough for you?"

Tongue-tied again, I quaked. My guilt became a fault line cutting me into pieces. Old Silver, new Silver. Which was worse?

The doorbell gonged. Time to line up the punching bags.

Chapter 8

I bailed my car out of the shop on Wednesday. If it'd been the Red Renegade, I'd have nitpicked every repair detail. I just wanted my freedom back and hardly paid attention to the new Camaro.

My three-sixty mood reversal and Beranger's glowing report of my recent session awed my parents. Maybe meeting Tara or pounding the punk thief's face into the ground released pent up emotive crud. Or saving Mikey Dalton from three bangers helped. Whatever. I felt awesome. I even stepped up physical therapy to return my sack of bones to human shape.

I laced up my boots, wondering how Silver or memories of her would spoil my day. As soon as the thought clouded my head, her image drooled at her reflection in my bathroom mirror. The usual midnight horror show. I shook the disturbing imagery off.

"Did you know Denny was suspended in L.A. for hacking into the school's mainframe? He's awesome on a computer. He has *two* in his bedroom."

"Jeez, *Sylvia* Rose." I spun to confront her and remembered her invisibility. I also remembered my same conversation with Denny. "Do you spy on him in the shower, too?" The words hemorrhaged out.

"Don't call me that." My just-combed hair rippled up as Silver continued, "At least he doesn't wank himself."

"Better than Ciara's one-on-one welcome to varsity football parties." I slipped on a nondescript navy windbreaker, tapped the switchblade in the pocket.

"She's still a virgin, more-on."

Wind blew through my hair. I'd need industrial gel if I had more of these spectral conversations.

"Don't get your thong in a twist," I said. "She's not all that. I dumped her if you recall. Too much competition if you know what I mean."

What Silver never knew was that Ciara tried to hook up with me on our first date. Talk went viral yesterday that she'd already moved on to Raymond after a short stint with Glenn. Ciara and Raymond deserved each other. Silver dumped Raymond for reasons that'd piss me off forever. Once I achieved vengeance on the gang, Raymond moved to the top of my hit list. The switchblade may come in handy for Raymond's Karma Day. My groin gave a sympathy twinge.

"You coming?" I reached for the door handle. In an effort to fit in, Denny volunteered to cart me to the park for Silver Ghost's first official meeting. Sand Bluff Park was in our neighborhood, but it earned its share of unsavories. The park drew more *cholos* to this side of town than a Cinco de Mayo celebration.

In a snit, she said, "I have an errand to run first."

Shock stopped my heart for a second. "Like what?"

"I may be dead, but I do have a life, you know." With that ominous statement, she vanished.

Her afterlife happiness gave me a skosh of comfort. I wish my afterlife did. With Tara in town, I was inching my way there.

A half hour later, Denny and I scoped out the park, our burger bags stashed on the grayish, splintery table between us. The picnic table sat away from the main barbeque area. Spruces and evergreen bushes circled us, providing partial seclusion. We went to town on our double cheeseburgers while we waited for the Nomads. Mikey Dalton couldn't escape his domineering father, but he was onboard with our nefarious activities. He planned a little reconnaissance of his own using his father's computer access into certain restricted websites.

Denny fit right into our clique of nobodies. He wasn't into any of the other groups either, although he did eye the geek squad a little too much for my tastes. Kev and Denny especially hit it off at the pool the other night as if they'd never spent time apart. Denny and I clicked from day one. I think it was because he shared Silver's techie traits—my total opposite. I wasn't going Brokeback on him, but fresh blood who didn't know my history or flinch every time Silver's name came up was A-okay in my game book.

What sucked most about the impromptu pool party was that Tara flaked. Something about helping her mom highlight her hair. Lame chick excuse, if you ask me. What. Ever. I refused to give up on her. That curious, zany radiance about her drew me in and left me thinking about her 24/7. I wanted to solve the mystery at a leisurely pace, the only pace I knew.

Darkness drew down the evening. Coastal fog settled below blurry stars, a soggy mantle on our official debut. A chill swept across my neck, and I was glad I wore my windbreaker and long pants. I kept my senses peeled for Silver. So far, she was a no show. Seriously, this was her revenge, too.

Kev and Chris squealed up in a white Chevy truck—one of Kev's dented and dinged vineyard work trucks—and parked next to Denny's SUV. With all the money Kev's parents bankrolled, they refused to buy him his own ride. Old incidents like borrowing his dad's Porsche when he was thirteen and driving it between the vines pinched a nerve. He was still paying for the paint job due to all the scratches. He borrowed whatever vehicle was available. None ever included the good family cars.

"Anybody bring any brewskies? Munchies?" Kev latched onto my wadded burger bag.

"I'm not getting busted for drinking in a public place." I never understood Kev's insatiable need to inhale everything in sight, or his ability to stay lean. Must be all those grapes he lugged.

"Here's the deal." I gauged Denny's reaction. I'd only told Kev and Chris about the gang attack. Trust must be earned. Denny hadn't paid up yet. "We need a diversion from the usual this year. Something to make our mark." The sly hint rolled off my tongue. "I want to form a secret vigilante gang. You in, Denny?"

Kev upturned the dregs of my French fry box into his endless pie hole. "So Silver Ghostman, what're our plans?" he asked through a mouthful of mashed potatoes.

"Oh mother," Chris muttered. A prickly silence rained down as we all followed Chris's gaze.

Seven Latinos ranging from fourteen or fifteen to twentyish advanced on us. Four of them wore black athletic jackets, the stylized black and red CrimsonX logo on the upper sleeve. Dead stupid giveaway. They rambled toward us, definite purpose in their arrogant struts.

"I told you we shouldn't meet in this park." Chris jumped off the tabletop and moved to my right. He used to wrestle on the junior high school team and still lifted weights to stay in shape. I felt comfortable with his shorter bulk by my side.

"Don't be a wuss." I shifted the switchblade in my pocket. "Just keep cool."

Kev stuck his hands in his pants pocket, drew them out, dug them back. "Looks like they want to bust some white-bread heads. Welcome to Sea Haven, Denny. Wanted dead or alive."

"Aren't those the CrimsonX dudes who hang on the bleachers?" Chris cracked his knuckles, flexed his beefy biceps.

"Yeah. Same pack of 'cans I saw smoking there yesterday." Denny folded his arms over his chest, following Chris and Kev's defensive stances.

"CrimsonX minions." I rested a hip on the table, opening my senses to Silver. What kind of errands do ghosts run? Spooking rugrats and old geezers?

Guarded, we silently waited for the advancing gang. They weren't brandishing weapons and we weren't turning tail without discovering what they wanted. Our club needed to make a stand from the outset or we'd never garner respect. Besides, Silver would never let me live it down if we scattered like pansies.

The sharp snap of a twig shattered the silence. Chris flinched. Kev staggered, losing his he-man stance. Silent, the seven CrimsonX members approached. They halted ten feet away. Some crossed their arms, others dangled them at their sides, fists bunched. Only Rico appeared familiar, not that I could ID anyone from the accident. Or batting practice on the front lawn.

"Wha'chu doing here?" demanded the oldest, a short, stocky light-skinned dude leading the pack. His muscles rippled up his biceps to the top of his clichéd wife-beater. Rico stood to his left.

"It's public property," I replied, my tone flat, steady.

"Not for you rich *white boys*. Go back to your country clubs," the stocky Mexican barked out, a scornful emphasis on "white boys" as he stared down a half-white Kev.

"Aren't you in the wrong part of town, *boys*?" quizzed Denny, as though he knew what he was yakking about. Kev must've schooled him. Or he had a death wish.

The stocky leader signaled to the others and spat out an order in Spanish to the tall, skinny pocked-marked dude on his right. They scowled and grunted like gorillas.

Too bad I skidded through Spanish class. Kev arched an eyebrow. I guess his half-Mexican blood had flown the chicken-shit coop. The guttural words spewing out of the leader's mouth weren't exactly words we learned in the required Spanish class.

"You didn't answer my question." Husky leader whipped out a black-handled blade. Recognition flitted across his face, but when he lurched toward me, uncertainty crinkled the lines bracketing his dung-brown eyes.

Total dick move. I hopped off the table and adopted a defensive stance, my sight pinned on the steel closing in at heart level. Tramping down a thread of fear, I hoped they only meant to scare us. Not normally a wuss, I didn't dig the seven to four odds. Other than my virgin blade, I bet not one of Silver Ghost's members carried so much as a penknife. Or a pen. After tonight, I'd check into obtaining weapons for self-defense. I hadn't anticipated one-on-one combat, let alone an altercation at our grand opening.

The spic stopped a yard away from us, reeking of tacos. *What else did a Mexican gang reek of?* My boys flanked me, the two stooges on one side, the newbie on the other. Surreptitiously, I calculated the distance between the picnic table and Denny's SUV. Fifty feet, give or take.

We were ready to fight or take flight, whichever worked in our favor. That night, I realized I'd made the right choices in bros. I wanted this kind of loyalty. If any one of them wanted to weasel out, he could've already scrammed.

Leading with a menacing growl, the leader said, "Who the hell you think you are *pendejo gringo*?" More Spanish expletives followed. He swished his switchblade in front of my face.

The deafening silence of the others tripped me out. I didn't think they'd connected me to the face-rearranging incident the other night, but Rico knew about it. I stepped back, the rear of my thighs bumping the edge of the picnic table. Stumpy Leader parried his switchblade inches from my windpipe, pinning me against the table. The other gang members crowded closer. Kev and Denny's sheer body mass on each side of me kept the gang from closing on my space.

"You know who we are?" Stumpy's dark, ominous eyes were unnerving as all get out.

Maintaining a passive mask, I answered with forced indifference. "Should I?"

"We," the leader gestured to his gang with a wide expanse of his left arm, "are CrimsonX and you honky *cabrones* are on our turf."

"You're mistaken, *beaner*," Denny spat out, obviously forgetting the danger to my lifeline. Newb white-bread needed blade etiquette lessons if we escaped alive, along with name-calling protocol.

Stumpy swung to his left, advancing on Denny. Fists curled and the Mexicans closed in. I seized Stumpy's arm and attempted to shake the blade out of his grasp. Cursing, he jerked his arm from my hold, slamming the knife downward. The blade sliced through my palm, opening up a gash to my wrist. Blood plopped in drops onto the ground at my feet. *Holy hell.* Who knew where or whom the blade had last cut?

Incensed by the stinging pain and the blood oozing between my fingers, I clasped the dude's arm. Raucous cries erupted from the peanut gallery on both sides, blades drawn, stances made. I swung Stumpy's arm so hard the knife sailed into the bushes along the wrought-iron fence.

Even though I'd gained a smidge of control, defeat slid through me as blood continued to drip from my palm. Mom was so going to go off on me. Beranger may insist on a padded cell.

The gang leader and I glared each other down, each waiting for the next blow. Refusing to leave without a fair chance, I lunged and rammed a fist into his muddy right eye. Streetlights dimmed as fiery pain radiated from my knuckles to my shoulder.

I vaulted onto the table, jumped to the other side, a jolt of pain shooting up my bad leg. Without a word, my gang bolted toward the parking lot. CrimsonX gave chase, tossing Spanish slurs as we fled. Damned if I'd further engage hotheaded Mexicans with one switchblade, little experience, and a gimpy leg on my side. Revenge front-listed my motives, not stupidity.

A whirlwind whisked up and rained dead pine needles and dirt in their faces. A Silver crop dusting?

"Good going, Silver—" I'd almost screwed up.

No one noticed my slipup as we scampered into our vehicles, seconds to spare. We rocketed away from the curb, tires chirping. Denny maneuvered into the sporadic flow of traffic, tailed by Kev's clunker and a plume of smoke from the clunker's tailpipe.

Victorious shouts rang out from the truck. "Greasers! It'll be a frozen day in Mexico—" Kev's words faded into the rushing wind. Roaring, the gang shook their fists from the parking lot. Now that sounded funny coming from Kev, being half-Mexican and all.

"That was hella close." Denny threw a wad of napkins at me.

Pressing them against my butchered hand, I felt the blood draining out of my head. Nausea rolled up from the pit of my stomach. Blood soaked the napkins in seconds.

Chapter 9

"Hey, you okay?" Denny sped up, bouncing the Tahoe in a pothole.

I gripped the seat cushion with my good hand, trying to stop the world from bobbing in a sea of gray. "Sure." Sweat poured down my face. I had to be okay. No way did I plan to spend another minute in a hospital. Already did my time.

Silver's voice floated between the front bucket seats. "It's bad, Lucas."

Son of a—. Those words haunted me every day. "Not so bad," I slurred, my head lolling against the headrest.

"You're losing blood like Dracula's midnight snack." Despite her joke, her presence soothed the burning in my hand.

"Silver, zip it." I meant to keep that to myself, but my mouth had a sudden alternate personality.

"Dude, you're tripping." Denny flashed me a quick look. "Um . . . you don't look so hot." The SUV's wheels squealed as he turned it down our street. "You sure you don't want to hit the emergency room?"

His concern dropped an endorphin in me. I straightened in the seat, blinked back the midnight sea. Threads of paranoia tried to whiplash my pain. Paranoia pussed out.

Once we reached home, Kev and Chris bringing up the rear, we weren't sure what to do without alerting either set of parents. Denny called his sister, and the goddess extraordinaire met us in the Harrison driveway. Tara took charge. All hail my savior. She could take charge of me anytime.

Tara shoved her glowing tablet device at Denny, and peeled off the sticky napkins. "Take him to the pool house."

She cared about me. Awesome. My legs wobbled like the newly risen as I leaned on Denny.

"Where's the pool?" Chris asked as they half-dragged me down the flagstone walkway past a dirt lot in the backyard. Trees hid the remodeled pool house from the main house.

Kev chuckled. "Previous tenants must've stolen it."

Denny and Kev helped me stretch out on the couch. I let them think I needed the assist. Really. Once they'd accomplished that magnanimous feat, they stood like simpletons watching me bleed to death.

"Where'd Tara go? *She'll* know how to wrap my hand."

"Off to get first aid supplies." Denny scuffed his shoes on the tiles. Kev ransacked the refrigerator and brought me a can of 7-Up, along with a horde of snacks for his bottomless pit.

Eons later, Tara returned, tossed a wet washcloth at Denny. "Try to stop the bleeding. I can't believe you dimwits didn't think of that."

"Well—"

"Hold pressure on it." She shoved Denny's arm.

Her voice cut through the stream of unconsciousness threatening to submerge me. I closed my eyes to end the immersion, sucked down soda to kill the turbulence in my gut.

Denny wrapped a ragged towel around my hand. "Did Mom or Dad see you?"

"No." She pushed in front of him and began doctoring my hand after his piss-poor attempt to save my life. "What happened?"

"Slight accident," replied Kev wryly, flopping onto the floor against an easy chair. "If you want blood, you've got it." The AC/DC reference slid by Tara.

"*Slight,*" Tara echoed in disgust. "He needs stitches. At least I stopped the bleeding." Like a born nurse, she cleaned and bandaged my hand. "His color's returning too."

"Martian green." Kev toed my leg, mimicked ET.

"Go get him orange juice, idiot," Tara commanded. Denny bolted before she destroyed his manhood. "Lucas, can you hear me?"

Silver would've loved Tara. They both got off on the name-calling. Speaking of which . . . I cracked an ear open. My head hurt to move it. I guess blood loss screwed with the wits. If I'd been conscious after The Accident, I might've remembered that tidbit.

Tara's velvety tan face swam above mine. I buried my right cheek in the pillow, weirdly ill at ease about my battered body, even though my scars were fading. Without another thought, I lifted my good hand and feathered it over her cheek. "Thanks," I croaked out. She gasped and stood to her full height.

Chris sighed out his relief. "Same old Lucas."

"When it comes to seduction, he's always ready, villain, and able." Kev cracked a hoarse chortle. With a meaningful look, Chris slugged him. I guess he was afraid I'd step off the mythical ledge again.

Tara's cheeks pinkened. Damned if that self-conscious bug didn't start a river of sweat down my back. Whole new feeling for me. Her floral perfume wafted over me, feeding me more sugar than any orange juice. Behind her, that shimmery air thing happened. Suddenly, Tara wrapped her arms around herself and the blood drained out of her face. *Whoa, dude.* She spun around as if someone had tapped her on the shoulder. Just as quickly she turned back to me, rubbing her hands across her arms.

"Lucas, Tara can feel me," Silver whispered in my ear, awe evident in her whispery voice. "I better split."

The air cooled. I met Tara's gaze. Her eyes were haunted, but she snapped out of it quickly. I wanted to question her, but didn't want to tip my hand. My buds saved me.

Kev straightened, tossed his empty soda can and snack wrappers on the coffee table. "We gotta bounce before curfew."

"You going to live?" Chris flicked a finger on my head.

"I'll stay with Lucas, make sure he gets home." Tara herded them out. "Back in a sec." The door thunked shut behind the trio.

Man, I liked her and I had no clue why. Totally not my type. Before Accident, I never went for the shy, smart, natural girls who had brains. What a loser I used to be. My hand flinched, throbbed. Tara's flip-flops click-clacked outside the door. For some weird reason, I felt a connection to her. Couldn't explain it even if I traded my brain for Einstein's.

The door clicked open and Tara returned to my side.

"Hey, thanks for patching me up." My smile evolved into a pained grimace.

Tara patted my shoulder, her warm fingertips lingering before she handed me a glass of orange juice and cookies wrapped in a napkin. "No problem." She piled the scattered medical supplies neatly on the coffee table.

I finagled myself into an upright position and downed half the juice. "You saved my life."

She sat on the edge of the couch, rolled her eyes. "Anyone could have done it." Her skin turned that edible shade of cotton candy again.

"Riiight. Not those posers."

Her hand alighted on my arm. Electricity arced between us. *Club Tara calling.* Her blush deepened. Then as if her internal light flipped on, she leaned against my side and mocked sternly, "Now, Lucas Alexander, tell me what really happened tonight."

"You sound like my mother." I groaned, dropped my head back on the couch arm. I probably turned as green as the vines snaking across the golden velour couch.

"I'm not, am I?" Her fingers trailed over the back of my hand ever so softly.

I hadn't planned to tell anyone else about my new "gang" or my reasons for vengeance, but when her expectant blue eyes reached into my soul, I confessed it all to Tara. Something about her drew me in like rain in the desert, kept my good hand touching her arm, and compelled me to open up in a way I hadn't ever opened to a virtual stranger.

Chapter 10

Denny's mom roped him into helping her on the computer and he never returned. Tara walked me home, mainly to keep me from snacking on daisies in the side strip between our houses. *I don't eat greens.* I felt better after sharing my wrecked life with her, telling her about the gang that caused the accident, ensuring her silence. To feel more life sprout within my barrenness.

Within seconds of entering the kitchen, Mom fixated on the bloody gauze around my hand and had twin cows. Time to up *her* meds. My stomach grew all gnarly again.

"What did you do now? Can't you go anywhere without killing yourself anymore?" Eyes blazing, she latched onto my arm. All of a sudden, she released me and sagged against the counter. Tears spilled down her cheeks. "Oh, honey . . . I didn't mean it. What happened? Are you okay?" She reached for me again.

Horror backed me against the counter before an arrogant rush drew my spine taut. The granite edge dug into my rear and I wanted to morph into the stone. "One day I might just get killed. Then who would you scream at? Dad?" I hugged my hand to my middle, smearing more blood onto my ruined A's T-shirt.

"Lucas!" Dad's berating voice boomed in the archway to the dining room. My bandaged hand forestalled his rant. After examining my wound, he ushered me to his car. Absolute silence kept our emotions in check on the drive to the hospital.

My initial nausea and dizziness stemmed from the idea of hospitals, not the sliced hand or blood. *Come on. I'm a dude. We don't get queasy over crap like that. Right?* Sea Haven General's emergency room door loomed alien-like. When I crossed the threshold, panic clawed up my gut. It felt different this time. For one, I was conscious. Second, I was more alive than dead.

I'd been a walking zombie until I realized Silver was still here in that weird way. When school started, I became the living dead, a vampire sucking up the emotions of those around me, trying to fill my never-ending emptiness. Tara edged my darkness with sunshine, warming the wintry, lonely muck of my innards. The blood dripping from my hand proved I wasn't the walking dead, nor the undead, but a living kid who had arisen from the depths of death. Yeah, that sounded dumb. Beranger said I needed a hobby, something to divert my troubles. Tara fit the prescription. Vengeance became an astounding second. Spouting poetry was becoming a perilous third. Maybe I needed my brain jumbled again.

Dad hovered at my side as I told the ER doctor that Denny had left a hobby knife on the couch, it slipped between the cushions, and I'd stuck my hand on it. They bought the story, hook, line, and stinker, although the doctor gave me a hairy eyeball. No tetanus shot necessary since I'd gotten one after The Accident. I suffered no nerve or tendon damage and ended up with sixteen stitches.

When I got home, I went straight to bed, willing Silver to appear. No such luck. I missed her every stinking day. One positive, though, my stomach no longer clenched every time she sprang to my awareness. What did ghosts do all day when they weren't haunting the living? Jeez, Louise, I needed a manual on Girls, Ghosts, and Gimps.

The weekend dragged onward. The pain injection wore off and my hand throbbed like a mother. I tore up my bedroom, scattering clothes, books, and bedcovers everywhere searching for the Vicodin I found shoved in my football gear in the rear of my closet.

Mom tripped over herself to make my favorite homemade pizza for Sunday lunch, slathered in salami, pepperoni, and sausage.

Dad gave her the leery eye and played handy househusband except for the fifteen minutes it took him to wolf down pizza and guzzle a couple of brewskies. Words grew scarce. Chris and Kev were on chore duty and out for the count. Denny and Tara got suckered into family plans. The weekend sucked ass.

At nine-thirty Sunday night, the bottom fell through my well of boredom and awkwardness. The doorbell rang, killer sounds echoing throughout the house, like a Metallica guitar riff to my ears. Mom and Dad were watching TV together, the first time in forever. Maybe they decided to play family for a while. Or they were watching a how-to on coping with loss, teenagers, and hauntings.

I lunged for the doorknob, hoping for any sign of life outside my prison of inequity. As I opened the door wide, surprise staggered me into the doorknob. "Aunt Serena? Alyssa?" My aunt and fifteen-year-old cousin stood on the porch, suitcases piled behind them. A green taxi burned rubber into the night.

"Honey, I'm so happy to see you mobile." Aunt Serena held a tissue to her red nose. Last time she'd visited was for Silver's funeral. I hadn't been much company being in a coma.

I hugged her and it felt like hugging my mother, her identical twin. "Mom didn't tell me you were visiting." Classic Mom move. Aunt Serena sobbed and clinched me tighter. Alyssa twirled her finger by her ear in a cuckoo gesture.

"What's going on?" I managed to pry myself out of Serena's arms. By then Mom and Dad had joined us in the foyer and a cacophony of voices grew loud enough to wake the afterlife. Speaking of which, Silver floated on the stairwell. Her elated whoops and our excited voices overrode any sadness in the room, feeding me a weird boatload of glee. One person's misery was another's happiness. The answer to our prayers. How many clichés could I think up to fit the sitch?

"Lucas, take the floral bags up to Silver's room for Alyssa." Mom's words sliced through the tangle in my skull.

"What?" I rounded on her. "No! It's . . . that's Silver's room."

Four pairs of eyes glommed onto me. Sorrow smashed the dead silence. Defiance drew Mom's lips into a grim line. Was this her way of coming to terms and moving on? Fill Silver's room with someone else. Fill her life with another teenage girl. *Ho. Lee. Shit.*

"It's okay," Silver whispered. "I don't need it anymore." The kiss of a breeze lifted my hair before she vanished.

"No big deal, Lucas," Alyssa said. "I can sleep elsewhere."

"It's a perfectly good room." Mom shot a scathing look at me. "Lyssa needs it."

Rattled, I snagged the suitcases, slung one over my shoulder. "Come on, Lyssa. You can give me the scoop."

I hadn't stepped inside Silver's room for weeks. Each time I tried to enter, I stood in the doorway and fixated on the dark purple comforter, the pewter bed, the scattering of makeup, nail polish, and perfume on her dresser, or the pictures of her friends and wannabe friends—movie and rock stars—plastered over her gradient purple walls. At some point, Mom had packed up a lot of the clutter, but the twenty shades of purple and silver was all Silver. I dumped the suitcases on the bed, diverting my focus to Alyssa, a much safer subject.

"What'd you do to your hand?" She slipped her pink purse off her shoulder and tossed it on the queen-size bed, avoiding my frank stare.

"Why are you guys here?" I crossed my arms over my chest, hiding the bandage under my pit. "Hasn't school started in Boston yet?"

"Mom left Dad." Her accent barely held a taste of New England since they'd only lived in Boston a few years after moving from San Diego. She plunked down on the bed and toed off her green and black sneakers. "Aunt Claire told Mom anytime she wanted to leave the prick, to come here."

Wonderful. Another girl to torment me. Lack of any evil intent accompanied my squint. Memories of Silver petting Alyssa's long brown curls—thick, shiny curls Silver always drooled over—surged into view. They used to spend hours braiding and brushing each other's hair in this room. Cobwebs in my brain knitted over the memories.

Alyssa didn't care much for her stepfather. No big surprise. Loser from day one, he'd adopted Alyssa when he married Serena five years ago, after Alyssa's real dad Uncle Nathan died from colon cancer. Simon lost his job two years ago as the CFO of a Boston high-tech. Serena worked two jobs to make up for his lazy-assness. They lost their monster house and had to rent a rinky-dink condo. Then he started boozing. Guess things hadn't changed.

Our families vacationed together every summer for a week and he never came. Instead, he discovered the Indian casinos and gambled away all their assets, hiding it from Serena. He'd ransacked Alyssa's college account. When he embezzled a mint from the company to pay off his gambling debts, the company fired him and settled out of court. Mom and Dad paid for Serena and Alyssa's plane tickets last year. This year . . . well . . . guess I killed the family vacations too. The old days of fun in the sun had bit the dust.

Maybe those days had just begun for Aunt Serena and Alyssa. New grains of sand to rebuild the shattered glass walls in the Alexander household.

Chapter 11

Sandwiched between Tara and Denny, I sauntered onto campus Monday morning. A new sense of belonging I hadn't felt since before the accident enveloped me. Gossip cannibals engulfed us before we rounded the first bend. Sea Hag was a small school, any newbie became instant celebrity—granting at least fifteen minutes of fame. Curious stares, jealous glares, and cheerful grins met us. It'd be a repeat performance when Alyssa joined the circus. Boys would clamor all over themselves to get at her. Might need my switchblade—or Silver—to scare them limp.

Despite my decreased popularity, peg leg, and villain scars—I should've gotten an eye patch and a parrot—the Harrisons fit among Sea Hag's admired and hated. Okay, Denny and Tara earned the drooling. The hallway of cooing girls vouched for Denny. I vouched for Tara. Not a classic beauty, Tara was the sun on a winter day. Sourdough to my salami sandwich. *That was gross, but you get my drift.*

Word spread like hotrods on nitro that I was hard for Tara. No need to drop pressure on anyone to steer clear since no one had the guts to usurp my claim. A bone for the poor accident victim? I'd gnaw on it.

Tara pulled her arms across her chest and she stiffened against my side. Nervous, her gaze darted around the perimeter before she dropped her arms. Shyly, she brushed her fingers over my good hand and split toward the girls' locker room without a word. We shared only one class, since she was a junior, which blew. Worst of all, it was Dalton's class. He'd keep us a mile apart.

"Lucas Alexander's in love," Silver chirped.

I shook off lustful thoughts of Tara and scowled. “School’s off limits.”

“Who you talking to?” Denny asked behind me. The first bell rang. Silver faded away behind Tara, purring over Denny.

Shit. Shit. Shit. Tara shot my concentration to the pits. My purpose for being had faded in the wake of my new purpose for living. I drew a hard breath, blew it out, wheeled around. “Just a pesky ghost buzzing me.” I adopted my best poker-stare.

He canted his head, snorted. “Dude, you’re whacko. Kev warned me you were a clown.”

Were, was the word. I took off toward calculus, the most useless class. EVER. Denny went the other direction. “Good luck with Dalton. You’re gonna need it,” I yelled at his back and finger-waved to Dalton as he hulked in the doorway to his room, glowering at me.

The morning zoomed by. When lunch rolled around, I was salivating to see Tara. The gang and Tara met me at our front corner table in the cafeteria for lunch. It became Grand Central Station as one clan or another skirted the table, assessing the fresh meat. You’d think we’d never had a new student before. Mikey Dalton never received that much attention. Everyone was too afraid of his dad. The football team scared all the boys away from the other new student, willowy Jillian. I shuddered. After lunch, I gimped to last period needing to purge the years I spent as chief of the jock clan. Had I been that much of a man whore?

Seconds before my fifty-five-minute sentence in Dalton’s Prison, I bumped into the nurse outside the counselors office. Nurse Nadia, one of Mom’s good friends, led me to her office. Denny sprawled on a cot, slits of white peering at me through puffy and bruised skin. Nice having connections. Nurse Nadia trusted me and dispatched me on an errand I hated to love.

I cut across the quad back to Dalton's room. As I was about to round the far corner by auto shop, voices caught my attention. Halting, I stepped behind a square pillar.

"Today's the day, *mijo*," Rico's voice wafted to me. "Your manhood initiation happens, then you can roll into the higher rank."

"It's cool, Rico. I stole a bottle from my dad. I'll get her drunk and she'll open her legs to anyone."

"We don't need *anyone*," Rico growled out. "Just you. Bang her and get it done. Be at Pine Cone in half."

Are you kidding me? Manhood initiations? The two split up. I waited until they cleared the hallway before jetting toward Dalton's room, revulsion fueling my steps. I strolled into room thirty-two. Disdain stained Dalton's spray-tanned face, plucked at his goatee. I tossed a ball of paper on his tidy desk. He smoothed out the crumpled note as I strode to Tara.

"CrimsonX beat up Denny," I murmured. "His house after school," I added to a slack-jawed Kev. Big ears strained to hear. Chattering bloomed, despite Dalton's black scowls.

I gestured to Tara. "You're excused from class."

"What?" She shoved her notebook masking her eReader into her psychedelic book bag.

"Your mom's driving home from Monterey. The nurse is letting us take Denny home." We meandered past a curious and crazy-irritated Dalton. Score one for the gimpster.

Once we entered the breezeway, she clenched my arm. "How bad is he?"

"Broken finger, broken nose, two black eyes, bruises. He's okay."

"*Okay.*" Her fingernails dug into the skin of my forearm. "You guys have a strange sense of okay when it involves bodily injury."

"Could've been worse. When four bangers pound on you, there usually isn't much left. Denny sailed through it."

"What happened?"

"They cornered him in the locker room after P.E."

"How did they recognize him? Wasn't it dark in the park during your confrontation?"

"Not that dark."

We hustled to my car. Scrunched on his side in the small backseat, Denny listened to hard rock from his smartphone through the car speakers. Exaggerated moans joined the guitar riffs.

"At least he can hear." Tara squinted. "Hey, how you feeling?"

"How do I look?" He flapped his left hand, careful not to move his broken pinkie off his stomach. Splotches of blood stained his white polo shirt. Nurse Nadia had cleaned and bandaged the worst scrapes on his arms.

"Like crap."

"Thanks."

"What will you tell Mom and Dad?"

"The truth, what else?" He unplugged his smartphone, tucked it in his pocket.

"They'll ask who provoked it and why." I pointed out, starting the car. The burble of the engine leveled to a quiet purr. I crawled over the speed bumps for Denny's sake.

"I got mad at one of them during P.E. and my 'tude pissed them off."

"They'll buy that, knowing your big mouth." Tara fastened her seatbelt, pulling it loose to enable her to face the backseat. "They might want the school to punish the gang."

I was thinking along the same lines. Great minds and all.

"I'll tell them the beaners got suspended. They won't pursue it."

"Did CrimsonX say anything?" I studied him in the rearview mirror.

"Yeah. We're even as long as we stay off their turf."

When Denny staggered into the nurse's office, he told Nadia he didn't recognize the bangers and it happened *off* school grounds. We didn't want school officials involved. CrimsonX would simply retaliate harder. Silver Ghost just got their next assignment handed to them on a silver . . . er . . . on Denny's broken nose.

Denny kept jabbering from a cloud of cluelessness, "I'm just sayin.' I'd rather we had a plan first before we knock heads."

I took the next right toward the coast, turning the corner slowly.

Tara rubbed her hands together, then pulled her sleeves over her knuckles. "Is this a shortcut?"

I sped up. "Something like that," I mumbled as we passed the sign pointing toward Pine Cone beach.

Pine Cone Beach adopted its name from the pines surrounding it. *Town planners hitting the weed again.* It's one beach up from the main sand drag where all the visitors hung. Townies preferred Pine Cone's better waves, less seaweed, finer sand. It was small enough that visitors preferred the larger stretch of beach closer to the restaurants, shops, and wharf. Bigger than Deadman's Cove, the rangers patrolled it regularly. Not as off the hook as Sea Haven Beach, where you couldn't get away with anything fun.

"This isn't a shortcut," Tara declared, confused.

"I want to show you guys this beach. We should hang here while Denny recoups from his war wounds. It's the townie beach. Tourists don't litter it much. Waves are killer. Great for surfing."

"Dude, I'm hurting back here," Denny griped lackadaisically.

"Grow a pair. It'll only take a minute." I parked in the near-deserted lot by the three-foot-high white fence separating the tarmac from the beach. A few people on the sand caught feeble afternoon rays. A trio of kids tossed a Frisbee back and forth. A woman and her yappy dog jogged along the waterline. A Latino boy who looked like he was twelve and an older blonde girl with major dark roots were making out in front of the rocks jutting from the low cliffside that traveled from this juncture of the lot. Our corner of the parking lot blocked them from most views. I doubt we were even visible to them.

"Nice beach, Lucas." Tara drummed her fingers on her thigh. "Now let's go."

Denny groaned as he lifted up on his elbow to peer out the window. "Killer waves. Do you surf?"

Seagulls wheeled overhead, screeched at one another. Waves pounded the shore and ebbed quickly to build into another white-capped curl. The Latino boy pressed the anorexic blonde full length onto a beach towel, his slight weight mashing her into the sand, her fists gripping his back. Lip-locked and loaded. They were into each other big time.

I replied to Denny, "Used to surf a little."

"Cool. When we heal you can teach me."

"Sure, then you can join the *Mavericks.*" Sarcasm lay heavy on Tara's voice. "Hey, that girl doesn't look like she's into that boy. Her face is wet. I think she's crying." She unlatched her seatbelt.

I grabbed her arm. "Hold on. Let me check it out."

The second I stepped out of the car, I heard the girl whimpering between the waves pounding the shore. The boy shoved up her blouse with one hand to expose her naked breasts. At the same time, he fumbled with his pants. The girl began beating her fists on his back, and I knew she hadn't been holding him to her, but was trying to push him away. Diving in for another hard, biting kiss, his mouth covered her cries.

I skidded off the grid. "Call nine-one-one," I shouted, hightailing it for the sand as fast as my limited mobility allowed.

The boy had already gone over the edge and wasn't returning. She cried out, "I said stop! Not here." He wrapped her in a bear hug to stop her from beating on him, using the full force of his weight to pin her to the sand.

Red-hot fury increased my pace. I ran in the shadows of the staggered cliffs. Intermittent sirens arose from the expanse of narrow sand that connected the beach to the main drag on the other side of the cliff. "Hey," I called out to attract the couple's attention.

Wind whirled sand at the cliff. It was then that I noticed the expectant audience. Four boys wearing CrimsonX jackets watched from the shadows of the rocky outcropping. They slapped at the sand blowing into their faces, knuckling their eyes. Finally, they all perked up at the sound of sirens. Still no one noticed me as I approached the scrambling couple. The creep was pulling his pants up, the girl sobbing on the towel, straightening her clothes.

He held his hand out to her and she slapped him away. "Just go, Ricky." He tried to lift her up, but she crab crawled away from him. Instead, he dashed toward his friends, and the five boys bolted . . . straight into a ranger's Jeep.

I didn't recognize the girl, but that didn't mean anything in Sea Haven. Despite the one public high school, there were private schools and home schooling here just like anywhere else. I waited until I knew she was safe before I nonchalantly retraced my steps to the car. But I was burning inside, sifting through the ashes of another life, a similar incident, fanning the embers of my hatred of violent, immoral gangs and their kind. And so much more.

My fists curled into my palm, ragged nails digging into my skin, pressurizing my bandaged cut. When I climbed into the car, Tara touched my cheek, her fingers trailing down my throbbing jaw to my knotted shoulder.

"Rangers caught the boys," she said.

I peered down the incline. "I should have done more." Two rangers had corralled the boys, and the girl stood off to the side glaring at Ricky, clutching her purse to her stomach.

"You did enough."

"Dude, you stopped whatever was going down *and* avoided a CrimsonX beating." Denny thumped the back of my seat.

No one spoke a word the rest of the way home. Reality had hit us at one-eighty.

I parked the Camaro in the Harrison's driveway. Mrs. Harrison arrived seconds later in her boxy Volvo. A slender, older version of Tara peered at us through the open car window. Other than a few light crinkles framing her eyes, her skin was smooth and youthful. Tara would be hot as she aged.

Tara slid out of the car and pulled the seat forward for Denny.

"My God, what happened to you?" Mrs. Harrison bounced out of her car so fast she almost took a header into the side of my Camaro. *Take it easy, Mrs. H. Precious is alive.*

"Wasn't my fault." Denny adopted a hangdog expression. He recited the semi-bogus story.

Mrs. Harrison squealed. "We better take you to the doctor." She frowned at my bandaged hand as I helped Denny into her car. *Welcome to Sea Haven. I'm the dark lord of trouble.*

Tara and I watched them drive off. "Do you want to go swimming?" I asked.

She cast her gaze down at her gladiator sandals, hugged her bulging book bag to her stomach. "I have a lot of homework."

"There's no one around to bother us." I managed a half-hearted wink.

"Until Chris and Kev get here. Sorry. No thanks." She walked away.

I sensed her irritation, knew I had to make another move. "There's a dance Friday. Do you want to go?" I chanced asking her. The gossip mill already spilled that she'd turned down two other boys. No girl had ever rejected me, if fortunate enough to get my invite. Of course, that was before my topple off the A-list. I had to keep reminding myself that I lived a nomad existence now. Only slightly better than the nerd herd, I guessed.

Tara's hand froze on the doorknob. Wheeling around, she flashed me a smile that sparkled in her eyes. I about melted. "I can't." A blush rose up her neck. "I didn't think you were interested. I mean, guys like you don't normally . . ." She cupped her hand over her mouth.

"What? Not interested." I whipped my head up. Then it dawned on me. "Uh . . . we weren't originally planning on going to the dance."

"Oh. Okay." She pulled her keys out of her book bag. "So what changed your mind?" she asked in a small voice.

I fought the random crick in my heart. "You."

"Oh."

"Why can't you go?"

Spots of heat burned her cheeks. "I'm going with someone else. Niles Randall, the owner of the resort getting the first expansion, is an old friend of my Dad's—"

My fist clenched against my thigh. "You're going with Raymond Randall?" Images and emotions I tried to forget swam to the surface, seeping lava into my phantom spleen.

"It was a set up. We're both stuck. I don't usually go to dances." She stretched her sleeves over her hands, gripping the ends of the pink material. "Mom wanted to make sure I found a good circle of friends right away after yanking us out of school in L.A." We held each other's gazes for eons, until her cell rang and she hesitantly waved me off.

How had I read her so wrong? Was she into the über popular jock crowd? My former clique that drew girls like vampires to a blood bank. My life blew. Same garbage, different day.

I slogged to the Alexander zoo. Another new life alteration I had to suck up. I used to enjoy my afterschool freedom, no one to watch me struggle with physical therapy, except my ghostly sidekick. Screams blasted my eardrums as I opened the front door. Auntie Serena was castrating Uncle Simon on the phone.

"Mom took Alyssa to the resort so Auntie could smack down on the loser," Silver's voice invaded my head.

I skipped a step on the stairs, landing heavy on my bad leg. Pain gushed through my bones, setting my teeth on edge. "Damn it, Silver." I flicked a mad-dog look over my shoulder. Dust motes rained on me from the light spilling through the windows above the door. I jetted up to my room and slammed the door shut.

My rumpled bed sank a foot under the weight of my backbreaking books. "Next time announce yourself or something."

"Where's the fun in that?" Cue the evil cackle. A new level of crazy. Or genius.

"I'm gonna get caught having a convo with you, then it's commitment time." Slumping on the bed, I rubbed my knee, wishing I'd lugged an icepack upstairs.

Like the old days, she'd balance on top of my desktop, legs crossed, kicking out her platform sandal. "If you're tired of me already, I'll disappear for good."

I shook my head of the vision. Had I really seen her? The band around my heart cinched. "No. That's not what I meant. It's just that you aren't here much anymore."

"Miss me?"

"Sometimes," I grumbled to the floor. "I worry."

"Worry?" She scoffed. "You're the one who needs fretting over."

"You know what I mean." I flicked a dead fly off the rug across the room. It blew into my discarded shoe. "You're slipping away."

A breeze lifted the blond hairs on my arm. "When you don't need me anymore, I won't have a choice but to leave for good."

Air plugged my throat. "What's that supposed to mean?"

I swear I heard the familiar jingle of her five silver bracelets. I'd given her the bangles when we turned thirteen. She never took them off.

"I'm here as long as you need me." Her voice softened. "We're in this together."

I looked at the desk, shook her off, fisted my hands on top of my rumpled comforter. For the first time since the accident, I really focused on a moment without my twin sister in my life. My head pounded, my heart wrenched.

Thoughts of Tara replaced the sadness. Pale lips spread in a shy smile, showing a hint of straight, white teeth. That indefinable sparkle in her blue eyes when she looked at me. Even the constant blush that stained her cheeks turned me on. It held mystery, reluctance, promises. Most of all she represented hope.

Chapter 12

Deep down I knew Silver wasn't real. But her memory lived on and using that as a sounding board had kept me lucid during the worst summer of my life. What happened when my memories faded? Would I lose her for good? *Don't get your shorts in a tangle over it.* Yet, I craved a normalcy I didn't understand any longer. *Calling Dr. Beranger. Prep the padded cell.*

When Denny and I hung out in the Harrison's pool house counting our war wounds later that night, I basked in a new familiarity.

"Broken finger." He held up his right hand. "Battered ribs, five cuts, eleven bruises." He sprawled on the couch, legs swung over the arm.

"You got lucky. Four to one." I slouched in the leather easy chair. "CrimsonX could've eighty-sixed you."

"They just wanted to scare us. Imagine if they'd seen you on the beach this afternoon." The door swung inward and we automatically zipped it.

"How's it shakin', homies?" Kev tottered in, a wine chaser on his breath, thirst quencher staple at the vineyard. Chris followed like a barnacle, tossed keys on the table. Wow, his mom actually let him drive her batmobile? Shocker.

We'd dubbed the Harrison's pool house Silver Ghost headquarters. When the parents started snooping, we'd move to the caves on Deadman's Cove. One day, I might feel at home on that beach again. Another sore spot. Silver and I used to host an annual beach bonfire the weekend after school let out. Epic failure this year.

"Hey, beauty pageant winner." Chris knuckled Denny's shoulder.

"I gave them a run for their drug money." Denny lifted his bangs to show off the bandage on his forehead. "My fist came into contact with at least one eye."

"Your own?" Kev threw himself onto the rug, stretched on his side. "Lucky you aren't traveling the stairway to heaven."

"Or the highway to hell." I rolled my eyes.

We continued teasing Denny about the thrashing, anything to prick holes in the cloud of foreboding hanging over us. He enjoyed the attention, proudly showing off his badges of war. Forming a gang on the wrong foot hadn't been our goal, but we'd tripped out the starting gate. The finish line was as far as the Mexican border. It flew way beyond Silver's revenge now.

The room quieted, all focus on me, expectant and keen. "We need a plan to tackle CrimsonX."

"On top of a plan to deal with the tire thief," Chris muttered.

"CrimsonX isn't gonna end it here." Kev picked at a scab on his forearm that never healed.

"They have one up on us." Denny waved his bandaged hand. He told them what happened at the beach this afternoon. I told them about Mikey Dalton's clash with a trio of fists. Another reason the world needed us.

"We can't get cornered alone." I pondered ideas. "CrimsonX never fights with an audience."

"We need more blades," Chris announced, although he had no problem taking care of himself since he'd learned self-defense in wrestling. Not sure about the rest of the gang. I might outrun a one-legged toddler, and my fighting skills were limited to smacking punching bags on the gridiron, or my newly invented bat tossing.

"Even if we got those puny legal switchblades, we can't bring them to school," Denny piped up. Affirmative nods went around the room. Any weapon on school premises promised expulsion or more.

"Let's keep the idea in the queue." Even with one blade, I refused to stoop to an aggressive gang. We needed to outwit them, not become them. But if we experienced more violent run-ins, we may resort to packing blades for self-defense.

"So what's our plan, Stan?" asked Kev. "Wait it out? Shoot to thrill."

"While they clean our clocks one by one?" Denny threw a rubber dog ball at Kev who caught it bouncing off his shoulder. "No thanks."

"Don't be a Debbie downer." Kev rolled onto his back, tossed the ball in the air. "We wait for the right time. Remain incognito. No direct contact."

"He's right." I paced around the couch, my bare feet soundless on the cool stone floor. "Timing's the key. Keep it on the DL and don't get caught alone until we nail down a solid plan. I bet they won't bother us again unless we hit them first."

"There's got to be a way to curb the crap gangs tote into any city. The graffiti and vandalism is as bad here as any large town. Just on a smaller scale." Denny scrubbed his head, goading his marbles to action.

"Sea Haven's resorts and tourists are crack for theft crimes. There's plenty of game." I fingered the switchblade in my pocket, digging the cool comfort.

"Not a half-baked idea if we recruited more people. Like a whole town." Kev clambered to his feet, tossed the ball into the cold fireplace.

"It's a start." Denny opened the door and led the way out.

"I think CrimsonX did more damage than we thought. Doncha think, dildo?" Kev nudged Chris in the ribs, pointed his index finger at his own head.

"At least he didn't get suspended." Chris rubbed his index and middle fingers together, sure sign of his paranoia.

"What's the deal?" I asked Chris, wondering about his nervousness.

"Just saying luck's on his side." He kept rubbing his fingers, but my thoughts skipped onward. Chris was a byzantine chain of emotions half the time. Too much for me to decipher. He'd spill his troubles when he was ready. I knew him too well to goad him further.

Denny had watered the seed I planted. Soon Silver Ghost would spoon-feed it into a real cause. After some well-placed vengeful appetizers.

I stretched my leg, increased my pace. "I have a lead on the ass-wipes who jacked my car. I know where they live. Tomorrow night, Silver Ghost goes knocking."

"Dude, how'd you score that?" Kev did a double take in front of me.

"You're never gonna believe this." I told my buds how Mikey and I knew each other. "The kid is trying to prove himself to me. I described the getaway Mustang to him and he tracked it down to a house in the east side of town. He discovered a garage crammed with stolen property.

I gave them the 411 on the sitch and my plan. *Coming soon to a police blotter near you.*

• • •

Tuesday after school, I withdrew money out of my savings and bought a prepaid cell phone loaded with minutes. I sent Denny to Walmart's paint department while I made a pit-stop in the automotive department. We stashed our toys in Denny's black-as-night Tahoe, sans license plates. Couldn't tell it apart from the other five black Tahoes I'd seen in town.

I looked forward to waiting out the evening in the den of lionesses. *Not.* I totally rallied behind Dad's killer decision to work late in Monterey. For an unwelcome change, Mom was coming home earlier than ever from work. Mom, Serena, and Alyssa stalked me the second I set foot inside the estrogen cave.

Alyssa bounded over and hugged my arm. "Guess what? We're in English together." You'd swear she'd just won *American Idol* by the wide smile on her pale face.

I wrung my arm out of her grip. "*Right.* That's senior English." Scorn edged my tone.

Mom beamed at me from the stove where pots simmered. "Alyssa took AP English during the summer."

Homemade Italian sauce rife with garlic permeated the room. One positive affect from Auntie and Alyssa being here. My stomach gave a hungry, appreciative rumble. "Great." *Let me go kill myself before Alyssa gloats me to death.*

Aunt Serena was unpacking reusable grocery bags. Green, red, and yellow vegetables littered the counter. Farmers market fare. Maybe she wasn't such a positive influence, after all.

"Hey, Lucas." Her cheerfulness belied the dark circles under her red eyes. "Think you can stand my special stir-fry?" She held up a bottle of low-sodium soy sauce.

"Raincheck?" I forced a smile, and she giggled. Literally, like an obnoxious girl. Like Silver. The large half-empty glass of wine on the counter hinted at her false cheer. Maybe I should start drinking.

Alyssa adopted Silver's know-it-all-cackle, reducing it to an obnoxious roar.

Mom pointed a wooden spoon at me. "Get used to it. Things will be different around here. Serena and Alyssa are staying until Serena's on her feet again."

"Can you believe it?" My cousin gleamed North Star bright.

I was so dead. "Whatever. Call me when dinner's ready. I have tons of homework." The hormones stayed behind in the kitchen as I slogged up the stairs. Well, at least most remained behind.

"It'll be good for Mom," Silver said.

"What about me? Dad?" I slammed my bedroom door shut. "Don't we matter? Mom needs to spend more time fixing her own marriage rather than helping Serena destroy hers."

"Dude, you know Uncle Simon's a Class-A jerk. You love Serena and Alyssa. What's the big frickin' deal?"

"Two more *chicks* in my business." I clenched my jaw.

"Oh. Nice. So now I'm in the way?"

A weird pressure pushed on my ribs. "You know what I mean." I toed off my sneakers. "You want vengeance or not? It means I have to be more guarded talking to you." I kicked a shoe across the room, bouncing it off a tottering stack of clean clothes. "With Mom and Dad spaced out in separate galaxies, it was cake. You heard Mom, 'things will be different around here.'" My mimicry gave a SpongeBob cadence to my voice.

A soft knock sounded on the door. "You on the phone?" Alyssa asked. Alarm tripped through me. "Your vegan plate's ready." Her snarky laugh wafted away.

"See what I mean?" I spit out.

"You really should quit talking to yourself."

I scrubbed my head and hoofed it downstairs. Alone.

Dad didn't show for dinner. Mom and Serena gibbered about how best to bust Uncle Simon. Guess he was plowing their neighbor. An odd expression crossed Alyssa's face as if she were trying to read my mind and halfway succeeding. I only opened my mouth to shovel in forkfuls of baked rigatoni, ignoring the medley of vegetables on my plate. By the time I was full, I couldn't wait to escape the suffocating trio. *Thanks, Dad. Wish you were here to enjoy the PMS Brigade with me*. It was my week for kitchen cleanup, but Mom didn't twitch into a tizzy when I excused myself to finish my homework. One more plus to the new female regiment.

Dad wandered in at ten. We traded hellos in the downstairs hall, bobbing dinghies in the night, as I hit up the fridge for a bottle of water on my way to bed. Too stoked to sleep—not like the nightmares allowed me much sleep—time crawled toward midnight.

Lacey veils of fog obscured the sliver of moon. I slipped out my second floor window, lucky my bedroom was at the front corner of the house, away from the other occupied rooms. I slid down the garage slope to the ladder I'd placed in the sideyard earlier. Since it was my job to keep the backyard clean, no one had touched the ladder. Or asked if I planned to throw my guilt-ridden, depressed self off the roof. Cool air blasted me, and I zipped my jacket to my neck.

The faint glow of a nightlight crept through Tara's white window blinds. Raymond and Tara? How'd the douche-tool lure her into his shit-web so soon? Or had she told the truth about the setup? I scratched the healing surgery cuts on my stomach, felt the twinge of pain in my knee and my endless emptiness. Suppose I was too tweaked to rate.

Denny waited in his SUV around the corner. As we raced off, he turned on the headlights. We fist-bumped each other and headed to Chris's house.

Since Kev lived eight miles outside town on the elitist vineyard, he was spending the night with Chris. Chris's mom had flown out a window to preside over a séance, exorcism, or some other bogus witchy ritual. Noisy, high on adrenaline, Chris and Kev scrambled onto the rear seat.

Chris's boots hit the crowbars, jangling the steel sticks. He lifted them up one by one. "Awesome. Are we using these?"

I faced the backseat. "Only if necessary." The creak of Kev's leather jacket set my nerves on edge. He'd gone unusually quiet. "Give one to Kev. He needs a whipping stick."

Kev smiled nervously. "I'm cool. I got my own."

"That's a crowbar in your pants? I thought you had a hard-on for my next door neighbor."

"Shut it." Kev punched Chris's shoulder, stuck his hand in his coat pocket. "I'm talking about this." He withdrew his hand, gloved around the handle of a small revolver.

Chapter 13

A jackhammer on nitro couldn't blast through the tense silence.

"Holy mother." Chris pierced the first hole. He molded himself against the door, his dark clothing morphing into the black interior. "Is that real?"

Kev spun the empty cylinder on the small revolver. "Hell, yeah. You've seen my dad's shooting range."

"Dick move." I laser-stared Kev down. "You want epic trouble?" Guns were so not part of our gang-banging arsenal.

"It's for backup. Don't pee your pink panties." Kev hid the gun in the backseat pocket.

For the first time, I wondered if this vigilante idea was a celebration of stupidity or brilliance. "Whatever," I breathed out the word. "Keep the gun hidden. Ditch it if you have to. Registered?"

Kev grinned. "My dad has an arsenal. What do you think?"

Wonderful. Small favors. Weird packages. His father was a member of the NRA and had his own shooting range on the vineyard. Kev actually knew how to use a gun, which was good. Not that I wanted any of us to use it.

We traveled to the east side of the original downtown area. Sea Haven's founding neighborhood of decrepit houses, jacked cars, and weedy yards. Like any other town's neighborhood of drug deals, overdoses, drive-by shootings, domestic violence. Okay, I exaggerated. I hadn't heard about any drive-by shootings. Not all of the small section of town was bad. Nice older people who'd lived in their homes since forever inhabited the neighborhood. Cruising the streets shouldn't dump us on the ocean floor. Quick stops might be another story. We were definitely too white-bread for this 'hood.

"Why haven't the cops busted them yet?" Curiosity rode Chris's attempt to defray our collective nervousness.

"Beats me. Guess a few lifted tires don't rate too high on their crime list."

Denny slowed, flicked the headlights off. The neighborhood wasn't too gnarly. Old, maintained cottages, some remodeled with second levels. Hedges bordered the driveway and trim lawn of the white ranch with a two-car garage. No lights glowed inside or out. A newer Beamer sat in the driveway next to an older Mustang, the getaway car that had abandoned the punk picking grass out of his face in juvie. Denny parked around a corner.

The Chevy's interior reeked of sweat and excitement. Chris handed Denny and Kev each a crowbar and took the third for himself. I patted my pocket where the switchblade seemed to vibrate against my side, stoking the adrenaline popping in my veins.

Clad in black from beanies to gloves to boots, we dodged between cars lined along the curb, working our way toward the dark house. We passed the house next door and a large dog woofed twice. Halting, I held my breath, listened to a distant TV over my pulse throbbing in my ears. I visually cased the house, then gave the signal.

The hiss of spray paint rose in the air as Chris began painting the CrimsonX logo on the left upper corner of the garage door in bright red paint. He formed the "X" first, then drew the "C" through it with black paint and dribbled drops of "blood" down the curve of the letter. Painted like an expert. Kev and I traded weapons. The snick of the switchblade opening eclipsed the hiss of the spray paint. One of the Mustang's tires earned his quiet frenzy. He planned to disable one tire on each car to prevent a getaway, or chase.

Denny and I found the sideyard gate padlocked. "I'll hunt for a key," I whispered, gesturing at the squat hedges between the two houses. I stepped to the corner where the two sidewalks met and dug my fingers in the dirt until I found the key. Got to give Mikey Dalton credit. His surveillance thoroughness served our mission well. The kid was a maniac.

Denny saturated WD-40 on the hinges. I unlocked the gate, sliding it effortlessly across the cement. Stacks of tires and wheels filled the sideyard along the windowless wall of the garage. I shone a penlight through my black T-shirt, counted over to the third stack, found my three wheels, the tires still attached. Right where Mikey had located them. I flicked the light over the wheels until Denny noticed.

A low male voice and shuffling from the depths of the backyard sent fingers of alarm squeezing my ribcage. We froze and threw each other a bug-eyed look. The neighbor's dog barked once before it rushed down the adjacent sideyard, toenails clicking on cement, a low snarling growl growing closer.

I flung my arm toward the gate. "Run!" I whisper-yelled. A radiant trail of light whooshed toward the rear of the house. Had my eyes played tricks on me?

Denny shot through the opening. Deep-throated, vicious barking at the end of the long sideyard shattered the night, joined by the dog snapping and snarling in the neighbor's sideyard. I managed to slide the gate shut before the dog—a Rottweiler by the sounds of it—leaped onto the fence, nails scratching at the solid boards.

"Rotty." The male voice yelled. The dog's barking morphed into a whimper and I heard its toenails click away, then back, a low, snarling growl building in its throat. A sideyard floodlight blazed on, blinding us. Pebbles pinged the fence, silencing the snuffling bark of the neighbor's dog. Silver's presence washed over me. I slid the lock onto the latch, leaving it unlocked, and shoved the key in its hiding place. Denny peeked around the side of the garage, gesturing for me to follow. Chris and Kev's heads popped up between two cars parked along the curb. Unable to contain my grin, I glanced at the one-foot high CrimsonX logo on the white garage door. Energy surged as we flitted between cars parked along the curb toward the SUV.

As soon as I settled into the front seat, I dialed 911 on the prepaid cell. It rang eight friggin' times. Random drug testing night? Snoozeville?

"Nine-one-one, state your emergency."

I placed my shirt over the phone to muffle my voice and dropped it an octave. "Two men with guns just broke into 5296 Harbor Lane. Backyard and garage are loaded with stolen goods." The garage was just a good guess.

"Please identify yourself."

"I'd prefer to remain anonymous. I'm afraid for my safety." I bit down on my knuckle to stifle my laughter. "Children live there. 5296 Harbor Lane." I clicked off.

"Dude, you're good." Kev slapped the seat.

"What if they think it's a hoax?" Chris drooped in his seat, his clinical pessimism piping up.

"Come on. Guns, children, Harbor Lane. Don't be a dumb dildo." Kev smacked Chris's arm. "Twenty bucks says five minutes or less."

Red lights bounced off windows, glinted off the trees in drops of blood. Two cruisers sped past us, lights spiraling on top, sirens silent.

"Yeah, baby! Pay up." Kev and I pounded fists.

I let out a subdued whoop. Neighbors drifted out of their homes, thrust aside window coverings. Most houses remained dark. I didn't blame them. Retribution was a bitch. Best to stay out of it.

We waited until the garage door at 5296 rolled up. Overhead fluorescent lights blazed. Plastic bins stacked from floor to ceiling burst with boxed smartphones, tablets, and more. A pair of cops pushed two cuffed twentyish guys—one Hispanic, one white—into waiting patrol cars. No way had the cops obtained a search warrant so fast. Had we busted open a theft ring?

"Boomerang," I said under my breath.

"Karma is indeed a bad, bad bitch," Silver's singsong voice replied. "You just busted a major theft ring."

Did ghosts read minds?

Twenty minutes later, I climbed through my dark bedroom window, yawning. The night's rush had sent me crashing.

"Lucas?"

I staggered against the nightstand, my pulses churning out palpitations. "What're you doing here?"

The comforter rustled on my bed. "Where'd you go?"

"Out." Reaching over, I turned on the nightstand light. Alyssa sat up, leaning against my wrought-iron headboard, clutching her stuffed baby sea lion. "What's wrong?"

"It feels weird being in Silver's room, and I'm nervous about school tomorrow. Just wanted to talk. I knew you were hiding something at dinner."

Alyssa and Silver were worse than two peas in a spacepod. They should've been twins. I perched on the bed, unlaced my hiking boots, and heaved them off. "Why're you nervous? Aren't you excited? You and Silver were always like that on the first day."

She twirled a curly strand of hair between her fingers. "It's different. I don't know anyone."

I gave her a look of mock horror. "Dude, I'm not just *anyone*." I lay back over her legs. She pulled a lock of my short hair. "I'll hook you up. Have you met Tara and Denny next door? They just moved here. Started school yesterday."

"Oh . . . awesome!" Alyssa wriggled her legs beneath my shoulders.

"Like I'd leave you in the dust." Lifting off her, I jostled her halfway off the bed, tossed her sea lion at the door. "Now scram." Stifling a yawn, I slipped off my sweat jacket and curled onto the bed. I zonked out before she shut the door.

Dreams of spiders crawling over my skin awakened me, leaving my heart racing. Only it was an insomniac ghost fanning my face.

"Are you seriously going to introduce Alyssa to Denny?" Silver's voice bit into my head.

I lugged the pillow over my face, groaned. "Duh, we live next door to each other. Besides you can't have him."

"If he was dead, he'd be all mine."

I flailed my arms. The pillow thumped onto the floor. Sitting up, I went bug-eyed, scanning the room for her. I seriously needed to get a grip. "You're not going to mess with him, are you?"

"Don't let your paranoia hurt you, Pippy." One of her favorite snarky sayings. "Kidding. I'm here for you. One for all, all for one. Oh . . . maybe for Tara, too."

I blinked and she vanished. *WTF?* Sometimes, I felt like telling Dr. Beranger about my daily moments of ghostly delusions. Then I checked myself. No sense in feeding the meter.

Chapter 14

Despite my latest early morning horror show, I introduced Alyssa to Denny. Instant lust for both. Further, Tara and Alyssa were on their way to becoming BFFs. Anything that got me closer to Tara was *numero uno* in my new playbook. Horn-dog Raymond was already sniffing around Alyssa too. Fortunately, Alyssa hated him on first sight. I wished he'd hook up with his hand and bugger off.

Silver accepted this new regime. Really, she had no choice. She stayed away for the most part, and I needed this time for me.

Life seemed good again. Beranger reduced my head shrinking to once a week. At the same time, he doubled sessions with Mom and Dad. But I refused to think about it. Call me an ostrich. Everyone agreed that going to the dance was another step in my recovery.

I decided to go stag rather than bury my head in the sand. Whistling Skillet's *Awake and Alive*, I crossed the driveways to the Harrison house, Alyssa shadowing me. My apprehension collided with my anticipation. CrimsonX liked dances. After busting the theft ring, CrimsonX and the Juggernauts, a rival gang, had issued an open call to war. I loved it, but it set CrimsonX on edge and they had crosshairs on trouble.

The door slid open before my finger touched the doorbell. Denny's face lit up as he inspected—salivating a little—Alyssa's tight black jeans, high-heeled black boots and a second-skin purple sweater. When I first saw her, my throat had grown chalky. Except for her auburn hair, she'd pass as Silver's sister. My sister.

Oddly disconcerted, I sagged onto an ottoman in the living room. Alyssa crossed the room to check out photos on the wall above a weird medieval table with dragon legs.

"We taking the Camaro?" Denny scrubbed his hands together. "Man, I wish my parents would drop a Camaro in my lap."

Alyssa turned, her jaw hanging. "Seriously?"

"Ah, dude." He whacked himself upside the head. "I'm such an idiot."

An awkward hush fizzled up to the vaulted ceiling. With a stiffness born of lingering pain, Denny sat on the floral loveseat and Alyssa sat next to him, her pinky grazing the side of his hand.

"Don't sweat it." I tossed a small pillow at him and he caught it before it thumped his skull. I gave him credit for trying hard to fit in. "I didn't even want a replacement Camaro."

"Talking cars again." Tara glided down the staircase. Her virtual radiance unfurled a fire from my chest to my groin. Her silky voice set my heart fluttering. Douche-jerk Raymond.

The dance was informal, but she wore a short black skirt, a flowing pinkish blouse, tall black boots over black tights. Everything in the room vanished, except Tara. Stars exploded inside me, warm and tingly tumbling around the two of us.

My jaw seemed to thud on top of my best Nikes. "Sure you don't want to go with me?"

As she descended the last step, her arm brushed against the back of my hand. Static burst between us and we both jumped a little, blinked back our surprise. We stood there, absorbing the heat of electricity.

Alyssa waved her hand between us. "Hello! Anyone home?"

I leaned around Alyssa. "Be careful with Raymond," I murmured to Tara. When her brow crinkled, I added, "He used to date Silver. There's a reason she dumped him."

"Argh, Lucas." Alyssa tugged on my hand. "Butt out."

When we arrived at the school auditorium, Denny and I left Alyssa getting to know a mob of sophomore girls I trusted. We split to find the Nomads. First stop, the food tables.

Bingo.

I spied Kev talking up the new sophomore transfer girl, huge plate of snacks in his hands.

"What up? Busting out all the moves?" I punched his shoulder playfully. Jillian shrank back as if she thought I might punch her squat freckly nose. She darted off before Kev recovered.

"Jillian," he called, but a group of giggling cheerleaders swallowed her up. "Thanks a lot. Your ugly mug scared her off."

"You sure it wasn't that bat in your cave?" Denny high-fived me. Kev turned twenty shades of red, fingered his nose. "Kidding. She probably couldn't cope with a gimp with a rap sheet a mile long. I rub off on people you know."

"You're the dark lord of badass now." Denny chuckled. "Where's your sister-wife, Kev?"

"Slaving at mommy's eye-of-newt shop. Inventory or some BS." Kev popped three Snausages-looking snacks into his mouth.

My forehead furrowed so hard, I might have done permanent damage. Chris's mother usually reserved Friday and Saturday nights for brewing toads and tots in the back kitchen of the shop. Not inventory. Whatev. Maybe he was her secret sacrificial toad for the night.

All of us were on guard. I hung with Kev while Denny returned to Alyssa. Kev trolled for prospects who might meet his standards, which barely scraped the sand in my shoe treads. He never really cared about the girls who hung with the football players, except for Silver. Everyone else seemed to want the hottest girl, all second to Tara in my eyes. Third to Alyssa, from what I overheard. Half-heartedly, I trolled with Kev, my eyes riveted on Tara. Occasionally, she glanced my way, waved once until Raymond flipped me double birds. He said something in her ear then towed her toward the jocks and cheerleaders grouped like royalty along the far wall. Twinges of regret ignited in my green-eyed soul.

Big turnout that night, as expected for the first dance of the school year, where everyone renewed friendships after a long summer. Splurging on San Jose's hottest indie band helped. Later dances always turned into wakes as radical home parties stole the limelight.

I bounced on the sidelines, chugging down over-sweetened punch, until I felt a tap on my shoulder. I spun on my heel to find Tara smiling at me, her face flushed and radiant. "Where's Raymond?" I asked.

"Took off with his minions for a few," she yelled over the booming rock song. Frenzied guitar riffs and pounding drums spilled into a rock ballad. "Looks like you need a dance partner." She took my hand. Sparks of electricity rushed to my nerve endings.

Tara tugged me onto the crammed dance floor. Not that I resisted. When I folded my arms around her waist, she leaned back into my embrace, putting distance between us. I knew without a doubt that she was different from any other girl I'd met. There was a curious shyness about her. On the flipside, her leading me to the dance floor showed a confidence I found hella fascinating. Loosely, she linked her arms around my neck. I eased back, leaving an inch or two of distance between our bodies, granting her the respect she deserved, even though I wanted her body plastered to mine.

Her heat drew me closer and her heart tangoed against my chest. She tipped her head back, exposing her inviting neck. Of its own volition, my hand brushed aside her scarf, fingers sliding into the silk. Unable to resist further, I kissed her neck below her left ear, feeling a long shiver rise from her toes. Her fresh floral scent invaded my senses, leaving me drowning in a warm, bubbly pool of ether. Drawing away from her neck before I fell into a drugged stupor, I lost myself in our slow dance. When the song ended, we swam in each other's presence until tropical storm Raymond blew over to us.

"Get away from my date, 'Xander." He teetered forward, and I maneuvered Tara away from the path of destruction. Drunk and stoned as usual.

His hand wrapped around Tara's arm, hauling her against him hard. She pushed at him, catching her balance, giving me an apologetic smile.

Raymond's mottled face lurched closer, reeking of booze, eyes popping out. "That Mikey punk wants to see you behind the stage, tool," he said for my ears only. Without squandering another second, he led Tara toward his group of little bitches. Several of whom, former friends of mine, gave me the bird. *WTF?* They all deserved each other. I wanted nothing to do with that life any longer. The phony and cocky dudes, the lofty queen bees and groupies were so yesterday. I couldn't even imagine I once belonged. Hell, I once ruled the A-list roost. Screw them. I had better in my new Reality.

Perplexed, I wondered about Mikey's secrecy. Maybe he'd hacked into some good info—vigilante style. Music bounced off the walls and dancers gyrated against each other in the center of the auditorium. I didn't spy Denny and Kev among the throng. I slinked past the stage to the door on the right, stealing furtive glimpses to ensure no one paid me any attention. Quickly, I stepped into the hallway. Canned ceiling lights illuminated the short corridor.

"Yo, Mikey?" No response.

I sidled to the first door on the left, a drama dressing room. Empty instrument cases lined one wall. Sport bags in various stages of disarray proved it was the band's room. The second costume room checked empty.

I waited five minutes in the corridor. "Raymond's so plowed," I muttered and sneaked back into the auditorium. The idiot probably screwed up the message.

Entrenched in limbo-land, I was unable to tear my sight off Tara swaying to the music, trying to keep space between herself and Raymond who kept grabbing and kneading her butt. His pawing reminded me so much of Silver taking the same crap from him that my stomach rumbled dangerously. The need for fresh air overrode my orders to remain in a group. No way was I going to toss my dinner in front of witnesses.

I thrust into the milling groups along the outer walls until I reached the doors to the anteroom leading to the quad. Abruptly, the music ended in the middle of a song. The din died. Anticipation grew in the hum and stilted laughter. Principal Wilkerson stomped on stage, thumped his hand on a microphone. The sound clunking out of the speakers echoed in my eardrums. The outside doors thunked closed, blocked by a security guard. Déjà vu slithered up my back in an icy path.

"Attention, please." Wilkerson cleared his throat. "A theft has occurred from the band's dressing room tonight." The drummer rolled three beats and tapped a cymbal. "I regret to say that you will not be allowed to leave while the matter is under investigation and everyone searched. If you saw anything unusual, please notify me immediately."

Jittery waves of speculation swept the crowd. Disgruntled teens from all cliques blasted Wilkerson's statement about the searches.

The principal turned to the drummer who approached from the rear of the stage. An argument erupted between them. I swear the drummer said "no police." Easy enough to figure out the band had pharmaceuticals of the illegal kind. An ageless stereotype. Off-the-charts dumb at a high school dance.

I sidled to the exterior door. The security guard sporting a buzz-cut blocked me. Instincts kicking in, my hand curled around the switchblade in my pocket. "You can't detain me."

"You have to wait like Wilkerson ordered," Buzz-cut said in a pipsqueak voice. He had a hundred pounds on me, and I had no plans to engage him.

"Unless I'm a suspect, this is what you call *false imprisonment,*" I said slowly so he understood the big words. Helped having a lawyer in the family. A sizable crowd gathered around me, some curious and others wanted to leave.

Two parent chaperones joined us. The older bald man said, "He's right. Wilkerson's not thinking. We can't keep everyone here indefinitely without the police."

Buzz-cut looked beyond my shoulders and adopted a typical Rent-a-Cop arrogance. That thread of déjà vu exploded in my gut. Footsteps approached. The crowd grew quieter. *Ah, hell.*

I wheeled around, stabbed my finger at Wilkerson. "You can't make us stay."

"Lucas, let's talk in private." The principal placed his hand on my arm.

I flung him off and held up my splayed hand in compliance. Silent, I followed him to the administration building. The drummer and Dalton waited in his office. The principal sat behind his desk, his extra fifty pounds filling his worn leather chair. I slouched on one of the cement-hard chairs in front of the massive, scarred wood desk. Dalton smirked at me from the right side of the room, and the drummer gave me bleary perusal from the left corner. I bet the Spanish inquisition felt more inviting.

Wilkerson picked up a pen, set it on top of a notepad. "I'll say this straight, and I don't want any of your usual antics."

"Who me?" I patted my chest, smiled a smile I didn't feel.

He slapped his palm on the desk. The ponytailed drummer flinched against the overflowing bookcase. "What were you doing in the band room tonight?"

"What?" My eyelids flicked up. *Set. Up. City.* "I didn't steal anything if that's what you're implying." I bounded up, hands fisted on my thighs, forcing them to remain there and not plant themselves in Dalton's gut.

"Sit, Lucas," Wilkerson commanded. "Answer the question."

My spine straightened. "Who saw me backstage?"

"No pretenses, Mr. Alexander." Sarcasm dripped from Dalton's mouth. "I *saw* you go back there."

"Big deal. There a law against walking the corridor?"

"The area's off-limits to students after school hours." Wilkerson exhaled loudly. "You know the rules."

I thought hard about my answer. Part of me wanted to give up the goods, the other part wanted to protect Mikey. At least until I discovered who set me up. Mikey won out. Raymond got lucky. "Some bozo freshman I didn't recognize approached me while I was dancing and said an unidentified person wanted to meet me in the corridor." I painted on my poker mask. No sense in displaying my thoughts like a radiation cloud. "Spiky red hair, freckles, my height, wearing a new green tee, dark jeans." I described one of the street racers rotting in juvie.

"I don't recall anyone of that description." Dalton impaled me with a contemptuous gaze.

"Who'd Denny Harrison bring to the dance?" I challenged his eye for observation. His stern, silent veneer burned through me. "Yeah. That's what I thought."

"Who did you meet behind stage?" Wilkerson's face wearied with every passing second. For the most part, we got each other. More so since my accident. He'd been involved in a car accident when he was sixteen that claimed the lives of his two best friends from a drunk driver. He'd covered up his grief by becoming a prankster.

My answer sealed my fate. "No one. Come on. Ever heard of a setup?" I tipped forward to force the words on the drummer, who seemed ready to pass out against the bookcase. *Yo, dude, smoke more crack or something.* "No one was there. I peeked in both rooms, waited five minutes. Then split."

"Why did you check to see if anyone was watching you before you slipped through the door?" A sneer traversed Dalton's face, tugged at his goatee.

"Riiight." Roiling disgust threatened to unglue me. Raymond was so dead.

"I saw you." Dalton waggled his finger at me menacingly.

"Maybe you need glasses."

"Watch it," Wilkerson warned.

"I'll watch it all right, but not from here. I didn't take anything. If you think I did, prove it before you toss more accusations."

"Let's check your locker." Dalton advanced toward me.

Idiot. Even if I stole the items, I didn't have time to stash them in my locker and jet back to the auditorium. "Let's go." I kicked aside the chair.

The firing squad marched me to my locker. Surprise, surprise, it was stuffed with books and a picture of Silver and me. I'd tossed out all the football and Camaro memorabilia on the first day of school. They joined the cold ashes of my letterman jacket in the fire pit.

"Go home, Lucas. You're not out of the woods until the items are recovered." Wilkerson waved me off. "Carl, do you want to press charges?"

The drummer yanked his head out of his sphincter. "Let the kid go. I actually believe his lily-white ass."

"One more thing." Dalton ran the tip of his index finger inside his loose watchband. He'd done it earlier. His tell? "Why were you leaving the dance so early?"

Fire raged up my chest as I stomped away. "Call my lawyer."

Cool night air calmed me. My car came into view, and I halted, stunned. "Tara," I breathed out her name. "Where's Raymond?" I forced the rancid name past my lips.

"Wasted. I left him with the football team." She rested her hip against my car, pulled the sleeves of her jacket over her hands. "Can you give me a ride home?"

"You never have to ask." I opened the door for her, my heart pounding. "Did you see Denny and Alyssa?"

"They'll hitch a ride with Kev."

"Cool."

"What happened?"

Caution schooled my newfound excitement and I loped to the driver's side. I told her what went down. "Dalton's already made up his mind no matter what evidence they find." I hightailed it out of the parking lot, cut my speed below limit, extending our drive time.

"Not much you can do tonight." Tara hugged her jacket tight.

"I know." I cranked up the heater. "Thanks for being here."

Ten minutes later, the Camaro crawled onto my driveway. I shut off the engine. "Sorry this turned out to be a screwy night for your first dance."

"You warned me about Raymond." She smiled, her rosy lips enticing me. "Thank you."

I couldn't stop staring at the opening of her blouse, the creamy upper swell of her breasts. "I wanted to take you to the dance." I wiped my sweaty palms on my jeans.

"There'll be other times, right?" she said softly, shyly, too freaking cute.

Endorphins sprang to life. "Definitely." Side by side, we walked up to her porch. Landscape lights radiated yellow beams across the walkway and newly filled planters of funky tall grasses and late-blooming flowers. "Tell Denny, case he forgets, we're not meeting tomorrow."

"Sure. Alyssa told me you're all going on a yacht trip in the Bay, an annual thing your father's law firm does. Sounds fun."

"Doubt it. But my parents insist we go as a family," I mocked with no real conviction. "I'll be hard pressed to keep my mind off tonight." I slanted toward her. "Or off you," I whispered in her ear, inhaling her tropical fruit shampoo into my senses, willing it to drown out the lousy night.

The length of her quaked against me. "Try. They have no proof."

"I feel guilty. And I don't even know what was taken." My lips toured her silky neck, along her jaw line toward her mouth.

"Dalton made you feel that way." Tara made a clicking sound in her throat. "I . . . believe you."

I touched my lips to hers, firm, soft, tasting spearmint. "Thanks," I said against her lips. Drawing closer, I kissed her gently. Her mouth parted slightly, her tongue darted out then hid from me as if afraid. A hot stream of desire fed my blood, and I was useless to cut it short. Easing away before I turned her off, I released her hand.

Dazed, I strolled home. Another seed of life sprouted in my barren soul, replicating as fast as those dragsters had snuffed out my light. For the first time since the Summer of Delirium, I felt like I might be okay one day. For real.

Chapter 15

The overnighter on the yacht blew chunks. Seriously. The dipping and rolling turned Alyssa into a cookie-tossing machine. Silver was still incommunicado. My parents snapped at each other like turtles all weekend. The yacht fest became a yawn fest. Even Aunt Serena begged out, citing excuses about a job prospect and a hot date. Newly separated, she wanted to circle the singles pool. I guess at the age of forty-one, she didn't have a minute to lose. Dumping the sleazebag husband was a no-brainer. I just hoped her divorce contagion didn't infect my parents. I hated seeing them at odds, especially when I was finally climbing out of hell. At least with Serena and Alyssa under the roof, Mom didn't dump all her attention on my mental state while avoiding Dad. Not that she wasn't avoiding Dad. Worst of all, I missed Tara. I'd never missed a girlfriend before from a couple days of being apart. How did I become so girl-struck?

By Monday morning, I was dying to go to school to see Tara. Sue me for being messed up. Yawning, I rubbed scar ointment on my face, my foot propped on the open toilet seat. A loud bang in the hallway nearly sent my foot into the water. I tossed the tube on the vanity and wiped my greasy fingers on a towel.

Mom's voice spiked, then Dad's angry monotone followed. A queasy feeling of unease overcame me. I slipped on my shoes and tiptoed out to the hall. One suitcase sat outside the master bedroom door at the end of the hallway. Dad finagled a second bag over his shoulder.

My hands grew clammy. "What's going on?" I sounded wimpy and lost.

"Lucas." Guilt swept over the deepening weary lines on Dad's face. "I have that trial in San Jose. I'll be staying there during the week."

"You're moving out?" I drove a fist into my front pocket. "Don't BS me. I heard you guys argue all night. All weekend."

"It's not what you think, honey." Mom shuffled out of their bedroom, cheeks puffy and pale. "We're only taking a . . . break. The trial seems like a good opportunity." Tears welled in her red eyes.

I totally skid off the rails. "Send me away." I pounded my fist against the wall. "I'm the one who killed her! Maybe if you didn't have to see me every day, you'd be okay." Bands tightened around my lungs, cut off my airflow. "I'll bunk with Kev and help out on the vineyard for a while."

"Lucas. It has nothing to do with you." Mom stepped forward, her hand alighting on my arm, sliding down to my wrist.

"But it has to do with Silver's death?" I kicked at Dad's suitcase on the floor. Spinning around, I snatched my backpack and flew down the stairs. They yelled at me to come back, but I kept going, bumping into Alyssa eavesdropping at the bottom of the stairs.

"Oww." She repositioned her backpack on her shoulder.

"Let's blow." I banged the front door against the wall, but nothing eclipsed the sound of Silver's crying on the banister here and now, her screams of agony echoing in my ears, the creaks and squeals of metal warping around us, driving into us on May 12. Or Dad's tired voice telling Mom last night how he didn't know what else to do anymore. Could I have screwed up my family any worse? I signed a discreet "I love you" in sign language toward the banister. Silver's crying stopped.

Alyssa and I walked to the Harrison's house to snag Tara and Denny. But we'd fumbled the ball and were too late. Raymond Randall scored again. *Just kill me now.*

We'd arrived home late last night. I wanted to call Tara, but I didn't know how her parents felt about calls after ten, or if she was asleep. I had started to text her, but chickened out and didn't hit send. Never had I fallen for a girl as quickly and in the way I'd fallen for Tara. If she didn't feel the same, she had a weird way of showing it on Friday night. Did my legal troubles scare her off? Could she not see past my healing war wounds? Was she seriously into jocks?

According to half Sea Hag's female population, Raymond had the looks and easy charm girls tripped over each other for. On top of that, he was the star quarterback and owned a hot ride. He also had an ego the size of the Pacific and didn't take no for an answer. It took Silver a long time to figure it out when she refused to listen to me.

"What's my problem?" I muttered under my breath. *I'm every bit as good. I'd be the hotshot football player if not for the bum leg.* I slapped my left thigh and winced, not at the pain but at the memories popping up like depressed zombies.

Alyssa beelined it for her locker, afraid I'd go postal on her. I spied Raymond turning the corner toward his locker ten down from mine. I darted after him.

Awkwardly, I fisted his jacket in my good hand, shoved him into the boys restroom. I threw him against a wall, jamming my forearm under his throat. Resentment easily trounced the wistfulness sprouting from the familiar texture of the letterman jacket.

"What the hell, 'Xander?" He shirked his shoulders, gripped my arm.

I made sure the stalls were empty, breathing through my mouth. Someone had dumped a deuce and it reeked.

"You tell me, asshole. You set me up at the dance."

His lips pulled back and the skin around his eyes crinkled up. "As usual, you skated right past guilty into innocence."

"Mikey wasn't even there." I bumped my chest against his. Of the same height, we were eye-to-eye with one another.

He body-bumped me back, but I stood my wobbly ground. "He gave me the message." Raymond's left eye blinked up a breeze, sending a twitch down his cheek. His tell. Unfortunately for me, his tell meant many things. He was lying, surprised, or pissed.

"What time did you talk to Mikey? What else did he say?"

"Why don't you ask him?"

"'Cause I'm asking you."

"I don't have to tell you jack."

The door swung open and I released him. His two bitches, tight ends on varsity, Raj and Nelson, barreled inside.

"Hey, Lucas," Nelson greeted, one of the few players who gave me the time of day. I nodded at him.

"See you, loser." I left the three lunks to stew in the stink.

Guess I needed to pick Mikey's brain. I shrugged off my backpack and opened my locker to exchange books for first and second periods. Lost in thought, I barely heard Dalton's taunting add another layer of frustration inside my muddled mind.

"Well, well, well, Mr. Alexander."

"Huh?" Preoccupied, I didn't notice him reach past me into my locker until he snagged a thin wallet and other items off my stack of books.

"What have we here?" he gloated.

Vaguely, I wondered if I'd opened the wrong locker until I saw the picture of Silver sitting on my shoulders at our cove party last summer. "Those aren't mine." Anger ballooned and my head thundered from the rush of blood.

"I know they're not yours." Dalton fisted the wallet, watch, and two pendants.

The tardy bell rang. Students milling in the halls scuttled to their first period classes.

Seething silently, I glared at Dalton's smirking face. Stalling, I shut my locker door, turned the dial slowly. "You know I was framed."

"Save it, Lucas." Dalton's use of my first name seemed perverted. "Principal Wilkerson will make the call." He wrenched on my shirtsleeve.

"Don't touch me." I jerked away. He clicked his tongue. "You think this is great, don't you?"

"As a matter of fact, I do."

"You're an asshole, you know that?"

"You don't have an exclusive on that one," Dalton replied, his casual intent unmistakable in his gloating. "But you'll be the first *not* to get away with it."

Chapter 16

Five days suspension. Three for the theft and two extra days tacked on for calling Dalton an asshole. Twice. The band declined to press charges. Five-day free pass. I texted Denny to gather the gang, including the nebulous Mikey, after school. Mom texted, grounding me until she got home from work. She also scheduled another appointment with Beranger. I called the shrink's office and cancelled all my appointments. I was so done with that pansy therapy crap.

Soaking in the hot tub loosened my stiff leg, gave me time to digest my life one sketchy piece at a time. My head rested on a plastic blowup cushion. Silver soon joined my misery. She tingled over my legs, and I felt her presence "lounge" in the chair beside the hot tub.

"You got busted for stealing."

"Yep."

"I'm sorry, Lucas." A soft breeze tickled my cheek.

"You have your own life now." In Heaven. The divide thickened between us. I blinked back a bug that flew in my eye. Just a bug. Nothing more.

"Don't say that," she wailed. "Don't you want me here?"

"Silver, I want you alive. I want May 12 to never have happened." Every word elevated my pitch. "Not gonna happen, is it?"

"No," she sighed, paused. "They're getting a divorce, aren't they?"

"You're dead. Why do you care?" Blood rushed to my face, a trail of fire stinging in its wake. Sadness stirred inside me. It tossed memories to the forefront, edged my hollowness. I huffed out a breath.

"Lucas?" Tara's curious voice wafted over before I heard the faint rustle of her backpack rubbing against her side.

Without moving, I asked, "How much did you hear?" Bubbles popping on the surface of the water grew louder. My heart tried to die. No luck there. It skipped a beat and the ticker restarted.

"Enough." Tara's clothes rustled, her shoes silent on the flagstone walkway. She sidled into my line of sight.

I flipped off my sunglasses and shielded my eyes from the sun. Tara still wore her school polo and weird skirt-shorts with bright pink and black checkered Vans. You wouldn't catch me dead wearing Vans, but they fit her to a tee.

"You think I'm crazy?" A ghost of a smile touched my lips.

She played with the strap on her matching checkered bag. "I'm not sure. Are you?"

The sun hung too high in a crystal blue sky for school to be out. "Why're you home so early? You okay?"

"I cut last two periods." She sifted her fingers through her short hair, leaving it sticking up above her right ear. "To come here." Gentle wind blew up and ruffled Tara's skorts. She eased out her hand as if to catch a falling leaf. To feel Silver.

I closed my eyes, opened them. The oddball urge to tell Tara about Silver, my strange problem, gnawed at me. Trepidation and excitement beat against my veins. This was major.

Tara frowned at a spider crossing her path. "How bad is it? Did this happen . . . from the accident?" She stepped over the spider and it skittered off into the safety of the lawn.

"Seriously?" I snorted. "You think I suffer from a mental condition?" I climbed out of the hot tub, pulled my long shorts up before the water dragged them to my feet. "What's the deal with you and Raymond?" I wiped my legs dry, rubbing the towel over the fading scars.

"Jeez, Luc. Just tell her." Silver's voice nagged me. "She's perfect for you. Ask her."

I flapped the towel at the air as if swatting a pesky fly. Silver, fly, same difference. It did the trick.

Cotton-candy pink stained Tara's cheeks. "Raymond just gave me a ride to school." She tossed her bag on a padded lounge chair and took up a perch.

"He doesn't give girls rides to school without *quid pro quo*." A glower tweaked the skin of my cheeks, tightening my scars. "He's pissed I took you home from the dance. I came to get you and Denny this morning but you'd already split."

A soft curve touched her frosted pink lips. "Really?" She sat straighter. "Raymond took us to the Surfside Theater on Saturday to apologize about the dance and offered to take us to school this morning. Denny's having trouble with the alternator on his Tahoe."

"That's it, huh?" Disgust and fury rocketed for the finish line inside me.

"What's the problem, Lucas?" Tara drawled with distinct mockery. Disconcerting at best.

"Don't be a goober and screw this up." Silver's voice invaded my space.

My dodge ball instincts kicked in. I had no right to grill Tara. "I don't know." I picked at a straggly loop on the terry towel.

"I'm not sure why I went with him. I . . ." she blushed. "It's hard to explain." She fluttered her hand.

Another stirring in the air swayed the long grass, caused Tara to rub her arms. Did Tara really sense Silver?

I tossed the damp towel on the cement, eased on my T-shirt. Sitting across from her, our knees met and that desire I'd never felt for another encouraged me. I trusted her. Call me looped. "I'll let you in on a secret. You can't tell anyone. No one knows about this, not even my parents."

"Will you kill me if I tell?" She dipped her head shyly. God, I loved that about her. So different from the brazen girls I used to date who had more spine than a T-Rex.

I grinned. "I'll find other ways to torture you."

Her eyes pierced mine. "Even if you stop talking to me, I won't tell a soul."

My knees pressed against hers. Her fingers feathered over my hand before she twined them with mine. Her touch was all the incentive I needed. I told her everything from the day of the accident until today. *Everything*. She remained silent, soaking it all in. I finished with a lopsided smile, feeling my dread evaporate.

Tara placed our linked hands on her knee, holding my hand prisoner beneath hers. "She was your best friend." She skimmed her fingers over her wet cheeks.

"Nah," I mocked, quirking my eyebrow. "Ya know, twin bond thing. I mean, we're only fraternal twins, nothing special." I dipped my head, hid my face. No way would I admit to a girl what I felt for my sister. I still had a pair. Jeez, unrelated girls were still number one on my hit list. A guy's got to maintain his bromance status too. "Certifiable, huh?"

Tara groaned, her relief skating across my skin. We fell into a balmy silence, the kind that relaxes every cell of your being. The silence two people with a bond share. The kind of companionship Silver and I used to sit in for hours at a time before our teenage social lives intruded.

"Explains a lot." Nervous, she pulled her hand from mine and twisted her hands together. "I need to tell you a secret too."

The second moment of truth had sprung. I sucked in a breath. Silver giggled. I shot her a death-ray look and pleaded with my eyes for her to leave. Lo and behold, the ghost followed orders for a change. A sudden cold snap replaced her lingering warmth.

"I can sense Silver, too," Tara blurted out.

I touched my fingers to the back of her hand. "I know. I saw how you reacted in the pool house the night I cut my hand."

Her mouth formed a big *O*. "I'm sensitive to spectral energy. But it's never happened with other people around. So when I felt her in the pool house, I almost freaked. Then I sensed her a couple of other times, including here today."

She launched into her own version of creepy. "For a year before we left L.A., I had a ghost attached to me." I drew back, sucker-punched. "He was my ex-boyfriend Vince's best friend. Vince was driving drunk one night when he dropped Eddie off at home. They were fighting. Eddie was jealous of Vince and me, going on and on with this stupid idea that Vince had stolen me from him. All lies. Eddie was a card-carrying whackjob." Her knees bumped hard against me, and I caught her weight with my legs. "Vince was leaving and plowed his car into Eddie as he stood behind the car egging Vince on. Then he drove over Eddie again." She flinched. "Vince insisted it was an accident. The night of the funeral, Eddie's ghost appeared in my bedroom. Scared me half to death." Another shudder sent goose bumps in a wave across her bare arms. "Eddie said Vince killed him to shut him up. He vowed vengeance. Said he'd haunt both of us until the day we died." Tara's bottom lip quivered.

I squeezed her fingers. Despite my horror-tinged sympathy, I vibrated with absolute glee. My curiosity must've showed on my face because she turned white as . . . well . . . a ghost. "Do you *see* ghosts? Silver?"

"No. Just a presence. You know, like how you get the feeling someone's looking at you, or someone brushes by you so fast, you miss them. Is that what you feel?"

I swallowed hard. "Exactly." I pulled threads off the towel, trying to wrap my mind around it. "Have you felt others?"

"I had a *good* ghost attached to me when I was eight. She was the ghost of a child who'd died in the house we lived in at the time. I was a loner. Always had my nose in a book, you know." She blushed. "So I wasn't into the dress up and make up thing girls seemed to be into. My parents thought I was pretending and had an invisible friend." Memories brought a fond, faraway expression to her face. "A psychic lived next door and she knew about the ghost. Told me I possessed a natural energy that attracted spirits. She also said they're attracted to a person for a reason. For help, solace, commiseration, kinship, friendship. In her case, it was the connection of the house. My bedroom used to be her room. Then there's evil intent like creepy Eddie."

"Huh." My life was too weird for words. "So what happened to him?"

"We moved, he stayed. Same thing with the child ghost." Her radiant smile lit my blood on fire. "Ghosts stay close to the people and places they were attached to in life." She leaned into me, laughed. "I'm as weird as you, I guess." Tara ran her finger over a stain on her skirt. "Silver was here when I first arrived. I felt her happiness. Why was she so happy?"

A flush scorched my neck. Tara made me nervous like no girl ever had. Stupid accident totally screwed up everything, including my ego and courage. "Tara, I like you . . ."

She giggled, a tinkling fairy sound I wanted to listen to forever.

"I wanted to ask you to go around with me, and I'm screwin' it up. Won't blame you if you think I'm a walking ad for a freaks holiday."

She suddenly wound her arms around my neck, her lips landing on mine. They were soft, yet firm, tasting of her bubblegum lip-gloss. After a quick kiss that left me starving for more, Tara edged back. She dropped her face in her hands. "Oh, God. I'm so embarrassed."

My pulse galloped. I resisted the crazed need to haul her onto my lap and kiss her senseless. I didn't think I'd ever experienced such a buzz. I hugged her close, feeling her sun-warmed body light my darkness. Tara was the first girl I'd ever truly desired and saw myself with far into the future. Sure, I'd gone around with others. *Duh.* I had a reputation to uphold as the star quarterback and class prankster. The A-list jerk. I played the part well. Yet I never burned for any other, never had my thoughts hijacked 24/7. Never thought the sun rose and the moon set on anyone except Tara.

"I'm here. You're not a loner any longer," I whispered, breathing her into all my senses. Our gazes locked.

"No. I'm not." Her voice trembled.

More of me awakened. The sky brightened, the sun grew radiant. I had no pain, no regret, no guilt. I was awake, alive again. As I moved in for another kiss, Mom's dreaded voice cut through the tiny bursts of electricity attacking my innards.

"Lucas," she screeched from the kitchen. The screen door practically popped off its hinges and she barreled out onto the patio. "Tara, I need to speak to Lucas alone," she said gently between mashed teeth.

Welcome to the firing squad. Tara gave me a sympathetic hug and I walked her out the sideyard gate.

I'd barely stepped a toe inside the French doors when the verbal hemorrhage began. "Why on earth did you call Mr. Dalton an asshole?"

"He *is* an asshole." I snatched a handful of Alyssa's white-chocolate-chip cookies from the pig cookie jar.

"That's no excuse. He's a teacher and he deserves respect. I've warned you about your smart mouth." She tossed her lunch bag on the counter. So palatable, her anger weighed me down. The disgust that piggybacked along for the ride chewed away at my newfound euphoria.

I swallowed a mouthful of cookie. "I didn't steal those things. Dalton's hounding me for no reason."

"Maybe you deserve it."

"Thanks for the vote." I grabbed the milk jug out of the fridge, gulped the last few swigs straight from the jug. "He planted a bead in the middle of my forehead before school even started."

Mom slapped the counter. "Come on. Do you expect me to believe—"

Swinging my arm wide, I flung the plastic jug into the sink. It clattered against dirty glasses. "No! You don't know me any longer. I don't even know me. Whatever. I stole those things. I called Dalton an asshole. Happy, now?" I shambled out of the kitchen. White as a ghost, Alyssa eavesdropped from the hall.

Mom reached for my arm from behind. I froze, strung tighter than an electric guitar. Alyssa shrank against the foyer wall, arms wrapped around her waist, her face green as if readying to launch more chunks.

"What's happening with you? I don't know what to do any longer. Every time I blink, you're in trouble or hurt," Mom spat out. "I'm sick to death of it. Sometimes I wish—" Her eyes popped wide. The revulsion of her implicit words hung between us as if tangible.

A strange calm claimed my anger, beat it to smithereens. In that moment, I believed Mom had no clue what Silver's death had done to me. She had no clue the connection Silver and I shared since she never experienced the same deep bond to Serena. Obsessed with her own misery and grief so much, she was oblivious to the fog surrounding the family. I think I finally understood she didn't place the blame on me. She'd taken the burden all on her own.

Calmly, I pried her tentacles off my bare arm one by one. "Mom. Silver's still . . . here." I thumped the left side of my chest, touched the side of my head. "Things are different. I won't ever be the old Lucas Alexander, that half of the Alexander twins. I'm the whole of us now. It's not your fault and *you* need to roll with it." Embarrassed, I clamped my mouth shut. I lunged up the stairs, turned at the landing, and saw the tears trickle down her pasty face. Alyssa went to her, waving me off with a wan smile.

Silver would never be dead. Not as long as I believed. And I refused to believe Mom ever wished I'd kicked it instead of Silver. That's just messed up. I had too much to live for now. Darkness had retracted its suffocating fingers from me that day. I refused to let it hurt me again.

Chapter 17

Before Accident, Mom would've stuck me on chore-duty as punishment. An old habit. I'd been suspended for throwing live ladybugs in a classroom, shredding test sheets and sprinkling the confetti throughout the quad, and letting tarantulas skitter around science lab. Innocent kid stuff. Blatantly mouthing off to a teacher and targeted for stealing kicked me squarely in the realm of bad boy. Text messages and voicemails from the Nomads proved my badassness. Just what I needed, more visibility—of the wrong kind.

Mom locked herself in her bedroom, refusing to talk to anyone. Dad called from San Jose and his firm, no-nonsense voice ordered me to stay out of Mom's hair. Although he believed in my innocence, he grounded me until noon on Saturday. No friends, no nothing. I had my computer, cell, and TV. Stick bread and water under the door and I was down with it.

Even so, the day sucked. I lay on top of my bed in the dark bedroom, both conjuring up Silver in my head and willing her away.

"Lucas."

I nearly pissed myself at Silver's soft voice. I turned on the bedside lamp. The dinner Alyssa brought me earlier congealed on my desk, the stench of festering tofurkey burger and wilted zucchini fries lingering in my room. Aunt Serena's vegan garbage.

"Do you think Mom wishes you had died instead of me?"

My gut pinched. "You're the *ghost.* Can't you see what's going on with her? Go be a fly on the wall." Trying to tune her out, I ratcheted up the TV volume.

"It doesn't work that way. Only you and Tara are sensitives."

"Dude, I don't want to talk about it. I'm moving on and she needs to do the same."

"But you have me in your life. She doesn't." The air whooshed, blowing loose papers from my desk to the floor.

"Leave it alone." I threw the remote at my desk. It clattered into the wall. "Mom has Dad. Now she has Serena and Alyssa. And I'm still here!" I swung my legs over the edge of the bed, stomped on the carpet.

"You're *not* here." Silver hiccupped on a sob. "You're not enough." As the air stirred wildly, I imagined her arms and hands flailing about, her bangles clanking together. "You're only a piece of that whole you mentioned. No one knows you anymore because you won't let anyone in. You used to be an open book."

An unnamed emotion thrived within my chest, coiling like a parasite on meth. For the first time, I wished the accident had killed me. If only to murder the myriad voices telling me the real Lucas Alexander had taken a powder. "You wanted me to lie about the gang initiation," I whispered through gritted teeth. "You wanted revenge. *You* needed a new phone." Spit flew as I spoke the words I vowed never to voice. A calm silence rode the air despite the guilt and anger knotting my intestines. A warm breeze whispered across my face as the heater turned on. Silver's presence lingered as if she were touching my cheek.

"Thank you. I've wanted you to admit that all along. It's all my fault."

A knock sounded on my door. "Lucas, can you turn the TV down?" Aunt Serena raised her voice over the blaring war movie I was wasting time on.

I lunged for the remote and shut the TV off. "Sorry, got carried away."

"Is someone in there with you?"

The door suffered my wry smile. "Just yelling at the TV."

"Oh . . . well, go to bed. It's late. 'Night."

I waited until the guest room door down the hall shut. "What should I do? Tell Mom and Dad the truth about the accident? Run away so I'm not in their business every day, forced to remember?" The weight of the world dragged my shoulders southward.

"Don't be a dillweed." The old Silver had returned. To lessen the impact of her mocking, tingles tickled my face, cheering me somewhat. "Involve Mom in your life again. Have a Deadman's bonfire Saturday. She loves cooking her famous snacks. Tell her it's in honor of me and a welcome to town for Alyssa, Denny, and Tara. She'll love that you asked for help. She wants to know you're going to be okay. That she won't lose you too." Silver's voice went shy, not a normal emotion for her. Scary stuff.

"When did you become Dr. Phil . . . Phyllis?"

"When I kicked it. See ya, Luc." A slight cooling in the air around me signified her departure.

My cell rang and Mikey's name flashed on the screen. "Dude, you have some explaining to do," I said without preamble. I'd been calling him all day with no success.

"My dad took my phone away." His annoyance spat the words out.

"Why?"

"Because he saw you calling."

"Screw that." I laid down on my bed, stared at the silver stars on the ceiling. "That's not what I meant. What happened at the dance? You setting me up?"

"No. No." The words tumbled out. "My dad saw me hanging around the backstage door and I couldn't get away from him."

"So you hung me out to dry?"

"Come on, Lucas. I'm sorry. I didn't know it would turn out like that. My dad's an ass."

I tossed a balled pair of socks up in the air, caught them in one hand. The sincerity in his tone spurred me on. "Did you steal the band's things?"

"I never even went back there. You were set up on that, but I don't know who did it."

Sue me, I believed the punk. "So what did you need to tell me at the dance?"

He chuckled. "My dad still has connections, you know, in law enforcement. With his ties to the gang crime unit, I have a lot of info at my tips. Know what I mean?"

Sitting up straighter, I tossed the socks on the bed, held my breath. "I'm listening."

"CrimsonX and the Juggernauts are the two main rival gangs in town. They're so big and badass, they won't let another gang in."

I exhaled slowly. "But they haven't been able to get rid of each other, right?"

"Yep."

"Do they do gang initiations?" I felt him out.

"Most gangs do."

"Do they ever play roadside games, like scare or harass people in their cars?" My heart thudded in my ears.

"Not CrimsonX or Juggernauts. That's petty crap for them." Mikey paused. "Why?"

"Nothing. Thought I saw a couple CrimsonX members harass some drag racers." The lie rolled off my tongue.

"According to deets my dad has on them, they don't get involved in racing."

"Low riders can't go over thirty." We snickered. "Hey, kid, you're all right."

"We good, now?"

"Sure. Keep up the good work Mikey Dalt." A smile tugged at my lips. "Keep your father off our backs. Know what I mean?"

"Cool."

"I'm having a beach bonfire next Saturday. You're in."

Suspension week dragged onward. Warily, I asked Mom if she'd cook the food for the bonfire. A smidgen of her former sunny self returned. Truce called. Aunt Serena offered to help, not that anyone wanted rabbit food. A former caterer, turned event planning manager, Mom had it in the bag. She'd teach Serena what real kids ate. Alyssa took to drafting invitations as if born to party plan. Of course, we had to prepare for the inevitable crashers, so the invite asked everyone to bring snacks or drinks. The idea of a party kicked everyone in a happy mood.

Questions bombarded me, and I called Chris on Tuesday after school. "Why didn't you go to the dance last Friday?"

Music blared in the background, which meant he was home alone. "I was sick. Didn't Kev tell you?"

I drummed my fingers on the phone. "I thought you were counting Ouija boards and spider legs for your mom."

"Oh, yeah." His voice took on a high frequency. *Dogs might rampage any moment.* "Lame stuff." Background music disappeared. "She wanted me to do inventory, but she was brewing some funky oils which gave me a headache."

"You heard what happened?"

"Kev gave me the DL. That prick Raymond's gunnin' for a bruising."

"He's definitely on my list. Hey, catch you on the flipside."

Raymond was so dead again.

During my mini-vacation, I spent the week extending my tan during the Indian summer days. My fingers remained glued to Silver's old laptop while I researched gang activity, known hangouts, and gang turf. I didn't find anything about a third gang. Whoever they were, they flew way under the radar. No problem. I'd work on a scheme to bust them wide open. Unfortunately, the scheme might include a trip down memory lane. Literally.

I shot the gang an e-mail link to last week's police blotter. "An anonymous tip to the Sea Haven PD helped solve a theft ring that has plagued the resort town since last winter." Yeah, baby! One down.

In my research, I stumbled across a San Francisco news article about a group of spiteful women who wanted to rid the town of prostitutes. They formed a vigilante club and spied on the prostitutes in a pay-by-the-hour motel they managed. Room dividers split the "guest" rooms in half, separating the dressing areas near the door from the beds. Surveillance cameras took pictures of the "Johns." The women sneaked into the rooms to copy IDs and credit card numbers while the pairs banged each other. Brilliant setup, if somewhat lame.

The vigilantes didn't nark on the Johns. Instead, they investigated them, contacted their wives and employers about the Johns' off- and sometimes on-the-clock shenanigans. The group of women thought it sufficient to scare away the Johns and boot a few prostitutes off the street. Worked for a while until one of the vigilantes got plastered and blabbed to a man dressed as a cop at a Halloween party. Only problem . . . the cop wasn't wearing a costume.

The prostitute-vigilante story lent me subliminal ideas of busting gang activity while staying safe and undercover. On top of handing out anonymous tips to the cops, we could blast out cryptic tips to other gangs, schools, and family members regarding their illegal activities. Our efforts might instigate turf wars, but if we caused enough damage between the gangs, maybe we'd do some good to the town at large.

With one more mystery to occupy my free time, I hadn't figured out who'd framed me at the dance. Raymond was my lone suspect. I doubted the gang members I'd ticked off would retaliate by petty thievery. They'd as soon knife me to death. Or beat up Denny. Dad also forced Wilkerson to conduct an independent fingerprint check. Whoever framed me had wiped clean the stolen items and my locker. Go frigging figure.

The sun warmed the fall air, soothing the throb in my knee, the haze in my brain. My eyelids grew heavy and the silence—absent Silver—towed me under.

"Hey, Lucas," Tara's soft greeting filtered into my sleepy ears. "Is it safe?" She called from the sideyard.

I seized the towel off the second lounge chair, loosely bundling it over myself, sucking in a groan. An epically vivid daydream, involving the make-out caves on Deadman's Cove, a blanket in the sand, the two of us alone, dissolved. No sense in showing her where my daydreams had taken me.

"Hey, babe." I waved her over. "My mom and Serena are at a new neighborhood watch meeting at the school. Dalton's some bigwig gang expert and he's leading the charge. Since our 'hood's on the list, they thought it a good idea. Alyssa and Denny are running errands for the bonfire."

Tara approached, vibrant and cute in her school uniform, green tennies, hair bound in a green scrunchy. "I know. They dropped me off." She flopped on the lounge chair, the puckering of her brow erasing her normal sunniness. "You'll need to sanitize your car. Denny drooled all over it." She tossed an envelope onto my chest. "Homework." Her gaze landed everywhere but on me.

I sat straighter, clutching the towel over my bare torso as a chill swept over me. "What's wrong?" I reached over and wrapped my warmth around her glacial fingers.

Her gaze finally paused on my face. "Promise you won't get upset?" She wound her purse strap around her hand.

"For now," I said slowly. "What happened?"

Tara tugged the sleeves of her green hoodie over her hands, sign of her agitation. "I was walking to Dalton's class past the smoking area where CrimsonX hangs."

My spine went rigid. I swung my legs over the lounge chair, planting my feet firmly on the ground. I tipped my chin for her to continue, a smothering weight pressuring my ribcage. If they hurt her, I'd destroy every last one of those beaners.

"One of them called me over."

My grip tightened on her hand. "Did they hurt you?"

"No." Her fingers brushed my arm. "The short, stocky dude said he'd heard my *boyfriend* had been busted. They all snickered like they knew something. Another one dangled a wallet and a watch. The stocky guy said 'now he knows what it feels like.'"

"*They* framed me? Doesn't make sense." I leaped up. My mind spun around the events of the last few weeks. Had they recognized me on the beach and pegged me the nark? Had someone seen us bust the theft ring? The police already corroborated that the kid they'd arrested stealing my tires had no gang affiliation. In fact, a CrimsonX beating awaited him when jail evicted him. Then it dawned on me. Interfering with Mikey's beating.

"Lucas." Tara grasped my arm. "The leader guy said it ain't over yet."

Chapter 18

The sky clouded up Friday night, and stacked, gray murk dampened Saturday morning. I lugged canopies from the garage and loaded them in Kev's borrowed junker. It'd drive me bonkers not to have my own vehicle. Once you've gone Camaro, there was no going back to anything else, let alone no car.

Wow, I could actually think that without choking up a hairball. Beranger should be so proud. *Next up: fixing my parents.* I buried thoughts of my family and hefted two empty coolers onto the truck-bed. Bad weather or not, we planned to party. Lousy memories or not, I intended to forget for a night.

"Dude, watch for scratches." Kev elbowed my arm.

I scrutinized the muddy white beater truck. "Any less scratches and it might lose its individuality. Heck, the only thing that makes this POS look good is distance."

"Least it ain't one of a million Camaro clones."

"Jeez, you sure know how to spin it." Chris burped in Kev's face. Kev retaliated by ripping some ass. I moved out of the bomb zone. No wonder they had no girlfriends. The Camaro comment didn't bother me much most days. Sure didn't hurt today. "It's cool," I said. "Once I sell my old parts, I'll have the dough to make mods."

"Did you bring soda?" Chris popped the lid off Kev's Styrofoam cooler next to my stack of empties, and gave a satisfied grin. Last party we had, Kev grabbed the wrong cooler. His little sister took a twelver of beer to a slumber party for ten-year-olds. He was grounded for two weeks and his parents put industrial strength locks on the refrigerators in the garage and lunchroom. Took Kev a week to find the keys. We kept moving the contents from one refrigerator to the other to prank on his parents. Drove them batty. They're still clueless.

"What's this small task you wanted Silver Ghost to do this morning?" Denny ambled over from his garage, arms laden with tiki torches and battery-operated lanterns.

My heartbeat accelerated as my mind latched onto Mikey's overheard conversation in the park. Poor kid was stuck on lockdown helping his father with neighborhood watch chores. He'd try to slip out and join the beach party later.

"CrimsonX and Juggernauts are both recruiting Juno Chavez," I said. "The nineteen-year-old serving his second senior term at Sea Hag, who keeps evading the cops during drug busts," I added for Denny's benefit. "He's a hot ticket, steering clear of gangs. Now he wants to join up. Both gangs offered him a high-ranking position. They've planned a fight-to-first-blood match of their strongest in the woods outside the fairgrounds tonight. Winner takes him."

Eagerness painted Denny's face. "We going?"

"Jeez, Louisa, we don't have a death wish." Kev lowered his voice as Aunt Serena strolled down the walkway toward Mom's SUV parked along the curb. We all waved. Kev whistled a shrill catcall. Apparently, she had another mystery date, evidenced by the flouncy skirt and snug sweater. And the overnight bag dangling from her hand.

"Watch and listen." I punched *67 to block caller ID on my prepaid cell. I tapped in the digits, then covered the receiver with the bottom of my hoodie. The phone on the other end rang three times. A woman answered, identifying Sea Haven Sheriff's Department. Faking a Cheech Marin accent, I said slow and succinct, "I want to report a gang fight going down tonight." The operator tried to get me to identify myself. After a quick moment, I said, "Name's Alex Silverstein." I kicked Kev before he busted a gut and blew my cover. "CrimsonX challenged the Juggernauts to a blood-match in the woods outside the fairgrounds tonight. Midnight. I overheard them talking about it on the wharf." Without waiting for a response, I clicked off, then dialed another number.

A woman answered. "Mrs. Chavez?" I said in my best Cheech-speak.

"*Si*. Yes."

"Tell Juno to choose CrimsonX or he'll spend time in lockup again." Without waiting for a response, I hung up.

Denny fist-bumped me. "Juggernauts will blame CrimsonX and vice versa."

"Hells bells. All we have to do is pit one gang against the other. Easy as ice cream pie." Kev whooped. "They'll regret ever messing with us. How'd you find out about the blood-match?"

"Silver Ghost hears all, sees all." The Nomads didn't utter a peep. They'd come to expect my newfound weirdness.

"I gotta jet." Kev slammed the tailgate shut. "We'll be at the beach at noon to snag the spot, take a snooze. I need my beauty sleep for tonight."

"All you ex-cheerleaders are alike." I fake-slugged his arm.

"I'm not an *ex*-cheerleader. I'm just good looking." Kev passed his palm over the top of his hair pretending to smooth down his shaggy mop.

"Go." I slapped the tailgate, wiped the dust off my hand onto my sweats. "I won't be able to stand looking at you if you miss your beauty rest."

My parents relented on the grounding early and allowed Denny to help with party prep. Tara and Alyssa took off to Wally

World for paper plates and stuff. Too wound up, I closed the garage door and we holed up in my room. Scents of taquitos, nacho sauce, and homemade salsa wafted up the stairs. Mom was in seventh heaven.

To pass the time, we logged onto an online game of Call of Duty. Seemed an appropriate appetizer for future club activity. I actually learned a few gnarly combat moves that might come in handy. Denny got me hooked on multiplayer games. I'd never been much of a gamer, being a jock and all. Silver, the computer geek, dug all kinds of electronic games, mostly the radical fighting ones. Also explained why she was crushing on Denny big time.

"This what you do all day?" I went commando on my onscreen attackers. "No sports ever?"

A quadroter buzzed Denny's man. "Kev and I played little league. Didn't he tell you? Ugh, take that sucker." His arm jerked into my side. "We got kicked off the team, then he moved. I played in L.A., then girls hit my radar."

I laughed. "Figures. Kev's not much of an athlete."

"Naw, wasn't that." A grenade shook the walls of my bedroom.

I turned the speakers down before my parents thought the house was under attack.

"We put pink dye in the chalk bags. Got busted by an assistant coach. He chased us into the next neighborhood and we hopped a fence to hide in a backyard. Everything was cool until a poodle's yapping gave us up." Denny whooped. "Dude, I just clocked you."

"Guess it's time to get the girls and split." I set my game controller aside. "Enjoy your win. Payback's a bitch." I chuckled as we grabbed our jackets.

Late afternoon turned into a drizzly mess. I had too much of my heart and head invested in forgetting the craptastic summer to let the soggy weather kill my excitement. At the beach, the wind buffeted the car. Waves pounded the shoreline as if the water wanted to beat the earth into submission. Whitecaps topped the sea, dipping deep and swelling high. A long horizon of soaked clouds spread out as far as the binoculars picked up.

Tara sprang out of the car and unfurled her arms wide, the wind fanning her soft golden curls around her head. She angled her face to the heavens, the sky spitting dew on her skin. She looked like the sun, my savior, a drug that built me up off the downhill slope of misery. How long would it last? Strange déjà vu overcame me, nearly forcing me to look inward for my disappearing sister.

"It's warm outside." Tara winked at me. She pulled the seat forward and hefted out a stack of tarps. Denny drove up beside us, Alyssa in the passenger seat. He'd finally gotten the alternator replaced in his Tahoe, and I reluctantly let Alyssa ride with him. As if I had a choice.

The horizon captured what little sun graced us that afternoon. Twilight painted dark bands across the ends of the sea. Fluorescent parking lot lights flickered on. A roaring fire blazed, casting dancing shadows on the sand. Kev and Chris had already hidden the beer-filled ice chests in the secret caves. Secret in that they weren't visible. Most townspeople knew they existed and avoided the haunted cove.

In the late 1800s, a high tide caught a group of homeless people living in the caves, and they all drowned. Throughout the years, numerous people have fallen off the bluffs overlooking the cove. The last death happened three years ago when a rogue wave knocked a drunken kid off the rocks jutting into the water.

Parks and Recreation posted warning signs along a fence around the upper cove, blocking the main path to the expanse of rocks reaching for the waves. The narrow cliff provided a death-defying nosedive for anyone on a suicide mission. *Best to do at high tide so the waves slammed your body into the rocks.* At least two suicides occurred off the boulders within the last twenty years. Bodies bouncing onto the rocks killed them rather than headers into the reef. Water levels had fallen, and the tide no longer neared the caves, providing a nice beach for the adventurous.

Townies named the small half-moon beach Deadman's Cove. Its real name was Sea Cliff Cove for, like, the sea cliff surrounding the patch of white sand. Tourists hunting paranormal thrills got off on visiting the caves ever since the town made it into several California guidebooks on haunted places. Small thrills for a dinky seaside town.

Was Sea Haven a mecca for spectral freakishness? Or did I hit the lottery? Did Silver hang out here?

Sketchy weather cleared the beach of the usual weekend crowds. I doubted rangers making their ten o'clock rounds to shut it down for the night would bother us. They only came to the cove if someone reported noise or unusual activity. If a body took a nosedive off the cliff, the deputies always arrived late to the party.

The rocky lower cliff walls provided a perfect windbreak. We strung tarps along the sides of the canopies, tying them to stakes buried in the sand to construct three-sided tents in case the weather went totally haywire. We also built a small fire inside the first cave. Body heat would keep us cozy if the fire and booze didn't.

I tied down the last tarp, wiped mist off my face. "Where's Chris?" I tossed Kev the hammer. "I thought he was hanging here."

"He split to snag a couple boogie boards hours ago." Kev stuck the hammer in his back pocket. Frowning at his cell, he checked for messages. "He was acting kinda weird. Like he was in deep, know what I mean? Then he called and said mommy gave him a boatload of chores."

"Nothing new there." Being the only child to a single working mother stuck Chris in sullen household slave territory on a regular basis.

"Last night he told me he had the whole day free."

Drizzle thickened into a steady rain. I wiped a hand across my wet face. Denny began turning on the lanterns scattered around the perimeter of the two canopies and the built-in granite steps leading down from the parking lot to the beach.

Kev and I stepped under a canopy. "He gets all weirded out about his mom. If he doesn't show by nine, call him."

Alyssa and Tara screamed and giggled as they bolted out of the caves waving a monster flashlight guaranteed to scare off any ghost, mouse, or bug left behind. Tara had never seen the caves and they toured all the make-out alcoves, which, according to Alyssa, Tara must avoid unless she wanted to risk becoming ghost possessed and insane. We traded a wink.

Tara whispered, "Silver's here. She's hanging in the caves, following us. Kinda making sure we stayed safe." She shrugged.

My eyes rounded. "Did you *feel* others?"

She flipped her hood up. "A little. None recognizable as a single being. Just imprints. Definitely a lot of spectral activity." Before I could quiz her further, Alyssa yanked her away and they headed to the food tables.

Legend held that ghosts had found a way to possess cave dwellers. Ten years ago, two spirits forced a pair of twenty-something's to bang each other. When the couple woke up buck-naked, they bolted from the caves, scared out of their red-faced gourds. The chick ended up knocked up and swore the baby was the Immaculate Conception Omen child. Cops busted them a year later on Ecstasy possession. Another reason why most townies shied away from the place. Might get knocked up by a ghost.

Despite Tara's natural tendencies toward the spectral plane, I hoped Alyssa wasn't scaring her. *I mean, come on.* A guy needed to hope and dream, once again. I hoped Silver had the decency to remain scarce if Tara and I got serious. Living in a ghost's fishbowl might actually be torture on my love life.

"Dude, you listening to me?" Kev punched my left arm.

Tara and Alyssa huddled by the gas stove. I beckoned Tara over again. "What?"

"Raymond got booted down to second-string. Glenn's the new QB."

I sniggered. "You kidding me?"

Tara looped her arm around my waist. "Everything smells great. Food's set out. Your mom's an awesome cook." She nudged a loaded nacho against my lips.

Opening my mouth wide, I chomped down on the gooey mess. Melted cheese dribbled down my chin. Mom's fire-roasted garlic salsa singed my tongue. I chewed slowly, savoring the homemade nachos. "Did Raymond receive an invite?" Half the school planned to crash despite the small list. Raymond used to top it. Too bad he sat alone on the shit list.

"Why wouldn't he?" Kev hefted a box of oak logs closer to the fire ring where Denny built up the mini bonfire. The beach had a gazillion bonehead restrictions against real bonfires, and we weren't chancing an early bust.

"Why, what's the deal?" Tara snuggled into my side.

I wrapped both arms around her, her down jacket a thick layer of padding blocking the body I hungered to touch. "Nothing." Leaning in, I kissed her hard, possessively. Hot and firm, her kiss captivated me. Flickers of lightning exploded in my blood. My tongue swept inside her mouth, tasting hot chocolate on her tongue tangoing with mine. Her hand cupped my cheek, light and tender, full of Tara.

"Ah, gross. Get a cave." Alyssa made a retching sound close to my ear.

Buzz kill. Easing out of the drugging kiss, I almost thought Silver had spoken. The two could seriously be twins, if not for me. Or the dead and alive thing. I peeked over my shoulder, caught her wide grin. Denny sneaked up behind her, wrapped her in a bear hug. Squealing, she wriggled in his arms. Anyone else and I'd be all over him like a spray of dynamite. But I trusted Denny, and I knew Alyssa's caution. Her stepfather's craptastic influence left her with a frosty shoulder where it came to the male species. Denny's ice pick chipped away at her every day. I was down with the slow thaw.

"Yo, Lucas!" The call stemmed from the granite steps. Half the varsity football team had arrived, Glenn leading the pack. Flashlights lit the group. No sign of Raymond. A breath I wasn't aware of holding blew out. Switch on the party.

The rain finally ceased, but a sporadic breeze blew through the cove. By the time the shindig was rocking, about fifty high schoolers pigged out, drank smuggled beer, cozied close to the fire for warmth and more. I disentangled from Tara's arms and struggled up from the damp blanket, balancing in the sand. Not prone to overindulging, I'd only guzzled two beers. Coach's healthy living scare tactics still lingered. Call me a dweeb. Wasted and losing control wasn't my idea of fun.

I signaled to Kev to turn down the music and still had to shout over the crowd and the surf. Party noise dwindled and curious gazes slowly encompassed me. Mikey had shown up a half hour ago. He held up a red plastic cup of cola, tipped it in my direction. No sense in angering his father further by drinking beer if he got caught slipping out of the house tonight.

Holding up my beer bottle, I shouted, "To Silver, the best part of the Alexander twins, the bright sun at every party. May you rest peacefully among the ghosts of Deadman's Cove." Hollers and chuckles rang out. "Love you, sis."

"Love you, Silver!" The shout erupted, bottles clanked, plastic cups clicked.

I raised my cup again. "And a big welcome to—"

"And a big fat thanks to Lucas for killing my girlfriend." The familiar voice boomed from the stone steps behind me. "You should've bitten it in that badass car of yours." Jealousy pierced his slurred wrath.

Chapter 19

All hail Raymond Randall, loser extraordinaire. He stumbled down the last three steps, reeling onto the sand. I almost wished he'd do a header and bash his brains in.

Nelson and Raj lurched across the sand to booster him up. Gibberish tripped from his open cavern mouth. I hoped he hadn't driven himself. A nail head was less hammered.

An excited thorny wind swept through the cove. Logs sizzled, popped. Remorse snipped a tight knot in my gut. BA, I never turned away from someone I once called friend. Once a friend, always a friend. But Raymond and the others on the team following his lead had dumped on me first. Doc Beranger labeled my reactions situational depression with antisocial tendencies. I called it survival of the crippled vengeful. What label did Beranger have for them?

Nelson and Raj dragged Raymond closer, and he raised his half-empty tequila bottle. The amber liquid sloshed, twinkling in the glow of the tiki torches.

"To Lucas! The one who has everything. Best quarterback in Sea Hag's history. Best pick of girlfriends." Leering at Tara, he swigged tequila, held the bottle out to her. She ducked behind Denny. The crowd grew silent enough to hear him swallow over the rumbling surf and restless winds. He elevated the bottle high. "Greatest Camaro. Scratch that. The greatest *piece of garbage* Camaro." He hooted so hard, Raj and Nelson hauled him straight to prevent him from eating embers. "To Lucas!" He waved the bottle high again, taunting. "Everyone's friend. The greatest prankster."

An amiable "woohoo" wafted up. Some kids raised their drinks. What could I say? Guilty as charged.

"Raymond." Barely restrained, I stuck out my hand for a handshake. "Thanks, but I think—"

Raymond listed against Raj, a floating turd in a sea of buoys. Firelight glimmered across the storm converging in his eyes. His pinched grimace set the veins along his neck throbbing.

"To Silver's brother." Conspiracy dragged down his voice. "Her favorite *boyfriend*." Ripples of shock assaulted the air.

White-hot rage flooded the desolation inside me where that part of Silver once lived. A buzz vibrated in my ears, drowned the escalating noise around me. Tara took my icy hand in her gloved grasp. Alyssa sprang for me, but Denny held her back. For his protection, I was grateful, since I didn't know if blows would fly. Kev sprang to my right, Mikey to my left. Silver floated above me, her disgust smashing into my chest like a bowling ball.

"Kick. His. Ass," she screamed so loud, I think Tara might have heard by her death squeeze on my hand.

The wind picked up, blowing a shower of sparks and a halo of smoke toward the frothing sea. A whirlwind spun up another round of smoke, sending my friends closest to the fire scrambling to their feet, hacking out lungs. Gusts of wind absorbed my ballooning anger. I grappled against the crushing need to bash Raymond's skull against the rocks. *Where's my baseball bat?*

"Must be true. Poor Lucas can't defend himself." Raymond guffawed, pressed closer to me, towing his bitches into my space.

Tara squeezed my hand. "He's drunk. He doesn't know what he's saying."

I flexed my fingers and released her hand. "Stand behind me, Tara."

"No. I won't let him sucker you in."

"Aw. Poor Lucas needs his girlfriend to tell him what to do. Just like he needed Silver." Raymond listed forward, poked two fingers into my shoulder. Tara scooted back and Denny swapped places on my left.

"You need to chill, man." Denny knocked his hand flat against Raymond's shoulder. "Back off."

"Screw you, Harrison. You don't know shit about the sitch. You arrive late to the game and drill your prick where it doesn't belong." He tilted his head slightly at Alyssa.

I'd be damned if he got his slimy paws on my cousin. "S'okay, Denny," I slurred between frozen lips. My roasting fury couldn't penetrate the bone-chilling cold of my indecision. Indecision in where I wanted to plant my fist first.

"Shut the hell up," Raymond roared. "Everyone flocks to you like you're some goddamned messiah." His flailing arm took in my army of newbies, Denny, Tara, Alyssa, and Mikey. His back straightened and a sneer traversed his face. "Yo, listen up." His slurring voice soared over the yammering crowd. "Luc was always there between Silver and me." He prodded the bottle into my shoulder. "You were always in her head. Silver didn't wanna break up with me until Luc told her to. Loser thought I was wrong for her." The bottle dug harder into my shoulder. I stood my ground, my fists raring to engage. "What's that all about? I was good enough to be *your* friend." He paused, burped, and I got a strong whiff of alcohol and ass. "You were all she ever cared about. You twisted twin queers. You wanted her for your—"

I chest butted him, my right hook going for his filthy mouth. I wanted the mother to take it back. He didn't know us, or the bond we shared. The bond defying normal, an empathetic connection we couldn't explain. We'd been stuck with it from birth. The sick bastard would never know the emptiness her death created. Not just in me, but in the world. I doubt his ego or perversion allowed a pinprick of vacancy for her loss.

A roaring beast pulsated within me. Dark red thunder shattered my emptiness, threatening to erupt in a tempest. Wind whipped my hair about my head. We rammed each other like bulls, chests bumping together. I wished I had horns to gut him in two. My bellow echoed in the cove as I reached for his beefy neck. Denny, Mikey, and Kev towed me off him while Raj and Nelson held him back, clawing to get at me, screaming a string of blue curses.

Through the storm raging inside me, "incestuous freaks" boomeranged from one ear to the other, until frantic shouts eclipsed the mantra. "The fire! Watch the pit!" We stumbled backward, forced down by the weight of my meltdown.

Girls screamed. My bad leg bent and I lost balance, lugging my three wingmen to the ground. Sharp pains shot up my left leg.

Wind surged up from the sand, an almost solid mattress of air pushing against us. An invisible force twinkled and tingled around me. The airstream helped roll our heads away from exploding brain matter all over the cement fire ring. We hit the warm sand beside the fire, my healing hand scraping along a fallen camp chair. Kev and Denny landed on top, knocking the wind out of me. My breathing grew ragged as I tried to gasp in diminishing air and suck down the renewed pain in my hand.

Kev and Denny rolled off me and clambered to their feet. Huffing, I rested on my side. Two other football players joined Raj and Nelson to restrain Raymond.

I wanted to beat a retraction out of him. Not for my sake, but for Silver. I'd suffer the fallout, but Silver's memory didn't deserve his sick, warped perspective on our abilities. My parents didn't even know about the strange bond we shared, each other's pain and emotions. The source of my new emptiness. How did he know? Was he talking out his sorry crack? I knew Silver never told him.

If we focused hard, Silver and I were able to block the bond. When Raymond and Silver hooked up the first time, I spent the night sick as a dog. Not because I had a jealous, disgusting incestuous bond to her or that I physically felt what she felt. We weren't that creepy. Her loathing and disgust had doubled me over. Raymond had forced her to go down on him, and she whimpered the entire time, almost to the point of passing out from her disgust and fury. He used her, another conquest among many. I'd warned her, but she was so stinking infatuated. All the girls were hot for him and he chose *her,* as if he were all that.

Later that night, I had to soothe her jagged edges, and I told her to dump him. After promising she'd listen to me, she sobbed herself to sleep. The next day she kicked him to the curb. Refusing to accept it, he hounded her, sent her chocolate, a pair of expensive boots she'd craved, and the latest video game. May 12 happened one week later. I tossed out the unopened bribery gifts the week after the hospital sprang me.

Kev extended his hand and hauled me off the sand. Tara dusted the sand off my leather jacket. Apprehension touched Denny's face as if I were the freak Raymond pegged me. Mikey handed me a hot poker. I waved him away.

Alyssa molded herself to Denny's side and said, "It's not true. Not Lucas and Silver. Never."

Denny shouldered Tara away from me. She slapped at him, stood her ground. He looked at me, really examined my eyes in the sputtering light of the tiki torches, and recognized the truth.

Relief burst across his face and he gave me mashed lip acceptance. Partiers huddled in small groups murmuring, ogling me.

I fought the urge to kick Raymond's 'nads out his ass. When he hurled all over the sand, I wanted to shove his face in it. I did none of those things. Instead, I turned to the group. "Guess someone can't hold his liquor any more than he can check his delusions." Laughter followed, but I heard more than my share of "what the hell," "do you think it's true."

"Party on. I plan to." I bent over to rebuild the fire and noticed Chris already stacking on logs. "Mother cut you loose?"

"Guess I missed the fun." Voice wooden, his movements were equally stiff. Poking the embers into a tidy pile, he ducked his head, totally avoiding eye contact.

Just as I opened my mouth to start the third degree, movement at the top of the stairs jerked my head up.

Silver uttered a short scream from behind me. In two seconds flat, her warmth was beside me. "It's them. Oh. My. God."

A dozen dark silhouettes jumped down the steps, following our trail of lanterns. In a short second of clarity, I recognized two of the three leading the charge. A freeze attacked my extremities, buried my feet in the sand. Molten blood swelled inside my dark hollowness.

The Pisser and his ragtag gang of killers. Could my night get any worse? Or my luck any better?

Chapter 20

The gang clomped down the steps. They cleared the last stone, checked out the dwindling partygoers. Moaning up a racket, beached whale Raymond flopped on the ground. Denny, Mikey, and Kev stepped into position at my sides. Chris remained behind me, his nervousness skating across my shoulders. I resisted the strange vibe to put him into direct view. My gaze met Tara's to my left where she and Alyssa watched while pretending to clean the tables.

"You know them?" Kev asked under his breath. Logs snapped and sparks puffed up into the air. He stomped a glowing ember into the sand.

"Who are they?" Denny snagged the hammer Kev had discarded earlier.

My throat made a clicking sound. Clammy sweat broke over my body. "The gang." The wind carried my low words toward the sea at our backs. Chris must've caught it. Next thing I knew he was wielding Mikey's smoldering wooden poker to Denny's left.

"This is a private party," Chris called out.

"On a public beach." The pissing gang leader snorted. "Guess that makes it a public party."

I held up a finger to forestall further commentary from my sidekicks. "Haven't seen you around here. Where you from?" The desire to know snowed my astonishment. Knowing their origins shot their territory straight to the top of my vigilante hit list. *If I lived to meet daylight again, that is.*

"Well, if you want to get friendly, toss over some of that brew." The short white guy to Pisser's left crossed his arms over his chest. They wore dark clothing, and differed in age from high school to a few years older. I made out several Mexicans, couple of white dudes, a ratty-fro black guy, and another dude of a muddy race. Hard to tell in the dark. Not exactly a typical one-race street gang. Lantern illumination hit knee level, painting their black shoes in tiny strokes of amber.

Thunderstruck, I hadn't prepared for the day we'd meet face-to-face. I didn't want them hanging out with my friends, nor did I want to lose sight of them. I gestured toward the ice chests. "Plenty to go around." Denny elbowed me, Kev grumbled.

"Right nice of you punks," Pisser said. En masse, his minions strutted into the party zone, immediately getting über friendly with a group of gaga, drooling girls.

Once again, the partiers quieted. Snoring drifted up from Raymond where the football team left him under a Shrek beach towel. *Make the asshole comfortable so he doesn't catch cold.* Shrek might not care for such willful abuse of his funky green image. The wind tapered to intermittent breezes. The surf boomed, thunderous applause to a wild night. A cold sweat coated my back.

Pisser, Shorty, and the third dark-skinned loser approached. My friends cleared a wide path away from the others trudging to the coolers. Light glinting on Pisser's single silver earring provided proof of their identity. The imbeciles I plowed the Red Renegade into. Murderers who needed to visit Davey Jones's locker in cement wetsuits. The Pisser, a lighter-skinned Hispanic, looked an awful lot like Raymond, who was half-Hispanic. They shared the same long, angular face, wide-set eyes, and low hairline.

The fire flared, burnished shadows chasing flickers of light across the sand, ending where the trio stopped ten feet away. Once again, their black jackets gave nothing away. They wore no other identification.

The darker kid freed his hands from his jacket pockets, leery and tense. "Do we know each other?" He cocked his head. The Pisser glanced down at Raymond and his hand twitched at his side as his face lit up in recognition.

He toed Raymond's arm. "Yo, cous. Raymond." He pushed his foot harder into Raymond's side, gave up when he didn't respond.

Cousin? *You've got to be kidding me.* I looked from the gang leader to Raymond. Despite the fact that Raymond was a whale and Pisser more slender, the family resemblance unnerved me. Had Raymond been with the gang on May 12?

"Hey, let's split." Shorty elbowed Pisser's side. He hadn't placed me yet, but the leader's eyes suddenly bulged out in recognition.

The crowd circling the food tables mingled, and buzz drifted over. Nelson recognized one of the interlopers as a friend of his older brother. Tara and Alyssa stood safe under the canopy. The party around us raged onward.

"I do know you from somewhere." A frown crinkled the skin between Pisser's eyeballs. Hopefully, the frown strained his brain enough to let a clue inside.

"Ocean Avenue and County Coast Road sound familiar?" The location avalanched out of my mouth. I tried to keep my cool, but my head spun and coherent thought refused to gel.

Silver Ghost closed in on me. The real Silver's ghost was a tense pressure on my back. A domino affect killed the crowd noise again. Only the crackling fire and the pounding of the surf broke the hush. To add to our misery, another rain cloud began to dump a load.

Visible in the glow from Chris's torch, I saw Pisser blanch. The other dudes slinked toward the steps. Raj, Nelson, and three other football players coincidentally blocked their way.

"Guess I was wrong." Pisser inched backward. His bootlickers followed.

"For once in your life, you're right." My feet propelled me forward a step. "Now, here's a fun fact for you. May twelfth, nine P.M. Ring a bell?"

Pisser held up his hand. "Look, man. Obviously, I was mistaken. We'll clear out." He slowly slid his right hand behind him. *Did they teach lessons in subtlety in Ganghood 101?*

Rainwater rolled down my cheeks into the neckline of my sweatshirt. "You sure? What's obvious about it?" My fists curled against my thighs, raring to curl around his throat.

The snick of a knife split the air behind Pisser. I waited for him to make the first physical threat. Lawyer in the family. Bonus. Nervously, he glanced over his shoulder. None of his friends by the steps gave a ribbon-wrapped turd about him. Murder had apparently bypassed their agenda on May 12. Pisser traveled alone in his guilt trip.

I lowered the boom, enunciated clearly past my chattering teeth. "Maybe I ought to call the sheriff."

Pisser lunged forward, brandishing a midget knife. Swiss didn't exactly make switchblades. His two goons yanked him back, and his other murderous allies scattered up the steps. Four against three, all bristling with repressed adrenaline.

"We didn't know." Squeaky Short-Shit blew his innocence. "We weren't out to hurt anyone. Just a scare. Wasn't our fault." He feinted right, then bolted toward the cliff. Chris gave chase. Afro Homie dashed off, Denny racing behind him, hammer clenched in his hand.

My sight never wavered from the Pisser, nor did his from me. Strung tighter than catgut, I hardly felt the ache Raymond and the stormy weather caused in my leg. This cat was ready to chase the mouse. His arm shot forward and steel gleamed orange in the glow of the fire.

"You gonna kill me like you killed my sister?" I badgered. The burden of the ensuing silence anchored me to the spot.

"Punk, I don't know what you're accusing us of." He bounced from one foot to the other. Rain glistened on his face. Camera flashes lit the night.

I forced out a cruel laugh. "You dumbasses really are too stupid to live returning to Sea Haven. I swear your parents are wasting their hard-earned cash keeping you alive." I bent slightly forward over the wobbling pocketknife. "Your boy already ratted you out," my tone leveled off. Water dripped off my slick hair down my temples. I shook my head to fling off the rain.

"If you're innocent, why the toy knife?" Kev smirked.

Whoa, Kev. The *toy knife* was poised to do damage. Been there, suffered that. All I cared about was getting a confession from the bastard. Before witnesses. Pounding him to dust . . . a well-deserved perk. Then Raymond rose to the hot seat.

Wind whipped up, showering rain onto the fire. Smoke mushroomed. I sucked in ashes and began hacking out a lung. My eyes stung, watered. A log cracked, shooting out embers. Pisser lurched at me, the knife aiming for my upper torso. Hopping out of the way, I bumped into Kev who thrust me aside. Asshat stumbled over the fire ring. He fell forward, caught his balance on an abandoned beach chair, and scrammed for the rocky cliff arm overhanging the sea.

No one had to kick me twice. I gave chase with Kev and Mikey close on my heels. Tara and Alyssa screamed at us to come back. So focused on the killer trio, I had no idea if anyone else remained at the party, and who wondered what really happened on May 12. I'd worry about damage control tomorrow.

"Beat the sucker down," Silver yelled after me.

Pisser leaped onto the boulders, clambering fast to the top of the rise. Toward oblivion. I doubt he knew he was ascending a one-way ticket to the sea. Death wish? One could only hope.

My numb hands found purchase on the first boulder. With sure steps, I climbed the sea wall, grasping wet handholds wherever I found one until I balanced on the first ridge. Strong gales blew sheets of rain on the cliff. Darkness camouflaged the Pisser. Loud panting gave him away to my right as he scampered toward the tip of the rock wall protruding out into the Pacific. Insanity must run in his family. Raymond contained a boatload of it. Kev shone a flashlight over my feet, bouncing light off the wet boulders.

"Light my path," I yelled over the roar of the tumultuous waves crashing on the rocks. The wind had picked up this near the sea and howled a sorrowful sound, the sound of death and vengeance. I staggered, steadied my hip on a boulder. I flung off the morbid thoughts, but they refused to die. Avenging Silver's death fueled the thread of control in my inner chaos.

The closer I scrambled toward the ocean the heavier the sea spray, soaking me to the bone. Kev flicked the light between the gang leader and me. Pisser stopped at the tip of the sea wall, dark hair plastered to his skull, moving left to right, trying to find another way down the rocks. Idiot had hiked straight into a lost cause. Unless he planned to take a header onto the rocks in the roiling sea.

Lost in my single-mindedness, I tripped and my right leg slipped in a crevice between two boulders. My knee slammed the rocks as I gained my footing, sliding my leg free. The icy wetness drove off the pain I'd feel in the morning. Waves pounded the rocks. I kept wiping the salty spray out of my eyes. Trapped like a caged lion, Pisser couldn't sneak past me on the twelve-foot-wide expanse. Sheer cliffs bordered our left side. The other cliff sides emptied out to sea, a killing drop into a rocky, churning cauldron.

Another light bobbed behind me. My vision adjusted to the murky night and I made out Pisser's silhouette. "Where you going?" Motionless, I stood six feet away from him. He feinted left, tried to rush me on the right. I lurched right, bowling him down. We fell on our sides, grappling with each other, rolling over boulders worn smooth by centuries of weather.

Pisser growled and roared. He gripped my upper arms and tried to knee my nuts. I easily thwarted the attack. Dumb girly move. My hands kept slipping off his slick rain jacket.

"You got the wrong guy." Rolling away from me, he struggled to his knees, panting.

"Then why'd you run?" I flipped to my feet, steadying my hip against a rock jutting from the cliff wall. "Your stupid game killed my sister."

One yard apart, we sized each other up. We were about the same height, but he had a good twenty pounds on me. My excitement fed me those twenty pounds and more. I'd use anything to crucify the soul-killing bastard.

"Drag racers killed your sister. They're doing their time." Wind flipped his drenched hair in every direction and he wagged his head to clear his vision. "You got your revenge, kid."

"Screw you." Satisfaction edged my bone-chilling shock. "Not until you and your rats pay for your part."

He shook back his shoulders, standing taller. "You'll never pin it on us. You can't prove anything. Your sister's dead, she can't narc. You didn't report us." Blustery wind carried his taunting laugh over the frenzied sea. "You killed her. *Your* car stalled in the intersection." He chuckled. "I bet she was a brat anyway."

I leaped at him, my fist hitting his face full force. I felt his nose fracture against my knuckles and the scathing chaser up my hand. He roared and shot an arm toward my gut. Lashing gusts forced us backward, and we rolled down the side of the cliff onto a narrow stony landing. The last firm footing before we tumbled into hell. That's when I noticed the ripping burn in my middle. Stunned, I felt the warmth of blood mushroom across my stomach beneath my cold, clammy shirt. He'd stuck me with the knife, buried so deep it appeared his fingers were digging inside my gut. My hands circled his neck. As I began to squeeze, a mountainous wave blasted the rocks and slammed us flat. Water sloshed over the ledge, dragging at us like an undertow.

He lost his hold on the knife. Pulling on my arms, he tried to loosen my grip on his neck. I dug for his jugular. Blinded by blood lust, I lost notice of everything except the sneering face pissing on my car, the lustful eyes staring at Silver, the gaping mouths when the two hotrods approached the intersection.

Another wave smashed into us, knocking us apart. He toppled backward, tumbled into the receding water. I fell forward on my hands and knees, gripping a sharp edge of rock.

"I'm gonna kill you." Pisser sprang up bowed over, prepping to gore me again.

I rolled out of the way, tripping him. He fell onto another flat boulder. I managed to push to my feet, the dark, tempestuous sea behind me an ominous threat. Pisser lunged for me, barreling us both onto the jagged rocks along the edge. He thudded on top. I rolled, flipped him on his side, my hand fisted on his jacket sleeve. His body thumped on another ledge of rocks.

Another wave towered up. Too late. It crashed down, a bludgeoning, suffocating weight pinning me to the boulders. Hanging on for what sketchy life remained, I waited for the wave to recede. It didn't. Another followed and a third. A triple threat.

I heard screaming. Tara or Alyssa? Strange thoughts of death flashed through my mind. A white beam lit the rocks lending their dark death a momentary glimpse of rebirth. *If I died, am I supposed to limp into the light or some stupid thing? Did Silver ever go into the light?* Where'd she go? She seemed to disappear when I didn't think of her. My mind rambled.

A hoarse, terrified voice spiraled above the storm. "Help me, man. You want another death on your hands?"

Water flowed, ebbed, and I lay half over the cliff, my right leg stuck between two rocks. Frozen fingers slid over my hand. I tightened my tenuous hold, reaching forward to grab Pisser's arm with my other hand. He dangled from the cliff, dead weight in my faltering grip. Without my help, he'd bite it hard. In one split second, I contemplated letting go, prying his fingers off the rock one by one, hearing his body plop to its death on the boulders below.

Silver checked my madness. "Don't give in, Lucas. Let him face his consequences. Make the scum-bucket suffer. I'm not ready for him to die so easily."

In a Hail Mary effort, I wrenched on him with all my waning strength. My numb fingers refused to work. I knew I'd lost blood and my body worked on borrowed energy. His weight was tearing my arm out of my shoulder socket. I tugged on him, unable to gain traction. He kept trying to secure a foothold and his jerking made my efforts harder. His wet fingers started sliding from my hold.

"Come on!" Tepid tears coursed down my frozen cheeks. "For Silver, you motherfucker. Revenge her way." A double wave crashed down on us. I lost my grip. Sputtering on salty water, the waves tumbled me over and over. My left arm caught in a gouge. My body moved one way and my arm remained stuck. Snap. One more bone down.

My head banged the rocks. Water engulfed me and the world went black.

Chapter 21

Positive I'd died quick, my death sure wasn't painless. My arm felt like I'd split it in two and my leg ached as if I'd broken it all over again. Fire smoldered in my entire torso. Guess my body should be thankful my stunt double days were over.

Silver's here-and-now voice vibrated in my ears. Which proved two things: I was dead, and I hadn't tripped into the killer light of heaven or the deathly heat of hell.

"Lucas, you with me?" Silver's tingly, calm warmth touched my right arm.

"I thought," I swallowed, mustering up moisture in my salty raw throat, "We weren't supposed to suffer pain once we bit it?" I lifted my right arm, the only body part that didn't hurt, and attempted to wave her nonexistent body off. *As if.* "Plus, you said you only hurt for a second."

"Lucas?" Mom stroked my cheek. I flinched. My scraped mug hurt from chin to forehead.

"Don't worry, son." Frogs had hijacked Dad's voice. "You'll be okay . . . again."

"Who were you talking to?" Mom feathered her fingers over my hair, the touch both welcoming and disconcerting.

My eyelids refused to obey my brain. Proof positive. Dead. I guess I should embrace death. According to Silver, ghosts had a blast. Dead people ruled. At least I'd get to see her for real.

"Lucas, can you hear us?" Dad asked. "Claire, call the nurse."

"Open your peepers. You're still kicking it." Air stirred my bangs against my eyelashes. "You didn't think I'd let you upstage *my* death, did you?"

Although my eyelids felt glued to my eyeballs, I managed to slit them open. Mom's face fluttered into view. Dad hovered over her shoulder.

"Thought I was dead, talking to Silver." Why bother sugarcoating it? My parents must already think I had a death wish. Call me Charles Bronson Jr. after the *Death Wish* movies I'd been watching late at night, my tutorials on all things vigilante.

Mom tried to hug me amid all the tubes connected to various parts of my upper body, her tears sizzling on my forehead. A fiberglass cast encased my left arm. Bandages plucked at my torso and a sling held my arm to my chest. Morphine, dripping way too slowly into my intravenous tube, kooked me out, turned my body to mush. I suspected if I wasn't pumped full of drugs, I'd be in several worlds of hurt. One world was enough.

"Do you remember what happened?" Dad squeezed safe real estate on my right forearm.

I remembered everything until the tidal wave crashed over me. And over the Pisser. *Oh, mother.* Did they haul him out of the sea? Was he alive? The heart monitor beeped into a jagged rhythm. Mom yelped for the nurse.

A blonde Amazonian swooped inside the room and slapped her frozen stethoscope on my left pectoral. Licking my dry, cracked lips, I lifted my eyelids. If Silver's Barbie doll lived, she stood in front of me in blue-eyed perfection. *Hello, Boobs.* Surely, I'd died and gone to heaven. But Nurse Barbie's deep, manly voice jolted me out of my hormone-induced daze. I double-checked her face for stubble. Nope. All woman.

"Hey, sweetie. I'm Laura. It's great to see you awake." She turned and addressed my parents. "Don't excite him. No more than two people in the room at one time." Her fingers were cool as she adjusted a tube stuck in my arm. "You relax. Let me know if the pain gets bad, okay?" She patted my arm and whooshed out.

Straining to smile and failing, I asked weakly, "What day is it?" Bracing for the answer, I held mummy stiff.

Mom sat by my side clasping my hand. "Sunday afternoon." Tension fled my board-straight body. "You weren't in a coma. You have a concussion, though. After the paramedics brought you in, you needed surgery." She choked up, brushed tears off her cheeks. "The knife ripped through your intestines. No permanent damage."

Dad laid his hands on her shoulders. His pale, misty-eyed look displayed his emotional state. "Your left collarbone and arm are broken. Clean breaks. You'll be good as new in a couple of months." Mom began to full-on bawl. Dad pressed a wad of tissues in her fist, and his fingers combed her hair.

Not as tough as I looked (BA), I couldn't master the moisture welling in my eyes. I forced out the two words begging for liberation. "I'm sorry."

Silver's voice resurfaced. "Buck up!" A frigid chill swept up my chest. "I need my Chuck Bronson, not some snively, whiney baby punk." She grew quiet, the chill evaporated. "God, Lucas. You scared me to death. Oops, umm, you know what I mean. I still need you. This isn't the end."

Through my watery gaze, I tried my best stink-eye. Of course, if she were alive, she'd play with the plugs on the monitor. *Dead-ass funny.* Man, I loved these drugs dripping into me.

After our moment-of-despair bonding, I garnered the nerve to ask my parents the other questions rocking my world. "How did I get out of the water? The undertow sucked me down."

"The surf rolled you back onto the lower ledge of rocks." Dad wiped his eyes then brushed his fingers on his sweat pants. I hadn't seen him publicly wear sweats in years. Wow, how'd I rate such slacking? Pride warmed my chest. "Kevin and Denny rescued you. Michael called nine-one-one before you went under. Those extra few minutes saved your life."

I swallowed the lumpy phlegm growing in my throat. Gross. "What happened . . . there was another guy—"

"The one who stabbed you?" Dad barked, his hands white-knuckling Mom's shoulders.

I nodded, waiting for him to tell me the police had locked Pisser up for assault.

"Boomerang," Silver whispered. "Karma's a sweet biotch, isn't she?"

Wagging my head side to side, I croaked, "He's dead?"

Dad held no punches. "His body washed ashore this morning."

Antiseptic mixed with industrial cleanser saturated the air, stung my nostrils. Pain invaded every cell of my battered body. I'd killed him. My blood beat against my veins, and I wanted to toss up my stitched guts.

Nurse Laura bustled into the room. Her face swam. "Sweetie. How many fingers am I holding up?"

Pockmarked ceiling tiles morphed into a gray cloud as my eyes rolled back into my skull.

"Lucas! No, no, no," Silver moaned. "You have to stay earthbound."

"Shut it, Silver," I muttered. "Boomerang." Red hazy pain joined the black oblivion swallowing me whole.

"Not you too." Silver's hysterical crying faded off.

Nurse Laura's deep voice dimmed. "Code Blue! He's coding!"

Chapter 22

My heartbeat ebbed and skipped. It thunked one last time. Peacefulness overcame me, eased my sore muscles. Pain vanished and I felt more limber and invigorated since BA. Death had called, but where was the light? Where were all the irritating dead people, aka Silver Alexander? Had my sins booted me straight to purgatory? Was I still stuck in a coma from the car accident? Maybe I'd been dead all along in a funky pre-afterlife?

I floated over the aqua Pacific, past the treacherous rocky cliff wall and Deadman's Cove in a la-la state as if I'd been smoking a joint. *No big deal. I'd tried it once.* Why wasn't I floating over my dead body in the hospital the way they did on TV?

The high school careened at me. Who filled my corpse brain with the idea that I wanted to visit the day-prison?

"Hey, Lucas." Silver drifted out of Sea Hag's quad in slow motion. Her lips kept flapping, her hands gesturing at warp speed. Air currents swirled her words into oblivion. She was real and solid. Alive.

The hand of déjà vu pushed me closer. Silver's blotchy face turned blood red. She must've busted a vein. *Prime yourselves for the gusher.*

"Don't you dare upstage my death, nimrod." An intangible wall holding us apart evaporated and a turbine wind blew us together. Silver pinched my arm. Hard.

"Cut it out." I rubbed my bare flesh. "I guess you're not the newb monarch of Heaven anymore." Glacial wind rolled up my backside.

Nearly jumping me, she hugged my waist. I folded my arms around her solid form, holding on tight. "It's not your time." She began to sniffle into my hospital gown. "As much as I want you here, I don't want you here. You're gonna kill Mom and Dad."

The thought tormented me, and my stomach did humongous flips. To immobilize the rising guilt, I focused on the obvious. "You got your revenge. At least we found the gang who caused your death."

"Your death too." She wiped her nose on the shoulder of my skimpy hospital gown, pulling it open in the rear.

No wonder that chill kept attacking my rear. The papery gown left my butt swinging in the wind. Thank God, someone let me wear my tighty-whities. Mooning and streaking never hit the top of my leap list. Reluctantly, I released Silver.

"That weasel, Raymond. Now the whole stinkin' town thinks you and I were boinking each other." Silver flitted around me in a circle.

"Um, Silver, about Raymond. Do you think he was part of the gang at the accident site?"

Silver froze. A mask of confusion descended over her face. "What do you mean?" She began to fade.

Indecipherable sounds grew louder. I recognized Mom's crying and Dad saying, "Come on, Lucas. Come back to us." Electricity arced through me, jolting my body off the skimpy mattress. The grass in the center of the school grew luminous. For a moment, radiant light dappled the cedars bordering the quad, reflected off the auditorium windows in gleaming waves. I easily resisted its lure as the magnetism to the hospital room gripped me.

"Told you it's not your time." Silver clapped her hands. Giggling, she play-punched my chest, a part earthbound punch that kick-started the ticker. "Gah. Can't you do anything right?" Light as mist, she kissed my cheek, her breath tickling my ear.

"I'll be back," she said. "You need to stay kicking. Plus, it's time to come clean about the accident. You're in major trouble with the law. Love you to death and back." She signed an "I love you" in sign language and vanished.

The jet-black abyss booted me earthbound. Mom was wigging out. Dad tried to remove her from the room while a slew of medical people surrounded me. Nurse Barbie aka Laura gave me a radiant smile. My pain receded, my heart rhythm returned to a slow normal. They'd stuck a new tube in my arm. Nitroglycerin to fuel my superpowers?

Had I truly died? Had Silver saved me? Did dead people lose their wits wandering the afterlife? I buried her words in a shallow grave to dig up later.

"Good to have you back." Dr. Sharma patted my shoulder.

"Lucas." Mom's broken voice exploded into the room, followed by her haggard body and Dad's distressed shell.

Dr. Sharma held up a placating hand. "Let's not excite the boy again. He's had enough for one day. No more than one person at a time in the room. Family only."

"What about the police?" Dad spoke quietly to Sharma off to the side, nodding toward the window separating my room from the busy hallway.

"Police?" I sputtered weakly. Two county sheriffs peered through the looking glass into my rabbit hole.

"I'll talk to them." Sharma's stumpy legs toddled toward the door. Yeah, the rest of his body was attached, too. *I'm telling you, these drugs are the bomb.* "They can obtain their statement in the morning when he's stabilized." The room finally cleared and Mom rushed to my bedside.

"Mom? What's going on?" I felt leaden on the slab bed, the scratchy sheets rough against my exposed back. I blinked rapidly to force my eyes to stay open.

"The sheriff wants a statement." She averted her gaze, tucked her hair behind her ear. The hair tuck was her avoidance tell. "They can get it later. You need to rest now."

On cue, I tumbled into a troubled sleep. My dreams honed in on Tara. I hungered to see her, to touch her. I wanted to fall and die into her radiance, to let the soul-deep warmth of her being bathe my body in life. Dreams of her helped keep my mind off the hospital, kept the jitters at bay, and prevented the nightmares of the car accident from propelling me into another drugged funk.

When I awoke later, morning sunlight filtered through the slanted mini-blinds on the windows to freedom. Sunlight left streaks of white in Mom's blonde hair while she snoozed in the chair beside the bed, her head resting against the wall. It reminded me of the highlights she and Silver painted in each other's hair last spring, which Mom kept up, not wanting the memory to fade with each inch of growth. Her eyelids twitched restlessly. Because of me, peace hadn't visited her in a long time.

"Mom?"

Her eyelashes fluttered up. "Morning." She smiled. "You look better, honey. How do you feel?"

"Can I go home today?"

"Maybe tomorrow." She adjusted my tortilla-flat pillow. "Dr. Sharma says you're doing great. No complications after our little scare." My actions put that waver in her voice, the mist in her eyes. Regret tried to drag me down again.

The door opened, disbursing the cloud shadowing the ray of sunlight. Dad entered and kissed the frown lines on Mom's forehead. "I need to talk to Lucas alone." They traded places on the edge of the bed. Mom shut the door behind her and stepped away from the sheriff glued to the corridor.

"Am I walking the plank? Do I need to lawyer-up?" I half joked, but a tightening fist in my stomach unfurled into full-blown jitters. "Are they charging me with murder?" Where'd Silver go? I had to bite my tongue to prevent myself from freaking out. *Man the hell up*.

"We'll straighten it out. There were witnesses. But you need to tell me the truth about what happened." He raked his fingers through his messy hair. "The *real* truth." His tone hardened. "Most of the kids questioned already told the sheriff you accused Dale Brisbin and the other boys of killing Silver." Lawyer Dad took over, an authoritative, emotionless man. "Several boys from the football team say you instigated the altercation and attacked Dale in retribution."

"Bullsh—" I blurted out, stopped as he went all Badass Lawyer, always worse than Hardnosed Dad.

"They say you pushed Dale off the cliff." He held his finger up to stifle the rant ready to erupt. "I want you to tell me what happened. First . . ." A fleeting look of discomfort crossed his features. "What *didn't* you tell us about the car accident?" Rising from the bed, he stepped aside, arms braced tight across his chest.

Like Silver said, if I didn't confess, trouble would snowball, boomerang, and I'd land in jail. Or kill someone else. I'd blown Silver Ghost's number one creed: avoid direct contact.

I fixated on the bleach scent of the pillowcases, versus the briny, salty sea springing to my senses. Dad's stormy face forced me to unload the truth about the car accident and the fight. Silver, the club, and our other activities remained my last secrets. My suspicions of Raymond remained a silent fixation, too.

Dad paced the room, his little-worn sneakers silent on the plasticky floor. "Why did you think you could go after the gang on your own? That's insane." He held my eyes for a second before his gaze bounced to the monitors, but not before I saw the gathering tears.

"The accident was such a blur, like they'd never been involved, as if I dreamed it. When I awoke from the coma, all I thought about was Silver being gone. I'd never seen them before. Didn't think I'd recognize them again. They didn't directly kill Silver and screw up my life." The white lie rolled off a sour tongue. I hated digging myself deeper into a mountain of crap. "I wanted to find them on my own, prevent them from harming someone else."

Dad puffed out a long exhale and the tension seemed to roll off his back. "At least your friends corroborated your story. Others confirmed the knife incident, and Alyssa snapped a picture of Dale threatening you with it. They also corroborated that Raymond passed out after your fight."

"Did the sheriff talk to the other gang members?"

Gullies formed between Dad's eyes. "The Monterey boys took off before the deputies arrived. You tell the sheriff exactly what you told me. *The truth*. No more lying or evading, Lucas. You say nothing about vengeance, got that? I'll coach you and then run damage control." Dad motioned in the sheriff.

After I gave my statement, a subdued repeat performance, Sheriff Masterson lectured me about due process and crap. "Hiding evidence is a crime. Good thing your dad's a smart lawyer."

I still owed him a Borla exhaust on his Vette. Once my broken body healed—repeat performance number two—I'd make good on my promise. My body was so going to kill me for hurting it again. I must've been a cat in a previous life. Nine lives and all.

The sheriff had barely escaped when the masses flocked in for the kill. Heaven for my gritty eyes, Tara waved to me outside the window, relief etched across her tired face. Alyssa, Denny, and Kev surrounded her. Even Mikey stood behind them, giving me a thumbs up. I smiled and motioned for Tara to enter. She was family.

The door opened and Aunt Serena barreled past Tara. "We drove back the minute we heard." She kissed both cheeks. I wallowed in her watermelon-scented hairspray, burying the gross, sickly odors of the hospital.

"We?" Smiling wanly, I wanted *any* conversation to settle on a path not related to my injuries or legal troubles.

"Hank took me on an overnighter to the opera in San Francisco."

Subdued talk filtered in from my gang waiting in the hallway. They sounded oddly stilted, forcing me to gaze past Aunt Serena.

"Hank *Dalton!*" I exploded, surprised the vein pulsing in my jaw didn't implode. My vision wavered. "You're dating Dalton?"

She backed off me as if I'd sprouted fangs and licked her neck. I saw his leering bronzed face through the window. Dressed in a rumpled suit, he looked like a *GQ* model, someone Aunt Serena would tie down in a heartbeat. He had the *cojones* to wave to me, his grin stretching his face into trouble territory. The hand he clenched on Mikey's shoulder tightened. Mikey looked ready to spew.

Chapter 23

Nurse Barbie and Mom conspired to keep everyone out of my sterile cage. Okay by me. Death followed me like a zombie chasing a brain. Too many people were dying and it scared me. I wanted everyone safe . . . from me. Bad karma had to quit boomeranging.

After a slew of medical tests, Mom split to handle insurance paperwork. Dad returned to his office to delegate lawyerly casework, then he planned to visit the district attorney's office. People scattered, the hallway emptied.

Dalton slipped inside my room. Too bad there weren't any banana peels in his path.

"What do you want?" *Jerkoff.* I tugged the blankets to my chin, wishing the anorexic cotton shielded me from the menace riding his pansy, floral cologne.

"Stay away from my kid. You're nothing but trouble." He snarled under his breath. "And don't ruin things between Serena and me, you little prick."

"Screw you. You're a time killer. Her *rebound.*" Ground glass accompanied my words. "She'll wise up and move on without my interference."

"Hank," Serena said from the hallway.

Dalton fingered the plug on one of the monitors. "Remember what I said." He slid through the door before Serena popped into view around the corner. He kissed her on the cheek, his arm possessively snaking around her waist.

Without skipping another heartbeat, I pushed the call button. Nurse Barbie responded pronto. I gave her an award-winning smile the girls used to love. Not so much anymore. Has-been football stars rated lower than the geek squad. "Can I use a phone?"

"You really shouldn't. Your mom's returning in a few minutes. Maybe she'll call for you."

"Please. I swear I won't get all hot and bothered. Unless you'll keep me company." I forced a grin I didn't feel. Pain had set up a rave in my body and the drugs hadn't arrived.

She clicked her tongue, scoped out the hall. Rolling the bedside table closer, she picked up the receiver. "Number."

"I owe you one." I recited Tara's digits. She punched them in, propped the phone to my ear and stepped to the door. Two rings later, Tara answered. "Can you come to the hospital later today? Bring your tablet," I whispered, not that she left home without her tablet and its million books. Sharp jabs of pain chased up my arm.

"Your mom's coming." Nurse Barbie seized the phone. "Sorry, Lucas can't talk anymore." She adjusted my pain drip, and a drugged stupor drifted me into la-la land. They ought to bottle this stuff.

Next time I awoke, the blinds filtered late afternoon stripes across the bed, illuminating Mom reading a book in the bedside chair. I hated the hospital, the complete lack of privacy, smells and tastes, the beeps and buzzing of the machines. The crying and mourning, the relieved sighs, and occasional laughter. They'd incarcerated me in a semi-private room alone, but healing and death haunted me every moment and from every corner. I wanted my reality back, whether before or after accident. Again, I'd lost touch with the world, and it sucked my soul dry for the second time in my short life.

"Mom? Can Tara visit?" I had to see her alone, at least one last time. A decision I wrangled over, hated with all my being. Too much danger surrounded me. If Raymond knew I found out about his involvement with the gang, it jeopardized anyone near me. I didn't see him letting it go any more than I would.

Mom jerked in her seat, the book clattering to the floor. "Hey, how you feeling? Will you talk to me first?" She traced her fingers over my cheek, brought a straw to my mouth.

The tepid water barely wet the dry gully. I wanted more but she refused. "I promise to answer questions later. Anything you want to know. But I need to talk to Tara." My fingers moved over her hand splayed on the bedcovers. "Please."

"Tara's in the waiting room." Her brows drew together. "About what Raymond said."

My face burned. I scratched the new road rash on my temple. "Eww, Mom, do you seriously believe Silver and I . . . oh, God, I'm gonna be sick thinking about it." I made a gagging reflex sound. Actually, I upchucked a little in my throat. "Raymond was wasted. He's pissed 'cause Silver dumped him. He's never been dumped before."

Mom sat, hands clasped on her lap, her normally perfect pink fingernails ragged against her denim capris. "He said something else, right?"

Which one of my *friends* ratted on me to my mother? My *mom* for piss sake.

The throbbing in my arm ratcheted up a notch. "Like what?" I deflected.

"About you and Silver having some sort of connection." She tipped her head to the side and wrinkles of curiosity edged her eyes. "What did he mean by that?"

I pretended to scratch my face. "Umm, nothing." My voice cracked. "He was just spouting off."

"Nothing more?" Her tone told me she didn't buy it.

"Okay. Okay." My face burned. "Silver and I had a twin bond thing. Nothing more. Raymond's full of himself. Always playing copycat. Well, he landed my spot on the team and screwed it up. He can haul my car out of the salvage yard. Now he wants Tara or Alyssa, and he thinks he can make me look like a perv with his big frickin' mouth."

Mom continued trolling. "What kind of bond?"

"I don't know. We felt each other sometimes. We weren't exactly normal fraternals." I rocked her boat. "We dealt with it, and it didn't interfere with our lives."

Her spine knocked against the chair. "An empathic bond?" The thin emotional connection that bound her to Serena had become second nature by their teens. Nothing spectacular or sketchy. Certainly not nearly as deep as the bond Silver and I shared as fraternal twins. We sometimes wondered if we were freaks of nature.

"Yeah, something like that." I buried my face in the pillow.

"You two never said anything about it. Why?"

"Because it was weird. Besides, had you told *your* parents?"

The corners of her lips curved up. "Point taken." She squeezed my hand. "Okay. I'm going home for a couple hours while you visit with Tara."

Tara breezed in, a large purse slung over her shoulders. "Hey." Bending over me, she pressed her lips to mine, tasting faintly of the bubblegum lip-gloss I loved.

I lived again, breathed in pure air. The anchoring weight of seawater filling my lungs became a recollection of another lifetime. Tara became my all. I touched the tip of my tongue to hers, reticent and possessive at once. After a drugging, airless moment, we drew apart. The lines on my heart monitor gyrated wildly. Tara's breath hitched. I thumbed the solitary tear off her cheek.

She was my reason for being. I couldn't stand never feeling this way again. Never touching her, seeing her, kissing her, drowning in her vitality. Never surrounded by the normalcy she provided. A lead sarcophagus pressed on my heart, and I knew I had to keep her safe from my life's insanity. Knew what I had to do. Later, though. After I escaped the disinfectant hellhole.

"You scared me. I'm so glad you're okay." She curled in the armchair, set Mom's discarded book on the windowsill. Our eyes met and I wanted to tumble into their watery depths, and soak her into me. I shifted my left arm with my right to hold her hand. Warm and vibrant, her fingers clung to mine. "Your mom said your heart stopped. Did you flatline?" She blinked rapidly to halt the tears threatening to waterfall.

Unable to utter an assent, I nodded, gulped down the rising sorrow. "Silver was there. Real and alive." As the story unfolded, tears coursed down Tara's cheeks. When I said the words, "I'd died and I was happy, whole, pain free." I shed a tear or two, hiding it from her. "When I awoke, you were all I dreamed about. I didn't want to be a ghost you couldn't ditch." I choked on a snort. Tara fed me a spoonful of ice chips. My whole torso burned when I moved or breathed, so for the most part, I lay like a frozen sack of broken bones.

"I'm glad I don't have to deal with another ghost." Her lashes closed over her ocean blue eyes, then swept up. She slicked her fingers over her cheeks. "The ghosts at Deadman's Cove have kinda latched onto me." My eyes grew wide. "It was spectral energy that pushed you guys away from conking yourselves out on the fire ring."

"Thought I felt something. Are you okay with the ghosts?" Unease fisted in my sliced and spliced gut. "Was Silver there then?"

"She was." She sighed. "I'm a sensitive, they sensed it. Silver threatened them if they spooked or hurt me. Ghosts don't usually hurt sensitives because they want us to communicate with them. They just can't help themselves from spooking us. We can help them come to terms with their plight. Just be with them."

"Like you helped the girl ghost?" She nodded. The ice melted on my tongue, cooling my runaway emotions. I rubbed my thumb across her palm. "I need to tell you something."

"There's more?"

I melted into her smile. I hated not being the recipient of that beautiful, slightly crooked smile ever again. The stitches on my arm burned. "It's about Raymond. The dead kid, Dale Brisbin, was his cousin."

She held up her hand. "I know. There was talk on the beach that they're morons forming a gang. CrimsonX and the Juggernauts keep driving them out of town."

I stifled a groan. Could I have outed myself anymore with CrimsonX? Again? Death wish much, as Silver used to say. "That's not the half of it." I sputtered. Tara handed me another spoon of ice chips. They melted courage on my tongue. "I think they were inducting Raymond into the gang the night of the accident."

Tara gasped, sucked in her middle. "Oh. My. God."

"He needs to pay."

Her eyes rounded. Red suffused her face. "Wasn't Dale's death enough?"

Recoiling, I closed my eyes for a second. Dale's death would always haunt me.

"Knowing Raymond as you do now, would that satisfy you?" I finally asked.

Chapter 24

Tara's nervousness rode the air, nearly thick enough to touch. She toed her chair away from the bed a few inches, as though the extra space blocked my cooties from jumping ship.

I needed to explain other stuff to her, especially Raymond's verbal spam about Silver and me. Instead, I could let her think the worst, drive her away to keep her safe. But I refused to tarnish Silver's reputation.

"Hey." I scrunched closer to the edge of the bed, wincing from the pain burning my shredded intestines. "About stuff Raymond spewed."

"That drunken blowhard?" She fiddled with her wristwatch, plucked her sleeves over her hands.

"It's not like he said. About Silver and me."

"I didn't think so." She chewed on her bottom lip, playing down the unsaid "but."

"What's the buzz?"

Her gaze glommed onto the tablet screen. "I don't believe any of it. When you're ready, you can tell me what you want. Several others have spread nasty rumors. Craziness between you two. Random stuff. Most are Raymond's buds—"

"Who's saying what?" Frost hung on the edge of my words.

"Someone said he'd witnessed you and Silver internally reacting to each other's emotions." She did air quotes with her fingers. "How you'd get angry or emotional at the same time."

"Big honking deal. Twins do stuff like that." Sort of. A vein ticked in my jaw. The monitors showed signs of an extra life, red and green lines gyrating and beeping insistently. I counted to ten, waited for my heart to slow, emotions to simmer. Amazonian

Laura stuck her head in the doorway, studied the machines, shook her finger at us on the way out.

"What idiot opened his cake hole?" Had to be someone close to me.

"Chris—"

"Chris?" I tried to sit up, suppressed a yelp. Total failure. "Did he breathe stupid dust or something?"

"He defended you but it came out wrong, his words got twisted. The whole thing went viral, now everyone's searching their memories." Tara plunked onto the bed. "It'll blow over. They'll latch onto the next big story. People love gossip."

Because ignoring the truth is too bloody easy. "What do you believe?"

"What you tell me. What Silver tells—"

The muscles in my shoulders loosened. "Do I scare you? Wait." I squinted my eyes. "Silver?"

Laura called from the doorway, "One more time and your girlfriend's barred from visiting."

"Sorry," Tara squeaked out, returning to the safety of the chair. "Silver latched onto me after the party. We talked. She didn't want the whole episode scaring me off."

"Are you scared off?"

She kicked out her feet, ducked her head. "No," she whispered.

Another knot unloosened in my shoulder even as I thought it would be easier if she were scared. "So what else did you and Silver *talk* about?"

A smile brought her back to me. "Girl stuff."

"Like what?"

Tara rolled her eyes. "It's personal, girl to girl."

"You mean ghost to girl?" My arm itched like crazy beneath my cast and my grimace put an end to the light-hearted conversation.

"She wants you to be right with the world again, you know," Tara said. After a moment battling my emotions, I nodded. "Anyway, you'll have damage control at school. Let's worry about it later. I want to get back to the other issue. What else does Raymond have against you? Was the initiation targeted toward you and Silver?"

"I think it was a fluke. On the flipside, Raymond's always been jealous of me. I was the star quarterback, school prankster who rarely got caught, had the hot car, all the hot girls." I smiled apologetically.

She wagged her head. "Yeah. I never would've talked to the *perfect* Lucas Alexander let alone date him."

"No kidding?" How'd I rate?

"Dead serious." Her fingers scrolled across the screen of her tablet device. "I'm not into competitive sports. I heard you were the number one playing field."

"Nah uh. I wasn't that bad."

"Riiight. Guess they called you King Renegade and named a set of pranks after you because—" She held up the tablet to show me the Pranx 'R Us forum. My escapades were on full display under my Red Renegade avatar.

My pain drip needed to catch up before I rolled off the rails. "That was the old me. Before accident."

"You threw a bag of ladybugs inside the school hothouse two years ago?"

I grinned. "Took janitors a week to catch them all. Never got busted. Officially."

"They flew through the ventilation system." She jiggled my good leg. "Seriously. You're done with that stuff?" she scoffed.

Pain stabbed my broken arm and my face grew clammy. Had I merely moved on from kid pranks to deadly retribution?

"Lucas? You okay? Do you need more pain meds?"

My arm throbbed like there was no tomorrow. I shook my head.

A rap on the door and Amazon Laura entered. "If you rest today and your tests look good, you're out of here tomorrow." She tapped her finger on Tara's shoulder and glided out to brandish her spear at the other jungle inmates.

"I need to get out tomorrow. Do you mind?" I gave Tara a weak smile I didn't feel over the guilt bouncing through me. "Keep this between us." I wanted to spend more time with her without Raymond hanging over me. The weight of two worlds sank my leaden body into the mattress. Silver's words flung from one side of my brain to the other. "Karma's like a boomerang" said it all. I kissed Tara goodbye, watched her trade places with Mom.

I didn't try to fall asleep. Instead, my body grew numb. I was totally freaking. How'd my life wind up so wrecked again? Bad enough I'd caused Dale Brisbin to eat it, in addition to Silver's death. I had to deal with Raymond, and I needed a way to cow him without it turning deadly. He may have been in the wrong place and time, same as Silver and me, but that didn't mean I had to drop it. Plus, I may have a new hit on my head from Dale's gang. My chest hitched.

"Hey, kiddo, you awake?"

Wanting to tell Mom everything, I wished she'd make the crap-storm bail. I'd kill one final time (kidding) for a do-over for the last few months. I examined her tired face, washed out from the light streaming through the window. "I don't want you and Dad to divorce. I'll go to counseling every day if you want. Please, can't Dad come home so we can be a family again?"

"Honey, nothing's your fault. Not then, not now. We never believed differently. If anything—" She hugged me, clinging tight, her fingers pressed into my back.

Weird how you don't miss affection after a long time without it. Then it became a welcome home after a long, harsh winter. You wanted more. You wanted to drown in it. If I could hug Mom, I'd do it, and never be an idiot again. *Okay, no one needs to know about the idiot part.*

She released me. "I told you we're just taking a break. Dad's going to commute to San Jose for the trial so he'll be home at nights now. I want you to get better and quit beating yourself up about Silver." Mom perched on the bed, stroked my hand. "Dr. Beranger thinks you're projecting your guilt in the wrong direction instead of in positive, creative ways. Personally, I don't think you've dealt with Silver's . . . death . . . properly."

"What's that supposed to mean? I'm moving on. What else am I supposed to do?" *Really. I'd like to know so I can add the Magnum Opus to the manual I'm writing on how to tackle death, teenagers, and ghostly delusions.*

"You've never returned to Silver's grave. You never talk about her unless you're feeling guilty. I think you need closure." Mom's voice wavered and she fingered her ear, telltale sign of her quiet conviction.

Beranger kept telling me the same thing. I ignored him. Silver hated that I'd never gone back to her grave. The twit found my lack of attention disrespectful of the dead. *Dead, my ass.* She just wanted more purple roses.

How do I bring myself to visit her grave when she sort of still lived?

My family no longer fit together. Like a puzzle missing the center, the edges jagged and thready. I couldn't ignore Mom and Dad any longer. They'd never heal until I did. My family would never find closure as long as I refused to play the grieving son in the dumb politically correct way.

Yet I refused to lie. Or tell the truth. "Silver will always be alive." I patted my chest over my heart, then tapped my head.

Chapter 25

The hospital released me the next day. Since I refused to see anyone else in the antiseptic, death-stinking room except my parents, the Nomads were chomping on my butt to catch up. I didn't feel like talking to anyone. Nor did I know what to say to Tara. I feared for her safety, feared I'd never let her go if I spent more time around her. Although I wanted her like mad, I avoided her. With a humongous crick in my heart, I texted her that I needed space; she wasn't safe near me; I was too dangerous and high maintenance. *Can dudes be high maintenance?* The agony of the message left a different kind of slow burn in my wounded shell. She never responded to my texts. I felt like a major douche bag.

Again, my world spun circles around healing and legal troubles. I used to love being the king of the school's rumor mill. Always in a wicked cool way, though. Today, I wanted to dig a hole in the sand and crawl to Australia where no one knew me. Inadvertently, I'd killed my sister, Dale Brisbin, my life. *Three strikes, you're out.* Beranger should sign my commitment papers to save the world from Lucas Alexander. I may as well have pulled the trigger on all three for all the guilt I felt from my collusion. Yet I planned to make it right if it was the last thing I did.

The minute I hobbled through the front door with Mom and Dad, Alyssa and Auntie Serena attacked, fawning and coddling. Despite my forced smile, I wanted to gag, rage, and throw things. Biting down my storming emotions, I gave into their rampaging hormones. Weird as it sounded, I might be the glue holding my family together. I realized the incongruity of the idea during my second—and final—stay in the hospital. *The next time I landed in the hospital, I swear, they better be embalming my body*. Knowing my precarious position, I refused to jeopardize my life or anyone else's life again.

My convalescing began anew. Serena made a bed for me on the couch in the family room and left to make my favorite raspberry lime Rickey. The smell of Alyssa's famous white-chocolate-chip cookies pervaded the house. Dad ordered pizza and garlic cheese sticks. Mom fussed and supervised. Her smile was worth my emo phase. She'd gotten her son back. Only took a Reality check, another death-defying dumbass play, and a real near-death experience to pound sense into my battered body. *Yeah, it takes me a while.* I am that creature inside me now, though. Sorrow, vengeful, and a skosh of hatred. But a thickening layer of hope glazed the clutter.

We sat around the coffee table eating, talking, and having a fun time. Dad and Mom connected in a cautious manner. They traded soft expressions, light touches, loving voices. The sight of them bonding buoyed my flagging spirits. I also ached to see Tara.

Dad gave my arm a friendly squeeze. "One of the partners is taking over my trial and I'm home now. You okay with that?"

Joy spiraled in my chest. Most teenagers loved that their parents weren't home much. *I may wish for it later.* "Thanks, Dad." I grinned, wiping pizza sauce off my chin. "Does this mean I'm stuck in club lockup?"

He laughed a carefree sound I hadn't heard in, like, forever. "Eat your pizza before the warden confiscates it."

Heaven-sent pizza filled me as much as the comfort of family. While I stuffed myself, *everyone* called or texted. Tara and Denny popped over, but Mom declared me off limits. I'd slammed four pieces of combination pizza when the doorbell rang for the *third* time. I girded myself for another rebuffed friend to talk off the ledge tomorrow.

"I got it," Serena called from the kitchen.

"Jeez, Luc, tell your friends to mellow out." Alyssa threw an olive at me.

I threw it back, bouncing the black slice onto her head. "You didn't give Denny the cold shaft."

Picking the olive out of her hair, she blushed. "We're just friends."

"Friends, my shiny white—" The word dried up, my eyes bugged.

Dad's head swiveled toward the archway connecting the family room and kitchen. "Hey, Hank, join the party." He pushed off the carpeted floor. "Pull up a cushion or a chair if you can't get down on the floor." In an exaggeration of discomfort, Dad stretched out his long legs.

Gnawing down on my tongue, I fumed. It took everything in my internal arsenal not to wig out. "Mom, can you help me upstairs? I need to chill."

"You don't look so hot." She pressed the back of her hand to my forehead.

"I'm okay." I let her help me stand, not that I needed it. She did.

Pure arrogance masked Dalton as he curled his arm around Serena's waist. You'd need a crowbar to pry them apart. Just so happened I had three in my car.

"Good to see you doing so well, Lucas. Let me help you upstairs." He reached for me and I bounced against the wall.

"Don't touch me." At least I got in one shot that simply earned a glower from Dad. "Lyssa, bring our drinks and cookies, we'll watch a movie."

Glowing like a jellyfish, Mom settled me onto the bed. "Your aunt's into him," she said unexpectedly. "He treats her like a queen."

"Doesn't mean I have to like him." *Freaking faker.* "She's not even divorced yet."

"Simon and Serena have all but been divorced for over a year. You know they held it together for Alyssa."

"Whatever. I don't trust him."

"Because he doesn't like one of his students? Come on. Give the man a break. He's new to town, and we all know your mile-long school record speaks for your character." Her eye-roll lessened the severity of her tone.

Alyssa arrived, a tray loaded with cookies, drinks, and a bag of M&M's balanced in her hands. "Look what I found? Silver's favorite black and orange M&M's."

"Thanks, Mom." I hugged her, feeling the tenderness I'd missed since May. Sometimes you had to fake it to recognize reality later.

The second the door closed, I pounced on my cousin. "Lyssa, we gotta get that jerk away from your mom."

She set the tray on the one vacant spot of real estate by the flat screen stand. As she straightened and turned, she tugged the bottom of her snug T-shirt until it settled above her belly button. Eyes widening, I recognized the screen-print tee I'd given Silver for our birthday in April.

"What am I supposed to do? My mom drools all over him." Alyssa sank onto the bed. "He's okay, I s'pose. I like Mikey, too. Wish he'd come over to drool all over you." She giggled.

I rolled my eyes at her, really noticing her. "Did my mom say you could wear Silver's clothes?" Mom and Serena had boxed up most of Silver's things after Alyssa took up residence.

She peered down at the shirt, her gaze sliding to Silver's favorite designer jeans, her face flushing. "Sorry. Do the clothes bother you? I don't have all my things and Auntie Claire let me take whatever I wanted."

"When?"

"Yesterday." She twisted the hem of the T-shirt. "Is it okay? Denny digs these jeans on me." Hope edged her voice.

My irritation boiled inside my chest, stewed, cooled. I didn't know why I hadn't *seen* her earlier. She looked and moved so similar to Silver in those clothes it creeped me out. "Whatever. They're just rags."

"Are you kidding me? These are awesome compared to my Goodwill wardrobe."

Reality Check. My family had so much while Serena and Alyssa lived on the few dollars they managed to scrape together after the Loser gambled away their life. Alyssa's entire wardrobe fit in the two suitcases she'd brought from Boston. Living with us must be paradise for them. They deserved a better man than a jerkoff English teacher toting a grudge stick.

"Wear whatever you want. Glad Silver's clothes fit." I tweaked her T-shirt, hesitated. "So Dickhead Dalton doesn't like me because I coached Mikey on online Camaro and pranks forums last spring. It was just a fluke they moved here. Mikey wants to get into hotrods and play some pranks for the cool factor, but Dalton wants him to play football like he did, which Mikey hates. He's dogging me. I'm sure he read my file, but I haven't done anything to him, nor have I done any pranks this year." I backed away, stuck my fist in the front pocket of my jeans. "I mean, things are different now."

Alyssa drew her finger across her lip, and her eyes went all puppyish. "He's just protecting his son. What's the big horkin' deal?" She handed me a glass of soda and the plate of cookies.

Jeez, she even sounded like Silver. "Whatev. He gives me the skeevies hanging around here without letting Mikey hang with me. Talk about double standard." I set the cookies on the bed, slurped down half the lime Rickey, unable to sluice the bitterness from my tongue. Raymond deserved my attention, not a loser teacher. Should I tell her? I ran the risk she'd blab to her mom. They were tight. *No can do.* I needed more time to plan the ultimate revenge, more Google-fu time. Time to figure out what Raymond would do knowing I had a hand in . . . I swallowed hard . . . killing his cousin.

All this took precedence over Silver Ghost's charter. I needed to keep Tara and Alyssa safe and ensure they didn't turn into slasher flick victims. Dad could handle my legal troubles. I'd already chucked the guilt over Dale's death into a temporary cavity in my thrashed brain. What I didn't suffer in nightmares, Beranger would siphon out.

I shrugged. Bolts of fire zigzagged down my left arm cradled in a tight sling. My pharmaceuticals had worn off. Grimacing, I slunk onto the bed, banged my elbow on the night table, unable to stop my sissy yelp.

Alyssa plumped my pillows. "Time to up your meds?" She giggled at her joke.

"Not yet." I absorbed the pain. Curious, I asked. "What's Tara doing tonight?"

The room stilled, quieted. I closed my eyes to slits and saw Alyssa freeze. Then she wrung her hands, unfolded them, scratched her cheek, and raked her fingers through her hair. She'd make a lousy poker player.

I opened my eyes all the way. "What?"

"Nothing." She crossed the room to my desk, snagged my iPhone, bounced it from hand to hand.

"Fess up."

"Don't shoot the messenger, 'cause I have no clue what's going on." Turning around, her knuckles whitened around my cell. "Raymond's been hanging with Tara at school, lying about you and Silver."

I bolted upright, sucked up the pain. "No frigging way. He doesn't know when to cut it loose. She doesn't believe him, does she?" Afraid the beach party had changed every aspect of my newfound life, rockets exploded in my pounding head as I waited.

Alyssa folded her arms across the wilted black and gray flowers screen-printed on the purple T-shirt. "They went on a date tonight."

Chapter 26

"What?" I hurdled off the bed, moved close enough to smell chocolate on Alyssa's breath. "Where'd they go?"

She sank backwards onto the mattress. "I don't know. Tara told me Raymond was picking her up at eight."

Blow me a new one. Tara said she believed me about Raymond's accusations. She knew I suspected him of being at the accident. What was she up to? Had she been hunting for an excuse for me to dump her or vice versa? Trippy girls! Were they all the same? I'd out Raymond before I let him hurt her the way he hurt Silver. Even though I knew Raymond wasn't a killer, he never even hinted he knew what happened at the intersection. That kind of load was too much for any girl to deal with, let alone take on his manipulative crap.

I stuffed pillows under my comforter, building a small, lumpy body. "Come on. You're best friends. Didn't she tell you why she went out with him?"

"Why'd you text her about needing space? Why are you avoiding her?" Alyssa set our drinks on the desk before my schizoid movements knocked them over. "Talk about crazy times ten."

"People die around me. No one's safe." I latched onto her arm. "Not even you."

She threw up her hands. "Give me a break. Your text was a dumb excuse to break up. You hurt her."

"Yeah, so she's burying her pain in Raymond?" I found my shoes halfway under the bed, shoved them on. "Cover for me. Put on a movie, and lay on the bed to block the pillows. If anyone asks, tell them I'm asleep." I rescued a sloshing drink off the desk.

"Where you going?"

I downed two Tylenol. They'd dull the pain without kooking me out like Vicodin. "To look for her."

Torn in two, I brushed hair off her check, compelled by the troubled faith in her eyes. "Raymond," I swallowed hard, "nearly raped Silver and she was totally gaga over him." Alyssa blanched. "I won't let it happen to Tara. You heard the BS he spewed. Nothing will stop him until he stomps me or people I love into dust."

"What does he hold against you? It's not like, you know, you . . ." Alyssa stammered.

"Have anything left?" I slammed the Tylenol bottle against the bathroom door. The lid flew off and tablets pinged the wall.

She locked the door to the hall. "You two were friends, though."

"He was the junior high class clown, the number one quarterback. Until I hit town."

She helped me stick my good arm through the sleeve of my zip-up hoodie. "Everyone flocked to you?"

"He was jealous of my relationship with my own sister. He wanted my Camaro. In fact, he tried to buy it before I did, but couldn't scrape up the dough. Then his parents turned around and bought him a Mustang after we won the district championship last year. We were friends because of football." I drew the side window blinds up. "He never visited me at the hospital, never called, texted, nothing. He never gave a rat's ass about Chris and Kev. They stood by me, even when I was bogged down with football." The words came out in a torrent. Raymond should be licking the dirt off my shoes for what he'd done to Silver. To my family. To my entire life. Was I wrong about him being at the accident site? I didn't think so.

"Try the pier. Tara mentioned clam chowder."

"I owe you one." I slid the window open. The ladder still stood in the sideyard. "His uncle owns a steak and seafood place, Surfing the Turf." With one arm, I leveraged myself out the window with as little pain as possible. "If she calls, scope her out, then call me. Don't warn her I'm searching."

"He won't hurt her, will he?"

I swung a leg over the rain gutter, easing down until my foot rested on the top rung of the ladder. "Just do what I say, Lyssa."

Moonlight bathed her nervous silhouette in the window frame. I didn't know what I planned to do, except rescue Tara from Raymond's bullshit. My right foot hit the last rung. I finger-waved to Alyssa and jogged to the gate.

Stealthily backing my car out of the driveway was a breeze since the family room sat at the butt end of the house. I wanted to slam my car into Dalton's Toyota, but I didn't want to infest my Camaro with his squirrely germs. Headlights remained off until I hit the street, then I gunned the engine into a quiet roar.

"Silver, you here?" The inside of my cheek suffered the brunt of my anxiety. "Quit playing games." Nothing. Had she tripped the light fantastic? Tight knots coiled my intestines. Although her presence diminished as I grew stronger, I wasn't ready to lose her—all over again. I rolled down the window. Damp air rushed inside. I dragged it down, the cold frosting my lungs.

I patted my hoodie pocket, feeling my cell against my side. The wharf lights loomed, rainbow beacons bobbing in the thin fog. Wispy, moist air roiled around the buildings on the pier and along the beach. It seeped into my pores, chilling me to the bone.

If I lost Tara to Raymond, to anyone, I didn't know what I'd do. I wished I hadn't sent her that text. Maybe I was wrong, or maybe I hadn't realized how much she was part of me. Way different from Silver, but a missing piece. I needed her like the sun orbiting me, the air filling my lungs, and the blood coursing in my veins. I wanted to feel her in my arms, her lips pressed to mine, to know she desired me the way I craved her. I'd fight for her and win her back. I couldn't deny the connection we shared, the ghosts of our pasts, the ghost of our present, or that she had brought me back to life. We needed to share the future, even if it meant we split temporarily to keep her safe from Raymond, Dale's gang, and CrimsonX.

The wharf area teamed with mid-week nightlife, almost as busy as the weekend. People from up and down the coast, including the local resorts, pegged the Sea Haven Wharf the best hidden touristy shopping and eating site between Monterey and San Francisco. Throw in Deadman's Cove and the town became the entertainment hub of central California.

I parked in an empty spot three doors down from Surfing the Turf. As one of the first eateries on the wharf, Raymond's family had opened the restaurant in the twenties. After football season ended each year, his uncle treated the team to all-you-can-eat crab and lobster. We broke the bank on those meals.

I slipped out of the car, holding my arm close. The Tylenol barely dented my pain, but I ingested the pain whole, let my boiling anger and anxiousness absorb it.

Noise wafted out the double doors of the restaurant. The hostess greeted me, wearing a skintight black tube cut to mid-thigh and a sympathetic smile. Guess the bruises on my mug sang my story. The dining room was packed, but I didn't spy Raymond or Tara.

"Raymond been around tonight?" I flashed the redhead my most charming smile, forced and fake.

"I recognize you. You're one of the football players." My arm sling earned her nod. "Tough game?"

"Something like that." Laughter from a loud party in the far corner drifted over. I leaned toward her to avoid yelling above the din. "I'm supposed to meet him tonight."

"He brought his new girlfriend for dinner." Wendy, her nametag read, tapped a long raspberry fingernail against the reservation list. "They left about an hour ago."

My blood simmered. "What'd she look like?"

"Short, cute brunette, blonde highlights." She gave me an exaggerated wink. "Bright blue eyes. She's totally into him. It's nice to see him with a girl after his girlfriend was killed in May."

Hot, angry bile rose up my gullet. I choked it down. "Do you know where they went?"

"Sorry." She shook her head. "A large party arrived as they were leaving."

I exited the restaurant, leaned against the weathered shingled wall. Once again, I called Tara's cell and got her voicemail. I was dialing Alyssa when Wendy rushed out the door.

"Good. You're still here." She rubbed her arms against the cool weather. "I forgot. Raymond ordered two coffees to go and grabbed some logs from the wood stack in the sideyard. Said they'd need to warm up until, well, you know." Her eyes sparkled from the icicle lights dangling along the length of the wharf buildings.

Phone at my ear, I bolted. Alyssa answered on the third ring. "Heard from Tara?"

"Not yet," she said in a sleepy grumble. "Where you at?"

"At the wharf. I think they're at Deadman's Cove." Hook-Up Caves. "How's my cover?"

"You're good. Your mom popped her head in. I told her we'd finish the movie then lights out."

I clicked off and rushed to the Camaro. My bandaged arm joggled against me, my lungs and gut burned. I longed for the day when pain no longer plagued me. *Damn you, Karma.*

Inching my car down the crowded street, my foot wanted to stomp on the gas pedal. Instead, I wound through the teaming streets until I hit Cliff Heights Drive, the frontage road overlooking the ocean. Soon as I hit the open road, I punched it. The Camaro's engine roared, thumping in tune with my angry heart.

"Raymond won't get his filthy hands on Tara." I refused to believe she wanted this. "Please God don't let me be wrong about her." I couldn't afford to lose my sixth sense along with everything else in my life.

My cell rang and I answered before the second ring. "Tara?"

"Yo, what up?" Kev blasted through the earpiece. "Long time, no hear."

"Where are you?"

"At Denny's. Dude, gotta tell you something you won't like."

I dropped my speed. "I know about Tara and Raymond." The words spit out like glass shards. I cut the lights and coasted into the parking lot above Deadman's Cove. Raymond's blue Mustang sat alone in the lot. After my party, Deadman's Cove became even more of a lonely, haunted spot. Locals weren't interested in partying with fresh ghost meat.

Denny's bitter voice wafted through the speaker. "Look, man, I don't know what's up between you two, but she's been hanging all over Raymond the last two days. That's not Tara. I didn't know she took off with him until Alyssa called. I don't like that prick. Any idea where they're at?"

"Deadman's Cove. I'm there now." I paused. "I think Raymond was being initiated into his cousin's gang the night of the accident."

"What?" Denny said on a heavy breath. "How do you know?"

"Things are clicking. The way he's acted since the accident. We used to be friends. Now everything I do pisses him off. I think he's deflecting, man." I raked my hand through my hair. "I don't want him near Tara."

"We're on the way." The line went dead.

The night wrapped me in a dank blanket. I slipped my fingers under the seat and gripped the switchblade, stuck it in my jeans pocket. I had no plans to use force, but you never knew with Raymond. Three beers and he turned into a toad with a bullfrog complex. I added a penlight to my pathetic arsenal. Cupping my hand around the beam, I followed the tiny pool of light to the steps.

Slow and easy, I made my way down the flat stones. Waves pounded the shore. A breeze hadn't stirred the air for days. Tara's sultry laugh floated to me, followed by Raymond's hee-haw guffaw. *Hello, jerk alert.*

Chapter 27

A light bobbed ahead of them in a white path to the water's edge. Raymond lumbered across the sand leading Tara toward the waves lapping at the shore, whooping it up, already tanked. I heard hesitation in Tara's stilted laugh. My internal stitches wrenched when I moved forward. Who knew if my intestinal shredding stemmed from anger or confusion? I'd lost the ability to read myself.

I took my last step onto the beach, my shoes sinking into the cold sand. I feared cutting my light. The last thing I needed was another broken bone. My body wouldn't make it to graduation at this rate.

"Come on, Tara. Take it off," Raymond cajoled.

Their flashlight hit the sand, a beacon pointing toward the ebony sea. Pieces of clothing fluttered onto a gnarled driftwood log. The half-moon slivered a pale glow across the beach, a slash glinting off the water. The cobwebby fog had moved on to plague another travesty, and my eyesight easily adjusted to the dark. I sidestepped the shadows of the fateful cliff. The name Deadman's Cove fit more than ever.

The sea wall blanketed me in shadows. Hidden along the base of the cliff, I watched Raymond strip and toss his clothes onto dry sand not far from the tide. Tara threw one glove, then another on the growing pile. Ever so slowly, she unbuttoned her jacket. For once, I was grateful her jacket had buttons versus a zipper.

Raymond's naked torso glowed vampire white. *Dude, wouldn't kill you to sneak out of the coffin during the summer.*

He stepped closer to Tara, one hand on his pants' zipper, the other he cupped around her neck. A slight crook of his head and his mouth pressed to hers. I clenched my teeth to keep my growl from escaping. The kiss ended and Raymond's lips slurped across her cheek. *Ah, gross.* Tara stroked her fingers over his arm. I seethed so hard, my arm and leg bones retaliated with surges of pain.

"Let's get into the water before I freeze my balls off," Raymond said. His crudity in front of Tara disgusted me. "The water's warmer than the air."

"I'm getting there." Tara breathed out a shivery giggle. "Take your pants off. I want to see all of you in the moonlight."

"Yeah, baby. That's what I'm talkin' about." Raymond peeled his pants down his pale, hairy legs, revealing hard evidence of the single idea in his pea brain. I was dying to slam my fist into his jaw. For Tara. For everything he'd done to Silver. For every girl who had fallen for his manipulative crap. Yet, I held my ground. Tara had an ace up her sleeve. *Let her play it.*

Part of me wanted to see the moonlight radiate off her soft and touchable naked body. On the flipside, I didn't want Raymond to lay eyes on her, to steal the reveal he didn't deserve. She sat on a log, struggling with her boots as if she were unlacing them. Too wasted, Raymond hadn't noticed she wore pull-on boots. He toed the waves washing over the sand, rubbing his arms.

"Go on in. I'm right behind you," Tara yelled over the booming waves.

"You're not gonna chicken out on me, are you?"

"Yeah, right. It *was* my idea." She tossed a boot at him. He caught it and threw it on the pile of clothes. "Isn't it romantic skinny dipping at night under the moon and stars?" Her voice splintered on the last word. She threw her other boot on the pile.

"Hurry, baby. I'm not gonna be any good later if I freeze up." Bellowing, he lunged for the surf, swishing his feet as the water inched up to his dead-white thighs. Pale moonlight sparkled off the surface of the swells rolling onto shore. I wanted that illumination to fall upon Tara only.

"Do it, Tara. Whatever you're up to," I whispered. "Or I'll blast him down a notch myself."

Tara spoke under her breath, but clear as day to me. "Silver, you're here." Excitement fringed her tone. "Why did you leave Lucas? He's missing you pretty bad."

"I'm still here." The air in front of Tara did that sparkly shimmer thing. "Lucas needs to find his way for a while. Can I haunt you instead?" They giggled.

"Anytime. I could use a best friend."

"Even if I'm not really here?"

"Especially."

Raymond whooped as the cold hit him.

"Be careful of Raymond. He's not what he seems."

"I know. Thanks for the warning." Tara cupped the air in front of her and waved discreetly. "Watch what happens. He's going to rue the day he messed with you." Tara rose off the log. "Hey, Raymond. Check me out."

Hand cupping his shrunken package, he jerked around so fast I thought his torso split off from his legs. A flash lit up the tableau, followed by two more. Tara lunged for the pile of clothes. She bundled them in her arms and bolted toward the cliff. Toward me.

"Tara!" Raymond screamed, knee deep in water, waves sloshing up to his thighs. "What're you doing?" Sputtering, he sprinted toward her. "Get back here."

I stepped out of the shadows into her path, grabbing for her. "Hold up."

"Lucas?" She stumbled forward. "Go, before he sees you." I caught her in my arms, the bundle of clothes between us.

"Too late." Raymond wheezed, barreling us to the ground. I rolled to my side to protect Tara from hitting the ground or Raymond from smashing her into roadkill. He hit the sand hard, barely missing my legs. The armload of clothes softened our fall. Thank God. I couldn't take another body slam.

"'Xander, you pussy. She dumped you. For me!" Raymond kicked sand at me. "She's done with your sick bullshit, you stupid killer. You'll pay for this, for offing my cousin." He snatched his pants off the beach, snapped the sand off them. We both scrambled to our feet, warily taking in each other. He held his pants over his crotch, spitting firecracker curses, duds in his case.

Tara pushed upright, brushed sand off her face, moving closer to me.

Raymond spun on her. "What the hell's wrong with you? You planned to leave me out here, didn't you?" Anger pulled his body taut. "You conned me, you dumb cow."

I sprang between them before he did something really idiotic. "Back off."

"Or what? Wussy gonna spit on me."

Speaking of spit, I wiped my hoodie sleeve over the drops on my chin. "Apologize to her."

"She can make it up to me by giving me a nice long goodnight kiss. If you know what I mean. Maybe then I'll forget this ever happened."

Blood boiled in my veins. My gaze settled on Tara's pale, appalled face. She grounded my sanity, stopped me from pummeling him into the sand. He so wasn't worth expending energy on or trying to put things right between us. I hadn't recognized who he was until he showed his true colors after the accident. Until my life flipped topsy-turvy and reality booted me into adulthood. Another broken cog in the wheel of my childhood left behind. With the secret he may be hiding . . . I didn't know what to do. I wasn't ready to show my hand until I had solid proof he was at the gang initiation on May 12.

Fisting his left hand at his side, Raymond puffed steam, a hornless bull eyeing its prey. Tara backed closer to me, her boots and jacket clutched to her chest like scales of armor.

"What's it gonna be, pansy freak?"

"Leave him out of this." Tara stepped between us. "I was teasing you, seeing if you'd give chase." The lies stuttered off her tongue. "But if you're going to be crude, I'm leaving."

"Not with him, you're not." Raymond reached for her.

I hacked away his arm, preventing him from touching her. "I'll take her home."

"Piss off, 'Xander. You're nothing but a freak show." Hopping in the sand, Raymond tugged on his pants. "She wrote you off already."

He was so busy jamming on his clothes that he didn't notice Tara's gagging expression. The final sign I needed. "Can we talk?" My fingertips touched her wrist.

"Talk all you want." Raymond huffed out a breath. "Then we're leaving. Together. Let the has-been go play with the asshole-rodeo."

Tara took my hand in hers. I squeezed her fingers, never wanting to let go.

"Better a has-been than a loser jock," she said in a low, ominous voice.

Raymond jerked up as if I'd shoved a steel rod up his ass. "What'd you say?"

"You heard me." Tara molded herself to my side. "I got what I wanted tonight."

"I knew it," Raymond roared, planting his feet in the sand. "You let your girlfriend do your dirty work?"

"Don't be a tool. Tara has a mind all her own."

"I'll ruin you." He leaned forward, his words forcing his threat upon us.

"Nah. I think not. In fact, I want a public retraction tomorrow of all the BS you flung about me and Silver."

Rustling noises drifted to us, followed by Denny's voice. "Tara, everything okay?" The Nomads circled us, the crash of waves upon the shore shadowing any sounds our small party made.

"You can eat shit and die before I give a retraction. I'll unload more about what incestuous circus tools you and Silver were."

"Lucas?" Tara hugged my arm. "You don't need to do this."

Breathing deep several times, my heartbeat evened out. A calm I hadn't experienced in days enveloped me. Tara's touch grounded me more than I had a right to expect. "Remember training camp last year? How 'bout the party earlier this spring?"

"What about them?" Wariness slunk into Raymond's tone.

"I have the pictures."

"Pahleez. Pictures of what?"

I tapped my head. "You. Steroids. Other things."

Raymond howled uproariously. "Good one." He rubbed his index finger behind his ear, gripped his neck. Proof of his nervousness.

"Pictures don't lie."

"Prove it. Fork 'em over."

"Nah. They'd make a good premiere on YouTube."

An evil, gleeful snigger overflowed Raymond's pie hole. "Lying sack of garbage. I took Silver's phone and erased them."

His words dropped anchor in my stomach, killing the buzzing wasps plaguing me. "You *what?*" I managed to croak out, my knees weakening. "*You* stole Silver's phone?"

He waved his arm in the air, his thin lips spread in an arrogant grin. "I swiped her phone, erased the photos, and binned it. So you ain't got nothing now, do you?"

I sprang for him, bulldozing him to the sand. My fist connected with his nose before Kev and Chris pulled me off, bristling for another go at him. He lurched up on rubbery legs.

"You stupid idiot." I chest-bumped him. "It's your fault we were on County Coast Road. Your fault we had to go to the mall and buy her a new phone. It's your fault Silver's dead." *As much as it is mine.* The unstoppable words rushed out, like an underworld beast ripping out a piece of my soul to join the other scattered pieces on Satan's puzzle board. "You killed Silver." I struggled against the octopus of arms holding me from drilling Raymond into middle earth. Clouds skated over the moon, obscuring it entirely, darkening our tiny dot on the world. Blotting my fury.

Raymond suddenly sank to the sand, blubbering incoherently. "It wasn't me. I swear I didn't do anything."

"Didn't do what?" My voice had calmed, though bitterness held it hostage.

He lifted his head, but it was too dark to make out his features. "I didn't kill her." Then louder, "You did. Just like you killed my cousin." His chin dipped to his chest. "Back off me. We're even."

In that moment, he knew what I suspected. He *had* been at the gang initiation. He watched the street racers barrel into Silver and me as he scattered from the scene. He'd kept it bottled up inside him. With Dale's death, his guilt had been erased. Screw that. I planned to nail his ass to the sand.

The clouds skittered off. The rays of the moon tumbled over us. A new sense of fulfillment streamed into me. I sound like a lame poet. Death did that to a person.

"Let me go. I won't hurt him." The Nomads released their hold on me, sandwiching me between them. I stepped aside, grabbed Raymond's short damp hair, yanking his head back. His eyes squeezed shut. "Look at me, loser."

"No. No. No." He tried to thrust out of my hold, but my clasp allowed no movement.

Tara crouched down to Raymond's level. "Do what he says and we'll leave you alone."

Eyes opened and a tear rolled down his cheek in a slow crawl toward his jaw. "I swear I didn't know. Luc, you gotta believe me. I didn't know." How easily his tune changed when the biggest secret of his life was about to spill.

"I'm not your worst nightmare." I shivered, remembering. "Karma's like a boomerang, it always bites you in the ass." I shoved him back, pressed my foot on his chest. "Got that, bitch?"

Chapter 28

We left Raymond slumped on his knees. I'd like to say karma paid him a visit. Unfortunately, for him, it had gone way beyond simple vengeance. Death did strange things to a person. Although my family and true friends had tried to console me in their own ways, I was alone with my remorse. I recognized it. Raymond needed to deal with his guilt his way.

"I'm okay." I wrenched out of Kev and Chris's arms. "I'm not going after him."

Tara's fingers feathered down my back. I rounded on her. "Do you want him?"

Without a second's hesitation, her arms twined my neck. Wrapping my good arm around her waist, I eased her into my side.

"Don't be a dolt." She kissed my cheek. "I tried to tell you my plans, but you refused to see me. You avoided my calls. Then I got your text." There was a catch in her voice.

"What were you doing out here?" Denny whacked her rear. "Skinny dipping? Have you lost your mind?"

"False rumors. You know how they snowball and explode. The risk was worth it. I wasn't letting another user play that game on someone else." She buried her face in my shoulder, and I wanted more than anything to kiss her senseless.

"But if he was at the accident site, what do you think he would have done to you if you blabbed?" Denny said under his breath.

"I was concentrating only on the rumors he's spreading about Lucas and Silver." She smacked Denny's arm. "I'm not stupid."

"Keep my suspicions on the DL." I stepped between them. "You guys take off. I'll bring Tara home."

The moment we got inside my car, I cuddled Tara into my side, planted my lips on hers. I absorbed her essence, and knew for real that my life was worth living. Hope sprouted in the shadows of my hollowness. The sun would shine on another day. *If the fog ever lifted.*

I rested my forehead against hers. "Next time let's talk before you do . . ." My voice hitched. Tongue-tied, I twined silky curls around my fingers until I got my act together. "I already had him. Silver downloaded the pictures onto her laptop. They're bad enough to expel him and kill his two scholarships."

"He's such a blabbermouth. I knew I'd easily coerce him to spin crap about you." She pressed a kiss under my chin, her velvety lips cool. "I wanted to flip him down a notch. You know I've been the scapegoat of vicious rumors." Her fingers dug into my arms, and I wrapped her into my warmth. "You have no idea how devastating they can be if left unrefuted."

"What did you hope to gain? Pictures of him naked?"

"No." She winced, smiled crookedly. "The skinny-dipping was payback. I e-mailed you a recording after dinner. The entire time, he gloated about how he'd keep circulating snarky stuff about you, making it sound like you always manipulated Silver, how she hooked up with him to get away from you. I flat out asked him if what he said was true. He skirted around it, made excuses. I knew he was lying." She tightened her arms around me. "Silver already told me the truth."

I cranked the heater, linked my fingers in hers. "You didn't have to jeopardize yourself that way, you know. I would've exposed his lies." I wanted to drown in her soothing lavender-vanilla scent.

"It had to end now." Tara fingered her eyes. "When Vince broke up with me after the accident, he totally believed I'd hooked up with his best friend. But I'd never gone out with anyone else. He was my first and only boyfriend. To cover up his own guilt, he talked smack about me sleeping with both of them. And other things. The rumors tailed me for a long time. I lost friends, holed up in my room, became a loner all over again."

Fire ignited in my chest. I set my finger on her lips. "Is that when you . . . befriended the girl ghost?"

"No. I was younger when I lived in Melanie's house. She was so sweet. The psychic neighbor told me Melanie died from leukemia. She'd been lonely because she was sick all the time and didn't have many playmates who visited her. We played word games and stuff. I like to think I gave her as much as she gave me. I was really sad when we moved. Weird, huh?"

Not knowing what to say, I shook my head. Weird defined me. I didn't plan to mention Silver unless she did. I wanted them to bond or whatever ghosts and sensitives did.

"Lucas," she murmured. I slid my fingers into the hair along her temple. "None of what Raymond says is true."

"I know." The car windows steamed up, and I turned the defroster on high. "The past is the past."

"Bad things follow and you can't always escape. You have to be ready and open for the good when it comes around." She cupped her hands around my face. I kissed her palm and felt her shiver deep into my soul. "Only the good can conquer the bad." Her gentle touch tingled where our skin made contact. "Can you let it go?" Her fingers on my chin prevented me from avoiding her intense gaze. "Are you satisfied now that Dale's dead and the street racers are in prison?" Silence took a spin and provided my answer. "You're still going after Raymond and keeping your vigilante plans," she finally said, not questioned.

Would Silver Ghost proceed with our plan of attack on the local gangs? Guess it depended if our continued efforts made a difference to the community. First, I had to untangle the mystery of Raymond and dump CrimsonX off my back. Those two monkeys riding me topped my to-do list.

Worst of all, I had to survive Silver's death all over again. Sorrow broiled my insides one minute, and then an icy wind doused the fire. I easily forced my mind off Silver. Hope was tantalizingly real in my embrace.

"Lucas?"

Thumbing her cheek, I said, "Silver's gone." I buried my nose in her hair, heaving in her perfume, burying myself in it rather than my grief. "The last time I spoke to her was when I flatlined."

"I'm sorry." Her fingertips scraped across my scalp. "You're stronger now. Dale's gone. I'm here. Your memories will never fade, but you can live with them in their proper place. Do you think with Dale gone, she went into the light, or whatever?"

I curled my fist, fighting my paranoia, not wanting to believe. "She would've warned me, right?"

"Wish I knew."

"As much as I hate that idea, I hope so. For her." I snorted hard, trying not to snot all over Tara's coat, trying to grow a pair. I kissed her, my lips lingering on her soft mouth, breathing her in, savoring. It was everything and I took no more. "I need solid proof of Raymond's involvement." I kissed a trail down her chin, across her silky jawline, soft baby butterfly kisses. "Will you help me? I promise that's all I'll do for now."

"Until your body's in one piece?" she replied shakily.

The silky lobe of her ear earned the attentions of my tongue. She quivered against me, propped her hand on my thigh to hold herself from melting onto me. "I can't make promises. Silver Ghost can make a difference in the long run."

"With a female brain running the show," she teased on a low, sultry voice in my ear before her tongue darted in, before her mouth locked onto my neck.

"Sure. Whatever you say." I groaned, making the mistake of spying Denny a couple of parking spots away. "Your brother's glaring at us."

Tara kissed my chin one last time before scooting to the passenger seat. I blinked rapidly, puffing out little pants until my airflow regulated. Pins and needles raked my entire arm. Even my leg hurt again. Somehow, I managed to get the car on the road, slow as a snail.

"I wish you had known Silver. You two would've hit it off. She's a lot like Alyssa, more outspoken, though. Loves to call everyone names, or at least me. Totally Denny's type. Into computers and war games."

Giggles swept away her surprise. "He'd die if he found out your—I mean, he'd love it if he found out a ghost liked him. But then, he might be scared witless."

"He'd think we're crazy. Talking to my dead sister." We traded an easy laugh. "Does he know you're sensitive to ghosts?"

"No way. Only you."

Honor deepened my internal connection to her. A trust I'd never betray.

"What should we do about Raymond's trash talk?" Tara nodded in the direction of the beach. "Do you really have Silver's pictures? If not, we can use my recording if he refuses to make a retraction."

I dug my cell out and handed it to her. "Take a gander."

Indecipherable audio overrode the empty silence. Video of Raymond at a party, smoking dope, shooting steroids, bragging. The pictures showed more of the same.

"How'd Silver take these?"

"She didn't. She was always leaving her phone in my car. I shot the snaps and video to prove he was a loser."

"Did she dump him?"

"Eventually, after . . . other things."

"What will happen if these leak out?"

"He'll get expelled, lose his scholarship."

"Huh. I didn't think he was good enough for a scholarship if they knocked him off first string. Do you have a scholarship?"

A reminiscent dull ache needled me even though the biting pang in my belly, every time I dwelled on the life lost to me, had lessened. "Stanford, UCLA, and Arizona were courting me with full rides. They retracted their offers after the accident."

"Oh. That stinks." She stuck the phone in the drink holder, her fingers brushing my leg.

"It is what it is."

"What will you do after graduation?" she asked with deceptive calm, as if she dreaded the answer.

I pulled into the driveway, turned the key in the ignition. "I think I may stick around home. Maybe go to UC, Monterey, study criminology or something. I kind of like this crime stuff." Tara expelled a held breath. Her face lit up in the amber glow of the coach lights.

"Good. I'm not done with you yet." Smiling, she leaned into me and kissed me soundly on the mouth, her lips hard and soft, shy and bold.

Another dose of the warm-fuzzies gloved me in the feel of Tara. At that moment, I held no doubts we'd remain a pair when college decision time hit me over the head. Plans beyond that were up for grabs. Silver's death taught me how fragile and fleeting life was. We had little control over so much. Sometimes, we just had to sit back and take life as it arrived. I planned to enjoy the future, including Tara, and never take anything for granted again. Temporary pawns on God's checkerboard, my grandmother used to say.

Unfortunately, justice hungered for Raymond. Bad karma controlled his next move on the board. I just needed to help karma along.

Chapter 29

For the second time *ever*, I wanted to go to school. I had to feel up my forehead to check if I'd contracted a case of nerditis. If I remained on bed rest the remainder of the day, Mom said I could return on Thursday. I owed Alyssa a gargantuan favor for keeping my cover. Otherwise, I'd be stuck in bed until Monday. One day, she'd collect. I hoped I didn't have to say no. Or that it included time alone with Denny . . . in his bedroom.

Like an industrious drone, I propped my pillows against the headboard and scoured the Internet for clues about Raymond, his family, and Dale's gang. Two hours later, I hadn't found anything useful.

Just before lunch break, Tara called. I'd given her a special ringtone. I had it bad. My heart flip-flopped like a love-struck fool. "Hey, babe."

"Log onto the student news video," her words rushed out. "I told Raymond I'd seen the video and pictures, and I played the recording from dinner. Gotta go." Click.

Sea Hag's website filled my screen. Raymond's phony grave face hogged the small video feed. *Dude, clean up the decomposing pizza snack on your chin.* Sound kicked in after a slight delay.

"I'm Raymond Randall, varsity football quarterback." *Liar.* "Last weekend I spread rumors about Lucas and Silver Alexander. The things I said aren't true and I regret saying them. I'm sorry, Lucas. Hope we can be friends again." The screen blackened. The last I heard was, "Tara, I'm sorry for being a dick last night."

Friends, my ass. Blackmail evidence had him running scared. He was worse than dog crap on the bottom of my shoe, yet I couldn't wipe him off and hose him down the drain the way he'd done to me.

Too bad his dumb confession didn't include the fact that he'd nicked Silver's phone. Or that his gang initiation put us in the path of a deadly drag race. I wanted him to eradicate my guilt, vacuum it from every cell of my being and absorb it inside him until he choked on it. Part of me wished we could all kick our guilt to the curb and get on with our lives. The other part kept winning. Yet he needed to take responsibility for his part in Silver's death. Eye for an eye.

Mom let Tara and the gang visit for one measly hour after dinner. To keep the peace, I let Mom have her way. I didn't get a chance to discuss Raymond with Tara alone. My half-baked ideas to flush him out weren't ready for prime time sharing with my buds, either. Silver remained scarce as Bloody Mary's ghost. I missed her. Not even Tara had seen Silver.

On Thursday morning, Denny and Tara picked me up. All too soon, I hobbled toward my locker high-fiving and fist-bumping the hallway chorus of well-wishers. Once again. It sucked. Despite Raymond's retraction, I received my share of snickers and creeped-out looks.

Chris and Kev met me at my locker. I winked at Tara, discretely rubbed her hand before she dashed off with Alyssa. Something about going to the nurse's office for cramp relief. I cringed at the girlie stuff I tended to avoid.

Mikey approached, lifted his fingers in a half-assed wave, looked around for his father, and sauntered past lugging his football gear.

"Your pal Dalton asked about you." Kev mimicked Dalton's sneer, giving us a toothy parody, a bogus goatee stroke. "He asked if you'd returned from your mini vacation."

"Dickhead," Chris tossed in. "What's it to him?"

"Maybe Dalton's hot for Lucas." Kev puckered his lips and made smooching sounds. He looked like he'd doubled up on lip injections.

I dropped my arm over his shoulders. "But I love *you.* Line forms behind me."

"Behind, the way you love it best." Chris's eyes darted right to left, and he rubbed his fingers. *WTF?* We still needed to hash it out about the party and his alleged alibi. That line formed behind crucifying Raymond, though.

"I bet his ex-mother-in-law called him son, but never finished the sentence." Kev brayed like a dying donkey.

We all laughed, needing it to alleviate the tension. Until Juno Chavez ambled past.

Shocked, my eyes bugged out. His mug looked like he'd kissed a meat grinder. Smiling, he sported a black and green Juggernauts jacket. "Whoa. Scoop me." I lowered my voice.

Chris leaned forward, his gaze finally landing on my cast, and said, "Juggernauts never showed to the blood-match. Police busted three CrimsonX members for beating Juno to a pulp. They think he narked."

The bell rang. The games began.

• • •

"Better hurry or you'll head up his tardy list," I teased Tara as she rushed around the corner toward room thirty-two.

"If I'm late, you're late." The inviting look in her eyes drew me closer.

"Me late?" I mocked, wrapping my one good arm around her waist, easing her backpack off her shoulder. "I need my afternoon *medicine.*"

Shooting a glance at Dalton's open doorway, she pressed herself against me. Our lips met tentative at first, then hers parted. Blood rushed southward. She tasted of wintergreen and sunshine. Dalton's scathing contempt intruded upon our moment, and our short burst of sun clouded over. The second bell pierced the halls.

Tara jerked back as if I were a vampire heading for a snack. She punched my arm, giving me a bitchy glower, careful not to bump my sling. "We're in for it now," she whispered. "Leave me alone, loser," she said louder for Dalton's benefit.

"What's one more tardy when you have a boatload?"

"I'm not joining your ranks," she flung over her shoulder as I followed her into the cave of murmurs.

Once my butt hit the seat, Dalton attacked. "Well, Mr. Alexander, one more mark to your growing list. Miss Harrison, since you were delayed through no fault of your own," Dalton landed a meaningful smirk on me, "we'll keep your slate clean."

"Thanks, Mr. Dalton." She turned, gave me a triumphant look of vindication. "The jerk deserves it."

A wave of speculation erupted around the room. Game on.

Dalton began writing our next twenty vocabulary words on the whiteboard. Listening to the quiet screech of dry erase pens, I had a tricky time breathing. Anxiety and I were intimately acquainted, and it struck at odd moments lately. Felt like I was having a heart attack. In stealth mode, I left my front-row seat to open a window, to ease the stuffiness and lighten the elephant lounging on my chest.

The window creaked as I pushed it open. I'd barely taken one deep breath of fresh salty air when Dalton spun around.

"Mr. Alexander, what are you doing?"

"Isn't it kinda obvious, *Mister* Dalton," answered Kev, my unappointed town crier.

"Mr. Alexander, I'm waiting for an answer."

Deprived of air, my mind let my mouth pass "go." "Trying to clear out the reek of ex-girlfriends." Irritation edged my tart answer. No other teacher cared one wit if a student wanted a window open unless the weather sucked.

"Since when do you leave your seat whenever you please?"

"Where's it written we have to ask permission to open a window?" *Oops, there goes the glower, the tick in his jaw. Run for your lives, he's going to blow.*

"This is my classroom. I make the rules."

"Hey," I addressed the quiet-as-a-mute-mouse classroom. "Did *Mister* Dalton ever say we had to ask to open a window?"

An indecisive hum spread among the students afraid to commit to an answer for fear of retaliation. Alyssa and Tara dipped their heads, avoiding me entirely. The consensus was a "no" from the subliminal head wagging.

"That's quite enough." Dalton slammed his clipboard on the desk, the sound cracking like thunder. Thing must be made of dragon scales. "From now on before anyone leaves his or her seat, for *any* reason, permission must be asked and granted. Is that clear?"

The inevitable buzz of disbelief and a heavy dose of disgust swamped the room. Dalton's list of commandments grew longer every day. Thanks to me, I supposed.

"As for you, Mr. Alexander," continued the spiteful warden, "gather your things while I write out a referral."

Sweet. Another ticket to party land. I marched through the door, smack dab into Denny careening down the deserted hallway toward the restroom next door. I waved the referral slip, told him what happened.

"What'd you ever do to him?"

I bit my tongue. "He's mental. Nothing I haven't done to any other teacher. Petty crap."

"Maybe you oughta lay off for a while."

"Me, Lucas Alexander, lay off? Kid, you've got a lot to learn." I slugged Denny's arm.

"I just thought—"

"Try not to think. It's too painful to watch. This is my style. Laying off isn't. Ask any teacher in this stinkhole who their favorite class clown is . . . was." I cracked a deflated grin. "Remain on high alert," I added as he saluted me.

I didn't like the solitary walk to the dean's office. CrimsonX never left my consciousness, and I was sure they still had me on their radar. Wariness bolstered my armor, kept my ears alert, and my toes bouncing. *Okay, you know what I mean.* Two near-death experiences booted out most of my bounce.

After the dean reamed me a new one, I practically bolted out the door, straight into Mikey. Perfect timing today, bumping into my friends. At least I knew they were safe.

"My dad busted you?" He shrank back into the lockers lining the wall. "Sorry, man."

"What's his prob?" I grabbed Mikey's arm and steered him to the secluded side of the teacher's parking lot. We stood between a row of cypress trees and the outer wall to the administration building. "If he's keeping you from joining my gang—"

"No way." Mikey's face drooped. I swear tears sprang to his eyes. "Just give it some time, then I can openly do what I want. He's just riding me to play football and stop playing with cars and pranksters. He sees all the trouble you're getting into. Scares him."

"Scares me, too." I winked half-heartedly. Dalton and the kid had a point.

"Are we cool?" Brow pinched, he held his breath.

"Sure." I play-punched his shoulder. "Keep feeding me stuff and it's all good." I heard footsteps, looked behind Mikey. "Aw, cripes."

Raymond headed toward Dalton's late-model Camry. He pulled out a knife as he neared the silver coupe.

Chapter 30

Mikey and I ducked behind the cypress hedge. I held my index finger over my mouth to keep Mikey quiet. Raymond just made my day. I pulled my smartphone out of my coat pocket and engaged the video recorder.

Raymond scanned the deserted parking lot before he squatted on the right side of the car facing us. He stabbed the blade in, first the front tire, then the rear tire, grunting with each jab. Then he pulled out a small spray can of paint. Before he began spraying, voices carried over to us from the front of the administration building. Raymond bolted, shoving the can and knife into his pockets. He crouched low between rows of cars, and I lost sight of him. Turning the video camera off, I looked at Mikey. Grinning, we shrugged in unison.

"What was that all about?" I asked. "What'd your dad ever do to him?"

"Beats me."

"Let's roll before we get busted." Slumping low behind the trees, we cleared the parking lot just as the last period bell rang. We split up into the noisy crowds teaming the hallway. I texted Denny to pick me up at five, then returned to the hedges to wait for Dalton. Ideas to bust Raymond brewed.

Word on campus was that Dalton graded papers until four-thirty. I pulled my reading assignment, *Of Mice and Men*, out of my backpack. Halfway through the required book, I'd gotten engrossed in the somber story, even looked forward to reading it. Silver would be proud that I lugged around her old tattered dictionary. One good thing about my imposed exile was it put me ahead of my reading assignments. Another lifetime first.

Teachers left, the parking lot emptied. At four-forty, Dalton emerged from the administration building. I thrust the book in my backpack and managed a clumsy climb to my feet. Broken bodies blew.

Once the coast cleared, I ambled toward Dalton's car in a sea of empty parking spaces. Head bowed, he dumped his battered leather briefcase in the trunk. All of a sudden, he unloaded, "What the hell?" I followed his gaze to his right rear tire, flatter than a smashed stingray.

"My bad luck must be rubbing off on you."

His head jerked up, the perpetual scowl marring his spray-tanned face. "What do *you* want?"

I skirted the rear of the car, blatantly checked out the flat front tire. "Ouch." The arrogance that followed me to the parking lot didn't have a chance. Glee exploded all over it. "Drive through Home Depot?"

"Go home and plan your next prank." He crouched beside the rear tire.

I leaned on the rear bumper. "That's no way to talk to a student asking for after school help."

"The only help I'll give you is a one-way ticket to juvenile hall."

I masked my disbelief. "I think it's time we put our gripes on the hood."

"Why would I waste time griping about you?" He passed his fingers over the flattened tire tread. "You're nothing to me. Or my kid."

A snicker escaped before I reined it in. "Come on, man. What's your prob?"

"I don't cater to hotshot jocks, pranksters, or spoiled kids with hotrods." He probed the grooves in the deflated rubber. "Three strikes, you're out."

"Hotshot jock? Last I heard thumb wrestling doesn't qualify as a sport. Case you haven't noticed I'm not exactly jock material. Now, Raymond Randall, he's the hotshot quarterback. Maybe Mikey should hang with him. He doesn't cause any trouble."

"You got that right. If that boy *applies* himself, he'll go far. He'd make a better role model than you." Rising to full height, he shot me a dick-deflating glare. "Know anything about my tires?"

"You blaming me?" I asked. His lips fluttered at the corners, but he didn't respond. Slouching against the car, I eased the pressure off my side, careful not to lean my backpack against the paint. Last thing I needed was accusations of scratches slung my way. My pranks never included deliberate damage. I plead the fifth on collateral damage.

"No. But I think you got my point." Crossing his arms over his chest proved his real point.

"Like I said, *Mister* Dalton," my voice grew light and amiable, "I haven't a clue what happened to your tires. Sorry I can't help you change them." I pointed at my sling, then hauled up my backpack for takeoff. "Gotta jet." In perfect sync, Denny's horn honked in the student dropoff adjacent to the teacher's lot.

I clambered into the Tahoe, wondering why Raymond slashed Dalton's tires. What flavor of crazy was he all about?

"Get your library time in?" he asked, bouncing the SUV over the speed bumps.

"Then some."

"So what's next on Silver Ghost's agenda?"

"Raymond. I plan to bury him." After making Denny swear on his life he'd tell no one, I gave him the scoop on my suspicions about Raymond and showed him the video.

Denny whistled. "Jeez. I bet Rayman's framing you."

"You think?" I traced over the red double hearts Tara had drawn on my cast. "Don't spill to Chris or Kev."

Denny's right brow arched. "Why not?"

"I'm getting a weird vibe off Chris. Since he and Kev are tight, I'd rather not stick Kev in a weird way having to lie."

"Thanks for dumping me in that position."

Groaning, I dragged my hand through my hair. "Can I trust you or not?"

Denny flicked his finger at my head since he couldn't whack the left side of my body for all my bruises. "Kidding. Don't bunch your shorts in a wad."

Hello, Raymond Randall. Welcome to Karma.

Chapter 31

Once upon a time, I didn't believe one was capable of falling for another person so completely. Then I met Tara, and I knew how fast and hard one fell. Like falling in an abyss of endless thrills. She was the sun that orbited me, lighting the dark corners of grief and rage. Spouting poetry again. I had it so bad.

Soon as I got home from school, I called and invited her over after dinner. After all, she wanted to help me choose my topic for my senior project out of ten focus areas handed out today. Maybe I'd choose the physical and psychological ways to destroy a family. Or how to go from Mr. Popular to Mr. Nobody in a hot Camaro moment. Or how gang violence was destroying the youth of America. Or how karma was a tool. Way too many choices. Silver would've nailed one in a heartbeat.

I missed studying with my sister. We used to make a great team. She was detailed, smart, precise. My devil's advocate sense dug for the angles and loopholes. I was the tail to her head. Tara patched the hole, except she searched for angles and loopholes the way I did. Yet, she couldn't ace a test if you wrote the answers on her test paper. She always sought patterns, trick questions, overanalyzed, doubted. At least that's what she'd told me when I saw the B-minus she'd gotten on her history quiz. We'd studied for it and we knew the answers. Even I got an A. Major shocker. She wanted me to help her focus and look a problem on its face. For a change, it gave me a sense of achievement to help someone with homework. Although much better reasons for our study sessions fronted the list, definitely allowing me to forget about studying with Silver.

The parentals worked late that night, so dinner was a shot-gunned affair. I ate Serena's disgusting tofu meatloaf in silence, stifling the occasional retching sounds. Excited beyond comprehension, Alyssa kept up the conversation about her and Tara's plans to raid the mall in Monterey on Saturday. Her first trip with a gift card Mom gave her for school clothes. The idea of them exposed to potential gang retaliation curdled the two bites of meatloaf I managed to choke down. I slammed the rest of my soda to rinse the taint from my mouth, dumped my dish in the sink. Alyssa and Auntie rushed through dinner and cleanup, then left for their evening power walk.

In the downstairs bathroom, I re-spiked my hair and swished mouthwash. When the doorbell rang, blood drilled my southern hemisphere. I tugged Tara hard against me, her resistance nonexistent. Her closeness was like a euphoric drug. I couldn't get enough.

"Ooaf." Her breath expelled in a huff of mint.

My lips trailed up her jaw. "Hey, I told Denny about Raymond and the accident." The smoothness of her skin felt like silk against my lips. I sucked on her ear lobe, planted a kiss on her neck.

"I know." Trembling, she danced her fingers over my chest. "We talked."

"What'd he say?"

"That you two are *taking him down*." Warm and electrifying, her fingers dipped into the top of my tee beneath my sling strap. "And to steer clear of you for a while."

Surprise drew my spine straight. Her teasing smile undid me. Again. "Yet, you came." I drank in her spicy, floral scent, nuzzled her neck. Sliding her book bag strap off her shoulder, I let the bag thump to the slate tiles. I stripped off her jacket, hung it on the coat tree.

"Um, Lucas. Is anyone home?"

"No." I took her hand, snagged her bag, and we streaked up the stairs. Fire swelled inside me, razing the bad thoughts, searing the edges of the massive crater of emptiness. Thoughts of Tara tumbled over each other.

The instant I locked the door, she surrounded me, wrapping her arms around my neck, the enticing scent of her skin overpowering the lingering slime of Tofu-ck Meatloaf, her heat thawing the ice layering my being. I fell into her, burying my senses in her silky hair. My one good arm curled around her waist, my hand settling in the small of her back. She wiggled her hips, lifting her midriff top to allow my palm to explore the downy skin of her back.

"Tara?"

She reached forward on her toes, pressed her mouth to mine. Our kiss grew hot, minty fresh, tangoing tongues, velvety lips giving as much as I took and returned twofold. Heart pounding, my hand traveled northward, slid up her tee, caressing her side.

Moaning deep in her throat, she inched away. Her fingers clawed at me, trying to ruck up my shirt. With the sling, it became next to impossible unless she ripped the shirt off. I was game, but she burst into giggles. We tumbled to the bed, her halfway on top of me, avoiding my gut wound. Light as a feather, she brushed her fingertips over the scar on my lip, setting it tingling.

We lay together, arms and legs entwined for the longest time, soaking in each other, our gazes never breaking contact. Our fingers grazed over bare skin, electrifying. Her flesh was softer than anything I'd ever felt, her touch on my facial scars mesmerizing. I left trails of gooseflesh over every inch of her back, and she left paths of fire where her tiny fingertips brushed my neck and arms.

I wanted her under me, around me, filling my cells with all of her. Wanted to glove her warmth within mine forever.

"Lucas," she whispered, planting tiny kisses from my jaw to my ear. "I feel such a connection to you. I mean, I want it to be you, but—"

I groaned, my hand settling into the precious hollow of her spine. She trembled down my length. "It's not just that ghostly sensitivity, is it? 'Cause it's more to me. It's everything. Is it the same with you?" My raspy voice sounded foreign.

She laughed a deep, sultry sound that undid me. "I've wanted you since the first day we laid eyes on each other. That doesn't happen to me." Her soft fingers wrapped around my neck. "Am I crazy, or do you feel—"

My mouth landed hard on hers, and I captured her tiny cry of pleasure, treasuring her senses. After eons of drugging kisses, I broke away. "You're not crazy. Freaky as this sounds, you're my touchstone," the frog in my throat croaked. We shared a gentle kiss, lips parted and locked together. My thumb wiped the tear leaking from her right eye. "I was dead until I met you, you know?"

"I never thought I'd meet another who understood the ghost thing. Someone who wouldn't freak out, or walk away." She kissed my nose. "You get me."

"If it wasn't for Silver—"

Tara stuck her index finger over my mouth. "Don't say it."

I couldn't say it let alone think it. Unable to quit touching her, I smoothed the goose bumps rising on her back.

Most people took life for granted. I had, even post-accident. In that moment, I recognized the true meaning of life. Tasted it on my tongue, felt it in the peachy flesh beneath my fingers, smelled it on the vanilla and lavender wafting into my senses, heard it in the little puffy breaths Tara took beneath me. Life was love. Love was Tara.

The front door banged shut, soon followed by Alyssa's knock on my door.

We were flushed, ecstatic, excited. We both let out muted laughs and reluctantly rose from the bed. Our grins faded in the wake of our fake anger, in the plan we'd concocted earlier.

"You need to leave." I forced winter's fury into my elevated voice. "If you don't believe me, then I'm done with you."

Tara slammed a plastic glass at the wall across the room. "Fine!" Flat Mt. Dew sprayed the carpet. "I should've never hooked up with you. You're such a jerk. Stay away from me."

The beautiful storm of Tara sailed past a trout-mouthed Alyssa frozen in the doorway.

Chapter 32

When I awoke the next morning, I realized that thoughts of Tara had chased my nightmares away. I felt more invigorated and alive than BA. We hadn't planned for yesterday to happen. Just laying eyes on her when she tripped through the door set off a craving I'd never known. Like the stars and planets had aligned or some corny stuff. Never had I experienced an all-encompassing desire for another girl. Every second of the day I wanted to see her, hear her laugh. Too trippy. Could it mean love? After everything that happened this year, I had a hard time believing I deserved her. It scared me to think how I'd feel after we went all the way.

For the first time, I was glad Silver hadn't haunted me. Imagine her ragging on my technique.

Five minutes before first period, Tara and I passed in the main corridor at Sea Hag, forcing phony glowers, sharing a secret smile. News spread like the zombie plague that we'd broken up. The external world witnessed our mutual antagonism, but not the inside of my soul. Nor did they read the semi-tame sext messages we traded at the opposite ends of the cafeteria.

Denny refused to buddy-up with me. Alyssa was pissed at me for screwing up the best thing to ever happen to me, in her clichéd words, and she rode with Denny and Tara to school. They refused me admittance into our clique. Mikey kept his usual distance to avoid Dalton's black looks. Left to Chris and Kev—playing Switzerland in the war—old times galore.

To the masses, Tara admitted to having mixed feelings about my varied psychological, physical, and legal issues. Rumors mushroomed that she wanted time alone to sort through those feelings, that I pressured her to stay, and she took the highway instead.

We hoped our ruse kept Raymond and his Mt. Olympus–size ego away. A shit storm was coming. *Yeah, I needed another storm of turds like I needed another broken bone.* Anyone close to me was in jeopardy of collateral damage. I wouldn't dump Tara in the crosshairs of vengeance. Denny and I'd have to watch Alyssa's back, too. Finally, I wanted both girls safe from potential gang threats. To authenticate our scheme, we kept our plan totally secret. Not even Denny knew about our phony breakup. Our perfect illusion of delusion. What straight guy in his right mind would let Tara—the sun who eclipsed my frozen moon—go? Let everyone think I was nuts. Shouldn't strain too many brains.

Outside first-period chem lab, Principal Wilkerson's voice spiked, followed by Dalton's angry sarcasm. Acid churned in my Swiss cheese stomach. Honest, I hadn't done a thing that morning except breathe. Breathing wasn't against Dalton's lamo laws.

When the door whooshed open, all attention swiveled from beakers of Borax, guar gum, and water to ogle the situation. Wilkerson motioned me over and said a few quiet words to Mr. DeAnza. When I passed the chem teacher, he patted me on the shoulder, gave me a tight-lipped smile. *Ah, Jeez.* Who said I did what? Better yet, who did what and blamed me? I'd never had DeAnza as a teacher, but he'd watched the volcano explode mud all over chem lab last year. Who knew lighting a homemade time-lapse super-volcano made it explode rather than drip lava down the sides. I guess using M-80s hadn't helped. No one got caught. They never suspected me, Chris, or Kev, since we didn't take chemistry last year. Yet, word on the street . . . me in a bulletproof nutshell.

"What's going on?" I closed the lab door behind me, studied Wilkerson in the breezeway between buildings.

"You know very well what's *going on,*" Dalton exploded.

"Hold on, Hank." Wilkerson stepped between us. "Let's handle this diplomatically."

Dalton groused. I almost heard the "pranksters don't deserve diplomacy" spinning in his weenie brain.

"Come along, Lucas." Wilkerson placed his hand between my shoulder blades.

In festering silence, we strode toward the teachers parking lot. As we left the haven of the school walls, the day's chill draped me in a thorny blanket. I hugged my slinged arm closer, wishing I'd grabbed my hoodie. Charcoal-gray clouds gathered in the sky, obscuring the late morning sun. Black clouds of hatred coagulated in Dalton's eyes, matching the spray-painted "bite me asshole" written across the driver's side of his silver car.

Raymond had struck again. I swung on Dalton, fisting my hand at my side. "You're not blaming this on me."

"Settle down, Lucas." Wilkerson held up his hand, forestalling Dalton from spewing out lies. "We'll get to the bottom of the matter." The message in the look he traded with Dalton told me they'd already reached the scummy bottom.

Dalton hadn't called service on his two flat tires. I bet he'd blame me for the tires, too.

Wilkerson continued, "What time did you arrive at the teachers parking lot yesterday?"

The lawn and bushes where I'd held my vigil didn't constitute "teachers parking lot," so I said, "Four-fortyish. 'Bout the time Dalton tossed his briefcase in the trunk."

The fingers of Dalton's right hand trembled slightly, and he ran the tip of his index finger beneath his watchband. *Hmmm, his elusive tell?*

"Go on. What happened next?"

"I wanted to ask him about our senior projects, to run a topic by him." Wilkerson sent Dalton a glare primed to melt his devil's scales.

Thank Karma for video. I fingered my smartphone in my front pocket. Raymond was so dead. Dead on my terms.

Right on cue, I spied Mom's Lexus drive into the parking lot. Un. Believable. I swung on Wilkerson. "You called my mother?"

"I had no choice. Destruction of property is a serious infraction."

"You can't prove I did *anything*." I crossed my other arm over my sling, holding myself from using my cast to bean Dalton. "I have an alibi for last night. I'm not the person you knew last year, Mr. Wilkerson. You know it." Despite the anger threatening to snap my rigid spine, I experienced an indefinable feeling of rightness. "I'm different."

"Mrs. Alexander." The principal held his hand out to Mom. She clasped it, her eyes flicking from the car to me.

"Principal Wilkerson. Hank . . . er . . . Mr. Dalton." Curt and preoccupied, she glanced at her smartphone. "What's this about?"

Wilkerson's recap of the court-of-no-law railroading brought her up to speed. I sidled to her side like a good little boy. *Yo, Mom, you got my back?* With everything that'd happened to me this year, I wanted her on my side for a change, without being forced to prove my worth to her like a lowlife crook to a jury of his peers' mothers.

"Did you do this, Lucas?" She flicked her hand toward the car. I shook my head emphatically. Tightlipped, Mom scrutinized the car again. "I'm sorry this happened, but it's not Lucas's style. Denny Harrison brought him straight home after the parking lot conversation and he never left the house. Search elsewhere for answers, but quit accusing my son of things he didn't do. That includes the theft at the dance, which I might add, you haven't investigated further."

Go Mom! Although I took umbrage—love the word now—at the "not his style" bit, I spun on my heels, wanting to dance a jig. The second I faced the car, the sprayed message on the side caught my eye. A small CrimsonX logo in black paint dotted the "i" on "bite me." The logo was missing the red drops. Totally bogus. CrimsonX never slacked on their tagging. Idiot Raymond.

I kept turning on my heel, not wanting to draw attention to the phony evidence. "Thanks, Mom," I whispered.

Wilkerson cow-towed to Mom a few more minutes and assured her he'd investigate the tagging further and that the theft investigation was ongoing. He dragged a fire-spewing Dalton by his pointy, forked tail toward the offices.

"Do you know who did it?" Mom brushed a lock of hair off my eyelashes. I let her caress my face. She deserved it. I actually longed for it.

My jaw dropped. "You believe I didn't do it?"

"Of course." Exasperation puckered her lips into a slight smile. I gave a triumphant fist pump. The alarm on her smartphone beeped. "Shoot. I'm late for a meeting. I'll be home early. I'm making Dad's favorite smoked salmon. We'll enjoy a nice family evening. I promise we'll talk more about this."

"Sure." I kissed her cheek. I swear the clouds parted, the sun exploded, songs of heavenly love descended in the smile she bestowed on me. Score! Major points. Good for another prank or two, another bruise or maybe a broken bone.

Unfortunately, our moment of trust and bliss lasted for that measly moment.

"Mrs. Alexander." Wilkerson jogged over to us, his potbelly jiggling over his belt.

Mom peeked at her watch, pulled her cell out. My feet bounced on the tarmac, dodging the daggers Wilkerson's eyes flung at me.

"Another urgent matter has arisen." This time the hand he positioned between my shoulder blades was iron firm, the pressure cutting my spine in two.

Jeez, Louise. What now?

Wilkerson, without the devil's sidekick, led us to the gym. Students and teachers crowded around the main doors. The stench of rotting seafood poured into the hallway.

Someone had pulled a legacy Lucas Alexander. *Karma's such a stinky player today.*

Chapter 33

At least I had the smarts to do my prank outside to avoid death by rot. Last year, I stuffed frozen shrimp inside the iron hand railings of the outside bowl bleachers. Took two weeks in January for the smell to build and the campus maintenance crew to find the stinky buggers. Bleach and a hose cleaned the rails spectacularly. I even volunteered for cleanup duty. Earned extra credit to boot. The funniest part was the growing smell and the inability of anyone to find the source. So how'd I get busted? I never did. Wilkerson suspected me and made a notation in my file. No proof meant no sentence. I never bragged on the Pranx forum. Yet, I made comments about the shrimp idea when someone posted a joke about a divorcing wife sticking shrimp in the hems of the curtains in the house she lost to her cheating husband and his newest hookup.

A copycat perpetrator had played the prank on the indoor gym bleachers. The stench overwhelmed, my eyes smarted.

"Did you do it here, too, Lucas?" Wilkerson asked. Janitors were already disassembling the bleachers, paper masks covering the bottom half of their faces.

"Do what?" I inhaled through my mouth, my face a blank slate.

Mom cupped a hand over her nose. "Mr. Wilkerson! Does everything bad happening around here involve my son?"

"Mrs. Alexander, I know your family has been going through a rough time, but you know as well as I do Lucas's propensity for pranks."

I breathed in fishy air. "Until yesterday, I haven't been at school in a week."

"It takes a while for frozen shrimp to rot in cool weather." Wilkerson argued with me like a teenager. I think his exasperation had reached the top of the volcano. Or an apoplectic fit seized his molten-red face.

"Not indoors in September," I replied.

Sighing, Mom asked for the sake of asking. "Did you do it, Lucas?"

"I haven't set foot in the gym since the dance." True that. We know how that fiasco turned out.

"Then we're done here." Mom steered me to the door.

"Hold on." Wilkerson put his hand between my shoulder blades. Man, I hated him touching me now. "We have video footage."

Video footage of what? Girls tripping over each other playing volleyball. The basketball team fumbling another game? Coach Burton feeling up Nurse Nadia behind the bleachers? Or maybe, just maybe, footage of the real culprit responsible for replicating my prank.

We passed Dalton lording it over a growing crowd of flies on the way to Wilkerson's office where school security had taken root. Mom and I were asked—ordered rather—to sit in the waiting area. Wilkerson shut the door on us.

Mom squeezed my hand. I gazed at her, flashing my best puppy eyes. "I swear I didn't do it. I'm not doing dumb stuff at school anymore." Not really a lie. I kept mum on my real hijinks.

"I know. You . . . things . . . changed after . . ." her voice trailed off. "You're not the same anymore. You've grown up more than any teenage boy should in the last few months." Her comforting hand on mine killed the intangible distance between us. "I'm able to say it now. God knows for a time I—" She wiped her index finger under her eyes. "You're still the son I love more than life.

Don't ever doubt it." She banged our twined hands on my thigh, gave me a triumphant smile as if it took all the effort in the world to utter that shiny, bright tidbit.

For the briefest moment, I wanted to confess my deep, dark secrets about Silver and Raymond. The words lodged in my throat, refused to budge. Revolting, my brain hauled back the escapee cells. Knowing I'd had whole conversations with Silver would reset Mom's recovery to the starting gate and send me to the loony bin. *No can do.* "Thanks, Mom."

The door to the principal's office swished open, ending further public displays of embarrassing motherly affection.

"Mrs. Alexander, we'd like you to view this video from Saturday night."

The night of the beach party. *Alibis 'R Us.*

As we watched the hazy surveillance videos, my alibis began collapsing like bodies in a zombie apocalypse movie. My limited edition, black Ed Hardy bulldog hoodie and a slight limp gave my phony doppelganger away. A tumultuous mix of shock, confusion, and anger rocked me to my feet.

Mom's face fell. Every word, every gesture, every loving thought we'd traded flew out the proverbial window. People say pictures tell a thousand words. This messed-up picture told the lie of the century. An imposter had stolen my hoodie—although I didn't know if it was missing since I couldn't wear it over my sling—limped along and mostly kept his backside to the camera while he stuffed shrimp after shrimp inside the bleacher rails.

Worst thing about it, I had worn my hoodie inside out when I played my prank last year. Three people knew: Chris, Kev, and Raymond. My prankster assistants. None of them had uttered a word for fear of reprisals.

Denials spilled out. I inventoried my alibis—my grounding, party preparations, surrounded by people all day and night, the hospital—and Wilkerson gave me some benefit of doubt. He'd investigate further. He didn't suspend me, but ordered me to leave school for the rest of the day. Half gone already, he gave me a free Friday afternoon. *Need I say more?*

Mom believed me. On her way back to the resort, she dropped me off and asked me to stay home.

"I can't." I hunkered down outside the car door. "Someone's got a moving target on me. Am I supposed to sit here and take it pointblank?"

Thoughtful, she gripped the steering wheel, searched my face. Apprehension swirled in her hazel-green gaze. "It was your jacket, right? The one you saved up to buy?"

"Yeah."

"Okay." Her expression stilled. "Do what you need to do. Stay safe. Keep it legal. No more trouble." Her hand closed over mine on top of the door. "No more scares. I love you."

I rose and kissed her cheek. "Thanks. Love you, too."

As I turned to go, she captured my hand through the window. "Go check if your hoodie's in the house. Then call me. I'll bring your father up to speed. If you're late for dinner, let me know." Mom was back among the living.

I ransacked my bedroom, Silver's—Alyssa's—room, the rest of the house. I didn't really need to search the whole house, since I'd scared the crap out of everyone about touching my jacket. I'd left it hanging in my closet the last time I wore it. I did hang up some clothes. The special ones. My search came up empty. When I called Mom, the relief in her voice scrubbed away whatever doubts we both held. She asked me to call Dad.

"Hey." Flying down the stairs, I greeted him on speakerphone.

"Why would someone do this to you?" The accusation in his tone set my teeth grinding. *Will the real Dad grow a pair?*

"Let's see. I have a rap sheet of suspicious pranks a mile long. I'm a killer, and I doubt my legal troubles are helping my cause. Not worth much, am I?" The words hemorrhaged out.

A pause grew so long I thought Dad had hung up. After forever, he said in the quietest, calmest way ever, "You're not a killer. Never say that again. Those were random accidents. *Accidents.* Do you understand? You're worth *everything* to your mother and me."

I blew out a breath. "I know, Dad. Don't go psychoanalyst on me." I lifted my keys off the coat tree by the door and started for the driveway. "I'm still me, believe it or not."

"That's what scares me." Dad forced a laugh. "Are we okay?"

"Do you believe me?"

"Yes."

"Good, 'cause I'm gonna bust the bastard screwing with me." The alarm chirped on my car. A flock of blackbirds took flight, flapping and squawking their annoyance.

"*Please*, Lucas, don't do anything stupid."

"What? Like chase a moron onto the cliffs in a monsoon?" The fist of unease started to thaw in my gut over Dale's death. "I can't afford another broken bone." Another lengthy silence afforded me time to strap in and start my car.

"Call me if you need backup. I'll bring the bats," Dad said. An honest-to-God funny.

In the ways of healing, my family had hit a milestone on the potholed road to recovery. And Raymond Randall better run far, far away. No amount of repaving would help him.

Close to two-thirty, I parked around the corner from Raymond's house and hoofed it to the porch to wait behind the square pillar near the front door. With no football practice, he'd go straight home after school to watch his little brother and sister till his parents came home from work. I had a half hour before the carpool dropped off the rugrats. The half hour he and Silver used to spend in his bedroom, sometimes ditching last period. The half hour that haunted me every day, a short time I had to control the rising hatred, and feel Silver's anxiety, her weakness. The time each day I wanted to strangle her for letting him coerce her before she was ready. When I wished he had died instead of Silver.

Although blind to his selfish arrogance, Raymond ceased being my friend that fateful day. When he never visited me in the hospital after the accident, I celebrated his absence.

Chapter 34

Raymond whistled up the walkway, keys jangling in his hands. When his foot landed on the porch, I stepped away from the pillar and tapped his shoulder.

He spun around, eyes draining of color as surprise set in. "Man, you scared the piss outta me." His eyes narrowed. "You following me?"

"Waiting for you." I thumbed on my phone recorder in my hoodie pocket. Another layer of icing on the evidence cake. He stepped backward, bumped against the double doors.

I crept closer. "What did I ever do to you? Is your life so pathetic you have to possess everything I have?" I swept my arm wide to encompass the large house. "By the looks of this McMansion and your new Mustang, things don't look half bad. Your parents aren't divorced. Your *sister's* alive. You can have almost any girl in school. The football team's yours. You got a full ride scholarship. Why're you dinking with me?" Raymond hailed from solid upper class, his family upstanding citizens in our small community. Far as I knew, he had no more problems than any other teenager. Barring me, of course. My problems stemmed from a bad karma playbook. So why the gang initiation? Only half-Hispanic from his mother's side, he wasn't your typical gang type, no more so than Kev.

The crimson tide slithered up his neck, painted over his vampire-tinged face. "I thought we settled our probs." He slipped his index finger inside the neckline of his polo shirt and ran it back and forth, dipping into the V, showing his discomfort. "I apologized in front of the whole school. You dumped Tara anyway. Get off my back."

The hackles, if hackles existed, rose on the nape of my neck. "Why do you always bring her into the convo?"

A shit-eating grin revealed a tasty snack for later stuck between his two front teeth. He wasn't a good enough friend anymore to tip off. "She said if I gave her space for the next month, she'd go with me to winter formal."

Fat frigging chance. "Whatever." Fake nonchalance rode my voice. "This isn't about her. It's about you and me." *It's about Silver, you moronic toad.*

A thoughtful expression, if ever a look in Raymond's tiny sack of emotions, scrunched down on his brow. "There is no 'you and me.' Take a hike, queer." He faced the door.

I grabbed his arm. Unfortunately, he easily jerked out of my paltry grip. Fortunately, he bashed his elbow against the wall of rocks to the left of the door.

"Son of a—" He cupped his elbow. "Get lost, 'Xander, before I pound what's left of you into the lawn."

"Why'd you do it?" I asked calmly. "You knew I'd take the heat."

"What're you spouting off about?" His index finger dipped into his neckline again, traced the V, fingered a button.

Hoping to throw his strained pea-brain off guard, I took another route. "Dalton harassing you, too?"

He waited a long moment before speaking, weighing his words by the indecision on his grim face. "The dude's got problems. I'd steer clear of him. That's your lucky tip of the day."

"And here's your lucky tip." I pulled an envelope out of my back pocket, tossed the blackmail photos at him. Still not willing to tip my hand about the accident, I kept that in my back pocket. He caught the packet against his chest. "Did *you* tag Dalton's car? Did you slash his tires?"

Color drained from his face as he flipped through the pictures. "You said you wouldn't show these if I apologized." His Adam's apple bobbed several times. "Don't be a Judas, man."

"Beg." The hated words rushed to the forefront. I loathed them as they barreled out. "Get on your knees. You know you want this. You're nothing without me. I'll make your life a living hell if you don't do what I want." I mimicked the fateful words Silver had written in her electronic journal.

He stumbled against the door, his mouth a flytrap. "She told you."

"Silver hated you that day. I've hated you every moment since."

"She wanted it." Sweat beaded his brow, threatened to rainfall. "At the last minute she backed out."

"You should've listened to her and accepted her decision." I wished the words were rocks peppering his blotchy face.

"We had a pact—"

I wedged my hand against his neck, shoving him against the door. "I don't give a flying fart about your six-month dating pact."

He gulped against my hand. "What do you want from me?"

"The truth."

"Fine." He didn't hesitate. "I tagged Dalton's car. But I didn't slash his tires."

"Liar." I pulled my phone out of my coat pocket, turned on video, and shoved it in his face. "What about the shrimp prank? Where's my hoodie?"

Confusion halted the alarm widening his eyes. His Adam's apple shifted against my hand, and I applied more pressure.

"Wasn't me. I swear."

The slight sagging of his body and his pathetic voice gave me pause to believe him. Until otherwise proven guilty. "Why the car tagging?"

"I can't lose my scholarship. Dalton's threatening to flunk me." Sweat dripped down his temple onto my fingers. "I want out of this hick town. I'm not getting stuck at state."

He'd lost me. My grip around his neck loosened. "I don't buy it. Your family's not exactly camped on the unemployment grid." His father owned the town's biggest resort, the one where my mother worked, and his mom was a doctor at the local hospital.

"My dad said if I didn't get a scholarship, he won't pay for any other college except state. He wants me to stay here and join the business. But he wanted me to go through the effort of earning a scholarship. Like he did." A vein in his forehead pulsed.

The somberness in his eyes bared part of his soul. Desperate to escape the stifling town he'd lived in since birth for big-city action, he'd probably stoop to shaking down old ladies for their social security checks. I didn't get it and had no desire to understand. Everyone needed to examine both sides of life and weigh their own choices. Not my place to figure him out. My own plate was toppling under the weight of crap loaded on it.

Then it dawned on me. The bruises he told everyone I gave him last semester. The reason why he lied to the team about me throwing the games. He tried to get me off the team as early as last season.

"You practice football with your father?"

"Huh?"

"The bruises."

"What are you talk—" He turned tomato-faced again.

My bewilderment took another spin around my aching head. "What about the theft at the dance?"

There went the facial tick proving his guilt. "All I did was relay the message."

"What else did you do?"

Raymond waggled his head, sweat flying like a sprinkler. "Nothing."

The bombshell dropped out of my mouth. "Were you with Dale the night of May twelfth?"

His throat bobbed up and down. He looked ready to spew. Finally, he managed to say, "Don't involve me in my cousin's trash. You killed him. You got your revenge." He pushed his fist into my shoulder. "*You* killed my cousin."

I shoved him back. "And you killed my sister." I flicked my finger on his forehead and walked away.

"What about the pictures?" he yelled after me.

Was that all he cared about? "While you're in my sandbox, I'm hanging onto them."

I'd almost reached my car when he sailed down the sidewalk. "For what it's worth, I'm sorry about Silver."

I got in and punched my steering wheel, absently waved to his brother and sister in the SUV passing by. "Everyone's sorry about Silver."

"I mean about everything." He drove his Vans into the tan bark, strewing it over the sidewalk. "I drank too much. I didn't mean to hurt her, to push her."

"You're always tanked." I fiddled with the stereo, wanting anything to distract me from the thoughts threatening to light me up. I needed solid proof. But I think I had him running scared. His useless apology was an attempt to steer me off course.

"I know," he said.

The angst riddling him reminded me of my own. I gunned the engine.

Truth healed. It was time I quit resisting. I sped off, the cylinders in my mind spinning as my RPMs increased.

Kev and Chris wanted me to hang with them that night. They believed I needed vigilante style consoling to get over Tara. Instead, I offered Saturday night to repurpose Silver Ghost's mission. Going after Raymond wasn't up for discussion. I planned to bag him on my own.

I arrived home in time for dinner. Mom and Dad gave me space without the Spanish inquisition. Aunt Serena invited Dalton over, but Dad nixed the idea. Family dinner meant family only and he refused to put up with the antagonism between Dalton and me. *Go Dad!* One-armed batting practice together might be fun later. Good bonding time, whacking down the unsavories.

One *person* was absent from dinner. I missed that goofy ghost. I rushed upstairs to clean up for dinner and called Tara. "I miss you."

"How much?" she said on an airy breath.

"More than I can voice. How 'bout I show you tomorrow?" Forcing myself to behave, I brought her up to speed on the day. "Did you agree to go to winter formal with Raymond?"

"I said I'd *think* about it if he gave me space for a while. Did the jerk drink all his brain cells away or what?"

"There's something weird going on with him and his family. Father's pressuring him, crud like that."

"You going soft on him? What about his involvement in the accident?"

"Not soft enough to let you go to the dance—"

"*Let* me?"

"You know what I mean." The persistent tight fist in my stomach locked in place.

"I have no intentions of going anywhere with him, not after the way he treated me at the beach. Tell me what's wrong?" she pleaded. "We'll take Raymond down, don't fret."

I chuckled. "Girl, you turning vigilante or what?" Alyssa called up the stairs for dinner. "I gotta go eat. Call you later."

"It's Silver isn't it?"

The back of my eyes stung. "Yeah. I miss her all over again. Dealing with Raymond brought it all to the surface. Reminded me that she's really gone now. Have you seen—"

"No. I miss her too," Tara whispered.

Not only does truth heal. Time healed. Absence healed. I had to carry on without her. I knew that then.

• • •

The usual nightmares plagued my sleep. I relived the accident for the millionth time. The scorching fire left me soaking in a feverish sweat. The stench of gas and smoke plugged my nose until I had to breathe through my mouth. The sizzling, jagged metal stabbing my gut turned my insides into ashes. A heavy weight crushing my knee flooded molten pain down my leg. Two hotrods slamming into us with a deafening bang, fire roaring, tumbling metal on asphalt, screeching metal into the ditch shattered my consciousness. Silver's screams drowned out the numbing noise. I welcomed the silence as oblivion scooped me into an ebony morass.

Jolted awake, I sprang upright, panting as though I'd run a sprint to the end zone. Sweat coated my bare chest, dripped down my neck.

"'Bout time you woke up." Silver's voice filled my head. Frantic, my beseeching gaze zipped around the room, dug into the dark corners.

"Silver? Where've you been?" Excited, I rolled out of bed, hugging my bad arm, ignoring the throb. I turned on the lamp, searched the room. "Where are you?"

"In your mind, deedle-dum. Where do you think?"

The back of my knees hit the bed, and I sagged onto my skewed covers. It had to stop. "No." I clutched my head. "Get out. You're not here. You're not real."

"Well, duh. I'm dead."

I pinched myself to ensure I was awake. The red mark could testify in a court of law. "Come on, dude. Where you at?"

"Same place I've always been. Exactly where you last saw me."

"In my head?" I ground my knuckles against my forehead, grinding sanity into me.

"The only thing in your head is a big empty place waiting for the marbles to return." Again, her gibberish flooded my mind, echoed from ear to ear. No telltale warm or cold prickly air. No sign of Silver.

I was totally losing it. Lying on the bed, I focused on the painted moon on the ceiling. "Stop screwing with me. I don't need this right now."

"Yes. You. Do." Silver's voice pulsated in my skull. "Return to where you last saw me," she whispered. "Please, Lucas. You have to go back. I need you to see. For you." Faintly, I heard the jingling vibration of her bangles. I shook the sound out of my head.

She wanted me to flatline and return to the border separating the living from the dead? Minutes crawled by. No response. "Silver?" Nothing.

"Is this what you meant by coming back? This is it?" I leaped out of bed and swung my arm, knocking the lamp off the nightstand. The bulb crunched, the room darkened.

Stars twinkled like diamonds in the pre-dawn sky. I stared out the window, trying to make sense of my bizarre night. A shooting star caught in my peripheral vision. It streaked through the black atmosphere to vanish in a trail of gray haze southwest of town, exploding over the corner of County Coast Road and Ocean Avenue.

I sucked in my stomach, gripped the wrought-iron bedpost for balance.

The last place I'd seen Silver. Alive.

Chapter 35

My summer motto: avoid life like an ostrich. I hadn't ever returned to the crash site. Summer had whizzed by. Fall leaves littered the ground. Seasons changed everything. Time changed me. It was time to suck it up and let the conflicts and contradictions duke it out in Reality.

Not bothering to sneak out the window, I stealthily crept down the stairs, noticed the empty den, glad Mom and Dad slept in the same room again. I skirted the car parts graveyard on the right side of the garage, untouched since spring. My auto dude Dean might want some of the unused parts. Dad might even be in for a garage cleanup bonding session once I busted Raymond. My recovered stolen wheels reminded me of Silver Ghost's derailed mission. The reason for my trip to memory lane.

Brisk and breezy, no fog or clouds marred the early morning. On deserted roads, I drove out to the crash site. I parked on the shoulder opposite from where Silver and I had idled in the Red Renegade. The county had replaced the streetlights, and an amber glow pooled at two corners. They'd repainted the white lines on the road and installed new deflectors. Although the perpetually humid air and time had erased the charred reminder of the car, time hadn't blotted the skid marks. I fixated on the fading sets of rubber deposits, clearly visible below the gray shroud of dawn.

The pressure on my bladder, more than anything else, forced me into motion. Facing the trench on the passenger side, I did the deed, shivering from the assault of frosty air on my skin. The ditch where the bogus dead body had sprawled drew me to the other side of the two-lane road. I shoved my hand into my front jeans pocket, more to halt the trembling than for warmth.

Brown, foot-tall stickweeds grew in the center of the trench. The shallow depression opened itself to me, dared me to blame it. Yet I held little blame for the span of earth, nor any for the intersection of County Coast Road and Ocean Avenue. Fault lay where it must: on Dale and his gang, on the street racers, on Raymond for several reasons. Even on Silver.

Fault lay on the idea of gangs, our trepidation and tolerance of them. Or I should say our blind intolerance, our ease at sticking our heads in the sand and letting others handle the riffraff. Blame lay on the parents of these kids who allowed them to run amok. On the press and those who victimized or vilified street gangs or street racers. I was getting good at this adult psychoanalysis. Silver would be high-fiving me.

Fault lay on me, for I embodied this behavior. However, I refused to take the entire burden. No more wallowing in guilt and allowing it to destroy the people I loved. I planned to use my arsenal against those who refused to understand how their actions snowball. That bitch Karma had already strung her permanent noose around my neck. And I had arisen from the beyond.

"Silver and her 'karma's like a boomerang' crap. Karma's like a tool is more like it." I kicked a rock into the ditch. It pinged against metal.

Light glinted off a small piece of silver about a foot into the trench. I crouched down and brushed aside the debris to reveal a tarnished silver earring. I scooped the cross onto my palm. Dale's earring? I rocked back onto my heels. He'd worn the earring in his left ear on the night of the beach bonfire. The memory I sought stabbed my head. He also wore it on the night of the accident.

That night, my headlights had bounced off the silver dangling from his left ear, twinkling in the dark. The lights had also bounced off something glittery on another gang member. I brushed the dirt off the earring on my pant legs, stared hard at it while my memory twisted and turned. It looked so familiar but my mind was a jumbled mess. Then a picture hit me of Silver remarking upon the sparkly glint of it one night. Shock yanked me straight. I pulled out my cell phone and thumbed through pictures until I saw one corroborating picture after another of Raymond wearing the cross in his left ear last spring. The proof I needed.

The impact the evidence made was much less than I had anticipated. I soaked it up, already convinced of Raymond's involvement in the accident. Relief surged heat through the icy landscape of my insides. It filled the empty cavities my twin's presence once occupied.

What I would do with this information was still a conundrum—Silver's word of the day. Go to the sheriff? Feed the info to Silver Ghost? Confront Raymond? Tell his parents? What was my end game? I didn't know.

Safely pocketing the earring, I swung around, swept my sight from one corner of the intersection to the other three. I strode to the STOP sign, rested my shoulder against the steel post. "I'm here, Silver. Let's do this. Time to come back." *Where I last saw you.* I didn't dissolve into a puddle of prissy sorrow. Heaven didn't smite me. I didn't stampede for the loony bin. In fact, another dead vein of blood burst new life in the inner recesses of my body. I'd accomplished an impossible feat. I lived to gloat. "Yay me."

"Silver," I yelled. "Come on, dude. It's freezing."

I strutted to the middle of the intersection. Then I followed the skid marks to the side of the road where the police report indicated my car had landed on its side, wrapped around a street lamp. Strangely, the wooden utility pole suffered no damage, as if an imaginary hand stopped the car's trajectory inches from hitting it. The pole could've split my body in two.

Dawn's gold hovered on the horizon, gobbling night's gray out of the sky, enabling me to see within the shallower depression. A floral engraved cross and several wilted wreaths marked the place of Silver's death, the death of my old life. Fresher carnations in a plastic vase stood at attention. I touched the plastic frame holding Silver's junior class picture. She'd been so excited in that picture because Mom had let her wear her silver diamond necklace. It dangled in the V of her purple blouse. Mom paid for Silver's salon "do" and her hair fell in spiral waves past her shoulders. Now you wouldn't catch her dead . . . oh well . . . you get my drift . . . wearing spiral curls.

Slumping to my knees, I studied the memorial markers, the outpouring of love on the laminated sign nailed to a post. I wept in a way I'd never wept, or ever wanted to again. Wiping my face onto the shoulder of my hoodie, I stood, my knees stiff and cramped. Swore that I'd never let myself breakdown again. Guys shouldn't blubber. But I made no amends for my runaway girly emotions. Besides, no one was watching. Apparently, not even Silver.

"Love you, sis." I pressed two fingers to my lips, then touched the picture. "Half of me." I waited to hear, "The pretty, smart half." A barnyard owl screeched across the sky in reply. I waited ten more minutes, then split.

I must've dreamed of Silver last night. Maybe I'd dreamed her all along. The visit to the crash site had been real, though. It felt right returning to the scene of death. Not closure in a strict sense, but another link on the chain of acceptance.

Later that morning, when normal people awoke on Saturday, I called Tara. "I drove to Ocean and County Coast Road this morning."

I heard her sharp intake of breath. “First time?”

“I dreamed of Silver. Hoped I’d *see* her there.”

“No luck?”

I dragged my brush through my wet hair. “No.”

“Do you want me to come over?”

“I’m okay.” I’d showered and soaked my face in cold water, yet I needed more time to cover my wussy tracks. “It was weird. I wanted to blame the intersection, the night, the burned-out light bulbs, everything, everyone.” I grunted. “Stupid, huh?”

“Not really. You still don’t blame yourself, do you?”

“In part.”

“Lucas—”

I cut her off. “I get it now. No *one* person is to blame. I suffered the accident all over again this morning. Saw the pieces fit together. Raymond taking her phone, Silver insisting we go to Monterey, taking no for an answer. She said I owed it to her. Raymond and the gang, the night, the street racers. My stupid car. Me. It all fits.”

“Very adult of you.” A hint of a tease lightened her voice. “Don’t tell me you want the street racers released from juvie, charges dismissed. Arrest the dead street lights?”

“I wouldn’t go that far.”

“Good. I thought you’d gone soft on me.”

“But Dale,” I stomped down the rising guilt, “didn’t deserve to die.”

“His death wasn’t your fault. Just blowback in his own prank that backfired. Didn’t your dad tell you the police ruled Dale’s death an accident? Do I need to come over and smack sense into you? Shall I bring Dr. Beranger?”

I laughed. Carefree. Untainted. “Please. No more doctors.”

A long pause ensued. The weight of the world crumbled across my shoulders, down my arms. Sunshine smothered the ebony darkness, liberating me from an emotional prison. Spouting off poetry again, I should start taking estrogen pills to rush along my transformation.

Finally, Tara spoke. "You don't have to tell me if you don't want to, but why did you owe Silver a ride to the mall? Did you always do what she asked?"

Fire enveloped my neck, and a hot flare of loneliness jabbed at me. Tara had earned my trust in ways no one had. She totally got me. Nobody ever asked me why I owed it to Silver. Not Beranger when I confessed it to him, not Mom when she tried to sooth my nightmares in the beginning.

"I asked her to forgive me for opening our bond when she," I coughed, "hooked up with Raymond. We swore we'd quit intruding on each other. She was so upset that her agitation opened the connection. Normally, I blocked her out. Instead, I fought to feel her emotions, wanted to drive to Raymond's house and rip him a new one. I told her I'd give her anything she wanted if she'd forgive me for butting in, and if she'd dump him. I showed her the pictures of him partying, warned her about the girls he hooked up with at training camp when he was with his previous girlfriend."

"She believed you, though. But she wanted *quid pro quo*."

"You got it." Bitter laughter followed my words. "Typical Silver. She took me up on the offer. Asked me to cart her wherever she wanted. I always had a hard time saying no to her."

"Oh, God. Lucas." Her voice wobbled. "I'm so sorry."

"Yep. I should've said no."

And I wanted to open the car up on the highway, take the Red Renegade for a test drive after my latest engine mods. Silver loved the speed, and it made her last night happy.

"One last thing," I whispered. "I found proof to implicate Raymond." I told her about the earring.

Tara sighed. "What . . . what are you going to do?"

"Do whatever it takes to make him fess up."

Chapter 36

I didn't want Chris and Kev involved in burning Raymond, so I avoided them with lame excuses. Fortunately for me, not so much for them, their own lives had taken over in the last two days. Chris's mom roped him into working at the witchy shop and Kev was stuck picking grapes at the vineyard.

Denny on the other hand, noticed Tara's phony depression. By the black look he tossed me as he flagged me backing out of the driveway, he wanted to ream me a new one. The beach bum was dressed in surfer shorts, flip-flops, and T-shirt. Like mine, his bruises and cuts were fading, but we shared so much more than flesh wounds. Our love for Tara. Yes, I could admit it. I had fallen into that elusive emotional vat called love. It oozed into every pore, every cell of my battered body. It coated me in the purity of the moonlight orbiting my world. I had no frigging clue love turned people into poets. I needed to do some He-Man stuff to get my testosterone back. My impending task provided me with the perfect outlet.

Clenching his jaw, Denny slapped the hood. "What the hell?"

"Shut it and climb in." I suppressed a chuckle.

The car was still rolling when he hopped in. "Tara's a zombie. What'd you do to her? I thought you two were in *luv*."

"A zombie. Nice." My grin refused to be checked.

"You think it's funny, dude?" He rounded on me, eyes throwing switchblades.

"Strap in. We're going after Raymond."

"No shit." Denny whistled and scrubbed his hands together.

I handed Denny the earring in a plastic bag and brought him up to speed on everything that Raymond had done, holding back my gut feeling that life was off-kilter in Randall-land. I wouldn't want my family business spread among the gossipmongers. Ah, who was I kidding?

"I knew it." He smirked. "You and Tara are faking it. Thought I heard her yakking to you this morning."

"Busted." I turned onto the frontage road, curving around the Pacific to my right. The aquamarine sheet of water stretched to no-man's land, until the road switch-backed and Monterey's wharf-side sparkled in the distance. Raymond lived in the ritzier suburbs, closer to the more expensive coastal 'hoods. "I want her safe. I got a bad feeling crap's gonna tsunami into the fan."

Denny tensed against the seat. "What about Alyssa? Will he hurt her?"

Alyssa's safety never left my mind. "I don't know how far he'll take it against me. I'm not chancing a thing. She knows to stay away from him."

"What if someone's home?"

"Everyone who's anyone in the resort biz around here is at that convention in San Jose today. Same place as your parents. And Raymond's working at his uncle's restaurant."

We snaked through a neighborhood park, passed by 3234 Black Gull Way, one of a half-dozen semi-custom home models. Birds and sea names. Someone needed to fire the town planner for acts of the mundane. We parked behind a white, long-bed pickup across the deserted park. Without being overly obvious, we cut through the small playground, stuck close to the overpowering eucalyptus, and dashed across the street to the Randall house.

Denny took watch, hiding behind trash bins reeking of putrid meat. I had to force my arms to my side to avoid lifting the lids. I slipped down the sideyard and peeked through the windows on the top half of the door into the garage. My lucky day. No cars. I motioned for Denny, and a quiet snick shut the gate behind us. Lucky for us, the Randall's didn't own a dog. Lucky for dogs the world over, except for the one possibly rotting in the garbage can.

Someone had left the garage door unlocked. Sea Haven wasn't a crime mecca, but the town got its share. *Like you didn't know already.* Enough natural light penetrated the windowpanes on the side door to illuminate the interior. If nothing else, the Randall's were neat freaks. Shelves lined the walls, stacked and labeled with plastic bins. Workbenches spread the length of the far wall, tools hung on pegboards.

Lava bubbled in my lacerated gut, triggering the willies. I tested the doorknob to the house. Unlocked. "Bingo." We passed through the kitchen and took the stairs two at a time to Raymond's bedroom. Blinds closed, darkness shrouded the bedroom, and we had to step over clothes and smelly football gear to maneuver in the space. I inhaled through my mouth.

"Check around." I gestured to the left side of the room.

Denny began sifting through the garbage littering Raymond's tall dresser. "What're we hunting?"

"Anything suspicious. My Ed Hardy hoodie. His phone. A journal even." I sneered at the thought.

"Who else did the shrimp prank with you last year?"

"Chris, Kev, and Raymond."

"Umm . . . I hate to ask, but Chris was gone on Saturday and you said he'd been acting weird."

"No way. He wouldn't do that to me." The idea had already occurred to me. The boy in the surveillance video looked smaller than Raymond, closer to Chris's size. Yet, I refused to believe the worst of one of my best friends.

Without touching a thing, I visually riffled one spot to the next. Then my eyes landed on the shrine. No other word fit. The wall above the desk was plastered with pictures of Silver, articles about the accident, notes she'd written and cards she'd given him, even a lock of her hair. My stomach somersaulted. Fists clenched, I stepped closer to the wall. Sounds of Denny's rustling faded away.

My heart hammered in my ears as I gazed at pictures of Tara and Alyssa walking down the main breezeway at school. I vibrated with anger. Pictures of the totaled Red Renegade and Silver's memorial at the accident site rounded out the freak show.

"Lucas." Denny shook my arm. "Dude, you okay. I've been talking to you." His voice filtered into my teaming mind.

Shaking off the new layer of ice attacking my extremities, I pointed at the wall.

"I saw. Look what I found." Denny lifted up a couple of snapshots to reveal a sticky note behind them. I read the words written in black ink. "You're up. May 12." Signed with the letter "D."

"Call Tara. Make sure they're okay. I got a bad feeling about today," I said in a calm and rational voice.

Driven into action, I shot pictures of the keepsakes with my cell phone, took wider shots of the room to place the wall. Before we split, I tacked the picture of the earring I'd taken front and center of the eerie shrine.

As we zigzagged across the park, the strong eucalyptus scent cleansed the fog curtailing my thoughts and emotions, granting me clarity to think of the implications of what we'd found.

Denny clicked off the phone and gave me a thumbs up. "Girls are still shopping. Where to?"

Relief cooled my boiling blood as I drove away from the neighborhood. "Beyond the Witches Brew. The New-Age store Chris's mom owns."

We parked on Main Street where the touristy shops were, lucky to score a spot in front of the inevitable T-shirt shop next door to the Witches Brew. Nauseating incense assaulted us three feet from the door. I threaded my way between the crammed shelves of potions, crystals, books, and jewelry. A display of fairy figurines caught my eye as I passed by loaded shelves to the antique counter at the back of the packed shop. Maybe later I'd buy one for Tara. She had a small collection of fairies in her bedroom. I owed her big time for helping me return to life. I'd start with a small fairy trinket and work my way up to bigger. She deserved bigger.

"Hey, Ms. Walsh." Younger than my mom by several years, Chris's mom wore a long braid swinging down to her butt. Dressed in a flowing tie-dye caftan, she totally belonged in Santa Cruz with the hippy brigade. She'd gotten knocked up with Chris at seventeen. No father figure ever emerged. I'd heard she was gay. Who knew? Chris got angry whenever someone mentioned it.

"Lucas." Her wintry tone sent the usual creepy crawlies up my spine. She'd never held much fondness for me. Too much testosterone? From the wrong side of town? Whatever. Lesbo witches weren't my thing. Denny got the warm Sabrina the Witch smile. "Hi, Denny."

"Chris around?"

"He doesn't work on Saturdays."

I hid my surprise. "Oh, yeah. Thanks." I half-turned to leave, stopped. "Was he helping out last Saturday?"

"No." The simple response called me an idiot. "He was at your beach deal all day."

I gave her a crooked smile. "Oh, duh. Guess, my memory's sketchy." I patted my splintered arm. "Thanks, Ms. Walsh."

We reconnoitered outside the door. I called Chris and rolled to voicemail. He must be with Kev at the vineyard. They actually paid him to work there. It was a good source of income when he wasn't slaving for his mom for a pittance allowance.

"Where to now?" Denny asked.

"I'm burning Raymond, tonight. You in for the ride?"

Chapter 37

Once again, I needed to prove I was a functioning human able to contribute to my skimpy society. *Genius brain cells claim your prize.* However, I wasn't a total moron. A sling, a gimpy leg, and head trauma flipped my A-Game into D-Game. I needed Denny to watch my back.

We took off to my house to brainstorm. Aunt Serena had accompanied my mom to the convention, and Dad decided to work a day at the law firm since he'd missed a few days dealing with my latest bonehead moves. Perfect day for vengeance.

Denny munched on potato chips, crumbs morphing into the colors of the granite counter. "What's our first move?"

I checked my watch. "It's almost five. Raymond's off work at six."

"How do you know?"

"Saw his schedule on his desk."

My cell had a dead battery. I called Alyssa on the house phone and rolled to voicemail. Guzzling half an energy drink, I left another message for her to call us.

"Call Tara," I suggested, maintaining our breakup game. I wanted to hear her voice so bad my throat ached. Nasty air from Raymond's room still burned through me. The bad vibes refused to take a hike.

Tara's voicemail also picked up. "Tara Laney Harrison, call me ASAP," Denny demanded.

My hands lost strength on my phone. I forcibly clenched it to check my escalating apprehension. "They should be home by now. You sure you didn't get any messages?"

Denny checked his phone and called home again. "Nada. Let's sit in the front room so we can watch the driveways."

I stared at my dead cell on the open phone book. What if? I plugged it into Dad's charger at the kitchen desk.

"Son of a . . . I have one message." Something fluttered in my chest. When Tara's voice rose from the speaker, relief swept through me.

"Hey, sorry I didn't call earlier, but we ran into Raymond at the mall." Shock tore at my gut. "He treated us to lunch in the food court. Said he was buying a necklace for his mom's birthday and wanted our opinion. Alyssa wanted to help. She doesn't know all the crap going on with him. It's not like I could've told her right then and there or cause a scene." Panic edged her voice, mingled with her annoyance. "They were gone when I returned from dumping our trash. I'm looking for them now. It was weird. Why would Alyssa just up and leave me like that? I can't get her on her phone either. Have you heard from her?" Her voice paused. "Oh! I think I see them. I'll call you back." Click.

Denny drummed the table.

A sick feeling of dread set up shop in my gut. "Something's messed up." We looked at each other, unsure what to do, other than go ape-shit on Raymond.

"Maybe he took off early to go shopping." Denny half-questioned, half-stated.

"My gut tells me different." Again, I called Alyssa and Tara's cells, to no avail. "Let's check your house. Maybe the car's in the garage."

The silent jog across the Harrison driveway felt like the Green Mile. I kept my eyes peeled, my ears tuned. We checked the house, garage, and answering machine. Nothing.

"Let's wait an hour. If we don't hear from them, we go looking." Denny's agitation pulled tight lines around his mouth.

While we waited, we called all their new friends, anyone who may have seen them. Then I called Mom. Without alerting her, I asked if she'd heard from the girls. No such luck.

Thirty minutes later of pacing, we were going bonkers. "I should call my dad. I really think Raymond took them. Dad's in Monterey. He can drive by the mall or look for them on the road. Maybe they broke down."

"They had two cell phones between them. We would've heard from them. Look, man, I don't want to freak my parents out. See what your dad says."

Dad answered his office phone on the third ring. More calmly than I imagined possible, I explained what happened that day, leaving out our breaking and entering crimefest.

"Why do you think Raymond took the girls versus them going along to the jewelry store?" Caution lay heavy in Dad's cynicism. Typical lawyer to play both sides of the jury.

Time to fess up. My reign as super sleuth was over. "Dad . . . I . . . um . . ."

"Come on, son, spit it out."

His exasperation kicked my mouth into gear. "Raymond is Dale Brisbin's cousin. I just found out he was with the gang the night of the accident. It was Raymond's initiation night."

"What? Doesn't make sense." Dad's icy words slowed to a crawl. "Raymond's not the type to get involved in a gang."

"Dale was half-white and yet he was a gang leader." I scoffed. "I have proof." I hated the defensiveness rolling off my tongue, the guilt threatening to engulf me again.

"What kind of proof? Why would he hurt the girls? Did you threaten to expose him?"

"I found proof today. I suspected him earlier and he may have fed off my suspicions." Fear broke me down. I told him about Raymond's involvement, about the earring, breaking into his house, the photo wall, the note. I sent the pictures of Raymond's room to his cell.

A long pause followed while Dad absorbed my crazy story. "Stay in the house with Denny. I'll call the sheriff. He can get mall security to check for the Harrison's car."

"I can't stay here doing nothing." I knocked my bad arm on the counter, letting the pain pound my dread into the ground. "I need to find them."

"Stay away from the Randall house. I don't want you kids getting hurt. Let the authorities handle it."

I banged my forehead against the doorjamb. "Okay. Thanks, Dad."

"Son." Dad huffed out a ragged breath. "I'm sorry I didn't believe you."

My mind was a whacked mixture of hope and fear. "Sorry I ever gave you reason not to." Drained, I hung up. My arm ached, and I resisted the urge to sit down. The relief I felt nearly undid me. As much as I wanted to, I couldn't handle this on my own, not without jeopardizing Alyssa and Tara's lives. I may as well kill myself if anything happened to either of them, if I caused another death. I ached for the girls to be okay.

I longed for Silver to return, if for a moment. Sue me, but I still needed her on some level.

"You got some Tylenol?" When Denny returned, I downed two tablets in one swallow. "I'm going after the prick." I snatched my keys off the counter.

We cruised the neighborhood. My sliced and diced torso stung since I had no more intestines to knot. I gripped the steering wheel until my knuckles cramped.

"Hey." Excited, Denny pounded his fist on the dash. "You think Raymond took them to the accident site? Dude's whacked."

"Eye for an eye? There's too much evening traffic. My dad will pass through the intersection on his way home." I flicked up my hand. "Besides, it's too obvious."

My cell rang and I about pissed myself. I whipped the display into view, closed my eyes for a second.

"Tara, are you okay?" I nearly yelled into the mouthpiece.

"Lucas, listen to me," she said in a frantic high-pitched voice. "Raymond took Alyssa. When they saw me in the mall, he grabbed her arm and I lost them in the crowd. She won't answer her phone. I've been following them in the car, staying way back. They're headed back to Sea Haven."

"Where are you?"

"Some obscure road that tracks the frontage road. We're not too far from the town line. There's not much traffic. He's going to see me." Her voice wavered. "I'm freaking."

"Tara, stay calm. Drop back. Don't antagonize him. We're on the way." I flipped a U so fast I might have shot my car out of alignment. And the rest of my intact body. Fire rolled up my arm.

"Oh, no," she wailed.

"What?"

"He stopped. Right in the middle of the road," she squeaked.

"Drop your speed," Denny roared. "Turn around."

"He's spotted me." Her voice broke. "What about Alyssa?"

Before we could respond, we heard a crack. An unmistakable gunshot. The echoing tire blowout and Tara screaming as brakes and tires squealed sent the bullet straight through my heart.

Chapter 38

Gunning the Camaro, I shot a murderous, panicked look at Denny.

"You think he's heading toward the intersection?" Denny slammed his fist on his thigh.

"Where else? There's only one other route into town from Monterey."

"Fifty-fifty odds. Not good." His voice wobbled as he dialed my dad on speakerphone. We told him what happened.

"Don't overreact," Dad said. "Stay away from him."

"Are you on County Coast?" I asked.

"Yes. Few miles from town."

Another lick of relief swept over me as I hung up. "We're heading to Gull and Piper Lane."

"Is that a gang initiation location?"

"Race location."

We hit a straight stretch of rural road and I accelerated to ninety. I'd install a million Borla exhausts if we found the girls unharmed.

Night shadows drew down twilight, forcing me to slow to forty-five. It became harder to see anything except what the headlights and the occasional streetlight illuminated. Houses sat way off the roads, distant beacons of normalcy surrounded by vineyards and orchards. An occasional vehicle drove past us. Not one Mustang. As we approached the intersection, my bowels churned. I pulled up at the stop sign on Piper Lane. Deserted.

"Should we wait?" Denny asked.

"No. He would have passed us already."

"Unless he turned around." His voice offered hope.

We turned right onto Gull and drove until we spotted Mrs. Harrison's Volvo on the left side of the road. My headlights lit it up. Denny checked inside the car while I examined the flat tire. When my fingers brushed against the jagged hole on the top side of the rubber, the bile churning in my gut rose up. Even though I'd heard the shot, I didn't want to believe it. I'd hoped Tara had merely popped her tire. To think that Raymond possessed a gun slammed the fear of Hades into me.

"Car's clean." Denny jogged over to me. "Shopping bags in the trunk. That's all."

I shone the light on the impacted area of tire. "Definitely a bullet hole."

Denny kicked the tire repeatedly. I pulled him back before he broke his toes.

"I'm gonna kill—" My phone rang, murdering the threat about to trip from my mouth.

Alyssa!

I jammed my finger on the speakerphone button. "Alyssa, you okay?"

"Hello, Lucas." Raymond's unnatural singsong tone gouged an arctic freeze up my backside.

"I swear if you hurt them, I'll—" I clamped down on my tongue. "Where's Alyssa, Tara?"

"Who said anything about hurting Alyssa and Tara. Saying crud like that generally lands you in trouble. You remember trouble, don't you? Considering it's a steady state of being for you."

I steeled myself to remain calm before I pissed him off further. "I'm listening. What do you want?"

"Awesome. Like Dalton's always telling us, listening's a killer skill."

"Okay," I managed to say through my clamped jaw. *Save the Communication 101 lesson for later, jerkwad.*

"Nice. Alyssa and I are having a great date. She reminds me of Silver. Doncha think? She's wasted on that loser Denny." His voice grew fainter as he shifted away from the mouthpiece. "Wouldn't you love having a new boyfriend, Alyssa?" He chuckled.

The itch to destroy him overwhelmed me. I fought the surge of emotion, eviscerated the rant begging to go off. Instead, I fixated on the muffled sound of the surf in the background, strained my ears to hear more. Since half the town sat along the edge of the Pacific, he could be anywhere along the coast. "Where's Tara?"

"Your little sleuth? If she hadn't been following us, she'd be home. Your mock breakup had me fooled. Otherwise, I never would've left her at the mall. Now I have a twofer."

"Don't hurt them. I'll do whatever you want, okay Raymond?"

"Who said anything about hurting Alyssa? She's not the one I want—" He stopped as though he'd said more than he planned.

Denny's eyes bugged out and he mouthed, "Tara?"

I clenched the phone so hard, the casing cracked. "May I talk to her?" Traffic seemed to pass by in slow motion.

"Nah, I think not. She's busy. You know, tied up, obeying like a *good* girlfriend."

"Can I meet you somewhere?"

"When I'm ready, I'll let you know what I want from you." Raymond's breathing grew heavier. Sounds of the surf rose louder, gulls squawked on his end of the line. He gasped and yelled, "Knock it off." Then he growled into the phone. "Don't you feel guilty about Dale's death? Think about death and guilt for a while." The line went dead.

I'd heard the unmistakable boom of waves slamming onto rocks in the background. *Holy hell.* "He's at Deadman's Cove." We raced to the car.

The Camaro shot in front of a pickup, and I ignored the blaring horn and screeching tires.

"How do you know he's there?"

"The waves on the rocks. Not a sound I'd forget in a lifetime."

Zigzagging in and out of traffic captured my concentration. Silence reigned. We remained on edge until Denny spoke the not so obvious.

"We can't just stroll up to him. We can't jeopardize the girls. Maybe we better call the sheriff."

"We don't even know he's there," I replied. "We'll park down the street and take the path on the other side of the cliff that cuts over to the caves. The rocks will hide us."

"What if he's there?" Denny crossed his arms over his chest. "Then what?"

I blew out a breath. Clues weren't washing up with the tide.

My phone rang, startling us like Mexican jumping beans. Denny handed it to me. "Tell him."

We passed the parking lot above Deadman's Cove. I took my foot off the accelerator. The amber glow of the overhead lights bounced off the dark Mustang. I relayed the conversation to my dad.

"Where are *you*?"

"Just got to Deadman's."

"Don't antagonize him." The authoritative fatherly voice arose. "Stay out of sight. I'm calling the sheriff."

Hiding like a wuss wasn't an option. Nor did I make promises. We parked in a shadowy corner of the lot. "Follow my lead." A frost chilled the length of me. The pounding of the surf obliterated any sounds we made.

This time, I chose the moment. The moment would not choose me. I refused to let it. I was so done playing a pawn in Karma's Boomerang Wars.

Chapter 39

Denny and I jogged to the scraggly footpath leading to the beach on the other side of Deadman's Cove. Halfway down the steep incline another path cut across the rocky hillside to the beach side. In the best of light, the rutted trail proved tough to navigate. I'd hiked it a few times, enough to remember the treacherous spots. Going slow, we used a single penlight to guide us. No sense in offing ourselves and giving Raymond the ultimate prize.

Huffing like stoners, we made it to the cove side. I illuminated the pebbly path to the top of the bluff, pushed hair out of my eyes. An orange glow close to the tip of the bluff overhanging the sea devoured a small area of darkness. Close to the spot Dale had bitten it. Where I'd almost lost one of my lives. The glow lit up two figures. One stood tall, close to the edge overlooking the rocky, churning sea. The smaller figure knelt on the ground, motionless. Alyssa's hair fluttered in the slight breeze, tendrils of copper framed in the firelight. My gaze bounced from one edge of the bluff to the others, frantically scanning, coming up empty.

Denny whipped his head around. "Do you see Tara?" he whispered.

"She's got to be around somewhere." I refused to believe Raymond had . . . I choked down the air in my throat, waited for my heart to regulate. "I'm gonna have a friendly conversation with him. That's all. No threats, no advances."

"What if he goes for Alyssa?"

"He won't hurt her. I'm giving him what he wants. Me. My silence."

"Maybe we ought to chill, wait for the sheriff, look for Tara."

"If the sheriff's coming." I bit back my frustration. I might need a new tongue by the end of the night. "I'm not sitting here with my thumb up my crack."

"Okay. Play it easy. Keep him calm." Denny's teeth chattered. "I got your back."

Gnarly jags in a rock loomed, the kind that reached up to my balls. We hopped up and over them. "You sure you want to tag along?"

"You need someone to watch your back, you one-armed maniac."

I'd almost forgotten my bad arm. The constant pain hadn't bothered me much, and I'd gotten used to clenching it against my body. We circled around, saw Raymond stare out to sea as if waiting for someone to return on the tide. Dale, perhaps. His sanity?

Under the cloak of darkness, Denny and I separated to approach Raymond from opposite sides, dropping to the lower ridges of the bluff. Fortunately, the deafening waves crashing on the cliffside drowned out any sounds we made. The pathetic glow of the manufactured fire logs extended out four or five feet. Alyssa spied me, uttered a gasp the wind carried away. Wearing an oversized parka, she knelt on a blanket three feet from the fire, her hands bound behind her, ankles duct-taped.

I held my finger to my lips, not sure how much she could see in the dark. Apparently, she saw enough, because she nodded twice. Denny and I crouched behind boulders. In the dark, the top of his head looked like a pimple on a rock. I prayed the boulders hid me as well.

Raymond whirled about, his phone to his ear. "Shall we play our next card? Another call to your precious cousin?"

Alyssa visibly struggled to stop her head from swiveling in my direction. I knew it was killing her. What had Raymond said to keep her from screaming her lungs out? Death threats? Or had he already scared the life out of her? I fought to control my rising horror over the morbid thoughts of Tara's fate.

Faintly, I heard my cell ring. Raymond stood too close to the edge of the bluff to hear it over the booming waves. I punched the off button through my jacket before he heard the ringing.

"Huh. He's not answering." Raymond shoved the cell in his coat pocket. He scratched his temple, tormenting his schizoid brain cells. I highly doubted he had any left. "We'll give him a minute. He should be at Ocean and County Coast Road looking for you. What'd ya think, Alyssa?"

"Why would he go there?" Her steady voice floated over. I felt a smidgen of pride that my cousin remained outwardly calm.

"You don't know?" The curiosity in Raymond's voice unnerved me. Did he think the world revolved around him?

"No."

While Alyssa distracted him with questions, I sneaked along the ridge of rocks, lowering myself as my cover diminished the closer I inched toward the sea.

Raymond squatted on the other side of the small fire. "He never told you about the gang initiation that night?"

"No." Alyssa's teeth chattered.

"Liar." In a blur, he lunged at her over the pitiful fire. "The reason he killed my cousin," he barked.

She screamed. He body-slammed her onto the rocky ground. In tandem, Denny and I rushed him from our shadowy cover. Startled, he stumbled away from Alyssa, balancing on the cliff's edge.

The horror of my fight with Dale and his ensuing death spilled into my senses. *Not again. It can't happen again.* But Dale never wielded a gun, nor threatened my cousin. I inched toward Alyssa, spitting hair out of my mouth. Denny plunged to the ground and rolled toward her.

"Get away from her. Both of you. Now! Now! Now!" The muffled crack of a gunshot split the night, ate away by the pounding surf. He'd fired into the sky. No telling where the bullet would land. Who else might become a victim of this insanity?

One hand in the air, I distanced myself from Alyssa. Not too far where I couldn't make a flying leap to throw myself over her if matters took a dive. Denny did the same, standing next to me, hands in the air. Over the briny sea air and the crashing of waves, Alyssa's sobs echoed in my head and Denny's fright skittered down my spine. Our combined torment fed my adrenaline, activated gelled thoughts.

Orange firelight glimmered off the gun's chrome barrel wavering in Raymond's hand.

I took a chance on my instincts. "You were looking for a place to belong, right Raymond? Now you have it. You have the football team. You don't need to do this. I'm sorry about Dale—"

"What do *you* know about being shut out? You had everything. The football team, the hot Camaro, Silver. And you got away with everything. Every prank, all of it. Hell, man, I couldn't even pin the dance theft on you. You got away with that too." He punctuated each word with a wave of the gun. "I got the leftovers. Second-string quarterback. Silver was never all mine, not with that freak-ass bond you two had. Not even Ciara Mitchell after you dumped her."

"But you have it all now." My voice came out serene. The way Dr. Beranger sounded counseling me. "The football team. You got your Mustang. Your scholarship. Your ticket out of town. You can even have Tara since she never wanted me." The lie tasted tart on my tongue.

He bleated out a harsh laugh. "What scholarship? I'm failing all my classes because of you."

Me? My mind reeled. Psycho dude.

Without any prompting, he continued to download. "You shouldn't have been on the road that night. Silver and I were patching things up. You killed her. You killed us. You fucking killed my cousin. He was my ticket into the majors. We were gonna rule Sea Haven."

Needing to stop his lunatic ravings, I held up my hand. He was twisted, sick. Required way more help than I had to offer. "Dale's death was an accident. Silver's death was an accident. Just like you being at the crash site was coincidence. We're square, okay? None of this needs to go any further. You let Alyssa go and we walk away." Right to the sheriff's office.

"Shut up." Raymond flailed his arms, his finger on the gun's trigger. "Shut up. You clueless freak!"

I inched closer to Alyssa. "I think you and I were a lot alike. That's what I'm talking about. We were lost souls trying to find our niche, our own way in life without something or someone defining us." Truer than Raymond ever imagined.

"What nonsense are you spinning now?" He advanced toward us, amber firelight gleaming off the turmoil carved across his forehead, crinkling his eyes. He cocked the gun's hammer, a faint click. He pointed it at me, then waved it at Alyssa.

Before I could react, a blurry shape rushed from behind me. Time stopped. The world quit revolving and hazed over. I leaped to cover Alyssa, missing her by a foot as she rolled away at the same time. I landed hard on the flat boulders, my good arm catching me from knocking myself comatose. A gunshot shattered the night. Alyssa shrieked. Another crack exploded across the dark, hostile seascape. Raymond fell to his knees, his gun dangling from his limp hand.

My cousin's screams evolved into soul-wrenching sobs, then her chest puffed out, sank, and she grew quiet. Her head lolled off to the side.

Raymond had hit her.

I scrabbled toward her, tumbling over the kneeling figure who'd fired the first shot, righting myself before I became another victim of a faceplant.

"Lucas. Oh, no. Oh damn." Chris catapulted toward me, Kev's "borrowed" revolver in his hand. Our eyes met, gilded shadows bouncing off his ashen face. Mikey raced onto the scene behind Chris.

All my focus shifted to Alyssa. "Sweetie." I cradled her in my arms, felt the sticky blood oozing through her blouse beneath my fingertips. "No, no. Not you too."

I wanted to die. Wanted the pain of death to fill me until I exploded into a million fragments and the waves swept the dust out to sea. I peered into the inky sky, hoping God looked down upon us and would halt the death and destruction my being on Earth caused. But all I saw was a shimmery sparkle in the dwindling firelight. I felt a barrel of sorrow mow me down.

Silver had returned. But it was too late.

"Silver, help her." My throat clogged up, grew strangled. "Don't let her die." Sobs convulsed me. I tightened my hold on Alyssa. She became dead weight, pulling down my arm.

"Watch out. He's got the gun!" Denny bellowed. He leaped at Mikey, barreling him to the ground just as Raymond fired at Dalton's son.

Beams of light illuminated the bluffs. Blinding, revealing. Floodlights, they told me later. Another shot boomed over the sounds of the melee and the surf. Raymond sagged to the ground again, slumped onto his stomach. The gun skittered across the rocks and over the cliff. My dad and the sheriff rushed onto the scene.

Gently, Dad tried to peel my arms off Alyssa. I refused to let her go. He pushed aside her jacket, his fingers gently prodding her blood-soaked blouse, traveling to her neck pulse. Dad's wide shoulders heaved. His ebony gaze landed on my face, Alyssa's death mirrored in his swimming eyes.

Chapter 40

A horrified grief paralyzed my arms around Alyssa's cold, lifeless body. Dad kept trying to take her from me, but my arms locked around her. Through a gray murk, I watched people converge upon us, Chris and Denny kneeling on the cold stone next to me.

"Silver. I need you," I cried into Alyssa's hair. That telltale tickly warmth surrounded me.

"She's not gonna die, Lucas. Not on my watch." Silver sobbed. "I won't let it happen. Hang on, Lyssa."

Sheriff Masterson rushed away from Raymond's body and joined us. Would Raymond go straight to hell? I hoped he rotted there for eternity.

The sheriff and Dad managed to pry Alyssa out of my arms and gently lay her on the blanket. All this happened within seconds, though it seemed hours. The wind carried sobs and murmurs toward the ocean. Numb, I gripped my bad arm and watched the sheriff perform CPR on my cousin. I held my breath until my lungs throbbed. Dragging in sea air, I let it bathe my frozen blood.

All of a sudden, Alyssa gasped and a violent shudder rolled through her torso, lifting her off the ground. Light spilled into her, and her chest glowed in a kaleidoscope of colors, as though the clouds had cleared and the sun beamed only upon her. My mind, hoping for divine intervention, played tricks on me.

I scampered the distance between us. "Lyssa!"

Dad blew out a heavy breath. "She has a pulse." Carefully, he cradled her body while the paramedics made their way onto the cliff. Relief softened the gullies bracketing his eyes.

Vaulting to my feet, I whipped my head around looking for Tara. Paramedics tended to Mikey. I rushed over to him. "You okay?"

"Shot only grazed me," he said weakly. I patted his shoulder gently and jumped back to Alyssa.

"Lyssa, where's Tara?" Denny's insistent voice rose before I uttered the words. I knew he had to feel like a machete had split him in two, one part wanting to stay with Alyssa, the other part screaming for Tara. It was what I felt.

"She's in Raymond's car," Silver said above me.

"Trunk," Alyssa sputtered, trying to say more the wind stole away, then she passed out. "Dad?" My knees took the full brunt of my sagging body. "Is she . . ."

He mashed his mouth grimly. "She's just out. Her heart's beating. Go look for Tara."

Denny, Chris, and I bolted toward the jagged trail leading to the parking lot. Lights lit up the rocky outcropping as emergency people converged upon the scene. The same lights marked our path, making it much easier to traverse than earlier. Sirens competed with the booming sea and the thundering of my heart in my ears.

"You think she's in Raymond's car?" Denny panted, easily keeping pace.

"Yes." No hesitation filled my voice. "Keep your eyes peeled just in case."

Emergency vehicles littered the parking lot, spotlights lighting it up like Sea Haven at Christmas. We raced toward Raymond's Mustang on the other side of the small lot. Sheriff deputies hadn't yet descended upon the car, concentrating on saving Alyssa and apprehending a dead Raymond.

"The door's unlocked," Silver said, hovering over the trunk of the car. "Hurry, Lucas. Raymond gagged her."

Without losing a step, I yanked the driver's door open and pulled the trunk latch. Denny shoved up the trunk lid as I bounded the three steps to the rear, heedless of the stabbing pains running up my leg.

Tara lay trussed up in a fetal position in the small space. My heart clutched up. Raymond had tied her ankles and wrists with duct tape. Eyes closed in a dangerously pale face, even her lips were turning blue. Chris dashed off to snag a paramedic.

"Tara, wake up!" Denny pulled the duct tape off her mouth in one fast swipe.

Tenderly, I eased her out and propped myself on the lip of the trunk, holding her against me, giving her my warmth. Denny pulled a nasty rag out of her mouth and she made a small sound in her throat. She remained lifeless, the same way Alyssa looked just moments ago.

All I could do was hold her close. I found a faint pulse in her neck. My spirits soared. Our hearts began beating together again. "Help me lift her out of here."

"Gotta get this tape off." Full of emotion, Denny's words were clipped.

As soon as he eased the last piece of tape off her ankles, we carried her to the pavement. A woman paramedic jogged over with a gurney. We lifted Tara onto the flat surface and the paramedic began working on her. Denny, Chris, and I held vigil around her, our fingers taut on the edges of the stretcher as we waited. I didn't even want to contemplate how Chris ended up here. How he shot Raymond. For Alyssa and Tara. For me. Most of all, for Silver.

Tara coughed and heaved in a breath. Then she took one more and another.

"She's fine. You boys got to her in time." The paramedic—Maria Salazar, her nametag read—beamed a smile on us. "Local heroes, I'd say." She bundled up her equipment and rolled the gurney to a waiting ambulance.

I gripped Tara's hand, leaned down. "Tara, you okay?"

"Alyssa . . ."

"Shhh, don't worry. She's safe." Denny stroked her hair. "Luc, one of us needs to check on her," he said in my ear.

Part of me was dying to make sure my cousin was okay. The other part couldn't let go of Tara's hand. But I knew Dad would take care of Alyssa. "You and Chris go. I need to talk to Tara."

Alone with Tara, I kissed her forehead, watchful of the oxygen mask. "You're safe." I rained more kisses on her face. "Silver saved you."

She lifted off the mask. "She came back. I felt her with me almost the whole time. She kept me calm. She sang to me."

Unable to find my voice, I nodded. "Off key?"

Tara giggled weakly. "Totally."

She lifted her hand an inch, dropped it. I gloved mine around it, giving her arctic skin my negligible warmth. "Thank you. I owe you big time," she said.

"You wouldn't be in this mess if not for me."

"Not your fault." She smiled. "Did we bust Raymond? Is it over?"

I coughed, averted my face. "Yes."

"He's . . . dead, isn't he?" Her fingers pinched mine.

My gaze drank in her wan face. I nodded.

Her eyes closed, opened. "How?"

I put my mouth to hers. "Later." We kissed. It was warm and soothing, hot and wild, lips pressed to lips, drinking each other in. When I drew back, I gazed into her pain-filled eyes. "You saved me."

• • •

My family and friends all paced the puke-green waiting room at the hospital. Everyone waited another lifetime while surgeons repaired Alyssa's spleen. They had to remove it, just like mine. Denny and Dad relayed the story to Mom and Aunt Serena. Kev arrived and Denny repeated another version, embellishing parts to make us appear the heroes. It freakishly excited Kev to know his gun had a part in breaking the case. Sheriff Masterson was less excited as he took Kev's statement about the confiscated pistol.

Serena kissed my head, ruffled my hair, her fingers trailing down my cheek in a soft caress. "Thank you for everything you did to protect her." Tears ran down her cheeks onto mine when she kissed me and rested her cheek against mine. It felt good to save a soul for a change, even if I caused it.

Dad took me into an empty room. "She'll be okay. You did good. But next time . . . God." He scrubbed his hand over his face.

"I'm sorry."

"I know." He pulled me into a bear hug. It felt right. "Luc, your mother told me about the empathic bond you and Silver had. We had no clue." His voice cracked, and his arms tightened.

I groaned and pulled away. We faced each other, a mirror of crimson heat. I didn't want this conversation, but I knew Dad needed it. Might get him off my back for a while. "We dealt."

"Why did you hide it?"

I shuffled my sneakers, kicked the frame of the bed. Testing out my dexterity in case I wanted to kick Nerf footballs around someday. Unable to avoid the question, I finally bounced the truth out. "We knew it was weird. We didn't want everyone to freak out. We wanted something that was ours alone."

Startled, Dad's eyes widened. "Then it's true about what you said after you awoke from the coma. About hearing her." He shook his head, jangled his keys in his pocket. "Are you okay with her gone? Really okay."

"Sure." I didn't know what to say. She's floating behind you yakking up a storm with Tara about riling up the Deadman's ghosts to kick Raymond to the curb didn't seem appropriate. "I'm alive. My family and friends are safe. That's what matters."

Despite the night's trauma, the relief that Alyssa and Tara lived hung like a rainbow over the room. As soon as the doctors quit poking and prodding Tara, I sat with her in the emergency room. I refused to let go of her hand, couldn't stop touching her. When the Harrisons arrived and the hospital released her, I had to let her go.

I pushed her wheelchair to the exit doors several yards behind her family. Denny regaled her parents with a toned version of our heroics. He didn't want to torture his parents too much.

"Where'd Silver go?" Tara whispered.

"Returned to Deadman's." I stopped the wheelchair just outside the sliding doors.

"Do you think we'll *see* her again?" She twisted the ID band around her wrist.

"I hope so." I knelt down and slid my arms around her, wincing at the pain on my bad side. I choked up hard. *Screw my sissy genes.*

Tara cupped a hand around my face. "You saved *me,* too."

My kiss found the center of her palm, moved to land on her cool, dry lips. I let them steal the pain, the nightmares. I wished to be a teenage boy with no cares except being Sea Hag's king once again, to fall in love, with a whole body and sane mind. Most of all, I wished to share it all with my other half. Tara.

Leaning in, I kissed her, soft and gentle at first, then heat formed between us. Our kiss became air and water, all that corny stuff of life. Strength existed in our kiss, each giving to the other. When she swirled her tongue around mine, I fell into her with all of myself.

Until her father's obnoxious throat-clearing and Denny's wolf-whistle spoiled the moment. Reluctantly, I let her go.

On the way back to the waiting room, I ran into Chris. "How'd you know what was going down?" Incredulous, I shook my head.

"Mikey planted a GPS on Raymond's car. He knew something big was going down. He called Kev and me as backup, but Kev was stuck at the winery. Dude, why didn't you tell us?"

A hot flush worked its way up my chest and neck. "Everything spiraled out of control. I'll tell you guys all about it." I steered him into an alcove where two gurneys waited for their next victims. "Chris, why did you do it?"

"What?" He shrugged, his face turning green. "Shoot Raymond? To save Alyssa, everyone else from his bullshit. Dude, I loved Silver too." After the look of disgusted shock on my face, he added, "Not like that. Silver was a good friend to me when you were tied up with football. She helped me deal with my mom. Geez, pull your head out of the sand. You weren't the only one who lost someone." He slugged my good arm.

He was right. I failed to realize how many people Silver's death had affected. I hung my head, bounced from foot to foot. "Sorry." Lifting my head, I met his gaze. "Thanks for tonight. I owe you."

"You owe me nothing. You would've done the same."

"I think I already did." We laughed. "Let's go see Mikey. I owe him one, too."

Chris tugged on my arm. "Um . . . Dalton's spitting bullets. I wouldn't go in there if I were you. Give him time to cool down."

"Wonderful. Another reason for the man to hate me. Get his kid shot up." We returned to the waiting room.

An hour later, Alyssa awakened. The doctor gave a glowing report on her recovery. "She wants to see Lucas alone first."

I bolted toward the recovery room. The same room I'd recovered in after the accident. Not that I remembered much, but the room number was stamped on my wrist tag. My chest constricted.

"Lucas?" Alyssa's weak voice drew me out of the morass of hell.

One foot before the other, I stepped through the door, breathing deep to maintain balance. "Alyssa?" I stammered. The Hospital Stench assaulted me. Ignoring it, I focused on my cousin.

"Is Tara okay?" she asked weakly.

"Yeah." I laid my hand on hers. "Her parents took her and Denny home. He wanted to stay, but they were scared and wanted him home."

"Scared of you?" She tried to smile. It failed.

"Funny, haha." A long pause ensued while her face scrunched up in deep thought.

Finally, she said, "I saw something tonight."

My guard went up. "What do you mean?"

"Silver."

"You saw her too?" My voice elevated and heat flushed my chest.

"Too? You saw her?" Confusion creased her forehead.

I deflected my mistake. "When I flatlined after Dale's accident."

The whites of her eyes grew rounder. “No way.”

“Way.” Grinning, I added, “If you tell anyone, I’ll have to kill you. All over again.”

Chapter 41

Tara and I lay out by the pool, basking under the weak rays of an autumn sun. The sunshine felt cheerful on our exposed faces, liberating and fresh. Alyssa was being released from the hospital in an hour. A small homecoming party awaited her.

Brochures for nearby universities were scattered on the lawn between us. With my life on firmer footing, I thought I better get busy and look at my options for the future. Football was done. Criminology and law school didn't require a top-notch body. Silver would be so proud of my choices. Mom was ecstatic that I planned to stick close to home. Dad was beyond stoked that I had an interest in law where before I scoffed at following in his footsteps. Death did that to a person.

"Silver's gone?" Tara asked.

"Looks like it." I settled into the lounge chair, snuggling Tara's hand on my chest. Silver was truly gone, safe and happy where she belonged. Something I took at face value. The other thing I took at face value was Tara's love for me. My love for her. Each day our feelings strengthened in the wake of the terrifying events we shared. We had an undeniable bond. I couldn't ever imagine a day not loving her. Yet, I knew how life changed at the drop of a dime. You had to just take each day and party it up. No regrets, no endless sorrow, no overwhelming guilt. You can't plan life. Life just happened.

I knew my future had possibilities. Life would go on. Just in a different way. Silver had buzzed around my room that morning in her tingly shimmery way and said, "When you need me, just look inside."

There was no denying that I would mourn Silver and the horrors of that summer forever. No person could skate by what

I did without it leaving permanent tire treads over their body. I hoped that Silver might return someday as the ghostly presence that helped slide me through the worst time of my life. If she didn't, I had the memories of her, the good days before the accident. I had my heart.

I also had my best friends who loved and honored her as much as I did. I owed them much more than I could ever repay. Kev, Chris, and Denny stuck by me when the world crashed down upon me. Something I would never take for granted.

We all decided to go to college together. Kev declared I needed babysitting. Chris the lost bulldog planned to tag along and attend community college. Denny was in for the ride. The four musketeers.

As if on cue, the French doors clicked open. Surprise jolted me upright. "Hey, Mikey Dalt. What's up?"

He strolled over the flagstone walkway, his arm in a sling. The bullet had only grazed his upper arm. Superficial flesh wound on the mend. "My dad dropped me off. He'll be back later once your aunt and Alyssa get home."

Tara and I traded speechless looks.

"Seriously? I thought I was on his permanent shit list."

"Nah. I told him all the stuff that happened. He's cool now."

"Like what stuff?" I cocked my head to the side, clenched my hand.

Mikey's eyes rounded and he backed up a step. "Just the stuff about Raymond targeting you. Why he did what he did. Stuff everyone knows. Nothing about your vigilante gang. He doesn't know I used his computer access."

"Cool." I blew out a breath and sagged into lounge position. I closed my eyes. "So he knows Raymond did the shrimp prank, the dance theft, the car, all that." I pumped my fist and grinned. "That Denny saved your life on the cliff."

Tension grappled with my relief. I cracked an eyelid, witnessed the torment etching Mikey's face. "What did you do?"

He scuffed his shoes in the grass. "I didn't do it to set you up or anything. I did it to fit in. Just like you did. I swear."

"The shrimp prank? But why the bogus limp?"

Mikey stomped on a soda can. "It wasn't fake. I got creamed in football practice."

I laughed, wiped my eyes. "Kid, you're all right." The funny thing was that I had found my Ed Hardy hoodie stuffed in the car parts graveyard in the garage. Guess I must've left it there before the accident. Mikey dressing up like me was creepy. We needed a little chat later.

The side yard gate clinked shut and the three stooges followed the walkway around the side of the house.

"Yo, *ladies*. How's it shakin'?" Kev called. Chris and Denny followed him into the backyard. Kev ruffled Tara's hair. She batted at his hand.

The sheriff had deemed Chris's shot at Raymond self-defense of some sort. The sheriff had actually fired the killing bullet. Again, I asked Chris how he felt about semi-killing somebody. We shared a similar bond, a two-man club. His skin had taken on a green cast, and I thought he was going to kiss the ground. Instead, he held his head high and said, "I had to stop him. We're buds." This was where his story got good. "Plus Raymond planned to sick CrimsonX on you and all your friends. Didn't Mikey tell you what he'd overheard in the locker room?"

I laughed so hard, I almost choked up a hairball. Hell had found its idiot. Raymond was a bug on my headlights. Life was too damn tenuous to hold a beef against a ghost.

"I ran into Rico yesterday," I said. "We all have a free pass from CrimsonX threats for a while. Apparently, Dale's gang had been tromping on their territory for a while. He actually thanked me for exposing them."

Kev grabbed a handful of over-buttered popcorn from the bowl on the table. "Having said that, we got Silver Ghost business to attend to. We're back in black."

"Dude, what's with all the AC/DC references lately?" Chris smirked at Kev. Kev slugged him. Just like old times.

"So what's the deal?" I asked before they embarrassed themselves in front of Tara.

"Juggernauts are harassing kids at Gulf Elementary. We need to drop the hammer," Chris replied.

"Tara, that's your cue." Kev swept his arm toward the house. "Shake a leg."

"Dream on. Silver Ghost needs girl power." Parading a big grin, Tara crossed her arms over her chest. "And a brain."

I gave her a teasing mad-dog look. "Seriously. We should rethink our mission. Keep it to playing legal watchdog. You know, keep a lookout for trouble where most people turn a blind eye."

"Come on, Skeleton Luc, you still have a few more bones to break," Kev wheedled.

"Revenge will never solve anything. Karma will," I announced. "I need to give my bones a rest."

"I agree." Tara trailed her fingers over my broken arm, giving me a thumbs up.

"'Fraid you're outvoted, dude." I shrugged my hands, grinned. Another day alive, another Silver lining.

Acknowledgments

As the saying goes, it takes a village to raise a baby . . . in this case to create a book. That cliché certainly doesn't minimize my appreciation to every person, whether I mention you by name or not, who helped me realize my dream and brought my story to life.

First, I'd like to thank my insightful and brilliant editor Jackie Mitchard who took a chance on me and my story and who didn't give up pushing for it. My appreciation goes to all the wonderful people at Merit Press who believed in *Vigilante Nights* and added their various talents to making my book a reality, including the stunning cover.

I'd also like to thank my agent, Natalie Fischer Lakosil, for being at the right place at the right time, and dropping everything to read *Vigilante Nights* well into the night.

Special appreciation goes to Jennifer, my awesome critique partner, and the fabulous people at the AW forums, where if you strain hard enough you can almost hear them say over the Internet lines, "Never give up, never surrender!" I'm grateful for all the reader and writer friends I've made online through various forums, who've helped, cheered, and motivated me.

Finally, I'd like to thank my mother and my friend Carolyn who both listened to me rant and rave about every step of my writing life. Even after all that, I'm glad you're still my biggest fans!